Progeny Unbound

Peace Be to This House

A NOVEL BY CHARLES LAW

*Behold, how good and how pleasant it is for brethren
to dwell together in unity! It is like the precious
ointment upon the head, that ran down the beard,
even Aaron's beard:*
PSALM 133, 1-2

 www.trafford.com

North America & International
toll-free: 1 888 232 4444 (USA & Canada)
phone: 250 383 6864 ♦ fax: 812 355 4082

For Saul Rose

For Sean Ross

THE HARTS AND JUDAHS
Ezekiel Hart married a sister of Abraham Judah in England

NEXT GENERATION
Aaron Hart = Dorothea Catharine Judah
(b. 1724)   (b. 1747)
Moses (1768)   Ezekiel (1770)   Uriah(1771)   Miriam (1772) Samuel (1774)
Catharine (1776) Charlotte (1777) Benjamin (1779)   Alexander (1782)
Elizabeth (1783)   Sarah (1784)

??? Hart = Naphtali Joseph
Abraham Joseph (17??)   Judah Joseph (1762)...Henry Joseph (1775)

Judith Hart = George Joel

Henry Hart = Elisabeth Visscher
Ezechiel (1783)   Harman Visscher (1784)

Moses Hart = Esther Solomon

Samuel Judah = Elizabeth Ezekiel
Bernard (1777) Abraham (17??) Catharine (1788)

Isaac Judah

Uriah Judah = Mary Gibbon
Henry (177x)   Sarah (1776)

Marian Judah = David Manuel
Hannah (1766) Catharine (1768) Dorothea (1771)

Dorothea Judah = Aaron Hart)
(see above

Elizabeth Judah = Chapman Abraham
(b. 1763)   (b174?)

THE HARTS/ JUDAHS/ DAVIDS/ JOSEPHS
THIRD GENERATION

Moses Hart = Sarah Judah
(1768-1852)   (1776-1827)
Areli Blake (1800) Louisa Howard(1801) Orobio (1803)
Other children of Moses Hart:
Alexander Thomas (1804) Benjamin Moses (1810?) Henry (1811?) Esther (1814?) Ezekiel Moses (1817)
Moses Ezekiel Moise (1818) Orobio Moses (1820?), Aaron Moses (1823) Reuben (1824) William (1826)
Thomas Nathan Vulge (1827) Elon (1829, d. 1830) Sarah Dorothea (1829)
Abraham Samuel Pierre (1830) Charlotte Matilda (1831) Elizabeth (1832)
Samuel Judah (1839) Andrew (1842)

Ezekiel Hart = Frances Lazarus
(b. 1770)   (b. 1769)
Julia (1795) Emma (1796) Samuel Bécancour (1798) Esther Elizabeth (1800)
Harriet (1801) Aaron Ezekiel (1803) Catharine (1804) Henry Ascher (1805, d.
1805) Caroline Athalia (1807) Henry (1808) Ira James Craig (1809) Abraham
Kitzinger (1811) Miriam Hadley (1812) Adolphus Mordecai (1814)

Uriah Hart = Miriam ?
(1771-179x)   (b. 177?)
Samuel Judah (1789)

Catharine Hart = Bernard Samuel Judah
(1776-1859)   (1777-1831)
Samuel (1799) Aaron Hart (1801) Jonathan (1803) Edward (1806) Miriam (1807) Abraham (1810 d.
1815) Alfred (1812) Washington (1814) Louisa (1818)

Charlotte Hart = Moses David
(1777-1844)   (1767-1814)
Moses Eleazar (1813)

Benjamin Hart = Harriot Judith Hart
(1779-1855)   (1786-1849)
Frances (1807) Henrietta (1808?) Ephraim (1810?) Aaron Philip (1811) Arthur Wellington (1813)
Baruch Frederick Weber (1814) Theodore (1816) Henry Naphtali (1817) Helen (1819) Benjamin
Moses (1820) Emily Abigail (1822) Julia, Joel (1823) Reuben (1824) Hannah Constance Halton
(1826) Dorothea Catharine (1828) Elizabeth Weston (1829)

Alexander Hart = Mary Ann Douglas
(1782-1835)
Alexander   Louisa

Elizabeth Hart
(1783-1840)

Sarah Hart = Samuel David
(1784-1831)   (1766-1824)
Eleazar (1811) Aaron Hart (1812) Moses Samuel (1816) Phoebe (1818) Frances
(1820) Sophia (1822) Samuel (1823)

Brandele Abigail David = Andrew Hays
(1762-1801)   (1742-17??)
Lazarus (1784?)   Moses Judah (1789)

David David
(1764-1824)

Samuel David = Sarah Hart
(1766-1824)   (see above)

Moses David = Charlotte Hart
(see above)

Frances David = Myer Michaels
(1770-1838?)   (1760-1815)

Bernard Samuel Judah = Catharine Hart
(1777-1831)   (see above)
Samuel(1799) Aaron Hart(1801) Jonathan (1803) Edward (1806) Abraham
(1810) Alfred N (1812) Washington (1814) Louisa (1818)
Henry Judah = Mary Gibbon
(177x- 1838)
Thomas Storrs (1804-1895) Henry Hague (1808-83)

Sarah Judah = Moses Hart
(1776-1826)   (see above)

Henry Joseph = Rachel Solomons
(1775-1832)   (1780-1855)
Henry (1806) Matilda (1807) Levy (1808) Catharine (1810) Benjamin Solomons (1811) Rebecca
(1813) Jacob Henry (1814) Abraham (1815) Jesse (1817) Sarah (1819) Gershom (1821) Esther (1823)

FOURTH GENERATION

Children of Moses Hart
Areli Blake Hart = Julia Seaton
(1800-1857)
Henry Thomas   William Blake   Christopher   Charles Edward   Amelia
Henrietta

Orobio Hart
(1803-1824)

Alexander Thomas Hart = Miriam Judah
(1804-1852)   (1807-87)
Moses Alexander (1841) Augustus (1842) David Alexander (1844) Lewis Alexander (1847)

Louisa Howard Hart
(1804-1857)

Benjamin Moses Hart =
(1810?)
Henry Moses

Henry Hart =
(1811?-1847)

Esther Hart
(1814?)

Moses Ezekiel Hart = Domithilde Pothier
(1817)   = Georgianna Pothier
Anne-Georgianna (1854)   Louis-Napoleon-Hormides (1866)

Aaron Moses Hart = Marguerite McCarthy
(1823-93)
Edward ( ) Moses Orobio (1847) Rebecca( ) Benjamin-Moyse (1865)

Thomas Hart = Agnes McCaffrey
(1825)
Alexander Thomas (1863-63) Emma Rosa (1866) Charles Ezekiel (1880)

Sarah Dorothea Hart = Neree Hercule Desilets
(1829-18xx)

Charlotte Matilda Hart = Joseph Ludger Desilets
(1831-18xx)_

Samuel-Judah Hart
1841

Reuben Moses Hart
(1843-1918)

Children of Ezekiel Hart

Emma Hart
(1796-1839)

Samuel Bécancour Hart
(1798-1859)

Esther Elizabeth Hart
(1800-1860)

Harriet Hart
(1801-1855)

Aaron Ezekiel Hart = Phoebe David
(1803-1857)   (1818-18??)
Frances Lazarus (1851) Sarah (1852) Asher (1853) Emma , Dorothea (1855) Sophia David (1856)

Caroline Athalia Hart
(1807-1883)

Henry Hart
(1808-1842)

Ira James Craig Hart
(1809-1883)

Abraham Kitzinger Hart
(1811-184x)

Adolphus Mordecai Hart= Hannah Constance Hart
(1814-1879)   (1822-1898)
George Ezekiel(1846) Abraham Emile (1847) Gerald Ephraim ((1849) Asher (1850) Harriot Judith
(1852) Miriam Hadley (1854)

Children of Benjamin Hart

Frances Hart = Raphael Schoyer
(1807-49)   (1800-1865)
Benjamin Hart (1836) David Arthur (1839) Ernest Augustus (1843) Albert
Asher (1845) Frank Reuben (1848)

Aaron Philip Hart
(1811-43)

Arthur Wellington Hart = Selena Ezekiel
(1813-91)
Harriet Blanche (1842-61)

Baruch Frederick Weber Hart = Elizabeth Johnson
(1814-94)
Katie (1865) Elmira (1873) Lucie (1878) Elizabeth Stringer

Theodore Hart = Frances Michaels David
(1816-87)   (1820-1844)
Sarah Harline (1842) Fanny Augusta (1844)
= Mary Kent Bradbury
(1812-92)
Charles Theodore (1846) Frederick L'Estrange Levey(1851) Robert Augustus Baldwin (1852) Edith
Marie (1854)

Henry Naphtali Hart = Jane Elizabeth Church
(1817-188?)   (1812-188?)
Isaac (1839) Maria (1840) Benjamin (1841) Louisa (1843) Caroline (1844) Aaron (1846) Arthur
(1847) Elizabeth (1852) Emily (1853) Blanche (1954) Henry (1857) Eugene (1860)

Benjamin Moses Hart
(1820-1891)

Emily Abigail Hart = Samuel B. Hort
(1822-18??)   (1816-1892)
Anne Julia, Harriet Frances (1842)

Hannah Constance Halton Hart = Adolphus Mordecai Hart
(1826-1898)   (see above)
George Ezekiel (1846) Abraham Emile (1847) Gerald Ephraim ((1849) Asher (1850) Harriot Judith
(1852) Miriam Hadley (1854)

Dora Catharine Hart = Alfred Waley Hort
(1828-1898)   (1817-1898)

Elizabeth Weston Hart
(1829-34)

Alexander Hart II = Mme Bouchette
(18??-18??)

Louisa Hart

Children of Charlotte Hart and Moses David

Moses Eleazar David = Rosina Florance
(1813-1892)
Charlotte (1848) Nina (1847) Arthur Meredith (1849)
= Ada Abrahams

Children of Sarah Hart and Samuel David

Eleazar David = Eliza Lock Walker
(1811-1887)   (1812-1887)
Gertrude Sophia (1840) Arthur Mamdro (1842) Ernest Wilfred (1843) Golde
Adela (1846) Carlo Grimaldi (1847) Marietta Beatrice (1849) Hilda Edna
(1850) Aleyda Eliza Winnifred (1852) Amy Lillian Ernestine (1854) Charlotte
Gwendoline (1857) Eliza Evelyn (1860)

Aaron Hart David =Catharine Joseph
(1812-1882)   (1810-1876)
Samuel (1837) Henry (1838) Monte David (1840) Sarah Mathilde (1842)
Tucker (1843) Moses Edmund (1844) Fanny (1846) Robert Sullivan (1847)
Esdaile Cohen (1849) Joseph (1850) Harline (1851)

Moses Samuel Hart David= Gertrude Virginia Joseph
(1816-1854)   (1825-1914)
Augustus (1847-50) Laurens Joseph (1848) Edith (1850)

Phoebe David= Aaron Ezekiel Hart
(1818-1882)   (see above)

Frances Michaels David = Theodore Hart
(1820-1844)   (see above)

Sophia Michaels David = Abraham Joseph
(1822-189?)   (1815-1886)
Fanny David (1847) Rachel Sarah (1848) Henry (1850) Montefiore (1851)
Andrew Cohen (1852) Helen Elizabeth, Catharine Octavia (1854) Crimea
Harriet (1855) Jesse (1858) Sophia Celine (1860) Stewart Scott (1862) Georgina
Patterson (1863) Martha Maud (1869)

Children of Henry Joseph
Henry Joseph
(1773-1832)

Catharine Joseph = Aaron Hart David
(1810-1876)   (see above)

Benjamin Solomons Joseph
(1811-1820)

Rebecca Joseph
(1813-1880)

Jacob Henry Joseph = Sara Gratz Moses
(1814-1907)   (1817-18??)
Rebecca (1849) Lizette (1851) Mathilda Inez (1854) Henry (1855) Horace
(1857) Caroline Muret (1859)
Abraham Joseph = Sophia David
(1815-1886)   (see above)

Jesse Joseph
(1817-1904)

Sarah Joseph
(1819-1903)

Gershom Joseph = Celine Lyons
(1821-1893)

Esther Joseph = Alexander Abraham De Sola
(1825-1882)
Aaron David Meldola (1853) Clarence Isaac (1858)

PART ONE

Entanglement
1838

One

Aaron Philip Hart wasn't certain of his ground. The streets in and about the racetrack bordering the Lachine Road were almost indistinguishable in the first rays of the morning sun. And he had the responsibility of directing his namesake and cousin, Aaron Hart David to their destination. The young doctor had been asked to be on hand if the duelists and the seconds couldn't work out an accommodation.

Aaron Philip had seldom wandered west of Rue McGill into the area between Griffintown and Pointe-Saint-Charles despite having worked with his father near the Old Port. The Irish laborers who had once been mobilized to dig the Lachine Canal were not his sort of people.

Robert Sweeny, a fellow lawyer, could barely be discerned standing at the edge of the field. Aaron Philip had felt an obligation to act as his second. How could he act otherwise given how other young advocates had stood with him in his earlier encounters with those whom he challenged as a matter of honor?

3

The relationship between Sweeny and him had grown over the last few months; both had been induced to represent several of the prisoners in Montreal's *Pied-du-Courant* prison. It was the relatively new facility overlooking the rapids characterizing the mighty St Lawrence River at this point in its flow. *Hence the name.*

It had been a most thankless assignment. Sir John Colborne, the emergency administrator of the province who ordered the constitution of 1791 be suspended, once had almost five hundred rebels behind bars. Since December, however, perhaps two thirds of these political prisoners had been released but over 160 *Patriotes* remained in jail awaiting trial. *Canadien avocats* were discouraged from offering their services; their loyalty to the Crown could not be vouched for. The burden fell on the British element, men such as he, William Walker and Robert Sweeny. But the latter was always happier behind his desk writing verse than consulting with the rough young men complaining about overcrowding, poor food and freezing nights in their tiny cells.

Almost eight years had passed since Aaron Philip was admitted to the bar. It had become a family tradition. His model had been cousins Aaron Ezekiel Hart, who now practiced in Quebec City and Tom Judah, who eventually migrated to Montreal. Subsequently cousins Eleazar David, Henry Judah and Adolphus Mordecai Hart joined the legal fraternity. It would have made quite a debate if they ever got into the same courtroom or the same living room. But distance and politics kept them apart. "Greetings, Sweeny! Is there any reason for me to try finding a way out of this mess?"

He received only a grunt though it was true that there was no reading the man's eyes. At five in the morning it was still too dark to delve into explicit passions. And it was passion at play here. The previous evening Sweeny described the offence that had engendered the challenge. It appeared that Warde, a popular Major in the garrison army, had done a most dishonorable thing. At the supper table on Beaver Hall Hill Sweeny had received a letter written by Warde to Sweeny's attractive wife, the former Miss Temple. The fact that Warde had never engaged with the woman didn't deter him from writing a steamy letter to her. His excuse was that he had been receiving flowers and messages from an unknown party and chose to have the courier followed. The trail led to the Leprohon house, where the Sweenys boarded. For some unexplained reason the letter was delivered to the lawyer, who was also a Captain in the local *Voltigeurs* as well as a published poet. Without finishing his meal he quickly jumped to his feet and searched out the culprit to issue his challenge.

Aaron Philip strode over to Warde's second. They knew each other because Captain Mayne had been part of an earlier duel, standing for a

Lieutenant Ormsby at the end of the previous October when the latter faced off with the *Patriote* Édouard-Étienne Rodier. That incident also occurred at the racetrack. "Are Major Warde pistols in good order?"

Mayne nodded. "He is prepared for the challenge though to his mind he did nothing he should be ashamed of. You know from personal experience, Hart, that nobody shoots to kill."

The soldier was alluding to the fact that Aaron Philip had been involved in duels with such notables as colleague Henry Driscoll, Francis Johnson and Bartholomew Gugy. The encounter with young Johnson had been at the corner of Sherbrooke and University and therefore not out of sight of Montrealers. (The Gugy affair had occurred in Quebec City.) In retrospect Aaron Philip had never anticipated serious harm as a result of these shenanigans. But Sweeny and Warde were experienced combatants; they had both returned from fighting the rebels south of the St Lawrence but a few months before.

Conforming to the rules of combat, Mayne and Aaron Hart handed each other the pistols that were to be employed in order to check whether these weapons were equally lethal. Sweeny, being the offended party, had agreed that at the sight of first blood, the duel would be ended even if the wound were minor. He could have demanded that the engagement go on till one man was so severely wounded as to be physically unable to continue the duel – or even until there was a mortal wound.

The parties themselves approached the seconds and stood back to back, pistols in hand. Sweeny had insisted on a relatively low number of paces, (The insult had been that grave.) They walked the set number and turned to shoot. *God damn! They're serious.* Warde had slumped to the wet ground and blood was flowing from his chest. Both seconds rushed to his side; he was indeed mortally wounded.

Sweeny seemed in a daze. As for his second, the shock was almost as devastating. He had had prescience in warning Aaron Hart David the previous day that there might be bloodshed. His cousin had promised to be ready to assist. *But what good was that?* The wound to Henry John Warde was obviously fatal. If only the army Major had not been so foolish as to send a love letter to Mrs. Sweeny!

* * *

Later that morning Aaron Philip appeared at the house on Rue des Récollets almost as a penitent schoolboy. Benjamin Hart would be less than forgiving. His father had become renowned as the leading magistrate in Montreal, the man whose rectitude had been tested by the events of the previous autumn. Though his son was not a principal in the duel, this participation in such a deed would be regarded as reprehensible by the many of those who already resented having a Jew speak for the British denizens of the city. As for the *Canadien* majority, the loathing of this particular justice of the peace could not but intensify. "I've always warned you, Philip, not to make 'honor' your cipher. And coming at such a delicate time."

"Do you think, papa, that my representations at the court-martials will be compromised as a result? I know that Warde was well liked by Clitherow and his staff." Aaron Philip realized that though he had proper sufferance as a defense counsel, the garrison officers had little patience for those who sought mercy for traitors. Major General Clitherow would probably chair the court procedures.

The interview was interrupted by the appearance of Aaron Philip's mother at the door. The imperious Harriot Judith Hart didn't often respect a closed door in her home. In any event, she was too disturbed to offer an apology. "What have you done, Philip dear? Everybody on the street is talking about the shooting."

"It shouldn't have happened, mama. But you do know Robert Sweeny. He is a jealous man; though not foolhardy. I think he will get out of the country before he is prosecuted."

Benjamin intervened. "That won't happen until there is an inquest. I will enquire whether old man Mondelet is ready to act with dispatch. As the coroner he is bound to proceed even if most duels are officially overlooked. A death, however, cannot be ignored."

"Is there anything I should be doing, papa? Will there be any guilt attached to me?"

"I think not, but everything is up in the air. A messenger reports that the new Governor sailed into Quebec harbor on the *Hastings* last Friday. I intend to travel to the capital to meet with Lord Durham before this week is out. It is so the case that Arthur Wellington is to sail from there to Portsmouth this very time."

"Do you believe you will be welcome? I've been told the new Governor is a well known Radical who had even quarreled with Earl Grey when they were in the Cabinet together. Will he be firm in putting an end to this insurrection?" Aaron Philip never had a high opinion of the Whig government in London despite the resolutions Lord Russell had introduced in the British Parliament the year before, the resolutions that had driven the *Patriotes* to violence. *How will young Durham, the son-in-law of Earl Grey, respond to this crisis?*

"I pray that he will. He must! Papineau is still at large and my sources tell me that the exiles are not reconciled to the defeat of their forces. Do you not think that it is on my mind when I go upstairs to our *shul* these mornings?"

Aaron Philip chose not to reply. The new synagogue at the corner of Rue Chenneville and Rue Lagauchetière was almost ready for occupancy. It would be incumbent on his father, perhaps the most dedicated orthodox Jew in town, to attend services more often than did other worshipers in the congregation. But he wouldn't have Arthur Wellington at his side albeit son number two was as devout as his father. God forbid that his brother's sojourn in England resulted in further embarrassment for Benjamin Hart! Papa could never accept such a possibility for his favorite son.

*   *   *

The sound of drumming resounded along Rue Notre-Dame as Aaron Philip took an unostentatious place on the sidewalk. Major Henry John Warde was being buried this first week of June. Aaron Philip felt his presence was essential; he was, after all, one of the last men on earth to see the Warde alive. *There is no escaping this incident.* The inquest had been conducted before a jury several days earlier. Cousin Aaron Hart David provided the testimony that demonstrated how Warde had met his fate. He actually opened the body in front of the jurors by introducing his finger into the gaping wound. The bullet had struck a vertebrae and the doctor had bone fragment in his hand to show the onlookers.

Nevertheless, Jean-Marie Mondelet, the rheumatic coroner of longstanding in Montreal, asked for a political verdict. He got it; the jury ruled that the late Major Henry John Warde came to his death, in consequence of a gunshot wound inflicted by some person unknown in a duel the morning of May 22. Aaron Philip grinned; *quelque personne inconnu* despite the newspaper accounts and the verbal evidence that had identified Robert Sweeny as the man firing the fatal shot. Sweeny, however, had conveniently skipped the country to avoid the possibility that there would be retribution.

The body of the slain soldier, encased in a coffin topping the wagon, passed by. His comrades, the 1ˢᵗ Regiment of Foot, constituted the firing party that accompanied the funeral. Major General Clitherow led the procession and all the other top-ranking officers in the district paid their respects to Warde. Dueling may be illegal, but the code required that they pay their respects to the fallen officer. The murmurs in the crowd suggested that not everybody was in agreement with that code. There had been too much death in recent months.

*With regard to the persons who have been apprehended for
political offences and are now in confinement, Her Majesty's
Government desires that such of them as you think it right at once
to liberate should not be brought to trial, unless they can be tried by
ordinary tribunals of the country. In case, therefore, a reference
to the ordinary tribunals should not, in your judgment, be
yet advisable, a law ought to be passed for the suspension of
the HabeasCorpus Act, which will enable you to detain
such persons in prison till the arrival of Lord Durham.*
COLONIAL SECRETARY LORD GLENELG
(letter to the Sir John Colborne, February 19, 1838)

*Eight prisoners held in Montreal are to be transported to Bermuda
under pain of capital punishment if they return without authorization.
Another sixteen exiles are under indictment for high treason;
they include Papineau, Côté, O'Callahan, Robert Nelson, Rodier,
Brown, Duvernay, Chartier, Gagnon, Cartier, the two
John Ryans, Perrault, Demaray, Davignon and Gauthier*
ORDINANCES OF JUNE 28, 1838

Two

Adolphus Mordecai Hart was no stranger to the *Pied-du-Courant* prison. Though he still made Trois-Rivières his home, the shortage of eligible lawyers able to represent the prisoners awaiting trial in Montreal gave him scope to advance his profession. His father had encouraged him to follow this predilection; Ezekiel Hart had long had some sympathy for the rebel cause despite his aversion to the violence. And he knew that three of his sons, Aaron Ezekiel, Adolphus and Ira Craig, had actively promoted the election of *Patriotes* to the Legislative Assembly.

The uprising in the district of Trois-Rivières last autumn had been limited to demonstrations in support of Papineau and his associates. One or two *habitants* on the other side of the St Lawrence had been brought up before Judge Vallières prior to the declaration of martial law. Adolphus did not hesitate to defend them with vigor in court albeit one result was that he was fined five *louis* for contempt. *And to think that my older sister once lived with Vallières!*

The admission to the *Pied-du-Courant* took longer than it needed to be even though the guards undoubtedly recognized Adolphus for who he was. Perhaps it was the early summer heat that was bothering them. Or they weren't ready to acknowledge somebody in his mid-twenties behaving so self-assuredly. Adolphus took all this in stride.

He was led to the appropriate cell on an upper floor. The malodorous product of unwashed bodies and stale urine saturated the corridor but Adolphus had come to expect these conditions. He had only to bear them for a very limited time. His client didn't have that luxury. In fact, his client was stretched out asleep on a cot when the turnkey admitted him into the cell. From then on everything said would be in the French language, though having grown up in Trois-Rivières Adolphus had no trouble with that. There was but one question on the mind of the prisoner and in his drowsiness he blurted it out. Would he soon be facing a firing squad?

"There have been executions in Upper Canada. Colborne has pursued a more prudent course. Nevertheless, the intention is to take you to trial. You and dozens of others. Who knows how the verdicts will go?" Adolphus thought he was giving the man an honest answer. He had not reckoned on how knowledgeable the prison population was; contact with the outside world was maintained through visits by family and counselors. "Is there not a new Governor in Quebec? Perhaps he will restore *habeas corpus* and allow jury trials?"

Adolphus was in no hurry to reply. If juries were drawn from the majority population, the Crown would probably fail to get convictions. A panel of British inhabitants, on the other hand, could not be expected to give the defendants a fair hearing. Lord Durham would be facing a conundrum unless he proceeded with court-martials rather than let civilian courts adjudicate. "Our best hope is that punishment will be restricted to the more prominent leaders of the revolt and that an amnesty will be declared for the remainder. Unfortunately I have failed to determine how you are regarded by the authorities."

"I fear, *Monsieur* Hart, that I am seen as one to be punished. The jailer has been pressing me to confess my guilt with the promise that there will be leniency as a result. It has been said that *Messrs.* Nelson, Des Rivières and Marchesseault have given depositions for this purpose."

The revelation shook Adolphus; Wolfred Nelson was not a *Patriote* who would cooperate readily with the British military. His reputation as an organizer of the resistance to the troops invading the Richelieu valley had spread up and down the province. A noted medical doctor, a leading citizen of Saint-Denis on the Richelieu, the brother of Robert Nelson, who had escaped to Vermont: *Was he so desperate that he would betray his own conscience?*

But Adolphus was there to give advice. Should he be advocating that this fellow cooperate with his jailer? Would this naïve rebel not be betrayed in the final analysis? The state may not be willing to show weakness when under attack.

*   *   *

The tavern was just down the street from the Courthouse on Rue Notre-Dame. Adolphus realized that if he dropped in for refreshments, he would likely encounter others from the legal fraternity. He could not have been more perceptive; sitting at a table near the window was his cousin Aaron Philip in the company of William Walker. The two Harts weren't especially close though there was but three years difference in age. Living a hundred and fifty miles apart was certainly a factor, but the contrasting political persuasions were undoubtedly an overriding consideration. The plight of the detainees and the need for them to have representation was only now bringing the two together.

Walker seemed friendly enough. He got to his feet to shake hands. Though his roots were in Trois-Rivières, the undersized lawyer had made his reputation as linguist, scholar and orator while practicing in Montreal. He had received province-wide attention because of his vocal support of the union of the two Canadas when it became a national issue over fifteen years before. Subsequently Walker led in the formation of Montreal's Constitutional Association and was its spokesman during a trip to London's Whitehall three years ago.

Another beer was ordered and Adolphus recognized that the two were celebrating. Indeed, Aaron Philip was jubilant. "We've done it. The confessions by the eight principal prisoners open the way for a settlement of all the outstanding cases. You have lost yourself a client, Dolph."

Apprised of who were included in the eight prisoners, Adolphus was secretly relieved that his client was not one of them. A *dilemma resolved.* "It surprises me that Wolfred Nelson would plead guilty. He's not that sort of fellow."

Walker drained his glass before replying. "True, there was not much contrition. In his private letter to the Governor he stated that he had rebelled against colonial *misgovernment.* Yet he doesn't deny defying constitutional order."

"What happens next?"

"This is Tuesday. Queen Victoria's coronation is on Thursday. The Governor has decided to issue an ordinance on that date. It will order the proscribed eight be transported to Bermuda. There will be amnesty for everybody else unless they participated in the execution of Chartrand and Weir." Walker was referring to two men, one a soldier, shot by the rebels prior to the skirmishes. The death of Weir, in particular, had become a rallying point for the British militias recruited to fight the rebels in November and December.

"And what is to happen to Papineau and the others beyond the reach of the Crown? My guess is that the Doric Club will be unsatisfied with such a resolution of the matter." Adolphus didn't hesitate to cite the Doric Club, the band of Anglo "constitutionalists" who had spearheaded the British opposition to the *Patriote* insurrection. Cousin Aaron Philip had been one of the organizers of this unofficial militia.

Aaron Philip scowled at the mention of the Doric Club. "You presume, but you are right. The exiles will not be ignored. Those who have taken refuge across the border are to be barred from returning here on pain of death. That includes Papineau, O'Callaghan, Robert Nelson and Côté."

Walker filled in. Actually sixteen of these rebels are to be banished for life. You know them: not only four just mentioned but also Rodier, Brown and Duvernay. I take great pleasure from Duvernay being on the list; his *La Minerve* has been the bane of our existence. Believe it or not, I have actually been in contact with Robert Nelson, who it seeking my advice. He may be setting up an army of exiles but at the same time he wants to recover the bail money he will forfeit if he does not return to this jurisdiction. A very complicated fellow!"

The discussion was interrupted by a beckoning from one of the tavern's patrons at another table. Walker got to his feet in order to satisfy his curiosity. As he departed, Adolphus was once more made aware of the man's chronic limp. It was public knowledge that it was the result of a duel fought some years before. Another affair of honor during which a fellow lawyer, one named Campbell Sweeney (no relation to the outcast Robert), delivered a bullet that shattered Walker's leg between the ankle and the knee. *What silliness!* Adolphus had never been a member of this fraternity. Walker, on the other hand, had helped organize the playfully named *"Brothers in Law"*, the Montreal-based social group justifying this kind of behavior.

Adolphus used Walker's temporary absence from the table to enquire about the health of Aaron Philip's immediate family. The latter did elaborate on his father's recent visit to Quebec. Adolphus was all ears; few had the opportunity of meeting Lord Durham. "Is it true that the new Governor is approaching the aftermath of the rebellion without prejudice?"

"Papa was both disappointed and confused by what he heard. He had traveled to the capital with the aim of having himself appointed to the Special

Council. He is of the opinion that Major General Colborne ignored his contribution in standing up to the French during the past several months. It was only logical that he should be one of those responsible for advising the new regime. Instead the Governor's first act was to dismiss the Special Council altogether."

"Was your father not impressed with the Executive Council Durham put in its place?

"The five were his own people. None of them has an intimate knowledge of Canadian affairs."

Adolphus could only guess at the degree of Benjamin Hart's disappointment. His uncle undoubtedly needed some sign of official approval to offset the disrepute in which he was being held among most *Canadiens*.

* * *

The last task left for Adolphus before his boarding of the steamer for Trois-Rivières was a call on Augustin Cuvillier, the president of Montreal's Board of Trade. Approaching Cuvillier's store on Rue Saint-Paul, Adolphus wasn't certain what to expect. The street traffic was busy enough; a mid-week walk on Rue Saint-Paul in late June was bound to be clamorous despite the current sour mood of many of its inhabitants. As for the Cuvillier establishment itself, the front door was ajar. Presumably the proprietor was at home.

An auctioneer, the man had reached the age of sixty having suffering many ups and downs. Once a staunch *Patriote*, Cuvillier had even traveled to London ten years before in the company of its other spokesmen – notably Denis-Benjamin Viger and John Neilson – to protest the rule of a former Governor of the province. But he was also a man of commerce and vehemently opposed to the agrarian philosophy of Papineau and his cohort. In fact, it was his performance in business that had brought Adolphus to Cuvillier's door this afternoon.

Cuvillier had issued paper currency during the recent conflict because specie payments to the troops had been suspended. It was to be redeemed once order had been restored, but the failure of a Montreal merchant set Cuvillier back about £3,000 and a run on his bills ensued. In Trois-Rivières Moses Hart had been holding some of this paper and wanted compensation from Cuvillier. Adolphus had agreed to act for his uncle.

The place was deserted when Adolphus entered the premises. Cuvillier emerged from a rear office. Introductions were exchanged and Adolphus thought it only proper to compliment the *Canadien* on the look of his store. It had been expanded a year or so before.

Cuvillier didn't mind explaining. "I've had a successful run in business over the past several years. Like your Uncle Benjamin I have become a leading importer of manufactured goods, fish, salt and liquors. I have even dabbled in the stock of bankrupt merchants and have been selling the shares of various banks. I have found that very satisfying. It was the Bank of Montreal that did me in during the '20s. Nevertheless, two years ago I was named a Montreal director of the Bank of British North America. They can't keep a good man down."

"And yet I'm here to collect on what you owe my Uncle Moses."

"Another bad stroke of luck! Never mind, I'll work something out."

Adolphus marveled at the equanimity of the man. So many of his compatriots certainly regarded him a *chouayen*, a traitor to his people. His recent actions spoke for themselves; during the rebellion he was a Major and commander of Montreal's 5th Militia Battalion. As a magistrate the previous November he had co-signed the requisition for military assistance that enabled British troops to march to Saint-Denis. In January he had helped found the *Association Loyale Canadienne du District de Montréal*. Adolphus enquired as to its program.

Cuvillier had no objections to expounding on it. "We are, of course, critical of the rebel leaders but at the same time we are dedicated to saving our constitution. I have previously campaigned actively against the prospect of uniting the two Canadas. You are too young, *Monsieur* Hart, to remember how strongly I argued against a parliamentary bill tabled in '22 that would have forced *Canadiens* to give up the protections written into the 1791 constitution.

"Is there much support for your position?"

"We are making common cause with the Bishop, who opposes talk of Union despite his support of the government during the uprising. Lartigue did manage last January to plead with Lord Gosford to keep the constitution in force, though once the Governor left for London the following month, it was apparent that General Colborne didn't see things that way."

Adolphus had never been informed on what was going on at the *Château Saint-Louis*. "Now that he is in London, will not Gosford advise against it?"

"That may be a waste of time. Gosford appears to have little influence with Lord Glenelg. The Colonial Secretary has been in correspondence with Colborne, who would have taken over mid-February if Gosford hadn't injured himself falling on ice. In any case, Gosford is gone and Durham is here. The new Governor, I suspect, may not have the same reverence for the Constitutional Act as written over forty years ago."

At this point Adolphus shifted back to talking about the debt. His Uncle Moses would never forgive him if he hedged on the matter. No moneylender could afford to be soft on the subject of repayment and Moses Hart was no exception.

I do not know if you have had news from Albany. I can tell you for my part that I am utterly disgusted with that source. Our friend Dr. Nelson has been there and has not brought back very pleasant news. On the one hand Maître O'Callaghan wailing that all is lost and looking for work in a print-shop; on the other, the great chief pacing from one end of his room to the other, barely willing to receive Dr Nelson whereas many strangers are admitted to his company.
DR CYRILLE CÔTÉ
(letter to Ludger Duvernay, January 26, 1838)

Papineau has abandoned us for selfish and family motives regarding the seigneuries and his inveterate love of the old French laws. We can do better without him than with him. He is a man fit only for words and not for action.
DR. ROBERT NELSON
(letter to J.B. Ryan, February, 1838)

Three

Cyrille-Hector-Octave Côté rose this morning less than appreciative of the early summer breeze sweeping in from the open window. He did, however, cross to the window to gaze down on the rushing stream; the Saranac River flowing into Lake Champlain was oblivious to the turmoil in his own mind. *Why can't my woes dissolve within nature's turbulence?*

It had not been an easy few months during this spring. He and Robert Nelson had yet to live down the abortive venture undertaken at the end of February. Several hundred of their *Patriote* followers had sought to cross into *Bas-Canada* from Vermont only to be scattered by British troops waiting in readiness. How could all of their planning be so easily compromised?

Of course, it was not a matter of abandoning the fight against British rule in their homeland. Preparations for an early return to *Bas-Canada* were underway, albeit it was far from certain that Côté's colleagues here in the Border States were close to consensus on how to achieve a true *Canadien* republic. The *Patriote*'s titular leader, Louis-Joseph Papineau, had demurred in

January when it came to the declaration of independence penned by Robert Nelson in anticipation of these insurrectionists marching onto Canadian soil. Others were also sniping at the leadership of Nelson and Côté. And to think that but a year ago Côté was still a family doctor administering to the medical needs of the *habitants* in Napierville and the neighboring villages of L'Acadie! Now he was ensconced in an upstairs room of a boarding house in Plattsburgh trying to oversee a conspiracy within a hostile environment. Along with Nelson, Lorimier, Gagnon and others, Côté had been arrested soon after the February fiasco for violating the American neutrality law, albeit a sympathetic Vermont jury quickly discharged them from custody. Nevertheless, the news from Washington and Albany was still discouraging. Not only had President Van Buren been successful in getting that neutrality law passed by Congress in March, but also New York Governor Bill Marcy, true to his membership in the "Albany Regency", gave short shrift to any overtures for support to the exiles.

Not that Côté was in serious physical danger. Plattsburgh was a creature of the American Revolution, founded by a Zephanian Platt after the 1783 peace treaty. The western shore of Lake Champlain still retained its frontier look: the Adirondack horizon; a series of river rapids that made the Saranac a haven for fishermen and frolicking canoeists; frame-housed villagers open-hearted in their acceptance of fugitive *Canadiens* in their midst.

Côté was still at the window when a rap at the door interrupted his reverie. *More bad news?* There was no good reason not to open the door. Lucien Gagnon was standing in the hallway, a beatific smile on his face. Côté reacted with unfeigned surprise. His boon companion was back from an incognito trip to their old stamping ground, the Richelieu valley's L'Acadie.

Their embrace was heart-felt. Côté had had cause to worry about Gagnon's travel. General Colborne had stationed troops at border points and the British settlers were generally eager to pounce on suspected insurrectionists. *But here he is, safe and sound!*

Once seated, Gagnon responded to Côté's enquires. "It was good to get back to L'Acadie. You know that Sophie returned to Saint-Valentin once repairs were made to our farm. It was *une joie!* She is counting on me spending time with them during the summer though I've told her my first responsibility is to the cause."

"I only wish all of our people were as dedicated as you."

"What are you implying, *mon ami?*

"Perhaps I'm too sensitive. But all I hear from Rodier is criticism. He is now living in Burlington. Being on the other side of the lake, he is less amenable to the discipline of the collective. He does agree with us on

Papineau's shameful retreat on our principles but at the same time he is suspicious of everything we say and everything we do."

"Does Édouard-Étienne not accept our new strategy?" Gagnon looked puzzled.

"He agrees that we failed in February because we neglected security. The concept of building up the *Frères-Chasseurs* makes sense to him." Côté did indeed take pride in pushing for an army practicing secrecy in an organized fashion. Under the *Grand Aigle*, the designated major general of the force, would be *Aigles* in as many districts as possible. The latter would form companies under the supervision of two *Castors*, essentially captains, and five *Raquettes*, each of which bringing together nine men under his command. Nelson and Côté could expect the populace to respond to the appeals of the *Raquettes* once hostilities commenced and arms and ammunition were made available.

Gagnon got to his feet. "There are risks in traveling north. They have a £100 reward posted for my capture. Even so, I am confident that whether I shall be in Laprairie, in Chambly or in Beauharnois, the farmers there will not betray me. We shall have many *chasseurs* ready to serve our *Aigles* when the time comes.

"*Bon homme!* Did you know that Lorimier is here in Plattsburgh? His Henriette joined him just a few weeks ago and promises to spend most of the summer in a boarding house down the street while he's off to recruit *chasseurs.*"

"Where will he go?"

"We think it best that he travel to the western counties. Deux-Montagnes, Beauharnois. What do you think?"

Gagnon didn't answer directly. He had a question of his own. "What are we to tell the *habitant*? Can we assure him that there will be the weapons and ammunition to make a success of any uprising?"

"I know what you are thinking, Lucien. But we must operate on the basis of the Americans eventually blessing our efforts by giving us tangible aid. They are already giving sanctuary to Mackenzie and his people." Côté had been in correspondence with William Lyon Mackenzie, who had retreated to Navy Island in the Niagara River following the failed rebellion in Upper Canada. Like Nelson, Mackenzie had set up a provisional republic and seemingly has the moral support of the administration in Albany.

Gagnon nodded in agreement. "I trust that God would not have me back away from such a just cause. And when I travel through our parishes in the next few weeks, I can be sure that there will be many willing recruits for the *Frères-Chasseurs.*"

"If only we can inspire them! Duvernay, who is also in Burlington, is determined to acquire printing equipment so that he can play his usual role in our struggles." A frown had returned to Côté's visage.

"Must we wait for Duvernay to use his pen? Even without a printing press, Brown has made himself noticed. In April he has, according what I've been told, published a long article on the rebellion in the *Vermonter*."

Côté shook his head. "It was addressed not for the readers we covet. In any case, Brown is departing for Florida. We are all without gainful employment."

"Can you hold out for long?" Gagnon's tone was solicitous.

Côté didn't reply immediately. Yes, he was still a doctor and there were limited opportunities to practice medicine in this community. But could he dare bring his family to Plattsburgh?

*   *   *

The phaeton hired by Coté and Robert Nelson was adequate for the journey that would take them as far as Albany. But this light four-wheeled horse-drawn vehicle had seen better days and their muscles were paying the price for having made that choice. Actually their destination was the Fish Kill, the river flowing into the Hudson at Saratoga, 40 miles north of the New York capital. On one bank of the river was the old Schuyler house, a reminder that the British contingent under General Burgoyne had surrendered here just over fifty years ago. It was regarded by just about everyone that this British defeat was the turning point during the American Revolution.

It being June and as yet no coordination between Louis-Joseph Papineau and his former acolytes, Coté and Nelson had reckoned that one more effort should be made to make peace with their leader, who was still revered by so many *habitants* in *Bas-Canada*. For that they had to take the road to the south. It had been fortunate for Papineau that a prominent Albany lawyer had befriended him some years before. When he had crossed into the United States the previous December, he was taken to the home of James Porter, register of the court of chancery in the New York capital.

The ride to Saratoga had been without incident. Côté and Nelson were, however, not convinced that Papineau would still be in the village. He had gone there with his eldest son, Amédeé, immediately after a confrontation in Middlebury in mid-January, but it was possible that he could have retired to Albany, where earlier he had resided as a guest of Porter. Subsequently Côté had learned that Papineau had gone to Philadelphia in order to consult with knowledgeable people in the federal capital. *Perhaps he can report some tidings as a result of this initiative.*

The phaeton came to rest in front of the Westcott house in Saratoga. Papineau's son, Amédée, was reportedly living there while he was studying for a law degree. Imagine their surprise when the servant at the entrance disclaimed any knowledge of Papineau. It took some time to ascertain that the latter had adopted the names of Jean-Baptiste Fournier, father and son. Amédée finally came to the door to clarify everything. "*Mon père* is at the moment entertaining family. He has just come back from Philadelphia. You will have to wait."

Young Louis-Joseph-Amédée Papineau had the look and temperament of his paternal forbears. Though not yet twenty, he was known to both Côté and Nelson as a conspicuous activist in their common struggle. Côté pressed for more information on the Philadelphia sojourn.

"It was all incognito. He traveled there under the name of Lewis. Only now can he resume his true identity. But that's beside the point. My mother and sister Azélie have first call on his time and they have also sent for my grandfather Joseph. He is 86 years old but it being June the trip should not be too taxing."

Nelson almost shouted. "Are we expected to wait for Joseph Papineau to show up before your father has time for us? I received the same treatment when I visited him during the winter. No wonder some refer to your *père* as a poltroon!"

Amédée was both angry and embarrassed. "You misjudge my father. He is pursuing alliances that are necessary for our success in defeating the enemy. Your maligning of the Church and our other national institutions serve only to make the task that much more complicated. Even so, I would personally be with you if I were not committed to the study of law. It is my only chance to work with men such as *Juge* Cowen, *avocat* Ellsworth et *Chancelier* Walworth."

Côté turned to Nelson. "Perhaps it was not wise of us to come. But I don't think we are misjudging this young gentleman."

* * *

Ludger Duvernay seemed more than a little tipsy. Côté had agreed to meet him at the local inn in Plattsburgh but hadn't expected him to be drinking even before they met.

"Have you had time to ponder over Durham's amnesty ordinance? I have a letter from Montreal actually praising the Governor's leniency, albeit I find little comfort in having so many of us left in purgatory."

"They could have been hanged. My guess is that those eight prisoners released from *Pied-du-Courant* are now on the high seas heading for Bermuda. Is exile to a faraway island much better than death? It still bothers me that they agreed to admit guilt. I would not have been so imprudent." Côté too had mixed feelings about the government measures. Durham had not followed in the footsteps of the authorities in Upper Canada; there were no summary executions in the lower province. However, he, Côté, was personally on the list of the sixteen prominent *Patriotes* who would have to remain in exile. Going back to *Bas-Canada* could result in his neck being stretched.

"Imprudent or not, we will have to live with this new reality. I am stuck in Vermont whereas Boutillier has decided to return to Saint-Hyacinthe. Some good may come of it. From there he should be able to collect some of the money owing to me. As it is, I have still not received enough contributions to obtain the necessary printing equipment to start a newspaper. I may not be ready to publish till next year." Duvernay was back to quaffing his beer.

"You would do that in Burlington, *n'est-ce pas?*"

Duvernay snorted. "Where else? On the other hand, we can hope that with our *chasseurs* in the lead, we will succeed where we failed last year. The name of Papineau does carry a lot of weight in *notre patrie*. If only our people knew how far he has stepped back in providing leadership! Boutillier still defends Papineau. Says that he has made mistakes, but is by no means a traitor to his country."

"We must do our best without him. Remember, we need money for other purposes as well. Especially for munitions. Nelson tells me that Beaudry in Montpelier is not limiting himself to asking for funds there. He is intending to tour other centers on either side of the Connecticut River to get the most he can from sympathetic Americans." Côté had been heartened by this news from the Vermont capital.

"Will he stick with it? He is not subject to arrest because he's not on Durham's list."

"Are you suggesting that he intends to return to Montreal?" Côté had never really got to know Jean-Louis Beaudry although the latter had been chosen as a vice-president in the *Fils de la Liberté* late last summer. Côté himself was a medic based in L'Acadie; Beaudry, who was about the same age as he, had been a successful merchant in Montreal. Such a display of militancy had appeared odd to Côté, who did not have a high regard for those in commerce.

"I would not be surprised. We all have to eat. Our mutual friend Rodier works as a waiter in Burlington." Duvernay's expression was almost cynical.

"Rodier is no longer a friend of mine! My guess is that at the first opportunity he too will retire to his old life." Côté was indeed in a funk. *Shall we be losing by defection as many as we hope to recruit by our forays into Bas-Canada?*

*More extensive changes in the Act of 1791 than were then in
contemplation seem now to be required, since it is hardly to be hoped
that when an actual conflict must have so greatly inflamed these
mutual jealousies and animosities between different classes
of the population which before obstructed the working of that
Act, it could, without very material alterations, be brought
again into beneficial operation.*
COLONIAL SECRETARY LORD GLENELG
(letter to the Earl of Durham, January 21, 1838)

*To become Masters of the Country has, I fear, become
a national sentiment with them.*
STUART DERBISHIRE
(letter to Charles Buller, August, 1838)

Four

Their embrace was heartfelt. Aaron Ezekiel Hart had grown increasingly fond of his younger brother even if circumstances had kept them apart for years at a time over the past decade or so. Adolphus too looked up to his sibling, the first family member – in truth, the first Jew – to be a member of the bar in Lower Canada. The eleven-year difference in their ages seemed less important as the years went by.

Adolphus did have to explain, however, what brought him to the capital of the province on this hot day in late July. Aaron Ezekiel had been counting on getting out of the Upper Town for the weekend to escape the elevated humidity so typical at this time of the year. Instead, he would be hosting Adolphus, who had just arrived from Trois-Rivières. Aaron Ezekiel had to be gracious. "Was it a comfortable trip?"

"I shared a carriage with Vallières, who has come here at the Governor's bidding.

"What does Durham want from a small-town judge?

Adolphus chuckled. "Did you not know that Vallières has been appointed to the Executive Council? The Governor believes our colleague can arbitrate the differences between the Quebec and Montreal jurists when they give advice to the Council during sessions of the Court of Appeals. For some reason Durham is convinced that Vallières has the finest legal mind in the province. Incredible, is it not?"

"You're prejudiced, Dolph. Just because he abandoned our sister for another woman." Aaron Ezekiel hoped his brother realized that he was joking.

"You're wrong, Eze. I have much admiration for Vallières even if he and Uncle Moses are constantly at odds. It took courage for him to grant a writ of *habeas corpus* to Pacaud knowing that Colborne had declared martial law."

Aaron Ezekiel concurred; if he were in Vallières' place, he would have been reluctant to let a brother of Louis-Joseph Papineau appear in court in defiance of the government's suspension of *habeas corpus*. In the event notary André-Augustin Papineau, a participant in the battle at Saint-Charles the previous November, was released from prison. Young Édouard-Louis Pacaud deserved credit for pursuing the writ. "We can be happy that Durham took over before Colborne took his revenge. Now Vallières visits the *Château* a hero!"

Having seated himself in his brother's bachelor apartment, Adolphus finally got around to revealing the purpose of his visit. "I too have business with the *Château*. Last month Uncle Moses sent the Governor a petition in the name of the citizens of Trois-Rivières asking for judicial reforms. He wishes me to press the administration to act on them."

"He has become quite cantankerous. He once praised Thomas Paine and the 'rights of man'. Since the rebellion he talks of England only as a charitable, high-minded and generous nation. In contrast Papineau and his disciples are 'hot-brained lawyers' prone to mischief."

Aaron Ezekiel's grin was sardonic. "When they get into their seventies, men become much more conservative. Uncle Moses probably regrets being a Deist and once a defender of the French Revolution."

"Our father's generation is certainly getting on in years. Papa is no longer himself and his cousin will not see the end of '38". Adolphus was alluding to Henry Judah, the parent of the two Judah lawyers operating in Montreal and Trois-Rivières respectively.

"These are different times from what we had earlier in the century. How do we explain civil war and economic recession after fifty years of a new Constitution? Perhaps Governor Durham will bring new thinking to bear. At least the suspension of specie payment has come to an end. Trade should improve as a result. Uncle Moses may yet make a success of his shipping business." Aaron Ezekiel had become quite contemplative.

"Tell me, Eze! No chance of refreshments for a tired traveler?"

"How inconsiderate of me! Alas, Marie, who cooks for me, left but an hour ago. But there is wine and brandy in the cupboard. Shall I pour you a drink?"

"When will you marry, Eze? You are already thirty-five. Do you want to be like our other brothers? Sam seems to be a confirmed bachelor and Ira Craig is showing no interest in settling down." Adolphus didn't mention another brother, Abraham Kitzinger, who had died at the beginning of the year.

"Who would I marry? Papa would never approve of me choosing a woman outside the faith."

"There are the David daughters. Phoebe is already twenty, Fanny eighteen. Even Sophia is of a marriageable age." Adolphus himself had had fantasies about seducing one or another of these cousins.

"I am not inclined to the wedding of cousins, though that appears to have been our lot. Aunt Sarah, if she were still alive, would never have agreed to having her children staying within the clan if it involved them hooking up with another Hart or Joseph."

"I'll have that drink now." Adolphus apparently didn't wish to pursue the subject of marriage if the specter of incest was being raised as a counterpoint.

Aaron Ezekiel went to the cupboard and brought out a decanter of Madeira along with wine glasses. *It is time to relax a bit.* "We might consider going down to the Lower Town to call on Abe. He has his office on Rue Saint-Pierre albeit we are more likely to find him at Lemoine's this time of day." Aaron Ezekiel regarded himself fortunate to have a cousin in the city; Abraham Joseph had located himself in Quebec over a year before, though he had often traveled to the capital in his capacity as agent for the Joseph family's tobacco business. Lemoine's was a boarding house on the Battery.

"How is Abe adjusting to living permanently in Quebec? I remember Ira Craig telling me that it was a momentous occasion for Abe transporting all his personal goods on the *British America* a year ago in May."

Aaron Ezekiel laughed. "It was even more momentous for him when last June, before the outbreak of hostilities, Abraham had shared wine with Papineau at a dinner given for the Assemblymen coming from Montreal to Quebec. The way he tells it, Papineau first declined to drink 'foreign liquor' but when no beer could be found, he took the wine."

Adolphus too found that quite amusing. The *Patriotes* could not always abide by their decision to shun goods not made locally.

*　　*　　*

Crossing the Place d'Armes, Aaron Ezekiel had an inspiration; he resolved to confront Judge Elzéar Bédard in his chambers. The courthouse off Rue Saint-Louis looked almost deserted this summer day. Perhaps Bédard would be willing to clarify a remark he had made during a recent session of the court. The right of *habeas corpus* was too important a matter in Aaron Ezekiel's view to be limited to an off-hand opinion.

Of all the justices seated on Quebec's Court of Queen's Bench, Elzéar Bédard was the one best known to Aaron Ezekiel. Not only were they about the same age – Bédard was born in 1799 – but also they both lived in Trois-Rivières during their formative years. Because Bédard was diverted for a while from his legal career by taking holy orders, the two happened to be admitted to the bar in the same year, 1824. Only protocol prevented them from being on a first-name basis.

When he reached the second floor of this forty-year old building, Aaron Ezekiel encountered nothing but silence. Nobody in the corridor; no bustle of clerks, litigants and their counselors as there would be when the court was in session. Had Aaron Ezekiel been misinformed? *Bédard may not be here after all.*

But he *was* there, seated behind his massive desk, poring over a book. He eyed Aaron Ezekiel and showed a hint of annoyance. "What brings you here, Hart?"

Aaron Ezekiel quickly apologized for his intrusion. He admitted to being disturbed by the remark the jurist had recently made about constitutional protection against arbitrary arrest. Was he implying that the government had acted illegally? Granted that the doing away of *habeas corpus* had occurred during the British war with the rebellious American colonies prior to Aaron Ezekiel's birth. But that was before the creation of the Constitutional Act of 1791. Too many *Canadiens* recalled the prolonged imprisonment without charges of Du Calvet and other critics not to ask themselves whether they were protected against such actions by the authorities. Yet Bédard along with fellow members of the court had raised no objections when General Colborne took that right away the previous winter.

Bédard heard him out. "No objections? No case has come before my court that required me to make an appropriate judgment. We were fortunate that most of arrests occurred in and about Montreal and not in this district. I'm not certain *how* I would rule if constitutional issues were raised during arguments. We were dealing with an emergency."

"I spoke with Aylwin about this. Not only had he taken up the cases of several of those imprisoned after last autumn's rebellion. He has even published his views in the press. Not cowered by General Colborne and his advisors. He expected some show of support by the court." Aaron Ezekiel had developed a friendship with Thomas Gushing Aylwin, who had been practicing in Quebec for more than ten years. The latter was treading where Aaron Ezekiel had been reluctant to go.

"You may note, Hart, that the point may be moot now that the new Governor has granted amnesty to so many of the detainees. Even our friend Étienne Parent is appeased. Didn't *Le Canadien* carry an ode to the Earl? Canada, it affirmed, would be the last defender of old England on this continent. Would you have the Court quarrel with the government in such circumstances?"

"At least Parent recognizes that the exiles have a point. As he said in print last February, we have only the name and shadow of a constitutional government. And a month later Colborne suspends the Constitution."

Bédard paused before replying. "Like Étienne, I am impressed with the impartiality showed to date by the new Governor. Needless to say, I wouldn't have gone as far as *Le Canadien* in its praise of Durham's measures. But I'm hopeful that the worst is behind us."

Aaron Ezekiel held his tongue. He realized that Bédard was being consistent with his reputation as a compromiser. The latter had participated in the development of the 92 Resolutions that the *Patriotes* under Papineau made as their rallying cry in 1834. Indeed, Bédard had introduced them in the Assembly. But he soon backed off in his support of Papineau and accepted the offer from Governor Gosford to be elevated to the Bench. His erstwhile colleagues received the appointment with great derision. "Do you not worry that the Special Council would approve such measures again if there is any further trouble? I read what Adam Thom has to say in the Montreal *Herald*. He reflects the opinions of Moffatt and Badgley, who appear to have the ear of the Governor."

"But Moffatt is not on the Council," Bédard was not conceding the point. The Special Council had been reconstituted in June with most of the original body serving on it again. They included men such as John Neilson, Andrew Stuart and other "moderates" who had once sided with the Papineau-led *Patriotes* but had been put off by the increasingly republican and anti-clerical tone of the Montreal faction within the Party.

"I am not convinced that Council would be steadfast in arguing for reinstatement of our Constitution. It is said that Andrew Stuart will be named Solicitor General for the province once he returns from England. I presume that is in reward for his presidency of the Constitutional Association and his support for a union of Upper and Lower Canada."

Bédard shrugged. "As you undoubtedly remember, I articled in Stuart's office. I still count him as a friend though he has pursued the political career that I gave up. Ease up, Hart! Why don't you call on our Chief Justice while you are here? Sewell is in failing health. I doubt if he will remain in office much longer."

Aaron Ezekiel was not assuaged. "I regard such a visit as being an instance of hypocrisy. Sewell's interpretation of the law of treason is much too severe for my liking. And this matters now that he has been reappointed to the Executive Council."

*   *   *

Everybody in this dining area off the foyer of the Union Hotel was in his best dress. This despite the late August weather bringing but a modicum of relief from the heat spell that had gripped Quebec for weeks on end. The formal dinner had been organized in honor of Stewart Derbishire, an Englishman providing advice to the Governor. Aaron Ezekiel sipped from an *aperitif* handed to him by a hotel waiter. He felt honored to be there, an invitation he attributed to the initiative of his cousin Abraham Joseph, who appeared to be well connected in the merchant community.

Abraham was in top spirits. He relished being in the presence of so many dignitaries: Commissioners, army officers, church leaders as well as the leading businessmen of the capital. "At the dinner the Chief Justice will be introducing Derbishire, who is reputed to have become very knowledgeable about the causes of the revolt. I only recently learned that Sewell was one of the founders of this hotel back thirty some years ago.

Aaron Ezekiel regarded himself rather ill informed on Derbishire's credentials other than he was subordinate to Charles Buller, who supervised the investigating committee set up by the Governor. Abraham did indicate that Derbishire was a bit of an adventurer. A qualified lawyer as well as a journalist, the fellow had previously gone to Spain to monitor a civil war that won him a decoration from the queen of that country. Subsequently he was recruited by Lord Durham to travel through New York and the two Canadas to get first-hand information on rebel activities and motivations.

The dinner went pleasantly enough and Derbishire entertained the guests with anecdotes acquired over the course of his travels. Aaron Ezekiel did have an opportunity to question him once everybody rose from table. He was direct. "Are you convinced you have enough information to provide the Governor with the foundation for a report to the Prime Minister?"

"I would say so. I've been studying the attitudes of these insurrectionists since I arrived in New York last April. It was my good fortune to talk to

Mackenzie, O'Callaghan and Côté even before arriving in Canada. In Montreal Denis-Benjamin Viger agreed to be interviewed." Derbishire was repeating what he had said at the table.

"That should be enlightening." Aaron Ezekiel had often wondered why Viger, not only a cousin of Papineau but also a long-time spokesman for the *Patriotes*, had not been incarcerated the previous November.

"Not only did I have several discussions with him. He also received Mr. Buller and Edward Ellice to dinner in June."

"Did he make a good impression?"

"More cultivated than most of his confreres. Nevertheless, I find the Canadians a sluggish race, fond of indolent pleasures, lighthearted and gay. And yet they consider themselves superior to all the other peoples, and too good to mix with any other race."

"Where did you find Côté? Is he still in Plattsburgh?"

"Actually we met at Rouses Point, also on Lake Champlain. Let me tell you that like so many of the rebels, he has no practical grievances. Yet he is primed for a fight. Determined to become one of the masters of Lower Canada by any means at his disposal."

"You have a most jaundiced view of the *Patriotes*. Have they no cause for complaint?" Aaron Ezekiel was seeking to find out what advice Debishire was giving to the Governor.

"Their grievances are insignificant. In fact I would argue that their condition, social and political, are an enviable one, as compared with that of all other people upon the face of the globe. They know not the sight of a tax-gatherer. Their imposts in the shape of rent are exceedingly light; and every man can obtain land in small or large quantities, or in addition to that which he possesses, according to his ambition or means of cultivation."

"And yet they insist on being masters of their homeland. His Excellency has before him an insoluble problem." Aaron Ezekiel wasn't taking much comfort from Derbishire's analysis.

Went to Synagogue in morning – first time I had seen the building –
it is certainly a beautiful edifice –plain & neat. I took possession
of my seat No.5. Prayers over at ½ past 12 – walked some way
with the D's [David family].
ABRAHAM JOSEPH
(diary, September 20, 1838)

Eveng walked down to Synagogue – went into Mother's – dressed–went
down to D's. Miss Frances, flower of the flock, sang for me – sweet girly–
Phoebe not to be compared to her. Got to Mother's at 11 pm
ABRAHAM JOSEPH
(diary, September 20, 1838)

Five

Abraham Joseph hadn't gazed on the interior of his mother's house on Place Près-de-Ville since before the uprising. (He had missed being home for the last Passover holiday.) The gathering this September evening should make up for his having been separated in Quebec for more than a year. Rachel didn't hesitate to remind her son that it was God's will that the family be reunited as they celebrated Rosh Hashanah, the beginning of the Jewish New Year. Now that the freshly inaugurated synagogue was virtually operational next-door, it would be the focus of their attention in the next couple of days.

Never in Abraham's memory was the dining area as crowded. Because his eldest sister, Catharine, had married Aaron Hart David two years before, it seemed only right that the *mishpokhe* should share places at their table. There were seven of them; all the Davids were orphaned years ago but were very much a close-knit group. In any case, Rachel Joseph was accustomed to having a flock at her table; eight of her own offspring had survived the cholera epidemic that took away her husband and oldest son.

A painting of Henry Joseph hung on one of the walls, a reminder that the assembled progeny owed their wellbeing to the business acumen of an immigrant who got his start in Berthier-en-Haut. A cousin of the Harts of Trois-Rivières, he had married Rachel Solomons thirty-five years before. In time he and two brothers became leading merchants in the province and Henry decided to live accordingly. In fact, he acquired the large property on Place Près-de-Ville back in 1825. Situated at Lagauchetière and Chenneville, it was then a tract in the *faubourg Saint-Laurent* just northwest of the Place d'Armes on Rue Notre-Dame. The family patriarch had purchased it at a sheriff's sale for £3000 when even his Trois-Rivières cousins doubted it was worth the price. (Moses Hart had declined to provide him with a loan for that purpose.) At the time the elder Joseph still lived most of his days at Berthier, where he and his first son ran their shipping and retailing businesses.

Now the second son had taken his place. Abraham looked up from his plate to focus his eyes on the young man at the head of the table. Jacob was but a year older than he but had taken control of the family's purse strings almost immediately after the death of the father and eldest son. Lately known as "Jacob Henry" in order to establish the continuity within the family businesses, he was already asserting himself as one of the majors in the province's transportation industry. Even more of his attention was being given to the wholesale tobacco trade.

Jacob took notice of Abraham's stare. He almost shouted a comment in order to be heard. "I suppose, Abe, you have yet to visit our new synagogue. I'm sorry you missed the dedication last month. The Board brought Levi in from New York to lead the ceremony."

"I suppose that would be Benjamin Hart's doing. At least he has been relieved of the responsibility of holding services upstairs in his house on Rue des Récollets." Abraham was acknowledging his relationship with his father's cousin.

Aaron Hart David spoke up: "Yes, the old man has been presiding over the Corporation of Portuguese Jews for over a year. The bylaws of the Congregation were published in July. My signature is on the booklet in my capacity as secretary of *Kahal Kadosh Shearith Israel*."

"A little young for being the secretary, wouldn't you say, cousin?" Jacob Henry, a scowl on his face, seemed primed for a quarrel. Abraham suspected that his older brother didn't have a high opinion of a professional undertaking tasks best left for men of commerce.

Rachel was quick to defend her Catharine's spouse. "It was only proper that my son-in-law should serve as secretary. His uncle provided the land for the *shul* and his cousin Moses Ezekiel laid the cornerstone. At least one of the Davids should be given due recognition. Besides, who says a medical doctor can't be a good administrator?"

"Isn't there room for a Joseph as well? At least one of our families is devoted to our faith." Jacob Henry looked mischievous saying this and Abraham realized the barb was aimed at him.

Rachel took the bait. "If Abraham were ever to return to Montreal, he would certainly serve on the Board."

"I am twenty-three years old, mama. Surely I can make that decision on my own."

The subject was quickly dropped and the eating continued. Rachel and her servants had made a sumptuous meal for the holiday. Most everyone preferred to enjoy it in peace. It was only after the males in the party broke away from the table to assemble in the smoking room that their conversation resumed its intensity.

The youngest of the Josephs started it off by enquiring whether the political discontent in the Richelieu Valley endangered the business prospects for the fledgling railroad. Gershom was about to enter his third year at the university in Toronto. He had secured his secondary education at Upper Canada College and caused a bit of stir by becoming the first Jew to be enrolled in the university there. He would once again be leaving home this September.

"I'm convinced we have made a good investment in the Champlain & St Lawrence. Railways are the future." Jacob Henry once again began enumerating the benefits of the line linking Laprairie on the river's south shore to Saint-Jean on the Richelieu. He did not fail to mention that he personally was on the ferry that took dignitaries to Laprairie for the official inauguration of the railroad in July 1836.

Jesse, Abraham's younger brother, interjected that Gershom might be worried that as a family "we have been compromised by our participation in putting down the uprising."

Jacob Henry answered with quiet fury. "I've received nothing but praise for my efforts in the Richelieu region during the fighting. It was my idea to conceal the dispatches in my leather linings when I traveled between Colborne and Wetherall. True, it was night but who knows what would have happened if the rebels had intercepted me and confiscated the letters."

Jesse tried to appease him. "I wasn't denigrating your battle performance, Jake. You showed great courage. But Gershom is concerned that there is likely to be more trouble and that our businesses may be vulnerable as a result."

"Maybe it is only you who is concerned. Overly so! Moreover, I have a complaint of my own. You continue to live at home, Jesse. Don't you ask yourself whether you are contributing enough to the household? Four women rely on our earnings." Jacob Henry was referring not only to his mother but also to three unmarried sisters.

Abraham hurried to intervene. "Calm down, Jake! You needn't be so derisive. The public may know us as Jacob Henry Joseph and Company, but remember that Jesse and I are your partners."

∗   ∗   ∗

The weather this Thursday morning was as pleasant as that of the evening before. Abraham rose early. Having yet to see the synagogue in its finished state, he needed the time to examine the building before settling down in seat No. 5, the location in the pew reserved for him. He already recognized the stone façade with its Doric columns framing the entrance, the synagogue's exterior having been defined even before he departed for Quebec. The interior too satisfied him; it was as dignified as he had hoped. He said so when he spoke to Aaron David

Aaron confirmed that the design of the inside had been a point of controversy. Moses Judah Hays, who had led the campaign to have the synagogue built, would have accepted a more embellished monument to his effort. But Benjamin Hart, who had long familiarity with the Sephardic style of worship, had insisted on a *décor* rather understated. He had already written into the rules of the Congregation that the rites of the Portuguese Jews be observed even if many if not most of the members were Ashkenazis originating in Germany.

Meanwhile, the rest of the David family had arrived at the synagogue as a bloc. They had come up from Rue Craig, not too far away. The three sisters then separated to join Rachel, Catharine, Rebecca, Sarah and Esther in the women's section behind the screen. Abraham shook hands with Major Eleazar David, who cut quite a figure even without his uniform. Mention was made of the evening meal still being digested. Other male members of the Congregation, Isaac Valentine, Benjamin Hart and sons, Esdaile Cohen, George Benjamin and Abraham's own brothers were now filling the pews. *Not a big Congregation but its members have contributed nicely to the building of this institution. And now there were enough for a minyan.*

Abraham took his seat. It was the beginning of the ten days of penitence; Adam's children would be judged before their God and emerge forgiven on the Day of Atonement. He accepted spending most of the morning reading the liturgy from the *machzor*. What he looked forward to the most was the blowing of the *shofar*. A total of 100 notes were to be played on this ram's horn in the course of the next hour or so. *Shall these unusual sounds encourage me to repent?*

Before the chanting commenced, Aaron leaned over to whisper in Abraham's ear. "The *shul* has already made an impression on our neighbors. It is by no means out of place. We now have the Scotch Secession Chapel on Lagauchetière. The *Wee Kirk* as it is called. And we are always in sight of the Friars roaming their garden across the street. This is a very spiritual corner of the city. Perhaps too spiritual!"

Abraham snickered. His brother-in-law retained some of the skepticism of a learned man. He would pursue the matter when they walked to the David's house on Rue Craig for lunch. Aaron had also requested that Abraham as an out-of-towner come over for dinner as well.

∗   ∗   ∗

The Davids had invited not only Abraham; already in their parlor were Benjamin, Harriot and Aaron Philip Hart as well as Thomas Judah, a second cousin Abraham had hardly gotten to know. He had, however, dressed for dinner and didn't feel out of place. He had noted the presence of the Harts in the synagogue earlier in the afternoon but hadn't been informed of their subsequent presence on Rue Craig. Thomas Judah, of course, had not been there; his parents had raised him as a Christian.

The three sisters took seats next to the pianoforte. Abraham had learned in previous times that the estate of David David included funds for the purchase of this musical instrument. Sarah Hart David had succeeded in having it delivered from England a few years ago in order that Phoebe, the eldest, could be taught how to handle the keyboard of a squared piano.

The sisters were soon asked to perform. Abraham had eyes only for the middle one, the shapely lass whom he had known as Fanny during their mutual childhood. Frances Michaels David was five years younger than Abraham but he had determined that when she was old enough, he would propose marriage. *If only I can prove myself while living in Quebec, I shall be able to support a wife.* Their recent correspondence had been minimal, but he had signaled his intentions before he left Montreal. And listening to her sweet voice this evening, he was reinforced in his passion for her.

Phoebe, at the piano, led off the entertainment with a few popular tunes that somehow didn't excite her audience. Only when Frances was prevailed upon to sing a song at Abraham's request did the applause rise above the courteous. She blushed visibly and resumed her seat quickly. Her performance, however, may have put off her youngest sister. Sophia declined to sing at all despite the urging of her siblings as well as Abraham. *She is sixteen; why the shyness?*

Within minutes Phoebe rose from the keyboard. She reminded everybody that she and her sisters had to be thinking about tomorrow. They would be walking to the synagogue rather early to be in time for the second day of services and they needed their rest. Abraham shifted his eyes to ascertain whether this meant that his Fanny would be withdrawing from parlor. *Alas, she isn't even looking at me!*

The guests were in no hurry to depart after the women excused themselves. Aaron Philip Hart and Tom Judah in particular chose to repeat some of the local gossip gleaned at the courthouse. Aaron Hart David appeared more interested in having Abraham report on what was occurring in Quebec. What was the Commission headed by Charles Buller up to? When would the Governor decide what was in store for the province?

Benjamin Hart, quiet through much of the discussion, finally sounded a sour note. "Lord Durham is acting as if law and order has already been established and he can write his report at leisure. He is blind to what is happening on the ground."

Looking at his elderly relative – Benjamin Hart would be seventy in the coming year – Abraham didn't know how seriously to take this warning. It had become a family joke that the old man wouldn't be satisfied until every rebel had been punished. His mood had not been improved when it became clear that the government would not be appointing him to the Special Council. It was Aaron Hart David, however, who did ask Benjamin to explain himself.

Benjamin obliged. "As police magistrate I receive regularly the reports from our secret agents operating in America. They are immediately forwarded to General Colborne but I do perceive that trouble is brewing in Vermont and New York. I could have foreseen all this by the confessions I recorded when interviewing so many of the rebels captured at the end of last year."

"But surely General Colborne has the forces needed to cope with any further insurrection? Papineau and his people must know that?" Tom Judah seemed to represent the general sentiment in the room. He did, however, betray a degree of uneasiness. Abraham recognized that Montrealers, with the experience of last November and December fresh in their collective memory, were much more aware than the citizenry in Quebec of the consequences of civil strife.

The subject was soon dropped. Benjamin hadn't expanded beyond what he had to say about the threat from below the border. Nobody wanted to speculate on the prospect of war when this was a time of celebration. Abraham queried Benjamin, the president of the Shearith Israel synagogue, as to the way forward. How could such an institution flourish without clergy?

Benjamin had a ready answer. "We shall find a qualified person to lead the Congregation. I have written to *Chazzan* Almosnino of the Bevis Marks Congregation in London. He has just replied; apparently there is a young man – one could almost call him a boy for he is not yet twenty-one – who impresses him with the depth of his knowledge of the Torah and the rituals of the Sephardim. And with a pleasing personality to boot. His name is David Piza."

Everybody in the room expressed their pleasure. Abraham asked the obvious question: When could they expect the arrival of a person who could combine the functions of *chazzan*, *shochet* and *mohel*? There was meat to sanctify, newborn boys to circumcise. They couldn't always count on assistance from New York.

"It will take time to get him here. There is space for another house on Place Près-de-Ville, but it has to be built. He does have a wife."

"Will he be leaving other family behind?"

"Actually he has no parents. Brought up at the community's Orphan Asylum."

*I am ever ready to spill my blood on the soil that gave me birth,
in order to upset the infamous British Government
– top, branches, roots, and all*
CHEVALIER DE LORIMIER
(letter to a friend, July, 1838)

*I warned Papineau that I had taken the oath of allegiance to Nelson's
provisional government, and that I was a member of the secret societies
of Albany ... I told him further that we were going to use his name
freely everywhere, except in the matter of money... So use his name
with discretion in New York, I am certain we
shall not be disavowed by him.*
THÉOPHILE BRUNEAU
(letter to Ludger Duvernay, October 11, 1838)

Six

The conspicuous markers of the autumn season were evident as Ludger Duvernay pushed himself into the stiff wind coming off Lake Champlain. Burlington appeared resplendent with its mottled leafy backdrop but it was Duvernay's guess that the threat of rain would still the sounds of building construction over this terraced strip of land between the bay and the Green Mountains range. His immediate concern was taking shelter, albeit the prospect of months of enforced idleness hadn't escaped his consciousness. There was yet no word on when the delivery of the printing press would happen.

What he needed now was a place next to a warm stove despite it still being September. *A warm stove and a glass of brandy is what the doctor ordered.* Once inside his room, however, the sight of a letter set on the table distracted Duvernay from this pleasure. He quickly split the seal. *Could it be another missive from Reine? She hasn't written for weeks.*

In fact his wife had sent the letter, albeit it was dated very early in the month. *Damn the postal service!* Once again she reported on the activities of sons Louis-Napoléon and Ludger *Fils* and daughters Marie-Reine-Joséphine and Marie-Adèle-Victorine. He and Reine had been married for over thirteen years and the four children could be their last as things stood at the moment. In this writing she once again raised the possibility of joining him in exile. *How should I answer? Who knows how the effort to create a new republic in Bas-Canada will work out?*

And what if an invasion failed as it did last year? Would he have to consider permanent residence in Burlington? Reaching forty years of age in January, Duvernay found it a frightening task to bring his wife and four children to a foreign land. Not that they couldn't adapt to an Anglophone environment and the town was certainly attractive enough. But as an exile he would never again play a role in shaping the future of a country.

Duvernay did pour himself a brandy and went to the window to look out at the steep hill behind the boarding house. Rather a different setting than the south shore of the St Lawrence, where he grew up. Since then it had been an urban life. Trois-Rivières, Montreal. Machines and sets of type. Now it was so different. During the summer months he had occasion to canoe on the Winooski River, which emptied into the lake about five miles to the north of the town. Even viewing the Winooski Falls at that point was an experience. Moreover, Vermonters in general were friendlier than most other Americans. Perhaps it was the legacy of Ethan and Ira Allen and the other Green Mountain Boys, who had treated with the British during the revolutionary period in 1780s. Furthermore, Vermont had refused to cooperate with the US federal government during the 1812 War. Returning to the bedside, he finished his drink and dosed off.

A rap at the door interrupted his sleep. Once he had gained admittance, the visitor – the broker he had been dealing with in Montpelier earlier in the year – shook off some of the water from his outerwear. The rain Duvernay had anticipated was indeed a reality. The fellow apologized for his unseemly state of dress. "Traveling down the Onion today was more troublesome than I expected." He was referring to the Winooski River, the gateway to the state's interior and the best route to Montpelier, the capital.

"Have you brought me news about my printing equipment?"

"Indeed! It will be coming up from New York within a week or thereabouts. However, I have even better news for you. It is reported in the New York press that the British government has rescinded all the sentences imposed on detainees such as you. The ordinances of last June have been cancelled.

Duvernay rubbed his eyes. Was he still dreaming? Or was this a practical joke? His interlocutor recognized this disbelief. He extracted a clipping from his portmanteau. "Read this yourself!"

Though the print was in English, Duvernay could take in the sense of the article. In Britain the prevailing opinion had been that Durham's actions were illegal. The exiled prisoners had not been properly tried and the Governor had no jurisdiction in Bermuda. And pronouncing death sentences on fugitives without their criminality having been tested in court was declared by Henry Brougham, the former Lord Chancellor in the first Melbourne administration, to be high handed to say the least. The Whigs in Parliament had gone along with his arguments.

*　　*　　*

It took more than a week or two for Duvernay to adjust to these new developments. In the interval he sent a note to Nelson and Côté in Plattsburgh. They must consult.

In mid-October Cyrille Côté did respond to this request. The ferry from Plattsburgh carried not only him but also Lucien Gagnon. Duvernay had thought that the latter had been in *Bas-Canada* setting up lodges of *chasseurs*. Apparently he had returned to New York. After the shaking of hands, Duvernay escorted the two to his room.

Finding two chairs on which to place his guests, he took the time to scrutinize their demeanors. How were they reacting to the surprise revoking of the ordinances? Would Nelson proceed with the declaration of a republic under his signature? Would Côté be a bit less stubborn about having his own way now that many of his compatriots had options other than obeying him? Duvernay hadn't forgotten their conversation in Plattsburgh earlier in the summer.

Distributing glasses of brandy, Duvernay found a place for himself on the bed. "Tell me, Lucien! When did you get back from the parishes?

"I've been here since late August. It has been a busy summer. Keeping out of the way of the British spies in order to recruit *habitants* in Laprairie, Chambly, Beauharnois as well as in L'Acadie. The result is what I judge to be an effective network of *chausseurs*. They will be ready when the signal is given."

Côté didn't let Gagnon finish. "And the signal *will* be given – perhaps in a matter of days. I too have traveled up and down the Richelieu. There is a strong sentiment for acting soon ~ before the Governor puts through the union of the Canadas. With Mackenzie in exile, the Tories in both provinces will close ranks and completely dismantle the Constitution."

Duvernay finished his drink. "My regret is that I will be of little help. My letterpress won't be assembled here until next spring though some of the equipment is on its way from New York."

"We do have Blanchard stirring the pot." Côté was referring to the editor of *The Canadian Patriot*. Duvernay had seen a copy of the sheet being printed in Vermont and distributed clandestinely in the border townships. Some of the rhetoric was certainly inflammatory. Duvernay recalled some of it: "Discard everything which advocates for aristocracy and beware the British yoke and galling chain." Duvernay planned to be much more subdued when he sought to drum up American support for the *Canadiens*.

"Has anybody been in touch with Papineau? Théophile Bruneau wrote me this very day that our chief's name is on everybody's lips. His popularity has not diminished because of the events of last November. Bruneau believes that the man will do nothing as reckless as to disavow his association with our cause." Duvernay had been in correspondence with Papineau's brother-in-law before and was intrigued by Bruneau's willingness to stand by his pledge to support Nelson rather than his sister's husband.

Côté shrugged. "We have heard nothing from Saratoga. You know, of course, that Julie has been there since June. I don't know what influence she has on him anymore. You know my opinion; he should be exposed publicly."

Duvernay rolled off the bed to stand up and face Côté. His tone revealed his dismay. "That would be ill-advised. Disruptive! We need every man we can muster to challenge the British. We may not have Louis-Joseph's money to back us, but his silence is to our advantage under the circumstances."

Gagnon also got to his feet. "Let's hold our tempers! As a matter of fact, Nelson agrees with you that now is not the time to have it out with Papineau. Our proclamation will address the question of seigneurial dues and tithes without pointing out the differences in our ranks. It is important to me that we are not put off by the lure of amnesty. As for me, my main objective is to maintain communications between Rouse's Point and Napierville so that we act decisively when it is deemed time to do so."

* * *

Duvernay finished his meal without trying to engage any longer with his waiter. He would wait until the inn's dining room closed, which it was scheduled to do in a half hour. The waiter was none other than

Édouard-Étienne Rodier, the erstwhile member of the *Patriote* leadership. Duvernay felt uncomfortable with being served by one of his own; too may of the exiles were being forced to find menial employment.

Nonetheless, Rodier was no stranger to manual labor. Before receiving his commission as a lawyer eleven years before, he had worked in a cooper's shop to survive. His fortunes improved immensely once he married a second time four years later. Elise Beaupré was the eldest daughter of a L'Assomption merchant. Now Rodier had just told him that Elise was on her way to Burlington. The children were remaining in L'Assomption. Duvernay tried to visualize the upcoming reunion; *What will Elise think of all this?*

This could be Duvernay's last visit to the inn before mobilization began. It was almost the end of October and a message from Plattsburgh, written cryptically, warned that the invasion was imminent. He would miss coming to the inn. It served a good beer and there was a supply of brandy in stock as well. Would Rodier be around to serve the drinks if he ever came back to this town?

Rodier had discarded his apron by the time he sat down at Duvernay's table. He had brought a glass of beer with him. They drank in silence for several minutes. Finally Rodier asked the question that was on both their minds. "When do our friends plan to cross the border?"

"I'm not exactly sure, Édouard-Étienne. Probably if I did know, I would be obliged to say nothing. They are insisting on maintaining as much secrecy as possible."

"I may as well tell you, Ludger; I may not ~ I probably should say, will not ~ be available for duty. Nelson and Côté really don't want me around, and there is no good reason to remain an *expatrié*. I intend to take up my life again in L'Assomption. The business there has suffered since old man Beaupré lost so much in the cholera epidemic. But I may be able to help revive it enough to keep my family together."

Duvernay hadn't expected such news. Rodier had indeed been alienated by what had been happening over the past year. *What a tragedy!* "Have you given any thought to living in Burlington? There are more *Canadiens* here than you might think. There is even talk of building a Catholic church in Burlington. This is a thriving city. I suspect it will be the biggest community in Vermont now that the shipping commerce at the waterfront is being combined with output from the mills operating at the Falls. Up the hill we have the University of the Green Mountains that Ira Allen founded at the same time that Vermont became a state in the Union. With your law degree and further study you should be able to make a living without waiting on tables."

"Always a possibility, *mon ami*, if all does not go well in *Bas-Canada* in the next few weeks. *Hélas*, I'm a skeptic. It may be wiser for me to make my peace with *les Anglais*. Now that the Governor's decree has been repudiated, I am free to return to L'Assomption. All I have to do is find the £3000 to post a bond."

Duvernay took another swig of beer. "You would pay a heavy price for such a choice. Could you accept being branded a turncoat by all your former colleagues? I know that I couldn't accept such a condemnation if I were to set out on an independent course."

*I shall not blush to hear that I have exercised a despotism; I shall feel
anxious only to know how well and wisely I have used, or rather
exhibited an intention of using, my great powers.*
LORD DURHAM
(September 28, 1838)

*[I have] re-established goodwill with the United States, and
rooted out from that people all sympathy with Canadian rebellion.*
CHARLES BULLER
(letter to John Stuart Mill, October 13, 1838)

Seven

On this early October day the steamship *Toronto* was making steady
progress moving downstream from Montreal to Trois-Rivières. From
the quarterdeck Alexander Thomas Hart peered at the receding shoreline;
he took comfort in the fact that to this point at least all the cabins were filled
and yet none of the passengers had registered any form of complaint. He and
his cousin Ira Craig Hart had been commanding vessels plying the waters
of the St Lawrence over a five-year period and both had become accustomed
to being bothered by some perplexity totally unforeseen. Owning one of
the dozens of steam-powered boats revolutionizing transportation in the
province, Alexander had raised his status within the Hart clan and in
the *Trifluvien* community as a whole. He was ready to deal with whatever
perplexity emerged.

The vessel floating from the river narrows near Sorel onto the widened
expanse of Lac Saint-Pierre, Alexander left the quarterdeck assured that
all would continue without mishap. He did feel the cold breeze, quite

uncomfortable despite the cloudless sky. He buttoned up his jacket and hurried down the main deck. There were dinner arrangements to be finalized, the Captain's table being open to the first-class passengers prior to the *Toronto* tying up at Trois-Rivières. Several of his guests were destined for Quebec, the steamboat's scheduled final destination during this run. They should be well fed before the boat passed Pointe-du-Lac.

Oops! He partially collided with a gentleman in his fifties; he had not been ready for this encounter with Judge Vallières, although Alexander had seen his name on the passenger list.

"Hart, isn't it?" Vallières seemed to be taking the mishap in stride.

Alexander chanced a chuckle. "You're the last man I want to upset. I'll be seeing you in court tomorrow. I've been served with a subpoena. It's the McClaren business. Ordered to testify as a witness to the fighting."

"Perhaps you can explain all this to me at the dinner table. You ought to know that I'm bringing Barthe along. He may want to read one of his poems to your guests." Vallières resumed his walk.

The jurist did make his appearance in the below-deck dining room at the appointed time. And with him was indeed Joseph-Guillaume Barthe, the young "poet" articling with lawyer Edward Barnard in Trois-Rivières. Alexander knew young Barthe – he was probably not much more than twenty years of age – as a *Trifluvien* whose parents lived in the Gaspé. The fellow was brash enough, albeit his scholastic record was rather indifferent.

Vallières explained that the two of them had traveled together to Montreal and were just returning after a week in the city. He indicated that their presence in the Court of Queen's Bench was not without interest. "At the Montreal assizes last week we saw Charles-Elzéar Mondelet and two colleagues defending four *Patriotes*. Mondelet made quite an impassioned speech on behalf of François Nicolas."

"What was Nicolas accused of?"

"It is charged that he executed Joseph Armand, the Loyalist they call Chartrand."

Alexander realized what was at stake. The government wished to demonstrate that the public trial in L'Acadie that fateful day last November was illegal and that the execution of the alleged traitor Armand was treason in itself. "You wouldn't want to express yourself on the guilt or innocence of the defendant?"

Vallières grunted. "That would be unwise."

"You know my sentiments. I am not bound by the same restrictions as the judge." Barthe spoke with vigor.

"Yes, it is said you spoke at a protest meeting in Yamachiche a year ago July. Letting the *habitants* of Saint-Maurice get a sample of your patriotic rhetoric." Alexander didn't hide his amusement.

Barthe laughed. "Most of them in that county can not read *Le Populaire*. For those who do, I've been using a pseudonym when publishing in Montreal. Marie-Louise, believe it or not!"

"And yet your talents are widely known. The last time we met, you were studying medicine with Dr. Kimber. Now I'm told you are in Mr. Barnard's law office. A change of course! When do you expect to be called to the bar?"

"Probably not till the spring after next." Barthe response was down to a mutter.

Vallières' mind was still on the assizes. "Charles-Elzéar is an enigma to me. I accept that as a counsel for a defendant, he may argue a case that he himself does not believe in. But he seemed sincere in his position that the *Patriotes* had committed political rather than criminal acts and should therefore be treated as political prisoners. And yet I remember the Mondelets, both he and Dominique, opposing the 92 Resolutions during the '34 debates. Dominique is so liked in the *Château* that he was appointed to the Special Council."

Barthe interrupted. "Don't be fooled by the appointment. He will never be part of this effort to suppress the voice of *Canadiens* defending the Constitution."

"I wouldn't bet on that, *mon ami*." Vallières sounded cynical.

Alexander brought the discourse to an end. There were other passengers to consider. And Trois-Rivières wasn't that far away.

* * *

Having a subpoena to obey, Alexander chose to remain in Trois-Rivières despite the *Toronto* departing for Quebec. With luggage in hand, he walked up Rue du Platon towards the main street, Rue Notre-Dame. His destination was his abode on Rue Alexandre. Though in his mid-thirties, Alexander Thomas still lived at home with his father. Moses Hart had long treated this "natural" son on an equal basis with the children born to Sarah Judah Hart. In fact, the proclivity of his half-brother, Areli Blake, for travel had the father turn to his "Aleck" for assisting him in handling much of the family's business affairs.

Alexander had in fact responded willingly to his father's invitation that he get involved in shipping. In May 1833 Moses Hart acquired a half share in the *Lady Aylmer*, a vessel built in the port of Quebec two years earlier. He immediately transferred his shares in the boat to his adopted son. The project had not gone that smoothly. John Miller, the other partner, had his own approach to the business and soon the two were in court to settle their differences. It was at this point that Moses and Alexander acquired the *Toronto*. The steamboat's cost was £2500, which was more than double what was paid for the *Lady Aylmer*. Alexander had still to prove to his father that running a service between Montreal and Quebec using the *Toronto* was a paying proposition.

Dusk had fallen by the time Alexander opened the front door and removed his jacket. Supper having already been served, he guessed that Moses and his partner had retreated to the parlor. The fireplace there was active, proof that the weather had changed enough to justify the burning of a log or two. Both Moses and Mary responded to his intrusion by greeting him warmly. They were surprised but pleased with his unexpected appearance. Mary McCarthy Brown in particular was prone to fuss about Alexander; she enquired about a libation and rang for a servant to have his selection brought to him.

"Will Areli and Julie be coming over this weekend?" Alexander suspected that they had been invited, Moses seemingly not able to get enough of interacting with his daughter-in-law. Julia Seaton had the elegance that came with being the daughter of a renowned soldier of the Crown. Alexander didn't share altogether his father's admiration of the woman; anybody who could be taken in by Areli's supposed charms couldn't be that discerning in spite of the elegance.

Moses, looking up from the journal he was reading, displayed a scowl. "Areli says that they are off to Quebec tomorrow. Silly boy! He thinks he can persuade the Governor to put an end to the administration's suspension of specie payments. I still think the answer for us is to get into the banking business ourselves. But let them enjoy themselves."

That's Areli, always aiming to enjoy himself! Alexander had held his tongue when almost ten years before Areli had taken off to Europe to see the world. The upshot was no end of trouble for the family, especially after Areli got into a relationship with a young Florentine. It took some doing to have this Italian marriage annulled, the woman in question threatening to go to court to charge desertion. Moses paid dearly but Alexander had stood by them. His papa Moses would occasionally remind him that Areli meant the "lion of God" in Hebrew. *Some lion!*

*   *   *

On a return voyage of the *Toronto* from Quebec, two of the passengers debarking at Trois-Rivières proved to be Alexander's cousins. Aaron Ezekiel and Adolphus had been in the capital through much of September. It was they who brought news of the uproar there following the Melbourne government's repudiation of Lord Durham's security measures. The Governor had resigned and was waiting to take the first boat back to England. Alexander suppressed his astonishment regarding these developments until he had consulted with Ira Craig; could his cousin stay in command of the vessel for the next hour or so in order to allow Alexander to hear out the two Hart lawyers? Receiving an affirmative, he accompanied the latter to the *auberge* across the street from the dock. There was much to talk about.

Traffic on Rue du Fleuve was light; the occasional dray did pass by, the sound of the horses' hoofs on the cobblestones announcing its presence. Alexander led the threesome into the dining area and called for a round of ales to be served by the bartender. He studied the faces of his guests; Aaron Ezekiel was older than he by a year but looked almost as young as Adolphus, his junior by eleven years. They had grown up together even if he, Alexander, carrying the stigma of illegitimate birth, often felt the outsider. Moreover, he didn't have the learning of these offspring of Uncle Ezekiel Hart.

After a few minutes of small talk, Alexander asked for more information on what had transpired in the capital. Why was the Governor resigning and was there any likelihood that the resignation would be accepted?

Adolphus responded with gusto. "Lord Durham appears to be adamant and most of us are taking him at his word. Last Wednesday we presented a petition to protest the parliamentary criticism of the Governor's actions. There were over four thousand signatures and I'm proud to say I provided one of them."

"You are satisfied then that Durham behaved properly when he issued the ordinances? I too have read accounts of what occurred in Parliament. It seemed to me that Lord Brougham had a point when he argued that the Governor acted illegally." Alexander's dissent was said with appropriate caution.

"Perhaps illegal but effective under the circumstances. Indeed, he has been a model of industry. Think of what he has done in a single summer! There are six working groups examining such matters as settlement, immigration, education, municipal institutions, commutation, registry offices, police, and the judicial system, not to mention a plan to alter the seigneurial *régime* on the island of Montreal. And yet he has found time to travel the country and meet with leading citizens in both Lower and Upper Canada. I deplore the treatment of the insurgents but I cannot deny that decisive action was necessary."

Aaron Ezekiel interrupted. "Here is where Dolph and I part company. I did *not* sign the petition."

"Brothers disagreeing! Tell me why, Eze!" Alexander had always thought the two sons of Ezekiel Hart were in full accord when it came to politics.

"I was led to believe in the beginning that Durham approached resolving the crisis with an open mind. Talking to Stuart Derbyshire recently, I discovered that the Governor has come here with a set purpose. While still in London he conferred with men such as Ellice and McGill, who offered prescriptions that tallied with the views of the Tory merchants in Montreal. You can bet on it: when Durham writes his report, it will recommend measures to reduce French influence in Canada. Union of the two jurisdictions; dominance of the English in all Councils. Unlike Adolphus, I am doubtful that the commissions will lead to anything that contradicts such an outcome."

Alexander was suddenly disconcerted. *Where do I stand in this matter?* Both arguments made sense to him and yet overlooked some of the realities. The *Canadiens* constituted the majority of the population and would not bow that readily to plans that were to their disadvantage. Trouble was very much on the horizon. He decided to say so. "Leaving Canada at this point in time may have unforeseen consequences. To my understanding there is strong sentiment in New York and elsewhere favoring American intervention on the side of the rebel *emigrés*."

Adolphus replied quickly. "Not according to Derbyshire. He assured Eze that Van Buren has promised that the United States will act against the insurgents crossing the border. Durham and the President drank each other's health when they met in Niagara Falls earlier in the summer."

"And I drink to your health, cousins. Even if I admit trepidation! We will be without a Governor at a most critical time. For the winter at least government will be back in the hands of the Special Council along with the generals and the judges. Will it be men such as Jonathan Sewell ruling on what happens in the colony?"

For some reason Adolphus though the question ridiculous. "I think not, Aleck! The Chief Justice is likely to leave the Bench before the month is out. He is a very sick man."

Alexander felt put down. He hadn't kept up with what was happening in the judiciary. Vallières hadn't said anything to him about a new Chief Justice even though they had been in contact in the past few days. "Who will replace Sewell?"

"My guess is that it will be James Stuart." Aaron Ezekiel spoke with conviction.

"I don't believe it. Stuart has been in private practice since he was suspended as Attorney General because of alleged improprieties. That was seven years ago and he still is very unpopular with the *Canadien* elite."

"Of course, he would be! His role in leading the Tory campaign for the Union Bill back in '22 hasn't been forgotten. But that is probably why Durham favors him. Stuart is, after all, a very accomplished lawyer and I suspect that the Governor likes the man's views on the joining of the two provinces into a single entity."

Alexander glanced at his timepiece. The steamship should be on its way if it were to keep on schedule. He quaffed the last of his ale and declared that he would have to be off. "Perhaps we can continue this discussion once I'm back in Three Rivers. It will be an interesting autumn for us."

Eight

The rendezvous had been set for Rouses Point. Close enough to the international border and within an easy ride from Plattsburgh, the village was also accessible by boatloads from across Lake Champlain.

Cyrille Côté had arrived early in the day in order not to miss teaming up with colleague Dr. Robert Nelson, the provisional president òf the nascent republic. He took heart from the fact that on this third of November the sky was clear even if there was a chilling wind coming off the lake.

Fixing the beginning of the invasion for today had not been without much debate and a series of compromises. The *émigrés* in New York and Vermont had spent almost a year preparing for the advent of battle. They also were aware that other *Patriotes* were assembling on this Saturday in the parishes along the border. In Napierville, Lacolle, Châteauguay and elsewhere they would constitute the reserves once arms and men arrived from the United States.

Nelson didn't disappoint him. Côté spied him conversing with a band of men dressed in dark jackets, the "uniform" that would identify them as a military troop. Most of Nelson's immediate subordinates, however, were elsewhere. *Perhaps in the inn at the end of the street!* So long as everybody is in place by sundown and so long as there was no US government interference during this mobilization!

The American federal presence at Rouses Point had, however, been minimal despite the government owning a military reservation beyond the shoreline. The fortifications of Fort "Blunder" had long ago been abandoned. The village itself, rising west of this "battery", had been settled immediately after the 1783 peace treaty by *Canadien* and Nova Scotian refugees awarded tracts of land as a reward for their services to the nascent revolutionary government. Now they and their descendants were witnessing the gathering of a new generation of exiles bent on returning to their homeland. Côté, engaging with Nelson, sought satisfaction on a key point. Were there the arms available to support the mission?

Nelson was gruff in his response. "The muskets have been loaded on a schooner up the lake. Ammunition too. There ought to be enough weapons to arm the *Chasseurs*. Our American friends assured me that the boat is on its way. Unfortunately they have to take precautions given the opposition of their federal government. It was not the same as last winter when we were able to take over the arsenal at Elizabethtown."

"And what if the schooner is intercepted or runs into foul weather? Ought we not to have a second source?"

"Cardinal does have in mind a second option. Once he is at Châteauguay, he proposes to push on to Caughnawaga to acquire weapons and ammunition from the Indians. They should have enough to arm the *Chasseurs* in that county." Nelson had seemingly met separately with his brigadier-generals, including Lorimier and Cardinal.

"You are recommending, therefore, that we proceed without waiting for the boat?"

"We have gone through this already. I have eight hundred men under my command. If we can reach Saint-Jean without serious fighting, there ought to be enough *Chasseurs* to augment our ranks for the march down the Richelieu to the St Lawrence."

That was certainly the strategy. If there were to be coincidental uprisings in Beauharnois, Châteauguay, Laprairie, Chambly, Boucherville, and Sorel, Colborne's regiments would be hard pressed to form a coherent defense against the main thrust of Nelson's contingent. True, that hadn't been the original plan. Côté and others had argued that there had to be close coordination with the force being maintained by William Lyon Mackenzie in the Niagara region. *How better to divide the British soldiers under the command of General Colborne!* It had, however, became obvious by the autumn that any raid into Upper Canada would not be happening. The opposition from the American government and the poor organization within his rebel camp had made Mackenzie himself reluctant to risk the loss of life and limb. And there wasn't the English equivalent of the *Frères Chasseurs* on the Canadian side of the Niagara River to support any serious enterprise.

Côté, therefore, knew it was a big gamble. The *Chasseurs* had never been tested. The *Aigles, Castors* and *Raquettes* had sworn oaths to stand by their comrades even if their property was destroyed by the enemy and sabers threatened their own throats. But well-executed oaths, secret signs and passwords might not prove enough when facing muskets and swords in the hands of trained troops.

There was no doubting the resolve of these *Aigles*. They were determined to make the republic succeed. Glackmeyer had even proposed that the assets of the province be marshaled for the good of the people. The Lachine Canal and the Laprairie-St-Jean railroad would be serving the populace at the will of the provisional government; the Molsons would part with some of their riches and the *Bank du Peuple* would replace the Bank of Montreal as the main financial institution. If the "Jew Hart" and his magistrate allies stood in the way, they would be dealt with ruthlessly. This thinking had not been altered by the fact that Durham was on his way back to England. His replacement, General Sir John Colborne, would be a tougher opponent.

Côté had cause to fear that not everyone was in full accord. He could attest from his own experience that Nelson was not the easiest man to get along with. In fact, Côté had to admit that he himself tended to be uncompromising when fundamental issues were up for discussion. Nelson was no less obstinate. Was he the right man to be leading the *Patriotes?* Nelson certainly had a presence. A vigorous man, swarthy and possessing medium height, he caught one's attention with his piercing glance and concise speech. But being so forceful and independent, he did earn a reputation of also being headstrong. *Two medical doctors accustomed to being decisive in their actions and brooking only a modicum of dissent.* Could their discipline be maintained in present circumstances?

* * *

The citizens of Napierville lined the sidewalks as the black-jacketed men strode down the main street. The marchers were dog-tired, having been on their feet throughout much of the night. The vociferous reception they were receiving did much to revive their spirits. Côté was among those seeking to connect with family and friends; he had lived in the neighborhood as far back as 1833 and achieved considerable stature not only as political leader but also as a physician. *And good fortune!* Margaret had brought the children with her from nearby Saint-Valentin; all could be seen vigorously waving their hands to attract his attention. *I'll embrace you, Margaret, at the earliest opportunity.*

It being Sunday, the denizens of the district had no other responsibilities to take care of. Mass was over. Most of the men had already been recruited as *Chasseurs* and were now answering the call to arms without need for passwords. Nelson and Côté mounted the steps of the church to read their proclamation; Lower Canada was now an independent country, and its citizenry would be exempt from seigneurial dues and the imposition of tithes. The subsequent cheers were gratifying to the two of them.

Napierville was but one assembly point. *Patriotes* would be gathering in Beauharnois, Baker's Camp outside Sainte-Martine, Saint-Constant, Lacolle and Châteauguay. Once they were supplied with the remainder of the armaments, which would be there imminently, the whole south shore upstream from Montreal might soon be in their hands. A scout was sent upriver to ascertain when and where the schooner was at this moment. In the meanwhile the contingent having traveled by foot from Rouses Point required some rest. Côté could attest to that; the fatigue was getting to him. Margaret would drive him home. He suspected he would be sleeping away the afternoon.

On the Monday morning Côté was back in front of the church anticipating developments. The expression on Nelson's face warned him that they were not all that positive. "The schooner has been intercepted coming down the Richelieu. The cargo is now in the hands of *les Anglais.*"

"*Merde!* We've promised our people that they would have the necessary muskets by now. This is disastrous news." Côté damned himself for not insisting that they wait in Rouses Point until the shipment was at hand.

Nelson nodded. "We need the arms and ammunition. We need them desperately. There are perhaps three thousand *Chasseurs* here ready to fight but they have very few weapons. I'm ordering that we send wagons and a few hundred of our men back to Rouses Point. We did hide some ordnance there. The lodges have the task of acquiring guns as well. It can't all depend on what we can bring from New York."

"Be realistic, Robert. Will a *Patriote* in the parishes take such a personal risk if there is no hope for success?"

"The news is not all bad. There is word from Beauharnois. Lorimier has seized the Ellice manor house and his men have boarded the steamship *Henry Brougham*." Nelson sought to be encouraging.

"Excellent! But what will they do with the boat?"

"Lorimier believes it can easily be converted into a war vessel. We should then be able to move down river to Montreal with greater impunity."

Côté shook his head. "Not without guns. We talked on Saturday of getting weapons from the Iroquois. Is that happening?"

"I'm waiting to hear from Cardinal. He ought to have close to four hundred men at Châteauguay. With that number he should make quite an impression on the Caughnawaga chiefs."

"In the meanwhile we wait in Napierville. An undisciplined and scantily armed *force de frappe* that will soon need to deal with Colborne, Clitherow and other experienced Generals. What have we done, Robert?"

"We do have officers with experience." Shamefacedly Nelson rebutted; he was referring to two French volunteers, one named Touvrey and the other Hindelang.

Côté turned away with disdain. *Are we waiting for a miracle!*

Towards evening Nelson and Côté learned no miracle had occurred. A message from the group that had returned to Rouses Point informed them that no cache of arms was available there – the American authorities had confiscated it – and also the *Patriotes* had subsequently been waylaid by militiamen, British settlers who had been recruited by the Odell family to battle the insurgents.

By dusk even more woes. A bedraggled *habitant* limped into camp. He had just come from Châteauguay. The man needing food and drink, it took some time to get his story. It was a sorry tale indeed. "It started off so well. We disarmed and arrested the leading members of the English party in the parish. But moving on to Caughnawaga in the early morning we soon found that we misjudged the temper of the Iroquois. While the detachment hid in the woods outside the reserve, *Messieurs* Cardinal, Duquette and Lepailleur went into the village to negotiate with the chiefs. The whole detachment was then invited to join our leaders. It was a trick! As soon as we were within the village, we were surrounded. I slipped away, but nobody else from our contingent escaped captivity."

* * *

The sky this Friday was overcast and the temperature had dropped even further. *Is snow possible so soon?* Côté trained his barrel-shaped eyeglass on the church that was the centerpiece of Odelltown. It was apparent that the British settlers in the Lacolle region had fortified this Anglican house of worship to make it a stronghold. They looked well armed even if their number didn't match what Hindelang had brought to the scene. And there was a cloud of dust on the eastern horizon. *More enemy soldiers on their way?*

The British regulars had yet to appear in the border area but the militia and volunteers in the Townships – British settlers in Wroxham, Covey Hill, etc – had reinforced the English-speaking locals. On Wednesday they had forced retreat by the *Patriotes* at Bullis Farm outside Lacolle.

Following this setback, Nelson, Côté and Hindelang quickly consulted. The 'provisional president' pushed for acting decisively. "It makes good sense that we reinforce our people at Lacolle. They took a beating from the settlers in Odelltown. If there is any chance of turning things around, it is an immediate defeat of these militiamen. And being somewhat closer to Rouses Point provides us with an easier escape route should things not go well."

As he put aside his spyglass, Côté gave further thought to Nelson's remark of that day. It implied the man's lack of confidence in ultimate victory. Was his colleague ready to run? Côté himself had concluded that the situation was dire, but he was ready for one more try. He had invested so many months in getting back to Napierville. But the battle plan was in tatters. *Ad hoc* decisions had become necessary. Côté still remembered the second message on Wednesday from the one other *Patriote* entrenchment of reasonable size. The courier from Beauharnois reported that a British infantry division was marching on Sainte-Martine. He was blunt. "Our force at Camp Baker there will soon be under attack. Lorimier decided to take a couple of hundred of his men to reinforce them before they were in the throes of battle. The men did stand firm. *Les Anglais* withdrew at nightfall. Yet he is a very unhappy man. Another regiment from Upper Canada is said to be on its way to the front. He is therefore not certain whether to consolidate his forces at Beauharnois. Says he has been waiting in vain for orders from here."

In the event several hundred *Patriotes* did depart Napierville Thursday morning and marched south to Lacolle to confront the militiamen, who were based in nearby Odelltown. Côté had long regarded the area as hostile territory; it was the growth of these British and Irish settlements over the last quarter century that had instilled in the *Canadien* populace of the Richelieu valley fear for its own long-term survival in the region. The *seigneur* of Lacolle and of Delery to the north was currently William Penderlieth Christie, the illegitimate son of the late British soldier, Gabriel Christie. The succession in ownership hadn't made that much difference in the treatment of the *censitaires*. "WP" may not have been as mercenary as his half-brother Napier, but he was still dedicated to populating his land tracts with immigrants from Yorkshire and other British counties and discouraging the *habitants* expanding the French-speaking communities on the west side of the Richelieu.

Hindelang climbed the hillock to join Côté. "I've ordered our men to commence firing on the church."

"It may be too late. I see enemy reinforcements arriving along the Lacolle River. We'll have a stiff battle on our hands." Côté suddenly felt queasy in his stomach. *Death is at the door!*

The exchange of musket fire continued for more than an hour. But once the reinforcements arrived, it was clear that the militiamen had the upper hand. Côté was conflicted. Ought he to join the fray if only to demonstrate the need for bravery? It was evident that the men were increasingly daunted if not actually disgruntled. Some of them had to resort to taking up the muskets of fallen comrades. The bodies of the dead and wounded littered the field outside the church. There was nobody available to lend succor. *Am I responsible for bringing on the angel of death?*

At last Hindelang was back at Côté's side. "We have probably lost up to fifty men. How can we persevere when we don't have enough ammunition to maintain effective volleys? I may have to order a retreat."

"I do agree, *mon ami*, that retreat is our only option. The invasion has failed. We must go back to New York."

"Where is Dr. Nelson?" Hindelang asked the question just as he readied himself to return to the firing line.

"He has left the field. My guess is that he is heading for the border."

Nine

The first Sunday in November hadn't seemed at first so different to Benjamin Hart from other autumn days of rest. The usual peal of Montreal's church bells, the clatter of horse hooves on the cobblestones at the corner of *Rues* des Récollets and Sainte-Hélene, the dissonance of a large family carrying out daily routines without the easy option of being outdoors.

Harriot, the mistress of the house, did maintain some order. Now in her fifties, she had learned much about how to handle the interactions of her offspring. She had borne sixteen children, albeit only half of them still came to the family table. Frances, Aaron Philip and Arthur Wellington no longer lived at home and five had perished at birth or in early childhood.

Benjamin, belatedly reading the Montreal *Herald* in his relatively quiet study, failed to pay much attention to horses coming to a halt outside the house. Daughter Hannah Constance poked her head into the room; she had noticed that the riders were no ordinary folk. A uniformed army officer was dismounting.

Going to the window to investigate, Benjamin recognized that the one now standing on the sidewalk was none other than the city's top soldier, John Clitherow. The Major General had arrived in Montreal the previous March to command the military district there. Benjamin had found himself dealing with him in the months that followed, Lord Durham having appointing Clitherow (along with three other military men) to the eight-member Special Council. Moreover, son Aaron Philip had to contend with the Major General when the latter presided over the court martial of the rebels still under indictment. Benjamin hurried out to greet him without waiting to don a cloak to protect himself from the cold.

Clitherow declined being invited into the house. There were other city officials to be visited. "We have reports from the Richelieu valley and from upriver at Châteauguy and Beauharnois that the rebels are on the march."

The revelation didn't shock Benjamin; he had been privy to the various reports from the British secret agents operating in the US. Indeed, it was knowledge of this rebel activity that had led to his frequent contact with the Major General at the Citadel. His immediate concern: how could he help?

"I have standing instructions from General Colborne to have you and your fellow magistrates arrest whomever you suspect of being a rebel leader. Otherwise, he will spread the flames of revolt throughout the district. It being Sunday, most of these suspects may well be found in their homes."

Benjamin was genuinely puzzled. "Why do you think that they picked a Sunday to start the uprising?"

"Perhaps they thought they could disarm the troops because they might be carrying only their bayonets during church services." Clitherow was only half joking.

Benjamin began shivering. He realized that he was too old to be there without a proper outer garment. *Or is it that I dread being in the middle of another crisis?* Not since almost exactly a year ago had Benjamin Hart been called upon to perform the role of a police magistrate in an emergency situation. He extended his hand. "You can count on me, sir. I will immediately get in touch with Leclerc and you shall have my list."

Clitherow gave only a ghost of a smile. Within seconds he was back on his horse and heading down the street. Meanwhile, son Theodore had joined Benjamin before the latter was able to take refuge in the warm house. The gist of what Clitherow had told Benjamin was relayed while they hurried back to the parlor. Theodore had become Benjamin's closest confidante since Aaron Philip and Arthur Wellington went their own ways. Though he was but twenty-two years old, Theodore was handling most of his father's affairs, both the mercantile end and the insurance business.

Benjamin knew that he required his son's assistance. Somebody had to call on Pierre-Édouard Leclerc, the superintendent of the police department, to set up a meeting. Meanwhile, he would need to go over in his own mind as to who should be arrested. At the same time he contemplated what might happen in the next period of time. *What a beginning for General Colborne's governance!* He was already stigmatized by the *Canadiens* for the behavior of his troops last December. *Le Vieux Brulôt,* they called him. Ironically, Benjamin feared that given the temper of the English-speaking communities, more villages would soon be on fire."

Theodore proved not to be over-excited. "You have always said, papa, that Colborne believes that firm military rule is required if only to provide our province with time to readjust to our colonial institutions. Lord Durham's resignation has permitted him to do what is necessary. Yet he probably didn't anticipate having to do so in the first few days of his taking over the reins of government. Let us hope that when Durham gets back to London, he will acquaint Melbourne, Russell and their fellow Whigs with the realities we face in the Canadas."

*   *   *

It was a fifteen-minute walk to Rue Notre-Dame and the courthouse. But now Benjamin was properly clothed for the chill, which he knew would intensify with dusk almost upon them. Theodore had informed him that Leclerc had arranged a meeting in the main conference room in the building.

Court activities not having been scheduled for this day, Benjamin noticed that there were not the usual quota of clerks, lawyers and litigants occupying the corridors. *Strangely quiet in view of what was happening elsewhere in the province.* The conference room, however, had been lit up with candles and there was some heat being generated from the newly fired hearth. Most of the few magistrates having jurisdiction in the city had gathered around the burning logs with hands extended for maximum warmth. Among them was Moses Judah Hays and Benjamin approached him immediately to shake hands. Hays was related to the Davids through his mother and thus was indirectly linked with the Harts. Younger than Benjamin, he had aided in getting the Shearith Israel synagogue build and was in fact president of the congregation. Hart and Hays were appointed as justices of the peace in August 1837 at the same time as most of the others in the room.

At last Leclerc was satisfied that all were present and called everybody to the chairs lining the central table. He was a man just entering his fortieth year. Though trained as a notary, he had been Montreal's police superintendent for just about all of the decade. A strong advocate of law and order, he had devoted much of his time in recent years trying to undermine the militancy of the *Patriotes*, including the infiltration of the *Fils de Liberté* just prior to the outbreak of last year's rebellion.

Benjamin didn't wait for any exposition by the chairman before voicing recriminations. "I tell you, gentlemen, that this should not have happened if we had taken heed of the warnings we received over the summer. Now the port of Quebec will soon close and General Colborne will need to depend on his own resources."

The mutterings from those assembled confirmed Benjamin's cry of dismay. It was Leclerc, however, who made the reply. "Like you, Hart, I have been convinced for some months that a terrible revolt would consume us. I would not be surprised if there are not at least five thousand rebels under arms and in the field. We did have advance notice of the uprising prior to the weekend so the army was on high alert but none of our troops was in place at the border."

Most of the subsequent questions centered on this lack of preparedness. Leclerc added to this melancholy. "We warned Clitherow two months ago that disturbances were in the offing. He did visit Île aux Noix to get confirmation of what was happening up the Richelieu but he came back saying that our concern was great exaggerated. And now we have this!"

It took Benjamin to change the mood. He proposed that they immediately assume that martial law would be in force and they comply with the request that known *Patriote* leaders be rounded up. General Colborne, he argued, was comfortable with a firm policy of counter-insurgency.

Leclerc appreciated Benjamin's different tack. "Our new Governor is without doubt a decisive man. To counter the rebel force at Beauharnois, he has not only mobilized the local militia but also ordered those in the counties of Glengarry and Stormont to come down from Upper Canada to join with whatever corps of volunteers can be raised here. One of Clitherow's officers tells me that a couple of thousand volunteers are currently guarding the entrances to Beauharnois and patrolling the streets in the village."

"In other words, we have martial law already in effect." Benjamin was buoyed by this latest information.

Leclerc at this point asked for names. Who ought they to pinpoint as potential enemies of the state? He started the process with his own target. "Denis-Benjamin Viger should be detained at once. He was not arrested last November though we did search his house."

Hays seconded the selection. "Since then, Viger has been coddled despite his owning more than one seditious journal. Last May he had dinner with Buller and with Ellice's son. What a waste of time!"

All around the table seemed to realize that this was a momentous decision. Other than Papineau, none was more highly regarded by the populace as the heart and soul of the *Patriote* movement than the veteran lawyer. Who in the room had not engaged with this man in court or elsewhere over the past thirty years!

Benjamin reminded all that there could be repercussions. "We would have to prepare for trouble. There will undoubtedly be a demand for bail."

"I would consider bail but not before he promised us good conduct." Leclerc appeared hesitant.

Benjamin was not hesitant. "I suggest that he not be permitted to see anybody while in prison. Our task is to avoid a contagion."

*   *   *

Harriot Judith Hart was clearly annoyed. Her husband had invited Adam Thom to the house without giving her due notice. Benjamin had also ignoring the sanctity of the Sabbath. She would have conceded that this had been an extraordinary week in their life. Rumors about what had occurred at Caughnawaga, Baker's Camp and other confrontation points circulated mouth-to-mouth and they certainly fueled apprehension and bitterness among the English-speaking citizenry of Montreal. Harriot, however, was confident that the new Governor, Sir John Colborne, had all in hand. Benjamin had assured her of that. So why household routines should be disrupted?

Benjamin dismissed her complaints; he noted that Thom would soon be embarking for England and that there was no other time for the editor of the *Montreal Herald* to meet with him. And did she not want to send a personal message to Arthur Wellington via the man?

Thom had been a frequent visitor to his home. Introduced to the Scotsman by Aaron Philip several years ago, Benjamin grew to be impressed by the fearlessness of the man's trenchant prose that so reflected Benjamin's own sentiments. The Anti-Gallic letters Thom wrote under the name of *Camillus* had rallied the merchant community to oppose the conciliatory policy that was practiced by the *Château* in dealing with the surging *Patriote* movement. Now he was leaving for London in order to help Durham shape a new colonial policy for the Lower Canada.

Benjamin did make certain that he spent enough time praying before his private *bema* upstairs before descending to the study in order to receive

Thom. The room not only had this raised pulpit but also an ark curtain and a rose window looking out metaphorically to Jerusalem.

Thom was punctual even though it was this Saturday morning that the momentous events at Odelltown and Beauharnois occurring earlier in the week required his journalistic skills at the printing plant. Benjamin had him seated in the study, closed the door and withdrew a bottle of Scotch from the cupboard. Thom raised his glass to indicate a celebration was in order. He informed Benjamin of what Clithertow had officially reported to the *Herald* but hours before. "This fellow Cardinal and his cohorts seeking to come down river from Châteauguay are now safely in jail in Montreal, our Caughnawaga allies having turned them over to us."

He was confirming what Benjamin had already known. "I've heard that Cardinal's house was set on fire by the militia in retaliation for his deeds."

The conversation shifted to Thom's impending voyage to the homeland. Benjamin inquired about the arrangements. "I trust your departure will not be affected by the invasion from the south. Nothing is more important than having Lord Durham develop a coherent policy to deal with a bad situation. You can contribute to that."

"Buller has asked for me specifically. I think he likes my writing skills." Thom had indeed cultivated that relationship with Durham's private secretary.

"You have much to say that will be valuable. Buller is, after all, an Englishman with no personal experience with the nuances of thought within the French element in the province." Benjamin was making no mention of his own disappointment with not being part of the policymaking process.

Thom took another sip of the Scotch whisky. "Like His Excellency, I am of the opinion that we have two nations warring in the bosom of a single state. We must bring such a contest to an end if only to save the economy. Nevertheless, as we are the minority, we cannot return to the constitutional arrangement that submitted us to French dominance. If the mother country forgets what is due to the loyal and enterprising men of our own race, we must protect *ourselves*."

Benjamin sighed. "That is happening. Just about every village sheltering rebels is being burned to the ground. From Laprairie down to the border our volunteers are exacting a high price for the French insurgency. I do pity the innocent; winter will soon upon them and there will be no roof over their heads.

"Everything now is under control. It is reported that the two militia battalions from Upper Canada arrived at Beauharnois over the weekend. The rebels there had already dispersed, probably because Nelson was known to have been defeated at Odelltown. Today I'm told that our volunteers are on Lorimier's trail."

"He will hang for his crimes." Benjamin's pity did not extend to the rebels themselves.

A rap at the door interrupted the *tête-à-tête*. Now it was Benjamin's turn to be annoyed. When a second knock suggested urgency, he rose from his seat to determine who was calling. Aaron Philip had apparently arrived at the house and seemed more excitable than usual. "I have just come from the prison. Hundreds of men are being herded into cells. Papa, are there actually warrants for these arrests?"

"I did issue warrants last week for a score of Montreal *Patriotes* but the men you speak of are obviously prisoners captured in the course of battle."

Thom had said nothing during this first interchange but he chose to interpose his view. "Be reasonable, Philip. In these circumstances the letter of the law can't be followed. These are terrible times."

"It has certainly been a terrible time. It is said that our volunteers know no constraint. They are putting to the torch every rebel house they come upon." Aaron Philip's voice was more high-pitched than usual.

"Even I deplore what is happening, son. Yet you surprise me. Last December you were among the most vocal in demanding punishment for the insurgents." Benjamin remembered being told of how Aaron Philip and his friends in the volunteers had jeered and hissed while prisoners were being escorted to prison. In fact, Benjamin had received an unofficial complaint over his son's behavior in harassing manacled *Patriotes* on the gangplank of the *British America* steamboat while they were being transferred from the Richelieu to Montreal. *Strange!* Had his association with the men he had defended in the court martial proceedings so altered his sentiments?

Aaron Philip looked sheepish despite his anger. "That was before I realized how badly we were treating ordinary Canadians. I've been talking to Drummond. We intend to defend these latest detainees most vigorously."

Benjamin and Thom exchanged glances. The reference to Lewis Thomas Drummond, the young Irishman who had not too long ago articled in the office of Tory attorney Charles Dewey Day, did shake Benjamin, who had long assumed there was unity of purpose within their community. The shaping of a new colonial policy was proving to be more complicated than he imagined.

PART TWO

Punishment
1838–39

The groans of the oppressed awaken remorse in the hearts of the oppressors, and bring a blush to their faces. . . . We should like to spare England the unenviable honor of seeing its name associated with that of Russia, the 'executioner of Poland.' There is all our crime. It is a great crime, we admit, in the eyes of all those who are plotting the annihilation of the Canadien people.
ÉTIENNE PARENT
(editorial, Le Canadien, December 24, 1838)

The country which has founded and maintained these Colonies at a vast expense of blood and treasure, may justly expect its compensation in turning their unappropriated resources to the account of its own redundant population; they are the rightful patrimony of the English people, the ample appendage which God and Nature have set aside in the New World for those whose lot has assigned them but insufficient portions in the Old.
LORD DURHAM
(opening of his Report, February, 1839)

Ten

Unlike cousin Aaron Philip, Aaron Ezekiel Hart in Quebec City had no immediate emotional response to the mass arrests in the days before November 12. The previous week had certainly been unsettling; General Colborne in the *Château* was dealing with a major crisis in his first days in office. Yet, in the Quebec region there were scant signs of overt rebellion. Aaron Ezekiel's priorities included preparing for his sailing to England in the next month.

He had prepared a list of tasks to execute once he traveled to New York and again when he landed in Bristol. Uncle Moses had business associates for him to visit; Papa Ezekiel craved certain delicacies that could only be fetched in the Old Country. And then there was the problem with Emma. Now in her forties, his sister's mental and physical health had been deteriorating over the years. The family was not satisfied with what the local doctors were advising even if it had a high regard for René-Joseph Kimber. The latter, like the Nelson brothers, was too involved in politics to be in the forefront of medical knowledge. Enquiries resulted in Aaron Ezekiel being advised to visit a district within Marylebone when in London. Doctors were setting up private practices on Harley Street.

It was late morning before Aaron Ezekiel reached his office, located in a building in the Upper Town shared by several in the legal profession. The clerk greeted him cautiously; a *Canadien*, the fellow was obviously preoccupied with what had been transpiring during the past few days. Martial law had been declared, arrests were being made and only a few official statements describing what was happening in the Richelieu Valley and environs were coming from the army officers at the Citadel. Aaron Ezekiel too knew he should be more concerned; the 2nd Battalion of the Quebec County militia could be called to duty. He was the Captain of that battalion.

His musings came to an end with the appearance of a fellow lawyer at the corridor door. Thomas Cushing Aylwin didn't have quite his seniority in the profession. But there was no denying that in the past ten years Aylwin had acquired a reputation as an excellent criminal lawyer. Nonetheless, the two men had often consulted when clients sought to defend themselves on charges by Crown prosecutors. Aylwin by his very facial expression was indicating that this was one such time. "John Teed was arrested yesterday for treason. John Teed of all people!"

Aaron Ezekiel confirmed the sentiment. "Colborne is going all the way. He has had so many of the *Patriote* leadership jailed. Not only Viger, but also La Fontaine, Berthelot, Girouard. Even one of the Mondelets."

Aylwin's laugh was sardonic. "Our new Governor has not forgiven Charles-Elzéar for defending Nicolas and his friends in the Chartrand affair. Imagine this Mondelet now in prison while his brother Dominique is acting as a Crown prosecutor."

"In my opinion Colborne will find it difficult to get any convictions even if the cases go before courts martial. And we know what would happen if they are tried by civilian tribunals. So tell me, Tom! Are you planning to represent Teed in court?"

"If only I am able to get a writ before the Court of Queen's Bench. With a new Chief Justice, that may not be possible." Jonathan Sewell had finally resigned his post almost a month before.

"Do you really believe that our new Chief Justice will rule any differently than Sewell would have had he remained in office?" Aaron Ezekiel was betraying his skepticism.

"But Sewell did issue writs of *habeas corpus* before martial law took effect. He may have been tough when it came to the law on treason, but I wonder if he would have approved of the course Colborne has taken."

"We may never know. But with Stuart on the Bench, the outlook is not good." Aaron Ezekiel had had little contact with James Stuart in recent years but one was not likely to forget that prior to Durham's arrival in the colony Colborne had named Stuart to the Special Council in April. The man's career had been characterized by pugnacity, so unlike that of his brother Andrew or even of Sewell himself. Over twenty years before he had been an ally of Papineau but ever since they had been bitter opponents. Was it not reasonable to expect that Stuart would take full advantage of his new authority to destroy the *Patriote* cause?

"If only I could bypass Stuart. We do have two Canadian judges. They may see things differently." A sly smile animated Aylwin's face. He didn't require any more advice from Aaron Ezekiel.

*   *   *

Not till three days later did Aaron Ezekiel learn of what was occurring in Montreal. A letter from Aaron Philip described the state of affairs at the *Pied-du-Courant* prison and his determination to defend the rights of the accused. A very contrite communication from a cousin who had for so long borne a grudge against him. *How different it had been five years before!* Aaron Philip, always cocky, had advised his father and Moses Judah Hays to decline appointments to the Montreal magistracy. As a newly accredited lawyer, he had declared that Jews could not in good conscience take the oath of abjuration to hold public office. It was that oath that had undermined Ezekiel Hart's bid to sit in the House of Assembly in Quebec thirty years before. In contrast, Aaron Ezekiel had encouraged his brother Samuel Bécancour to demand court approval of an appointment as a Justice of the Peace in Trois-Rivières. In fact, it was the testimony of Aaron Ezekiel at a sub-committee of the National Assembly that aided the *Patriotes* in clarifying legislation that entitled "persons professing the Jewish Religion to all the rights and privileges of the other Subjects of His Majesty in this Province." He had argued without specifically mentioning names that "the law had been improperly construed and incorrectly comprehended by a young man who has scarcely been admitted but two years to the practice of the Law, and who is far from being celebrated for the consistency of his opinions, and for the solidity of his judgment." Aaron Ezekiel could well understand why his cousin resented such a characterization.

Yet this news from Montreal didn't shock Aaron Ezekiel as much as what occurred a week later. On the Wednesday, November 21, Aylwin reappeared at his office door. "Judges Bédard and Panet have assented to my request for a writ of *habeas corpus* on behalf of John Teed."

Aaron Ezekiel was flabbergasted. "You must be joking. *Habeas corpus* has been suspended."

"That may be, Aaron, but Bédard and Panet are not accepting ordinances of the Special Council that are plainly unconstitutional."

"Where is Teed now?"

"He was moved to the Citadel as a military prisoner soon after he was incarcerated ten days ago. I was up to the Citadel to visit him. He is not in the best of shape. Being a tailor and American born, he was not given much sympathy by the officer brotherhood. The warrant for Teed to appear before Panet and Bédard has been served on the jailer. He refused to release the prisoner, having been ordered by the commandant not to cooperate. The two judges have had no other recourse but to arrest the jailer and to hold him, Colonel Bowles, in contempt of court. What a mess!"

Aaron Ezekiel didn't know Philippe Panet well, but Elzéar Bédard was a friend of long standing. Even when they were playing games in the woods about Trois-Rivières Bédard demonstrated his independence of mind. But in the current climate the authorities would not readily accept moving a case to the ordinary civil court for trial by jury. "Does Bédard believe such a judgment will hold once Colborne and the Special Council retaliate?"

"And they will. I have already talked to Andrew Stuart. The Solicitor General warned me that the Governor can't retreat without losing everything. We can expect the same objections from the Montreal court. O'Sullivan is the new Chief Justice there and I know what he thinks."

"A mess indeed! I suppose I should have guessed Bédard's attitude. There has been some ambiguity in his remarks over the past year. He was after all once a *Patriote* leader albeit he eventually began collaborating with the *Château* ten years ago. Panet is a different sort, even if he is the son of the first Speaker of the House. He was appointed to the Executive Council and was responsible for delivering the Governor's messages to the Assembly. All this tells me that our *Canadien* friends are sick with worry. Their influence in government may not survive these insurrections." Aaron Ezekiel had seldom been so sick at heart.

Aylwin had taken a seat and seemed unusually contemplative. "You may be on to something, Aaron. Our masters in London are hell-bent on ending an impasse that has lasted for a quarter century. My father warned me as a child that English merchants like him could not abide being subject to French law. He never forgave me for being sympathetic to the *Patriotes*."

Aaron Ezekiel could empathize with his colleague despite the fact that papa Ezekiel had never turned his back on the *Canadien* majority living in Trois-Rivières. Two languages. Two cultures. A religious divide. One had to be very strong to overcome prejudices. But the confrontation was now never more intense.

* * *

The denouement was not long in coming. On Monday, December 10 Aaron Ezekiel was informed that Colborne had suspended the two judges from office. The details had come from Étienne Parent, whom he had encountered while taking a meal at the Union Hotel.

The dining room there was only partially filled, a not unusual circumstance on a Monday evening. It would be very different in a couple of weeks, Christmas being almost upon the denizens of the city. Parent stood out; nobody else had quite his massive head and thick hair. He was alone. Aaron Ezekiel felt no compunction about proposing that they share the same table; they had done so on other occasions over the past decade and a half. Parent, looking up when Aaron Ezekiel hailed him, appeared somewhat dazed. But an invitation to be seated soon followed.

Aaron Ezekiel immediately sensed that Parent was upset. He had a reputation for being a bit of a recluse; his intellectual gifts showed up in his writing and social talk did not come easily. Tonight was an exception. He blurted out what was on his mind. "You may not have heard: Bédard and Panet are off the Bench."

"It's gone that far?" Aaron Ezekiel anticipated retaliation but this was extreme.

"Total repudiation! The judgments of Bédard and Panet on the Teed case have been quashed. The Special Council has set aside all of their orders."

"Dare you condemn this action in *Le Canadien*? Colborne has the authority under martial law to condemn anybody giving comfort to the insurrectionists." Aaron Ezekiel was mindful of the past. *Le Canadien* was actually a journal with a revolutionary past. Pierre Bédard, the father of the current judge, had had a war of words with the reigning Governor thirty years before. The upshot was his imprisonment in 1810 and the suspension of the paper. A dozen years later Étienne Parent, a seminary student, was recruited to write for a revived *Petit Canadien*. Another reincarnation of *Le Canadien* came in 1831 with Parent as its main printed voice. In subsequent years he came to reflect the views of most educated *Canadiens* with his watchword of "our language, our institutions, our laws."

"I feel I have no choice but to risk censure or worse. The dissent by our two jurists goes beyond Quebec. I understand that last week Vallières in Trois-Rivières also granted a writ. I fear he too will be punished for his impudence." Parent was staring in to space. Yet the intensity of his look chilled Aaron Ezekiel: what he would write in the next edition of *Le Canadien* was certain to be inflammatory.

"The Archbishop is strangely quiet. Don't you expect him to come to the defense of the judges?" Aaron Ezekiel himself had come to accept that Joseph Signay, who had succeeded to the Quebec episcopate several years before, would not be challenging the undermining of the constitution, much less any disciplining of judges. A year ago this very day Signay had denounced the insurrection as "criminal in the eyes of God and our holy religion." In contrast, Lartigue and his coadjutor in Montreal made a point of supporting the *Patriotes* who were filling the prisons, this in spite of their open opposition to the insurgency from its very beginning. Thus Lartigue was increasingly showing himself as an Ultramontane determined to be independent of the state even if that put him in conflict with the Crown. Sisnay wasn't made that way.

Parent sighed. "He is indeed a man of the *status quo*. I can't imagine him scolding the men in the *Château* for their attack on our institutions. He isn't the only disappointment. You will remember that I greeted the arrival of Lord Durham to our shores because I saw him as a check on the ambitions of the Tories in Montreal. In my editorials in *Le Canadien* I chastised my colleagues who foresaw nothing but more oppression of our people. Now I look foolish, betrayed by a man claiming to be liberal-minded."

"Have you spoken to Bédard? You once were very close."

"Not yet, but he's taken his stand. I would not be surprised if he sailed to England immediately to defend his legal prerogatives."

"He'll have to go via New York. All ships destined for Portsmouth have already departed our port. I should know, having booked passage on a boat leaving from New York next month."

Aaron Ezekiel was to recall this dinner conversation two weeks later. On December 24 Parent's editorial did appear in *Le Canadien*. It was a bitter reproach, citing the "groans of the oppressed" at the prospect of the annihilation of the *Canadien* people. He was still a free man on Christmas Day but on the 26th he was arrested along with the printer of *Le Canadien*. Such "seditious schemings" said the warrant, deserved prison.

The Court having found the prisoners, individually and collectively, guilty
of the charges preferred against them, with the exception of Édouard
Thérien and Louis Lesiége dit Laviolette, and the same being for
an offence committed since the first day of November last, in furtherance
of the rebellion existing in the Province of Lower Canada, do sentence
them, the prisoners, viz: -- Joseph Narcisse Cardinal, to be hanged by
the neck till he be dead, at such time and place as His Excellency,
the General Commanding Officer, so chooses, etc.
COURT MARTIAL PROCEEDINGS
(Eighth day, December 10, 1839)

Vous êtes une femme et vous êtes mère! Une femme,
une mère poussée par le désespoir .. tombé à vos pieds,
tremblante d'effroit et le coeur brisé, pour vous demander la vie
de son époux bien-aimé et du père de ses cinq enfants!
MADAME EUGÉNIE CARDINAL
(letter to Lady Colborne, December 18, 1838)

Eleven

Aaron Philip Hart had cause to be apprehensive. The tribunal constituting the court martial had accomplished what it had set out to do. The dozen *Patriotes* on trial this first week of December were going to be hanged so as to assert to the populace how British justice handles instances of treason. Aaron Philip had only to examine the mien of Major General Clitherow to be advised that mercy was but a distant hope. *Am I only complicating my life in pursuit of a lost cause?*

The lead prisoner, Joseph-Narcisse Cardinal, inadvertently touched Aaron Philip's hand as they rose to their feet to make their appeal. Clitherow, presiding over the trial, was in the midst of explaining to the Solicitor General, the prosecuting attorney, that the court had given the defendants and their counsel permission to make statements prior to the passing of sentences. There was enough time for Aaron Philip to have several of the events of the past two weeks pass through his mind as a series of tableaux.

The first image recalled was that of Lewis Thomas Drummond making his request that Aaron Philip join the defense team. Papa Benjamin was in the room and clearly indicated that in his view this 25-year-old Irishman was being presumptuous. It was already near the end of November and opined that the army had been too slow in exacting punishment on the insurrectionists. The name of Benjamin Hart had already been associated with the arrest of so many of the *Patriotes*. Would a Hart progeny being linked with the defending of traitors make him look foolish in the eyes of peers?

Aaron Philip had glared at his father before responding to the request. *Surely papa understands that if lawyers like me don't speak for the accused, justice would be tainted.* Already the court had decided that "rebels could not defend rebels" when *Canadien* advocates offered their services to the prisoners. Eventually Clitherow and his fellow officers allowed the presence of lawyers Joseph Moreau and Drummond at the hearings provided they were not to cross-examine the witnesses but rather to help prepare statements by the defendants. Drummond now wanted a more experienced barrister –Aaron Philip was two years older than he – to address the court.

The first December visit to the *Au Courant* prison had been Aaron Philip's opportunity to size up Cardinal as a client. The interview hadn't gone well at first. The name Hart was obviously distasteful to a leader of the rebellion. Cardinal, a notary practicing in Montreal, had engaged with Aaron Philip on occasion but only as legal and political adversaries. How was it possible to have this son of Benjamin Hart represent him fairly and effectively?

But what was there to lose? Cardinal overcame his animus in the course of Aaron Philip's inquisition. They were about the same age and both sons of Montreal merchants. Cardinal had lost his parents and one of his brothers in the cholera epidemic in 1832 but soon after became politically active. In fact, he was elected to the Legislative Assembly for Laprairie County in 1834 and became so much a part of the *Patriote* leadership that he chose to give up his captaincy in the local militia. Even so, he had not participated in the first rebellion, fleeing to New York instead to avoid arrest. Nevertheless, his commitment to the insurrection resulted in his leading the brigade that occupied Chateauguay. The arrest at Caughnawaga had proved to be his undoing.

Aaron Philip had explained to Cardinal the need to have more facts around which to prepare a commentary for the court. Why was witness John McDonald so certain of the words used in a conversation at Châteauguay after eight days of imprisonment, excitement and confusion? What had John Lewis Grant actually witnessed the night of the fourth November last? What does Tenihatie's claim of seeing Cardinal a prisoner in the house of an Indian at Sault St-Louis prove?

Prevented from challenging by themselves the nine witnesses for the prosecution - three of them Iroquois from Caughnawaga - Hart and Drummond were depending on Cardinal cross-examining these men on his own. Cardinal did get permission to take 72 hours until December 4 to prepare a defense and it was at this point that Aaron Philip was officially admitted as a third attorney for the accused.

The harshness of the gavel striking the platform table broke the reverie. At last Clitherow had turned his attention to the defendants and their counsels. The time had come for Aaron Philip to speak his piece. "Gentlemen, we are now about to conclude our address to you, previous to closing our defense. That done, naught remains but for the Judge Advocate to answer us, and you will then be called upon to fulfill the most awful part of this imposing trial. Yes, Gentlemen, the most awful part, at which any human being must shudder when required to perform. To dispose not only of the lives and properties of twelve fellow-creatures, but perhaps to make their unprotected wives widowed, their innocent children fatherless. - to fill to overflowing that cup of human misery, which they, by the visitation of Providence, have already too deeply quaffed. Great God, in his mercy, we must hope, will temper the wind to the shorn lamb."

The main argument chosen in consultation with Drummond was to distinguish between treason and mutiny and to stress the flaws in the procedures. Aaron Philip registered the charge that the defendants had been exposed to every disadvantage. "The earthly tribunal to us has been a strange one: were we soldiers, accused of mutiny, we should be prepared to be tried by this Court - we should know what judges would sit in judgment upon us - we would know what fate must await us, should that crime be proved. But, Gentlemen, you will recollect, that we are civilians, tried for an offence not mentioned in the Mutiny Act or Articles of War. We are accused, as the copy of the charge served upon us states, with Treason committed against the peace of our Lady the Queen, her Crown and dignity, and remark, Gentlemen, against the form of the Statute in such case made and provided - that statute, according to the forms prescribed by which we have not been tried.

"We, Gentlemen, are the first who have been selected to be tried by this, to us, strange tribunal, - we are the first of the inhabitants of this Province, who, since the conquest of the Colony, have been subjected to the jurisdiction of a Military Court, - and who are we? - many of us peaceable agriculturists, poor and uneducated, - we are required for the slaughter, and had it not been that the usages even of military tribunals permitted us to have the assistance of counsel, how were we situated? - unable even to state our own defense, unable to combat the arguments of the learned men who have for this occasion, contrary to the usual rule, selected to aid the military prosecutor, ~ unable to detect the inaccuracy, the inconsistency, of much of the evidence adduced against us."

Aaron Philip had begun to perspire despite the chill of this Saturday morning. He had never before argued with such passion. He finally raised the possibility that good sense would lead to a decision different from what he knew was inevitable. "Should we be set at liberty, then prayers, then blessings shall attend you, and may the great and wise all powerful Being direct you and guide you in your judgment."

He resumed his seat, exhausted by the effort. The summation of the Judge Advocate that followed barely penetrated his brain. What he did remember was the attempt to claim reasonableness. "We abstain from referring to books of authority in support of the opinions which we may have occasion to express on legal points, yet that such opinions have been formed with deliberation and research, and under a full sense of the grave responsibility of our present position."

*　　*　　*

Sunday was the day of rest, but Aaron Philip was restless. Had he and Drummond missed something in the comments they were allowed? Despite the demand by the deputy Judge Advocate, Charles Dewey Day, that the accused be sentenced to death, the tribunal did admit that the sentence attached to high treason was out of all proportion to the offence and that at least eight of the defendants ought not to be subject to the rope. Alas, Cardinal and three other were deemed ringleaders who had to pay the ultimate price for their deeds.

A week went by and only later did Aaron Philip learn that on the following Saturday, December 15, Governor Colborne called a meeting of the Executive Council to examine the verdict. Colborne was successful in getting the Councilors to agree that if high treason had been judged as proven, death sentences were mandatory. Furthermore, an example had to be made of rebellious citizens. But at the last minute Colborne relented; for eight of the prisoners were to be transported to Australia. On Friday, December 21 the scaffold would be ready to hang Cardinal and his clerk, Joseph Duquette.

For Drummond and Hart the decision prompted them to seek a last-minute reprieve for Cardinal and Duquette. They petitioned the Governor by voicing doubts about the legality of the court martial. Couldn't the executions be delayed until the courts ruled on the question?

Meanwhile Aaron Philip was given the task of convincing Cardinal's wife to make a woman-to-woman appeal to Colborne's wife for clemency.

He dreaded the assignment. So much easier to prepare petitions than to face a wife and mother broken hearted and desperate. *Will I not feel better if she is out with friends and not at home?*

She *was* home when he knocked at her door. Ushered into the parlor, he spied her prostrate on a sofa. Women friends were tending to her children, who seemed bewildered by what was going on in the adult world. *Madame* Cardinal recognized the visit by getting to her feet, but she was obviously grief-stricken. Aaron Philip felt a twang of regret. Here was an educated *Canadienne*, the wife of a professional who once sat in the House of Assembly in Quebec, reduced to such a wretched state.

He explained the purpose of her making a plea to a woman she had never met. Their conversion was totally in French, albeit Eugénie Cardinal was the daughter of an interpreter with the Indian Department. What shall I say, she begged him.

"Write to her that as a woman and a mother, she ought to understand how cruel it would be to deprive you of a husband, the father of five children! As simple as that!"

"Will the Governor listen to her?" Her sad eyes told him she doubted that he would.

Aaron Philip sought to give her encouragement. "Did you know that the Caughnawaga chiefs have also begged for the state to show mercy? This in spite of the fact that they had made the arrests that resulted in Cardinal's imprisonment."

On the Thursday, the day before the execution, the two lawyers played their last card. They maintained that since the proceedings followed in regard to the prisoners were illegal, unconstitutional and unjust, the Governor must understand that taking their lives "raised them from the status of persons presumed guilty to that of martyrs to an odious persecution." There was no response from the Citadel. And reading the *Montreal Herald*, Aaron Philip was to get a typical view from his former friends. "We have seen the new gallows. The rebels behind bars enjoy a perspective that will obtain for them agreeable dreams."

*   *   *

The funerals were indeed an occasion for protest. Most *Canadiens*, men, women and children, filled the street outside the Cathedral even though there was little chance to participate in the Mass. But there was no violence. The soldiers of the 1st Regiment of Foot made a show of force on Rue Notre-Dame. For the young members of the banned *Fils de la Liberté* there was no willingness to go up against bayonets when two attempts at rebellion had been so cruelly crushed. Moreover, a light snow was beginning to fall, a shroud for so disheartening an event.

Aaron Philip realized he was offending his parents and probably many of his friends by stating that he would attend the church services and even follow the cortege to the Catholic cemetery. A year before he had been willing to defend rebels while having little or no sympathy for their cause. But this December the circumstances were so different.

To his relief Drummond was also standing on the sidewalk outside the Cathedral. He had attracted a small coterie of *Canadiens* aware of the role he had played in court. He hailed Aaron Philip as he approached. They embraced. Hands shaken all around. They were led to the church's apse, which was relatively quiet.

Once inside this house of worship Drummond did not refrain from commenting again on what they had gone through over the past few weeks. "Never before have I seen so clearly the flaws in our justice system. Men act regardless of the law."

Aaron Philip found it difficult to come up with a fitting response. "At least it was a pleasure working with you, Lewis. There will be more trials ahead. Let's hope the result is not the same."

Drummond nodded. "The Indians of Kahnawake responded to the executions more sensibly than did many of our compatriots. I read what they wrote to Colborne and remember it word for word. 'We come to our father to beg to save the life of these unfortunate men. They didn't do anything bad to us. They have not soaked their hands in the blood of their brothers. Why shed theirs?' Shall we find our pew? They are saving places for us."

*Congratulations on the publishing of your poem. You have
had your baptism as a patriot and a political martyr.*
JOSEPH-RÉMI VALLIÈRES DE RÉAL
(conversation with Joseph-Guillaume Barthe, December 1838)

*Later I will trace in zigzag the straight line of conduct that
I propose to follow in the future.*
NAPOLÉON AUBIN
(writing in Le Fantasque, May 1839)

Twelve

The two cousins had almost never converged on the courthouse at the
same time. But this mid-December morning each had reason to beat
a path to the door of Trois-Rivières' resident judge albeit their purposes
might not have been the same. Actually Adolphus Mordecai Hart had
encountered Alexander Thomas Hart at the bottom of the steps leading up
to the entrance of the two-story building. Snow that fell the day before had
been cleared away but Adolphus was climbing the stairs gingerly when he
noticed his cousin's presence. *Quite a coincidence! A month earlier Aleck would
have been at the helm of his steamboat.* "What brings you here?"

"To see Vallières before he holds court."

Adolphus made no comment and they moved quickly to the judge's
chambers on the upper floor. The suite of offices were well appointed; the
courthouse had been built in 1821 and designed to provide much more space
than was available when the court operated in the old *Récollet* monastery on
Rue Notre-Dame.

The clerk meeting them at the entrance wasn't quite certain how to handle the unannounced presence of the two gentlemen. He undoubtedly suspected that Joseph-Rémi Vallières de Saint-Réal, having had an off-and-on association with the Hart family since his arrival in the town almost ten years before, had learned from experience that their demands on his time and attention could be significant. Adolphus, being one of the several *Trifluvien* lawyers having to appear before the bench frequently, was likely to be acting in his professional capacity. Alexander Thomas, on the other hand, often behaved as a stalking horse for his father. And Vallières' clerk knew enough about Moses Hart to believe the judge would be wary of the son as much as of the father.

Another obstacle to an immediate interview by either of them presented itself. Waiting in the anteroom was Pierre Vézina, the veteran Queen's Counselor. Adolphus guessed that he too had business with Vallières. They greeted each other cordially enough. Vézina had been his father's rival when Ezekiel Hart had contested the seat in the House of Assembly thirty years before. Nevertheless, relations had always been good over the years. His late daughter Clarisse had married Tom Judah in 1827 and there was a son as a result of that union.

Adolphus checked his timepiece. If Vallières didn't emerge from his inner office soon, there would be little time for any of them to get access to him before he was due in court. "Will you be long with the judge, *Monsieur* Vézina? I hope I am not offending you with the question."

"I am not offended, young man. Yet I can't predict how the conversation will go. It is no secret that I still intend to find a place on the Bench. I am here to enlist him in support of my endeavor." Vézina's disclosure reminded Adolphus that the veteran *avocat* had had only mixed success over the years in getting recognition for his devotion to the law.

The door to Vallières' inner sanctum opened at that moment. The judge, looking even more frail than usual, was already in his robes anticipating an imminent walk to the courtroom. He scanned the room. "I apologize, gentlemen. A request from our Governor has suddenly occupied me longer than I thought."

He first eyed Vézina, who repeated the purpose of his visit. Vallières looked very sober. "I do not hold out much hope for success in getting such an appointment. *Canadiens* are now required to demonstrate their loyalty to the Crown in the most obsequious way, the Constitution be damned!

Adolphus appreciated what Vallières was hinting at. A couple of years previously his health had so failed him that he had to be temporarily replaced as the resident judge in Trois-Rivières by Jean-Roch Rolland, the

Montreal-based jurist. Rolland was of a different breed: a lawyer grown rich defending seigneurial and merchant clients – rich enough to be able to buy the seigneury of Sir John Johnson a dozen years before. He had no use for writs of *habeas corpus* because, in his judgment, the relevant British statute on the subject wasn't applicable in the province.

Meanwhile Vézina introduced his own take on the situation. "I was in Montreal two days ago. Did you know that La Fontaine has been released from jail? They couldn't find anything with which to charge him."

"That hasn't stopped the Governor from incarcerating *Patriotes* during the last month or so." Vallières replied gruffly.

"That may be the case, *mon ami*, and La Fontaine did tell me he had been questioned by Leclerc for days to get him to admit that he was involved with the *Chasseurs*."

Vallières was visibly angry. "Leclerc is so cruel. It is said that Viger is being kept in solitude. No paper, no pen, no newspapers. They won't even allow him to play the flageolet to ease his mind. So there it is; Viger isn't as cooperative as La Fontaine. Demands a trial and that raises the question of *habeas corpus*. Leclerc undoubtedly has orders not to yield in that matter."

Vézina was thoughtful in his response. "That reminds me of our old chief. Pierre Bédard sat in prison for months back in 1810 because he insisted on a trial. The then Governor would not give him that pleasure! La Fontaine, on the other hand, is a born conciliator. When he was in London he engaged himself with men such as Gosford, Ellice and Hume, and back home he has spent many hours with Buller and Wakefield."

Alexander spoke up for the first time. "We do have martial law. The suspension of *habeas corpus* is not unusual in such circumstances."

Vallières stopped him short. "It may interest you, gentlemen, that last week I accepted a writ of *habeas corpus* for a farmer from Rivière-du-Loup. That is why I am in correspondence with the Governor. He wants the details of the case. I did indicate to him that such an investigation by the Executive tends to lessen the independence of the Bench."

Silence descended on the room. All realized that at least one member of the judiciary was challenging government in a most direct way. At last Vallières brought the stillness to an end. "What is it that you are after, Aleck?"

"I think we must speak in private. You do remember that my father has a number of accounts to settle with you."

"Sorry, *mon ami*! I have more important matters to attend to." Vallières strode out of the room.

*   *   *

The next time Adolphus sat down with his cousin Alexander was on Christmas Day. The court having closed because of the holiday, he had accepted an invitation for drinks at the Rue Alexandre home of Moses Hart. Mary McCarthy Brown was the only woman in the parlor, but she didn't seem out of place. She was a keen observer of the political scene and this day she brought news of what was happening in the capital. "The suspension of Bédard and Panet from their judicial duties has aroused Parent to fury. I have a copy of *Le Canadien*. He minces no words."

Adolphus surveyed the room. Uncle Moses was a little detached from the conversation but his two sons, Areli and Alexander, could hardly wait to engage their stepmother. Alexander spoke first. "Parent will pay for his indiscretion. Colborne does not do things by halves. His action against the two judges may prove to be mild compared to what could happen to *Le Canadien*."

Areli concurred. "Vallières is also asking for trouble. Can you imagine men like Ogden, the Stuarts and O'Sullivan advising the Governor to back off in today's political climate?"

Until that moment Adolphus had said little. But he got to his feet to replenish his glass of brandy at the side table and to grab a sweet. "Things will get worse. Twelve Patriotes already condemned and more trials to come. I may be going up to Montreal to defend some of the prisoners before the courts marital. Our cousin Philip has gained some notoriety defending Cardinal and his friends caught at Caughnawaga. I never thought he had it in him to take such an unpopular stand."

"That is so unlike Philip. I remember him berating me for speaking kindly of the *Patriotes*. He was active in the Doric Club and eager to volunteer for the militia when the fighting broke out last year. Why this change of heart?"

"Some lawyers do respect the law, even if they are weak in learning it." Adolphus was providing a barbed assessment. He too was thinking of the bad advice Aaron Philip had given his father Benjamin and to Moses Hays with respect to their original invitation to become part of Montreal's magistracy.

The one person reacting to Adolphus' characterization of Aaron Philip turned out to be Moses Hart, who seemingly was paying attention to the dialogue after all. His pique was evident. "I cannot believe, Adolphus, that you would repeat Philip's folly by defending the rebels. The province is caught up with debating the causes of the insurrection while trade is down and so many of us are threatened with ruin. Think again about what you will be doing in the coming months!"

It was at this point that Moses Hart raised himself from his seat – apparently a strenuous act for a man just turned seventy – and shuffled off to his bedroom. Alexander offered an explanation for this unexpectedly rude behavior. "Papa is most disturbed by the state of the economy. As you know, the government decided to suspend specie payments as of the day after the second insurrection. It has thus repeated what it did in May of '37 and then it took a year before the banks could do business as usual. Who knows how long the suspension will last on this occasion."

"Can't he do what others have done in this situation?" Adolphus had in mind the practice of some the leading merchants in Montreal. The Thomas and William Molson Company, for example had been issuing notes on which was stamped the words "Molson Bank" despite it having no government sanction to do so.

It was Mary who responded. "He has done so to some extent. But paper money is suspect even with the good reputation of the Hart name. Currently the Governor is tolerating all this because of the scarcity of specie. But in the end such notes will have to be converted to coin. Moses still holds the opinion that we need a proper bank in Three Rivers. He would require a license to operate one, but he may be able to convince the authorities that with his holdings in real estate and secured credits, a private bank here is financially feasible."

Adolphus said nothing but he was dubious that permission would be granted. It was common knowledge that the *Banque du Peuple*, launched a few years before to compete with the Bank of Montreal, was a thorn in the side of the government and of the Anglo-Scottish Tories who dominated the Montreal merchant community. Louis-Michel Viger, a member of the Papineau/Viger clan, was implicated in both the first and second rebellions and was currently in prison despite being president of the "peoples" bank.

*   *   *

A few days later Adolphus was back at the courthouse to see Judge Vallières but circumstances had changed from what they were earlier in the month. Word had reached Trois-Rivières of Vallières being suspended from the Bench just as Bédard and Panet had been a week earlier. Jean-Roch Rolland, the bearded jurist from Montreal, had been selected to replace Vallières. Not too surprisingly Vallières had already vacated the chambers. The clerk appeared disturbed but did speak without hesitation. If Adolphus wished to communicate with the man, he would need to go to Vallières' residence on Rue Notre-Dame.

Walking down Rue des Champs Adolphus pondered whether he too was treading on dangerous ground. Colborne was obviously intent on stifling any overt opposition to the regime. With Vallières absent from the Bench, there would be a less sympathetic ear in the district courts and an uncertain prospect to say the least if Adolphus had to argue before Anglo judges in Montreal or Quebec. Though not clear in his mind as to how to proceed, he did find himself before the *Maison de Gannes* on Rue Notre-Dame. Just about every *Trifluvien* knew about Georges de Gannes, a career officer during the French regime of the previous century, a man who had built the dwelling and lived there for almost two decades. To them Vallières was a *nouveau venu*. For Adolphus the house was the place where his older sister, Esther Elizabeth, had resided as part of a common-law marriage that lasted a few years. But that was the past. His sister was back in the Hart household on Rue des Forges and Vallières, now in his fifties, was married to the widow Jane Keirman. *No wonder Eliza's spirit has been so low since then!*

Notwithstanding this history, Vallières had showed no resentment towards Esther Elizabeth's siblings in the last couple of years. He greeted Adolphus graciously when the latter was ushered into the parlor. There was, however, another guest in the room. Ensconced in a corner seat was Joseph-Guillaume Barthe, the young *protégé* of the judge. His demeanor suggested that he too had been beset by troubles. Vallières was quick to explain. "You come at a delicate time, Adolphus. Perhaps you can help us. You may have been informed that Parent was arrested the day after Christmas. Jean-Baptiste Fréchette, the printer of *Le Canadien,* has also been thrown into jail. Sedition is the charge."

Adolphus feigned surprise albeit he had already assumed there would be retribution for the publishing of Parent's tirade. "And to think that Étienne Parent had praised Lord Durham when he first came over."

"This may not be the end of the repression. Ask our friend Barthe why he is here!" Vallières looked grim.

Barthe obliged. "One of my poems, the one titled *Aux exilés politiques canadiens,* was printed in *Le Fantasque* on the same day as Parent was arrested. I may be naïve for I did think the poem quite innocuous. Now I'm not too certain of that. If *Le Canadien* is regarded as subversive, *Le Fantasque* may be likewise judged. I am here to get the judge's opinion."

Vallières jumped in. "I have not been encouraging. Joseph-Guillaume may have to accept being imprisoned as a martyr. Knowing how Young thinks, I believe he will act against *Le Fantasque* and quite possibly against my friend here. Young and I were at dagger points when he was in the

Assembly in the '20s. He has always been hostile to the *Patriotes*. And now he has his chance."

Adolphus had met Thomas Ainslie Young several times when he clerked in the office of the Attorney General a few years back. His credentials as a Tory were well established; the son and grandson of leading Quebec merchants and a son-in-law of the late François Baby, he served as sheriff in the capital city for several years even while sitting in the Assembly. Currently he was superintendent of the police.

"*Hélas*, I fear there is a personal element. Young would like nothing better than to put Aubin behind bars. All through this year the *Le Fantasque* has been poking fun not only at Durham and Colborne but also at Young and his assistant." Barthe was seemingly in close contact with Napoléon Aubin, a journalist and lyricist who had settled in Quebec but a few years before and began publishing *Le Fantasque* as a satirical journal.

Le 8 janvier 1839 je reçus l'ordre de me tenit prêt à comparaître devant la cour martiale; onze de mes compagnons de captivité recurrent aussi la même injunction. Le 9 janvier, nous fûmes, conduits liés, dans une voiture rellulaire, à la prison du Pied-du-Courant...Quelques heures après notre arrivées dans ce lieu, MM. Drummond et Hart vinrent nous rendre visite dans nos cachots, et nous demander les renseignements dont ils avaient besoin pour notre defense.
FRANÇOIS-XAVIER PRIEUR
("notes d'un condamné politique prisonnier", January, 1839)

The procedures with regard to the prisoners were illegal, unconstitutional and unjust.
LEWIS DRUMMOND, AARON PHILIP HART
(appeal to the court, February 14, 1839)

Thirteen

The cell caging Chevalier de Lorimier stank of stale urine but Aaron Philip Hart had over the months become accustomed to the foul atmosphere in the *Pied-du-Courant* prison. He had Drummond's concurrence with him doing the first interview with the most prominent of the dozen *Patriotes* scheduled for the court martial on Friday. This was Wednesday, the 9th; over a week had passed since the New Year celebration and Aaron Philip was being reminded that the gaiety of his evening with the Davids and Josephs contrasted so markedly with the sense of futility in this corner of Montreal.

Aaron Philip's eyes adjusted to the little light in the cellblock. Chevalier de Lorimier was of medium height and had a dark complexion. So were his hair and eyes on the dark side. He was almost a decade older than Aaron Hart. He had made a name for himself in Montreal first as a notary and then as a political activist supporting *Patriote* candidates in two successive elections. Aaron Philip recognized that the prosecutors regarded Lorimier as a prime target. He had led the Beauharnois *Patriotes*, one of the last insurgent groups to surrender to the British army. He had almost escaped its grasp; he was caught at the border and therefore not able to join Nelson, Côté and the others in a continuation of their exile.

In other circumstances Lorimier might have rejected legal counsel from a man such as Aaron Philip, but the latter's reputation had been reassessed by *Patriotes* following his widely publicized defense of Cardinal and the others in the earlier court martial. "Take the chair, *Monsieur* Hart. You may not be happy with listening to your new client. We were told yesterday that we should prepare ourselves for trial on Friday. The prison van brought us here this morning and passed under the scaffold that took the lives of our friends Cardinal and Duquette. We *know* what is in store for us."

Aaron Philip had expected such a reaction. Most of the insurgents he had dealt with did not lack fearlessness. Lorimier was no exception. He seated himself as requested. "You do understand my purpose. *Monsieur* Drummond and I have been retained to defend you. We suffer under a handicap since we personally are forbidden to interrogate the witnesses for the prosecution. Yet there is this opportunity to gather whatever information can be used in your defense and prepare you to make the best use of it."

The actual events of that fateful week were reviewed. It had all begun with Lorimier standing next to Nelson and Côté on the Sunday morning in Napierville while the declaration of independence was uttered. It was followed by the march to Beauharnois, the occupation of the Ellice manor house and the steamship and concluded with Lorimier's thwarted escape. "I thought I had a charmed life. Last year I survived a bullet through my thigh during the clash with the Doric Club ruffians. That was before they ransacked the offices of the *Vindicator*. A week or so later I escaped Saint-Benoit prior to Colborne putting the village to the torch. But then I got myself lost in the woods trying to avoid capture at Beauharnois. I had to walk back to Napierville. Charmed life? Look where I'm now!"

"Will your wife be permitted to visit you?" Aaron Philip was taking a liking to the prisoner, who was describing his travail with eloquence. *What would I have done in his circumstances?*

"I doubt it. My greatest worry is that I have failed my family. Henriette did join me in Plattsburgh during the summer but caring for our two girls required her to come home. She has suffered much in recent years, losing our only son plus two other daughters to childhood diseases. It is fortunate that she inherited the house on Rue Saint-Jacques. Still, I know not how she will manage when I'm gone."

"I remember that house. Stopped in once to get a document relating to the American Fur Company. You were well located." For the first time Aaron Philip acknowledged having had previous contact with Lorimier.

*   *   *

The Friday morning was blustery. Attending the court martial required a willingness to brave the frigid January air until one was safely in the courthouse and once seated to exercise the feet until the chamber warmed up decently for the hearing. Aaron Philip recognized that most of the spectators were either army officers or the English-speaking officials attached to magistracy. He could anticipate hostility to any effort by the defendants to appeal for a humane understanding of their behavior.

A door at the rear of the chamber opened and everybody was ordered to rise to their feet. The Judge Advocate, President and members of the court filed in. Major General John Clitherow was once more presiding over the court and took his seat with deliberate dignity. Charles Dewey Day, the deputy Judge Advocate, had his own place of honor. Once the other members of the court were settled, arranged on both sides of the President and presumably in accordance with their military rank, Clitherow declared the proceedings should begin. On signal the twelve defendants were marched under escort to face the President. Day rose to his feet to read the Convening Order to the accused at which point the dozen *Patriotes* were instructed to step back to the table where Aaron Philip and Drummond were already located. It was an extension table covered with green cloth and occupied much of the room's middle.

Lorimier, speaking for his co-defendants, preempted the prosecutor by asking to be heard. "We have before us written pleas prepared by our counsels, Messrs. Drummond and Hart. You will observe that once again the jurisdiction of the court martial is at issue. We demand a trial before a civil court, which is our right under the Constitution."

Clitherow didn't take long to rule on that demand. "We have previously considered that argument. Needless to say, it is dismissed. Please proceed!"

Lorimier did not sit down. "We then ask, *sieur*, that prisoner Perrigo be excluded from this trial. The indictment is not applicable to him."

To Aaron Philip's surprise, the President responded favorable to this appeal. The judges had obviously come to the same conclusion by the time the trial opened. James Perrigo, a merchant at Sainte-Martine, had dissuaded the *Patriotes* at Camp David from pursuing a detachment of the 71st Foot once the soldiers had been repulsed after its first attack. Lorimier didn't agree with Perrigo's passivity, but that didn't matter. One life saved!

The way was now open for the prosecution to make its case. Though he was relatively new to general courts martial and the military setting, Aaron Philip was familiar enough with evidentiary matters. They were governed by military rules of evidence by which the prosecutor used direct examination of witnesses and the submission of documentary evidence.

Lorimier was not shy about cross-examining the witnesses and succeeded in several instances to have them contradict themselves. Aaron Philip could see that the former notary was comfortable in a courtroom albeit that didn't change the fact that the hostility of the court and the assembled spectators led to violent interruptions that would have tried even the most experienced lawyer.

The trial went on during the following week. The prosecution doggedly continued its examination of parties present during the occupation of Beauharnois. The proceedings were coming to a close and Aaron Philip couldn't be blamed for concluding that Lorimier had made good progress in disputing much of the evidence. He was not prepared, however, for the prosecution calling a surprise witness. A *Patriote* called Jean-Baptiste-Henri Brien, a doctor at Sainte-Martine, disclosed that Lorimier had come to Camp David from Beauharnois to encourage the insurgents to remain firm and not to give up the fight. Aaron Philip whispered to Lorimier to challenge the witness; was the man's "confession" being rewarded with leniency by the prosecutors? Nevertheless, the testimony, though challenged, made an obvious impression on the court. This was confirmed when Day, the deputy Judge Advocate, made his address to the court. Lorimier had been shown by the evidence to be a dangerous criminal who had fomented the rebellion. He deserved to die on the gallows. Drummond, who had articled in Day's office, groaned. "Just like the man – Tory to the core."

On the 21st of the month, ten days after the opening of the trial, the verdict was as expected. The court found all of the defendants guilty of high treason and therefore subject to the death penalty. For Lorimier there was no recommendation to the Executive for clemency; he alone deserved the harshest punishment.

In a court martial there was no requirement for unanimity in any judgment. The President and members of the court needed a simple majority to reach a decision and collectively they imposed a sentence. The two defence counsels now had their opportunity to have the last word by delivering summations for the accused. But what else could be said that was different from the arguments they had presented at the conclusion of the trial of the Cardinal twelve and as part of the last-minute appeals made in December before the hanging of Cardinal and Duquette?

* * *

The judges of the Court of Queen's Bench were expressionless. Aaron Philip Hart realized that appearing before them was an act of desperation. But the occasion of the quarterly assizes did give him and Drummond a chance to ask for a writ of prohibition, which granted would allow a civilian court to intervene in the judgment of a military body. Almost two weeks had passed since the sentences on Lorimier and six of his seven co-defendants had been pronounced. The two lawyers had followed the same appeal procedures as before to get the Governor or the members of the Special Council to lift the death sentences. But reiteration of the plea that the whole process had been illegal, unconstitutional and unjust hadn't moved these authorities. Would legal minds think differently?

The quartet that made up the Court didn't show much promise in this regard. The Chief Justice, Michael O'Sullivan, had been on the bench less than five years and no longer showed any sympathy for the *Patriote* movement. In any event, he had his health problems; a bullet lodged against his spine, the outcome of a duel of twenty years before, caused him frequent bouts of agonizing pain. Samuel Gale's elevation to the Court had been challenged by the *Patriotes* back in 1834 because he had once been a spokesman for the Townships' English settlers before the British House of Commons. Only last year he had submitted a written judgment maintaining the right of the Crown to establish martial law and suspend *habeas corpus*. George Pyke had the longest tenure on the bench but had always voted with the government when he was in the Assembly prior to the 1812-14 war. And then there was Jean-Roch Rolland, who even denied that *habeas corpus* applied in the province in spite of it being part of the British Empire. In addition, he was due to be leaving for Trois-Rivières in the next few weeks.

Lewis Drummond had argued that the effort was worthwhile. He was betting that O'Sullivan, a fellow Irishman, would remember his roots. He was quickly disabused of this notion; the Court of Queen's Bench rejected the writ within minutes. The seven condemned – Chevalier de Lorimier, Jean-Baptiste Brien, Joseph Dumouchelle, Toussaint Rochon, François-Xavier Prieur, Joseph Wattier and Jean Laberge – would be executed as ordered by a military court.

The two men left the courthouse without saying anything until they were on Rue Notre-Dame. The sharp February breeze caused Aaron Philip to shiver despite being well clothed. *How long will this business go on?* "What we need is a drink. Let's visit the *auberge* down the street!"

Occupying a table waiting to be served, they seemingly had lost the zest for conversation. For his part, Aaron Philip had neglected most of his clients in pursuit of justice for the condemned insurgents. At one time he had reasoned to himself that there would be compensation for the lost income; he had made a reputation among the *Canadien* shopkeepers, craftsmen and members of the liberal professions living in the town and island of Montreal. It occurred to him that these were the very people who had done business with Lorimier when he plied his notarial trade. On further reflection, he reckoned that he had burned many bridges by taking a stance so odious to members of the Doric Club. *I've made my bed.*

The two lawyers made an ironic toast to justice by clicking their glasses. Drummond got to the subject at hand. "This is Saturday, the ninth of the month. I think the Governor will decree the execution date next week. That leaves us just days before they go onto the scaffold. So little time left to come up with another motion."

"Perhaps we ought to do what I did for Cardinal? Have Lorimier's wife make a personal appeal for clemency."

Drummond's smile was more morose than encouraging. "I'll give you that task if you have the courage to do it."

My dear Baron: In a few hours, everything will have been said for me in this world. We just separated, I received your last kiss as a brother and a friend, and I still have the desire to talk. So let's talk.
CHARLES HINDELANG
(letter to Baron Fratelin, February 14, 1839)

A la veille de quitter mon lugubre cachot pour monter sur l'échafaud déjà rougi du sang des nobles victims qui m'ont précédé, mon coeur et le devoir m'engagement à t'écrire un mot, avant de paraître devant Dieu, le juge suprême de mon âme. Dans le peu de temps qui s'est écoulé depuis le jour de notre union sacrée jusqu'á ce jour, tu m'as rendu, ma chère femme, vraiment heureux.
CHEVALIER DE LORIMIER
(letter to his wife, morning, February 15, 1839)

Fourteen

It was on the Tuesday, twelve days into February, that the inmates in the *Pied du Courant* were told that seven coffins were being prepared for the executions slated for the Friday morning. François-Xavier Prieur had difficulty digesting his supper ration; for the last three weeks he had dreamed that all seven convicted in the court martial would not suffer the same fate. Now it seemed certain; he would mount the scaffold that was visible from their cell windows. Prieur foresaw himself sleeping badly this night.

An exclamation from the prisoner sitting next to him brought him out of his reverie. "The jailers play games; do not lose hope." Prieur hadn't realized until that moment that he was sitting next to Denis-Benjamin Viger, the venerable *Patriote* leader who, according to prison gossip, was also incarcerated in the *Pied du Courant*.

"But why seven coffins?" Prieur was still stuck on the coincidence in numbers.

"That is all the executioners can handle at a time. More than seven have been condemned to death."

He inspected Viger more closely. For a man in his mid-sixties he looked surprisingly fit. His eyes were clear; his face though hirsute not totally unkempt. Prieur tried to remember how he had appeared before being jailed; he had seen him only once before standing on the rostrum along side his cousin Louis-Joseph Papineau and other spokesmen for the *parti Patriote*. Prieur had traveled to Montreal, a young merchant from Saint-Timothée, the upriver village west of Beauharnois; to participate in a rally protesting the "Russell Resolutions" that had so riled most *Canadiens*. Papineau was the most articulate in expressing their common outrage but Viger was remembered as giving the most lucid explanation of the implications of this new government policy. And here he was, dressed in prison garb. "I had not noticed you as being one of the detainees."

Viger showed a wry smile. "I am fortunate to be in this *cantine* these days. Though arrested last November, I was not permitted to see anybody – even fellow prisoners – until recently."

"But you have not been charged with treason, have you?" Prieur had no knowledge of the dean of the *Patriote* movement having actually been involved in the uprisings.

"*Nullement!* Charged with nothing at all though the *Herald* denounces me as the owner of seditious newspapers. I wish to contest that view in court but with *habeas corpus* suspended there is no judge who will order a trial. This has happened before. You may remember Pierre Bédard, the late father of Judge Eléazar Bédard in Quebec. He insisted on being tried before a civilian court but the Governor of the day denied him that wish."

"You are referring to Governor Craig. I was not born yet when he put Bédard in prison. I am not yet twenty five."

"May I ask, young man, what brought you to this state of affairs?"

"I was not content just running my business in Saint-Timothée. Chevalier de Lorimier came incognito from Beauharnois last spring to tell us that preparations for an uprising were in the works. I agreed to be a *castor* for my district." Prieur went on to explain that sentiment in these parishes south of the St Lawrence River was strongly for independence from the British Empire.

"Were you not on trial with Lorimier? I understand that it was a travesty of justice. In keeping with the mood of the British when their interests are threatened."

"Our lawyers argue that all the *procès* was illegal, unconstitutional and unjust, but the military does what it wants. I am just one of many victims in this tragedy. In another time I would have lived to your age." Prieur suddenly felt a tear on his cheek.

*　*　*

Prieur's initial fear was realized; he had not slept well on the Tuesday night. Nor was he heartened by the news during this Wednesday afternoon that the Judge Advocate had come to the office of the jailer to identify who was to be the victims in Friday's execution. These unfortunates would thus have time to prepare for the rope. *Seven coffins! Will I be laid out in one of them, my neck stretched beyond the breaking point?*
Conversations among the prisoners suddenly seemed stilted in Prieur's opinion. Not knowing their personal fate was indeed depressing, albeit some spoke with what was surely a false sense of bravery. Prieur was especially impressed with the posture of the one foreigner in their midst, the condemned Charles Hindelang. A few years older than Prieur, the Paris-born soldier was his very antithesis, a Calvinist with Swiss ancestry, well educated and an extrovert. He had come to the province looking for a fight. At Odelltown he got it.

Apparently other prisoners had heard tales of Hindelang's exploits during the French Revolution of 1830. He gave up an officer's post in the post-1830 army there to come to the United States as a commercial traveler. Ludger Duvernay had recruited him in New York to become a member of the army of *Canadien* exiles; he combined revolutionary sentiments with military experience. Prieur enquired of Hindelang as to the possibility that he might be spared at the last minute.

"I think not, *jeune homme*. In my case, they intend to hang me as an example of what happens to a foreigner challenging the British flag. Especially one who acted as a General on the battlefield! I accept that verdict and take sweet satisfaction in having done what I could to bring good will to this accursed colony."

The main entrance to this section of the prison finally opened and the jailer appeared standing in the doorframe. His voice was clear enough: "Charles Hindelang!"

Two guards moved forward to accompany a subdued Hindelang to the exit. Several of prisoners shouted defiance; the Parisian had won friends among them in the few months they had shared these quarters. Prieur was not about to forget the words just uttered by this fallen General.

Ten minutes later the door opened again. Once more the jailer, seemingly oblivious to the tension in the chamber: "Chevalier de Lorimier!"

Prieur could detect muffled sobs from among the onlookers as the guards led Lorimier away. The latter looked neither left nor right. His face was a mask. The door had scarcely closed before the anger of the inmates developed into a clamor of utensils striking the stone cell walls.

Many more minutes passed without another pronouncement. Prieur decided it was safe to move to the back of the room in order use his saucepan to warm water for the cereal he had saved. Unfortunately, the door opened a third time. He couldn't hear what was being announced. Leaving his utensil in place, he walked forward quickly to approach the jailer. "*C'est mon tour?*"

The jailer looked confused. Prieur wondered if he should repeat what he had said. Does he not understand my question? He does speak English only.

It was Prieur who had to admit to confusion. The jailer, speaking in English, was visibly annoyed. "It is not you that I called. It is Mr. Lepailleur. Simply in order to deliver him some provisions that his parents sent him."

To add to his confusion, the door was once more ajar. There stood Lorimier and Hindelang, who were ushered into the cellblock. The executions were indeed scheduled for Friday. Prieur gasped as if he was seeing ghosts; two men he had mentally classified as already dead.

The prisoners gathered about the two of them; handshaking; embraces; undisguised weeping. Lorimier had a message for the assembled men. "Rejoice! We are the only two victims chosen in this section. But there are three others elsewhere in the prison. They are Rémi Narbonne, François Nicolas and Amable Daunais."

At that moment Prieur noticed that others, including two women, had followed Lorimier into the prison area. He soon learned they were his sister and cousin along with a male member of their family. Recognizing that these grieving relatives wanted time alone with the doomed Lorimier, just about all of the prisoners retreated to the end of the room. Prieur stayed close enough to hear Lorimier console the women. "*Mon sacrifice est fait.* I hope to go to see my God. Only one thing darkens my last moments. It is the thought of the fate awaiting my wife and children. But I entrust them to Divine Providence."

Prieur slipped away, greatly disturbed. Would he have had the same faith in Divine Providence if the jailer had called out his name earlier in the afternoon?

Soon it was dusk; six o'clock in fact. The guards arrived to tell the prisoners that they would have to return to their cells. The grief-striken visitors had no choice but to retire from the scene.

*   *   *

"May I ask you a favor, Prieur? Could we exchange beds for the next two days? I don't have the taste for sharing space with a condemned man on his last nights."

The request caught him by surprise. Dr. Jean-Baptiste-Henri Brien had shared the cell with Lorimier since the January trial. Unlike Lorimier himself, Brien was for several years known to Prieur, the doctor having practiced in Sainte-Martine, not too many miles from Saint-Timothée.

"Ah! Is it that you have a crisis of conscience?" Prieur's outburst was unpremeditated. He had not fully forgiven Brien for the statements he had made to the authorities following his arrest at Beauharnois; they had been used with devastating effect by the prosecutor during the trial. Prieur remembered how shame-faced Brien was during that testimony. Now this remorse was being played out in that Brien was likely to suffer no more than exile whereas his comrade would die a victim of his treason. No wonder Brien didn't relish being in Lorimier's proximity during the latter's last hours on earth!

Nevertheless, Prieur didn't spend the whole night in Lorimier's presence. That evening a priest arrived to listen to the prisoner's confession. Prieur stood in the corridor for about an hour. When he returned to the cell, he could not but be impressed by the sight of a man so at peace with himself. The two of them prayed together for part of the night before sleeping peacefully side by side.

The mood hadn't changed by the Thursday morning. More praying; more talk about Lorimier's wife and children, whose fate he could leave to Providence. Prieur took Lorimier by the arm and together with Guillaume Lévesque, Hindelang's roommate they walked with the condemned men to meet with several discrete groups of prisoners. Lorimier was resigned and dignified; Hindelang, noisily courageous. Prieur prepared some breakfast but Lorimier ate little.

Towards three o'clock in the afternoon *Madame* de Lorimier entered the cellblock accompanied again by a sister and two cousins of the condemned prisoner. Prieur would long remember the grieving expression on the wife's face. Yet she did not cry even as her companions wept.

Prieur and other had arranged for the prison to provide a goodbye dinner for Lorimier and Hindelang. The table was placed in the corridor near the entrance door. The prepared meal was set on it for a four-o'clock serving. Hindelang presided over this "banquet" but Lorimier declined to take the seat assigned to him. He did, however, come to the table for a glass of wine. Before that he walked the corridor with his Henriette arm in arm.

It was already known that a last-minute appeal to Governor Colborne made by her on the advice of Hart had not been responded to.

To Prieur it was all a spectacle. Not only the sad gaiety of Hindelang as he forced conversation; the jailer had admitted six strangers for a few minutes. He was to learn later they were touring the prison, including the scaffold outside, and that one of them was the editor of *The Herald*. Prieur sought to suppress his anger at the intrusion. At least they have the decency not to say anything. An instant later he was told that *Madame* de Lorimier had fainted and taken to her husband's cell.

As the evening began Lorimier's confessor was once more at his side for some time. He had already conferred with Hindelang, who didn't pay him the same attention. Prieur, still in the corridor, picked up the word "courage", which the priest repeated to the wife before taking his leave.

At 10 o'clock the jailer arrived to order Prieur and Lévesque out of the corridor and into their respective cells. At the same time standing at the entrance appeared Lorimier's children and other family members to complement the threesome that had been there since mid-afternoon.

At last Prieur had the opportunity of returning to his cot. Lorimier confided in him: "The hardest blow has been given." His tone was firm but his face pale as death.

There was still time before dawn for Lorimier not only to pray but also to write a letter that was his political testament. Then he slept tranquilly for three hours. Prieur, however, remained awake watching over him.

By daylight on the Friday morning all of the prisoners were sitting up in their cots in anticipation of what was about to happen in the yard outside. The confessor came once more to give communion and to prepare Lorimier for his walk to the scaffold. Prieur helped him wash and dress. As he fixed a little white *cravate* at Lorimier's neck, the latter could only say "*Laissez l'espace nécessaire pour placer la corde!*" Prieur was shaken as never before. It was the same reaction he had when he read Lorimier's goodbye note addressed to him. *Soyez courageux! Adieu.*

Sitting in despair on his cot he could hear through the window the words of Hindelang, ever the martyr. "The cause for which I sacrifice myself is noble and great. I am proud of it. I don't fear death. The blood that is spilled will be washed away with blood of others. Let the responsibility fall on those who deserve it. *Canadiens*, my final farewell is the old French cry: *Vive la liberté!*"

Dear Aaron: Esther wrote you to go by the R.Williams a week past.
I had only a place to write in her Magilla that all your Letters
were received, even the one you doubted from Bristol.
EZEKIEL HART
(letter to Aaron Ezekiel Hart, January 21, 1839)

I know of no national distinction marking and continuing a more hopeless
inferiority. The language, the laws, the character of the North American
Continent are English; and every race but the English (apply this to all
who speak the English language) appears there in a condition
of inferiority. It is to elevate them from that inferiority that I desire
to give the Canadians our English character.
LORD DURHAM
(report to the Melbourne government, February 1839)

Fifteen

The City of London was frankly a wonder to Aaron Ezekiel Hart. Perhaps because it being still winter, he should have expected disparities. *So many handsome edifices mixed with the grime of Old Country living!* The boots he wore served him well at dodging pedestrians, excrement and other detritus of this otherwise magnificent city. Whether or not he was properly dressed for an unusually cold March day was another matter.

Aaron Ezekiel hadn't been lodging long in the British capital. The journey from New York had put him first in Bristol and Exeter, where he attended to some family business. His Uncle Moses had retained him to check on some of the correspondents whom he dealt with over the years. Aaron Ezekiel had long recognized Moses Hart's reluctance to work with established agents in Montreal, Quebec, New York and Halifax. Over the past decades he had developed a network of British agents – including family members living in London. First it had been George Joel, Aaron Hart's brother in law, who had represented him until the uncle's death twenty years ago. A longer lasting relationship was with first cousin Judah Joseph, although he too was now buried. Uncle Moses wasn't comfortable without a trusted relative looking after his affairs.

Today he intended to pay a courtesy call on Judah Joseph's widow. The former Catherine Lazare deserved some commiseration, her husband having died only months before. He had lived into his mid seventies so that it had been a decent life for the both of them. In contrast, Judah's older brother, Abraham, had died almost twenty-five years before. (Abraham Joseph's widow, Hannah, perished not much more than a year before, the woman accidentally falling into a water-filled cellar.) And then there had been Henry, the youngest of the three Joseph brothers settling in Berthier before turn of the century; he had been a victim of the cholera epidemic of 1832.

The Joseph family, related because one of Aaron Hart's sisters had married Naphtali Joseph in London, was less than a day's journey living just upriver from Trois-Rivières; they had in fact migrated to North America at the behest of Aaron Ezekiel's grandfather. While Aaron Ezekiel was growing up, the Harts and Josephs often celebrated major Jewish holidays together. The only sour note during this time was that Judah Joseph had married a Christian and agreed to raise their children outside his faith.

The visit being over inside an hour – Catharine was too ill to have Aaron Ezekiel remain for dinner – the return walk to the inn where he was staying was accomplished in enough time to have him ready for his evening meal. Indeed, there was the opportunity for a short rest in his room. An opportunity to contemplate some of the instructions he had received from his father.

Yet it wasn't the listing of items Ezekiel Hart had requested that aroused his interest. He reread the letter. Dated in late January, it did make mention of Emma. *Poor daddy! Always so hopeful. Does he not accept the inevitable?* Aaron Ezekiel had always felt guilty about his lack of feeling for his older sister; she was now over forty years old and always mentally retarded. Lately her health had been declining and he didn't think she would last more than a few months. But his father could only write that she would have a "long life".

And then there was the usual appeal for him to search out a bride among the eligible Jewish daughters in Britain. He mentioned the Phillips girl, but he would be satisfied with just about anyone who would carry on the Hart line. (Neither brothers Samuel, Henry, Ira Craig, Abraham or Adolphus had yet to marry.) When last in Trois-Rivières, they had agreed that there were few options open if he were to choose a woman living in Lower Canada. *If only it were permissible to wed a Canadienne! Or even a British Colonel's daughter!*

What also struck him was the letter's addendum, which was written by his sister Esther. "You see how well our old Daddy writes. He is enjoying excellent health." *Was this more wishful thinking?* In any case papa Ezekiel was playing his usual game of being a friend to everybody of importance in the community. Esther referred to his entertaining judges Gale and Rolland even though the old man had for years taken a liking to the "defrocked" Vallières when he was in office. A leading property owner in the district, Ezekiel Hart was not willing to snub well-connected jurists.

*   *   *

This was the day that Aaron Ezekiel would finally lunch with his one cousin living in London. Arthur Wellington Hart had also been traveling elsewhere on the island so that today was their first chance to get together. Selected for the rendezvous was an eating place in Aldgate. Aaron Ezekiel was pleased; for it being late March the weather wasn't too threatening and the hackney reached the East End in good time.

Wellington, called so by family, was now in his mid-twenties. He had apprenticed as an insurance agent in York beginning in 1833, a year before the town was renamed Toronto. Five years later he had sailed for England, papa Benjamin encouraging him to negotiate with various insurance companies in Britain as part of the family business. Wellington confirmed that he was still at it. "I was in Edinburgh meeting with managers at the Standard Life Assurance Co. Later this week there will be a visit to Minerva Assurance on Stone St. here in London."

Midway through the meal Aaron Ezekiel enquired as to how Canadian affairs were engaging the powers-that-be in Whitehall. Wellington warmed to the subject. "It is said that Durham's report was submitted to the Colonial Office and then to the entire Melbourne cabinet at the end of January. Sections of it were leaked to the London *Times* so that its contents have already been disseminated in Quebec and Montreal. Some see Ellice's hand in all of this."

"I'm quite aware of the press reaction here but what will it be back home? From what I know, the report will be badly received by just about all *Canadiens*. They may welcome the granting of responsible government to colonists, but the submerging of their province into a unified country is bound to enrage them. Does Lord Melbourne appreciate such a consequence?" Aaron Ezekiel suspected he and his cousin were not in accord.

Wellington proved him prescient. "Durham argues that the reforms he proposes will put an end to what had become sterile debate and violence. He is counting on the *habitants* learning English ways."

"And do you believe that, Wellington? I have lived in Trois-Rivières and Quebec. In Montreal you may not comprehend how attached *Canadiens* are to their language and religion."

"As are *we* of British stock ~ attached to our traditions. I concede, Aaron, that as Jews we have not fared well. Papa is furious that among the Special Councilors of Lower Canada are men quite ignorant and illiterate and having no attachment to any property in the province. Why is he, an honored merchant in the colony and once an associate of Edward Ellice, overlooked? Obviously he has been debarred from honors because he is an Israelite."

Aaron Ezekiel hadn't realized that Benjamin Hart was still upset at not being rewarded for his service to the Crown during the rebellion. His uncle had already suffered widespread abuse for his partisan role in the events of two successive autumns. *No wonder he feels an injustice had been done!* "An Israelite who has enraged many Canadians. Even Londoners seem appalled by what is happening in the colony."

The execution of a dozen rebels in Montreal was being reported in the British press over the past couple of weeks. Universal acclaim of such action did not prevail. There were immediate protests from pundits contesting the legality of such measures. Speeches in Parliament reflected such sentiments and Wellington guessed that the Melbourne government would have no choice but to stay the hand of the colonial Governor.

"Won't the Queen have something to say about that?" Aaron Ezekiel played the innocent.

"It'll be Melbourne's decision. He has Victoria doing whatever he wants. She is still too young to oppose his wishes. Moreover, she apparently is very fond of the man though he be forty years her senior."

Aaron Ezekiel was intrigued by the suggestion of a sexual connection. He did remember being told that in his youth Melbourne dallied with the Romantic Radicals and that the man's wife had a scandalous affair with Lord Byron. Much later Melbourne himself was accused of being intimate with a leading London socialite and novelist. Perhaps now was the time to move on to less controversial subjects.

Arthur Wellington seemed to be of the same opinion. "Passover is almost upon us. I'm going by carriage to Exeter on Wednesday. Henry Ezekiel is holding his *seder* there and I've been invited. I am almost certain that I could bring along a guest if you were willing to accompany me on the trip."

"By coincidence I was in Exeter last month. I know of the Ezekiel family. Elizabeth Judah was an Ezekiel before she married my late Uncle Sam in London. That was a long way back!" Aaron Ezekiel knew from his grandmother that her brother Samuel Judah, who had gone to England just before the start of the American Revolution, ended up in New York after that war and had a family there.

Thus the luncheon ended without further acrimony. In fact, the two would be seeing much more of each other over the next week or so.

*   *   *

The sight of the flood plain and estuary of the River Exe thrilled Aaron Ezekiel. He had previously visited the city, which sat on a ridge of land backed by a steep hill. Exeter was an old community – the beautiful cathedral built in Norman times attested to that fact – but there had been considerable industrial development based on water power from a fast-flowing but navigable river. The carriage took them to the Ezekiel residence, which was magnificent enough in its own right. Henry Ezekiel himself came out of its main entrance to greet them despite a brisk breeze that was typical of Devonshire in late March.

He was an impressive man, clean-shaven with dark eyebrows and certainly well dressed – a most fashionable cloak showing off a white cravat. Aaron Ezekiel estimated that he must be in his sixties but looking much healthier than papa Ezekiel. There was enough time before the festivities began so that the two guests were treated to a tour of the abode itself.

Aaron Ezekiel and Arthur Wellington were then introduced to the mistress of the house. Servants were scurrying about on all floor levels. She was obviously in the midst of preparations for the *seder* and had her eyes on the clock. Henry Ezekiel took on the task of showing the two London visitors not only the various rooms but also some of the furnishings.

His pride and joy was a mahogany eight-day arch-dial long-case clock with a single-sheet silvered brass dial. Ezekiel pointed out that the dial was engraved with double Arabic numerals for the hours and minutes with separate seconds and date ring. In the arch there was an engraving of a muse-like figure holding a medallion bearing the words "Trade & Commerce." The host confided that he had acquired it in the previous century when he was in his twenties and his older brother, the late Ezekiel Abraham Ezekiel, was in the clock and watch-making business.

There was still enough time to dress for dinner. When he entered the dining hall, Aaron Ezekiel found himself rather shy being faced with so many bodies of every age and description. It did not escape his attention that among there were young maidens of some attraction. He was introduced to all of them but the one who intrigued him the most was an Ezekiel going by the name of Selena. She didn't have the flair of some of the others but her brown eyes and gentle smile struck him immediately. *Now there's a Jewish daughter papa would be proud of!"*

Nevertheless, there was no hope for an uninvited guest to choose where he might sit. And Selena was seated far enough down the table that he couldn't keep an eye on her even if he so wished. *Oh well! Maybe later I can engage with her.* Meanwhile he paid scant attention to the usual rituals of the Passover meal. Henry Ezekiel was an old hand at orchestrating the ceremony but the visitor from Lower Canada had heard it all before and never did take it seriously.

The fellow across the table from him introduced himself as an Ezekiel cousin who had also come up from London to participate in the *seder*. He proved to be a well-connected man from London. Not only was he asking Aaron Ezekiel incisive questions about Canadian affairs. But also he was able to offer gossip relating to what was going on in Whitehall. Like others he wasn't that enthusiastic about the Durham report. "I talked to Ellice, who prefers a federal union of the Canadas rather than a legislative union. A cabinet committee sees merit in a proposal to that effect. Last week I ran into Thomson, who is on that committee. He was once close to Durham but they don't see eye to eye any longer."

"You mean the Thomson who is the president of the Board of Trade? I didn't realize he was that intimately involved with the crisis in the Canadas." Actually Aaron Ezekiel had heard that Charles Edward Poulett Thomson in his capacity as head of the Board of Trade had involved himself in a dispute with the Upper Canada's House of Assembly over currency and banking legislation. But that didn't extend to having any role in putting down the rebellions.

Others at the table were rather subtlety demonstrating their annoyance at what they undoubtedly considered as inappropriate behavior in the midst of the *seder* meal. But the two men were undeterred. *It is merry when gossips meet.*

"May I ask, sir, what Lord Gosford is saying about the crisis? Surely he is being consulted?" Aaron Ezekiel had gotten to know that former Governor in Chief rather well and had high regard for his acumen.

"A good question, young man! He is quite upset about the direction Durham has taken as his successor. The English party in Quebec is anathema to Gosford so that the Durham's appointment of James Stuart, so outspoken an opponent of the *Patriotes*, as Chief Justice is regarded by him as sheer stupidity. And he regards the actions of Colborne and the volunteers he has mustered as unnecessarily savage. But his views don't carry much weight when men are being charged with treason."

"Will Durham consider returning to Quebec?"

"As you know, he is not a well man. A consumptive no less! He has lost a father, a wife and four of his children to the disease."

Aaron Ezekiel could attest to that fact. When in Quebec during the previous year Durham had been occasionally forced to take time off work because tuberculosis was getting the better of him. Aaron Ezekiel distinctly remembered the Governor once having a bloodstained kerchief at his mouth when they chanced to meet.

The last course served, the guests moved to the salon where a string quartet had set up to entertain the guests. Aaron Ezekiel Hart made one more attempt to intrude into a grouping surrounding Selena Ezekiel. But it was no use; *hanging and wiving go by destiny.*

PART THREE

Abutment
1839–42

*It may happen, therefore, that the Governor receives at one and
the same time instructions from the Queen, and advice from
his executive council, totally at variance with each other. If he is
to obey his instructions from England, the parallel of constitutional
responsibility entirely fails; if, on the other hand, he is to follow
the advice of his council, he is no longer
a subordinate office, but an independent sovereign.*
COLONIAL SECRETARY LORD RUSSELL
(letter to Charles Edward Poulett Thomson, (October 14, 1839)

*A despotism would be by far the best thing for Lower
Canada for the next ten years .. but that cannot be.*
CHARLES EDWARD POULETT THOMSON
(letter to Lord Russell, November 25, 1839)

Sixteen

With the final days of summer passing by, Abraham Joseph took heart that business activity was picking up. His wholesale operations in the Lower Town of Quebec had been slowed by the lull in trade but with the resumption of specie payments by the banks beginning in June Abraham could report to his brother Jacob Henry in Montreal that imports of tobacco products had indeed been facilitated.

Abraham had gotten to his office later than usual this morning. He always had to make time to *daven* before breakfast. The praying this day took longer than usual. He had become even more observant after having a *contretemps* with Aaron Ezekiel Hart. Only last Tuesday, the September evening prior to the Day of Atonement, he had made a point of seeking out his second cousin. "I'm not able to get back to Montreal for the High Holidays this year. Come to my place for *Yom Kipur*! We'll do the candle lighting."

There being no synagogue in Quebec, Abraham had to make do with using his small parlor for ceremonial purposes. Despite Aaron Ezekiel being a dozen years older than he, the cousin was still rather uneducated when it came to Jewish prayers. Abraham was determined to instruct him. With Aaron Ezekiel doing the actual igniting of the tapers, Abraham repeated the words *Barukh ata Adonai Eloheinu melekh haolam, asher kid'shanu b'mitzvotav v'tzivanu l'hadlik ner shel yom tov*, the blessing associated with the lighting of holiday candles. What Abraham hadn't counted on was his cousin's lack of piety and his insistence on talking about events more political than sacred.

"Did you know, Abe, that it has finally been decided? Almost sixty of the prisoners in the *Pied du Courant* will be transported to Australia. It is exile during their lifetimes and they must depart immediately." Aaron Ezekiel had intimated previously that his conversations in London with highly placed government officials suggested that Parliament would not countenance further executions; the death sentences imposed on dozens of rebels were in all likelihood to be commuted. Nevertheless, nothing during the summer months had prepared the prisoners for the ultimate verdict.

Abraham wasn't sure how to react. "At least it's not the rope. Perhaps everything will calm down now. Our Governor can get down to reviving the economy. You must admit, Aaron that there is less repression today. Didn't Parent get out of jail in April? Barthe too is no longer behind bars in Three Rivers."

"True, the writ of *habeas corpus* has meaning once more. I met with Parent recently. His months in our Quebec prison, cold and clammy as the cells are, have made him almost deaf. As you can well imagine, he is not well disposed to Governor Colborne."

"Which is why *Le Canadien* is again berating the *Château* for its policies."

Aaron Ezekiel replied with a sardonic laugh. "Parent didn't need to be released from prison to have *Le Canadien* print what it wanted. Did you know that he wrote his articles for the paper from his cell? A regular visitor, young Drapeau, brought Parent the newspaper clippings he needed by stuffing them in a baked tart. Corrected proofs went back to the print shop by the same message system."

Abraham tried to bring Aaron Ezekiel back to the purpose of this appointment. "I think it is time do do the *Amidah*. Let us stand to face Jerusalem and recite all of the blessings!"

Aaron Ezekiel immediately signaled his reluctance to go beyond the candle-lighting. "I'm not that religious, Abe. Don't press me!"

"It would seem, Aaron, that your father has failed in his duty. Or is it because you have been too long away from Three Rivers?" Abraham regretted these admonitions almost as soon as he uttered them.

"Too long away from home? You may be interested to know, Abe, that I am seriously thinking of settling in Three Rivers permanently. My father is not well and there are always the affairs of Uncle Moses to consider."

"I'm sorry to hear that, Aaron. Though I do see a lot of Ira Craig when he comes to Quebec, I've always regarded you as the one relative I could look to here in town. Which reminds me: will the fact that Dominique Mondelet has now replaced Vallières as judge there have any effect on your decision to move to Three Rivers?" Abraham was acquainted with Mondelet as the deputy judge advocate who had prosecuted rebel prisoners earlier in the year. He had been somewhat amused that Charles-Elzéar Mondelet, the younger brother and partner in the same practice, had defended some of these prisoners in the courts martial.

"Not really. But it did surprise me that Mondelet is in Three Rivers. With Michael O'Sullivan dying last March, I would have thought that Mondelet was in line to be the Chief Justice in Montreal eventually. And I have a good feeling about him even if we don't always agree politically."

So ended Abraham's attempt to bring his second cousin around to his way of thinking. That was last Tuesday. But certainly it was a new century for Jews, 5600 by the Hebrew calendar, and he would make a good start for it by maintaining the faith.

*   *   *

The levee at the Governor's residence was blessed with good weather considering that it was well into October. Charles Edward Poulett Thomson, designated as the new colonial administrator, had arrived in Quebec on Saturday, the 19th without much forewarning. Today was Monday; his stay in the capital would be short for he was bound for Montreal in a day or two to take up residency there.

A brief ceremony preceded the festivities; the erstwhile Governor Sir John Colborne was being invested with the Most Honourable Military Order of the Bath, best known to soldiers as the GCB. It was his compensation for yielding office to Thomson. The newly knighted General could now sail back to England with head high. Indeed, many in the crowd rushed to his side to show their loyal support for his tough stance against the rebels.

Not all the guests were Tories. Abraham noted that John Neilson was attending the levee. The Scot, now in his mid-sixties, had already made it known in the *Quebec Gazette* that he opposed union of the two Canadas and that the Colborne regime had gone too far in suppressing the rebellion.

The new Governor was not shy about ingratiating himself with his guests despite whatever political differences existed. He had all the confidence in the world; just turned forty, he was still unmarried and uncommonly handsome for his age. Once the investiture was completed, he moved purposefully from one group to another in the chamber. Meanwhile Abraham latched himself onto Thomson's civil secretary, Thomas William Clinton Murdoch, who had accompanied his superior on the long voyage. He was the loquacious type, not hesitant to give details of Thomson's rise to his lofty position even to a total stranger. For example, Abraham learned that the latter was offered the Chancellery of the Exchequer during the summer but being opposed to some of the economic policies of the Melbourne administration, had instead settled in early September for being commissioned governor-in-chief of British North America. Abraham offered his opinion. "I would have thought he is risking much. Governors have not fared well on this side of the ocean and conditions are no better than they were before."

Murdoch shook his head in denial. "He will be well paid. A salary of £7,000 they say. Plus an outfit of £3,000 and casual expenses covered besides. He may not have a title as yet but who is to say that he will not insist on one?"

He went on to explain that Thomson was the baby in a commercial family that had been firmly engaged for several generations in the Russian-Baltic timber trade. During his years in the British Parliament the young Thomson had stood for free trade and thus was at odds with his father, but timber merchants in Quebec were not convinced that there wasn't bias towards continental interests.

William Price in particular was suspicious of the man. The William Price Co, based in the Saguenay Valley, specialized in exporting timber and reportedly was shipping over a hundred shiploads of logs and lumber annually across the ocean. Abraham overheard him complaining to a fellow merchant. "He is a Whig who has actually lived in St Petersburg. How can we trust him?"

Murdoch had also listened to Price's remark. His comment was intended for Abraham. "No need to worry on that score. The irony is that the timber merchants in Britain opposed his appointment for the very opposite reasons your friends here fear him."

Meanwhile Thomson was still performing for his audience. Abraham found him rather obnoxious, playing the aristocrat, flattering all the women and receiving adulation in return because of his good looks. At least one of the guests intimated to Abraham that the man was an unashamed coxcomb.

His voice thin and effeminate, he hardly gave the assembled merchants confidence that he could govern effectively in these troubled times.

At that moment Thomson was being confronted by Neilson, who demanded clarification on the policy the new government intended to pursue. Thomson obliged. "I have met with Lord Durham. We both agree that our main task is to get the support of the French for a union acceptable to the government in London. Your friends, Mr. Neilson, must be made to understand that such a union will be less onerous to Lower Canada once there is an Imperial guarantee for a large loan to offset the provincial debt."

*   *   *

The snow did not desist once there was daylight but Jonathan Sewell had to be buried with full honors regardless of the weather. The former Chief Justice had died on the Monday, November 11 and the funeral had already been delayed in order to accommodate officialdom from Montreal and other population centers in the province. Abraham had arranged to meet Aaron Ezekiel, who felt duty bound to be at the service given the years he had spent under Sewell's guidance. They plodded through the snow to get to the chapel at the proper hour.

The Holy Trinity chapel on Rue Saint-Stanislas was perhaps a dozen years old and came into existence through the benefaction of Sewell himself. At least one of Abraham's business associates had confided in him that the former Chief Justice spent £3500 of his own money to have it built to his specifications. He had been intrigued by the design of the Ranelagh chapel in London's Chelsea district, a modest building erected for the Congregationalists in 1817. While walking to the chapel, Aaron Ezekiel recalled seeing HolyTrinity for the first time soon after being admitted to the bar in 1824. He was aware even then that Sewell had an ulterior motive; the incumbent would be one of his heirs. In the event Edmund Willoughby Smith proved be less than adequate as the vicar.

A few dozen mourners had already assembled in the foyer by the time Abraham and Aaron Ezekiel entered the building. Spotting John Neilson among them, the duo realized that the Quebec members of the Special Council had indeed returned home in time to participate in the memorial.

Neilson looked somewhat distraught. Aaron Ezekiel took the initiative of enquiring about his trip to Montreal. (Neilson and his father, Ezekiel Hart, had been friends for years.) Neilson was bitter in his response. "The Special Council was convened on Monday and we were given two days to debate the terms of the union of the Canadas. It was a travesty. Only fifteen members were at the meeting, the snow being a disincentive for travel. And our new Governor argued that the issue of union had already been settled and all that was necessary was to approve a proposed deal between the two provinces."

"And what is that deal?" Aaron Ezekiel interjected.

"Not a good one at all from the perspective of Lower Canada. In spite of having a smaller population, our neighbors to the west are to have equal representation in a new legislature and have their high debt charged against the united province. We were being asked to accept a permanent civil list drawn up at the discretion of the Governor. No wonder *Le Canadien* is attacking Thomson as *le poulet* scratching on the liberties of a disarmed majority in Lower Canada."

Abraham could not suppress a smile. Thomson's enemies making fun of the Englishman's surname. "Our Governor can't be happy with that kind of criticism."

"Indeed he is not! He regards it as insubordination; thus he feels justified in continuing the holding of Viger in prison without trial. And now he has ordered the arrest of Morin." Neilson was particularly incensed by Morin's incarceration; The *Patriote* stalwart Augustin-Norbert Morin had been in hiding since the first rebellion; he returned to Quebec from the countryside in late October on the assumption that he would be judged innocent of any participation in the armed struggle. He guessed incorrectly.

"In other words, sir, the new Governor intends to rule much as Colborne has been doing for the past year." Aaron Ezekiel sounded dismayed.

"There are different views on that. In any case, Colborne has left the scene. He and his wife boarded the frigate *Pique* in Montreal almost as soon as he got back from Quebec last month. Many of the people here regret his departure. Judge Bowen is saying publicly that recalling Colborne to England was a mistake."

"Damn it! Judge Bowen at this moment is staring at me as if I don't belong here. Let's take our seats!"

Aaron Ezekiel's outcry reminded Abraham that there was quite a history between the judge and the Hart family. Irish-born Edward Bowen was a longstanding *puisne* justice of the Court of Queen's Bench in Quebec, having served a quarter of a century as an associate of Jonathan Sewell. He had a reputation of being both tyrannical and unpleasant and had a special dislike of the two Hart counselors, Aaron Ezekiel and Adolphus Mordecai. In fact, the latter had gone to the House of Assembly to challenge Bowen's conduct on the bench. The dissolution of that body two years before probably saved the judge from censure.

The eulogy from the pulpit forced Abraham to concentrate on the deceased rather than on the living. He knew the former Chief Justice only by reputation. Though born just outside Boston, Sewell had been brought up in England and immigrated to New Brunswick before he was twenty years old. Settling at Quebec once his law studies were completed, he became a favorite of the then ruling Chief Justice (he eventually married William Smith's daughter) and rather quickly was appointed Solicitor General and then Attorney General of the province. Thirty years ago he ascended to the post of Chief Justice for the Quebec region while still in his early forties. James Stuart, his successor, had big shoes to fill.

As they filed out of Holy Trinity, Abraham felt the hand of somebody on his shoulder. "May I have a word, Mr. Joseph?"

"By all means, sir." It was not often that Abraham conversed with Thomas Ainslie Young, who was inspector of the Quebec police for the past couple of years. The son of one of the richest merchants in the city, Young had been trained to be prominent in government. Abraham remembered being told that Young was being schooled in London during the very years that Abraham was born and that at the age of 22 he received the post of controller of customs at Quebec a few months after the death of his father in 1819. He had been a leading spokesman for the city's Anglophone minority ever since.

"I noticed you in conversation with Mr. Neilson. You ought to know, young man, that though he is a Special Councilor, his views do not accord with the majority opinion in the community. We do not look kindly on those too lenient with rebels." Young's warning shook Abraham. He had never shared his cousin's affection for the old Scot, but he had not anticipated being upbraided for speaking to one of the most acclaimed man in the city.

*I have the honour to acknowledge the receipt of your Lordship's dispatch of the 24th of November enclosing a letter from Mr. A W Hart complaining of the exclusion from the special council of his father Mr. Benjamin Hart of Montreal. This complaint of Mr. Hart is evidently made under a misconception of the nature of the office of Special Counsellors and of the qualifications or disqualifications attached to it...
I freely admit that his religious persuasion ought not to be a barrier to his admission to the Special Council, I must at the same time consider that it gives him no claim independent of other considerations to be admitted to that Body.*
CHARLES EDWARD POULETT THOMSON
(letter to Lord Russell, January 23, 1840)

*I do not believe that any in our Colonies Her Majesty has more loyal subjects than the French Canadians of Lower Canada...
[The inequality of representation] could be nothing more arbitrary and unjust.*
LORD GOSFORD
(statement in House of Lords, March, 1840)

Seventeen

The hour was late and the only lit candles at his Des Récollets home were in the study. Benjamin Hart had determined that he must write again to his son in England before the morning post left Montreal. The political tactics of the discontented Canadians had to be countered at once.

A mammoth petition had been circulated throughout the autumn and winter pressing the Imperial government to reject any union of the two Canadas. Archibald Acheson, the 2nd Earl of Gosford, was seemingly selected to be the bearer of that petition to the Queen and Parliament. *What a disgrace!* Gosford's weak-kneed policies as Governor in Quebec had brought about Papineau's revolt. *How dare he exacerbate the crisis by going over the heads of those in charge at the Château?* Arthur Wellington should undertake the expense of printing an open broadcast to the British people.

Previously Benjamin's appeal had been to the Colonial minister and was restricted to objecting to the fact that he personally had not been nominated to the Special Council despite his services to the administration.

Son Wellington had been instructed late last summer to write to the minister making that very point. Benjamin could visualize his son addressing Lord Russell by letter. True, a face-to-face meeting was impossible; Wellington had established himself in Liverpool for the past several months. But that didn't prevent him from being forthright with Her Majesty's principal Secretary for the Colonies. He had promised to be blunt; for many years past the intolerant spirit of the Lord Bishop of Quebec has served as a serious obstacle to the advancement of his father to whatever office and immunities were enjoyed by his fellow citizens of Montreal. *All on account of his religious tenet!* Lord Russell would have been reminded that on the occasion of the late rebellion in Lower Canada, Benjamin Hart as a Constitutionalist took on his responsibility as a magistrate and dispensed justice to the entire approval of Governor Colborne.

Discrimination had not disappeared. Twenty years ago Benjamin had to suffer barbs from Jacob Mountain, the Anglican Lord Bishop in Quebec. His death in 1825 made life easier for prominent Jews albeit George Jehoshaphat Mountain, one of the Bishop's sons did act as his father's secretary and expressed similar views in high company. For years the son was preoccupied being the principal of McGill College but in 1836 was consecrated Bishop of Montreal and a year later acceded to the see in Quebec.

And then there was the Attorney General of the province. A dozen years younger than Benjamin, Charles Richard Ogden had been schooled in Trois-Rivières for a time and subsequently as a legislative deputy of that riding had interacted with the Hart family for decades. Benjamin blamed Ogden, who had been the government's chief legal officer beginning in 1833, for delaying his entry into the magistracy. Ogden had accepted the argument that Jews could not take the oath of allegiance in good conscience.

In the aftermath of the rebellions Ogden had become an intimate adviser to Governor Colborne, which suggested to Benjamin that it was he who advised the government not to include a Jew on the Special Council. Benjamin had yet to learn whether Wellington's intervention on his behalf would make a difference in this matter.

But that was in another year. On this January night, the freezing temperatures keeping the domestic servants busy feeding the different stoves with wood, Benjamin had another message to deliver to his son. Governor Thomson was at that moment in Toronto meeting with his Council whereas nothing was being done to challenge the petition circulating in Lower Canada. A most urgent task would be to ridicule any effort by Gosford bringing the petition to the House of Lords. Britons must know what was being perpetrated. Benjamin laid down his quill.

*   *   *

The walk to the courthouse was slow going, the accumulation of snow on Rue Notre-Dame being more than Benjamin had bargained for. He had already sent a note to William Walker asking that they rendezvous; hopefully the lawyer didn't mind waiting a bit.

Walker had indeed waited. He was seated in the office he shared with other counselors in the building. A law clerk was frantically scribbling on a notepad to keep up with some dictation. Within a few minutes the young man was dismissed and Walker gave his attention to Benjamin. His smallish frame seemed almost lost in the big chair behind his desk. Limping as usual, he offered to take Benjamin's outer gear to hang up on the corner clothes stand. "You caught me, Hart, trying to do too many things at once. There are deeds to record and I'm also writing an opinion piece on the Governor's latest actions. You may not know that I will be editing a new journal, the *Canada Times*."

"That is one reason I sought you out. If I'm not mistaken the paper's proprietor is John James Williams, who is opposed to the union of the Canadas." Benjamin had been appalled at the news that his long-time ally, one of the mainstays of the Constitutional Association in Montreal, had ventured into journalism – and on the wrong side of things!

"You are quite right. In spite of where I stood many years ago on this issue, I've concluded that we have everything to lose by merging with Upper Canada. The draft bill on union has been submitted to the Colonial Office as of last week. Thomson has strayed from the program outlined in the Durham Report and his changes are not to the advantage of our people on this side of the Ottawa River. Lord Durham promised responsible government, but that is not the message I'm getting from our new Governor. He thinks he has the right to make appointments to office even if the men he chooses are mere adventurers."

"In other words, you don't trust Thomson to act in our interest. Is it not true that he has to take into account the sentiment in Toronto and Kingston?"

Walker nodded. "You have a point, Hart. In Upper Canada there is no unanimity with regard to union. In fact, Thomson had a mixed reception when he reached Toronto. Your friend John Macaulay writes that the Governor was greeted with an abortion of a cheer. That was worse than silence."

"Are we ready for responsible government? The French are still the majority in this part of British North America. Do we want another

Papineau?" Benjamin was expressing doubts that he had been nursing for years.

"You will then be pleased by what is about to occur. The Governor insists that it is unsafe to leave the government dependent on the Assembly. And like our Chief Justice in Quebec, who advised him on text of the draft, he prefers that existing institutions be preserved. Legislative Councilors will continue to be life members."

Benjamin replied without hesitation. "Furthermore, it is said that there will be a £500 property qualification for assemblymen. To my way of thinking that will keep certain unworthy agitators out of office. I'm not forgetting that there is a powerful group here in opposition to the proposed union. Men like Neilson, Caron, Parent and Cherrier; men cleared of any taint of insurrection but dedicated to protect French dominance."

Walker interjected. "That is exactly my point. Even La Fontaine, whom I know is more conciliatory than his confreres, will not abide some of the provisions in the proposed legislation. Thomson is asking for trouble. All records are to be published in English. Canadians will gag at that provision in the bill, even if they are allowed in any new legislature to debate in the French language."

Benjamin was still bewildered by the arguments emanating from a once trusted colleague. He would have challenged those arguments but for the fact that they were interrupted by the opening of the office door. Standing on the threshold was none other than Aaron Philip Hart. Benjamin suppressed his immediate annoyance; his son was appearing at a most inauspicious time. The two of them had seen very little of each other following the execution of Cardinal and Lorimier. Benjamin no longer believed they were on the same side. It was one thing to defend rebels in court as a duty. But Aaron Philip had made it a cause. And here he was, obviously chummy with Walker. *They probably agree politically.* "I think I've taken enough of your time, Walker. Don't count on me being a subscriber to the *Canada Times.*"

With that riposte, Benjamin rose from his chair. He walked past his son with nary a glance and disappeared down the corridor of the courthouse.

*   *   *

A letter had arrived from overseas; Benjamin beamed with pleasure. Wellington had done what he had been asked to do – he published a broadside in Liverpool admonishing Lord Gosford for presenting the *Canadien* petition to the House of Lords. *A dutiful son without doubt. If only Philip were of the same character!*

In the same letter there was also encouraging news on another front. Wellington made mention of going to Exeter for the Passover. He had been calling on Selena Ezekiel throughout the winter and was on the point of asking for her hand in marriage. *Perhaps grandchildren at last!*

His son also described the arguments he had used when writing to Lord Russell regarding his father's claim to a seat on the Special Council. "*I mentioned that you were the oldest merchant in Lower Canada and that you are known to the Right Honorable Edward Ellice, with whom you have transacted business for many years.*"

A day later came another communication; Governor Thomson requested the presence of Benjamin Hart at the *Château* Ramezay. *Had Wellington's intercession brought success! February was not ending badly at all!*

Though the government house on Rue Notre-Dame could be reached easily by walking, Benjamin decided to be driven there by coach. It would not do having his best overcoat soiled by puddles of melting snow lining the sidewalk.

The halls of the *Château* Ramezay were filled not only with uniformed soldiers and civil servants. Office-seekers sat in a long line of chairs waiting to be interviewed. Benjamin would have to wait his turn.

At last his name was called and he entered Thomson's inner sanctum. The Governor looked fatigued. He was also in obvious pain. His face, which Benjamin remembered as being so handsome, was quite contorted. Moreover, one of the man's boots had been removed. The exposed foot was swollen. *That seems like gout to me.*

Thomson finally recovered his composure. "Pardon me, sir! It has been a trying time and I am not at my best. I left Toronto on Tuesday and arrived here the next day. They say the sleigh trip was done in record time. In thirty-six hours no less! But I am feeling the consequences."

"Most unfortunate! You were in a hurry to return to Montreal no doubt. You have been absent for almost a month."

Thomson scrutinized Benjamin as if he were being criticized for his absence. "Before leaving Montreal last month, Mr. Hart, I received a letter from Lord Russell informing me that an Arthur Wellington Hart had written him regarding your status in the colony."

"I am aware of that communication, Your Excellency. My son was advising him that I was passed over each time that the composition of the Special Council was determined."

"So it seems. You apparently blamed the Bishop of Quebec for his interference. You know, of course, that Bishop Mountain's predecessor died prior to the formation of the Special Council. Are you suggesting that the incumbent took a hand in this decision?"

"I cannot confirm that Bishop Mountain was ever consulted, albeit his bias against Jews is well known. On the face of it, there appears to be no other reason for my exclusion from the Council than the fact that I am of the Jewish faith."

"I freely admit, Mr. Hart, that your religious persuasion ought not to be a barrier to your admission to the Special Council. I must at the same time consider that it gives you no claim independent of other considerations to be admitted to that Body. I have written to Lord Russell in that vein."

"It is my understanding that the recommendations to such an appointment pass through the hands of the Attorney General. Is it possible to know whether my name was submitted for your confirmation or rejection? Mr. Ogden has on other occasions regarded my religious affiliation as a bar to advancement in government."

"The initial recommendation would have gone to either Sir John Colborne or to Lord Durham in '38. I was not privy to the bases for making those selections. At this point in time more relevant matters occupy my attention."

"You are speaking of the union of the two provinces?"

"Indeed! Reconciling the French element to union will not be easy. I am aware that Vital Têtu is carrying anti-union petitions to London with the plan to put them in the hands of Lord Gosford. In the end this effort will fail. I control the Special Council and will have it act to accomplish the union *de facto*."

"But not before Parliament passes the required legislation. There is opposition to such a union among certain members of the two Houses. My son writes from Liverpool that a parliamentary majority for the bill is not assured."

"Meanwhile, several bills have been prepared *here* for submission to the Council. It is no secret that I intend to reorganize the judicial system, incorporate Quebec and Montreal and extinguish seigneurial dues here in Montreal. These acts will harmonize with what is to be done in the two provinces and make their union more practical."

Benjamin Hart now recognized that history was passing him by. He took his leave with that in mind.

*I regret extremely to be compelled to call the attention of the President
and trustees of the Congregation of Shearith Israel of Montreal
to the singular and most extraordinary course of conduct
adopted relative to the legal proceedings which
at times have been necessarily connected with
the existence of the Congregation of Israelites in this City.*
AARON PHILIP HART
(letter to Benjamin Hart, May 14, 1840)

*I and sisters have left the place of our nativity and have come down
To Three Rivers to live. My reasons for doing so are very numerous.
I was living far beyond my means in Montreal and without any prospects
of my practice increasing sufficiently to enable me to meet the required
expenses of an increasing family; the reason for which I
attribute to religion. People have such an aversion to a Jew.*
AARON HART DAVID
(diary entry, June, 1840

Eighteen

The infant had awakened again; the crying emanating from his crib
could not be ignored. Catharine Joseph David struggled to regain her
equilibrium; the disruption of her sleep had become too frequent; Monte
David was into his third month and still unable to sleep the night through.
Samuel and Henry, on the other hand, had adjusted to decent nocturnal
hours much earlier in their maturation, even if the latter lived but a year.
Why are my boys so different? She had once asked mama Rachel whether there
had been any sleep problems during her own infancy. Her reply: "You were
the best of the lot in sleeping the night, Kitty."

Thankfully, Catharine no longer had the task of preparing breakfast
for the whole family. The three sisters of Aaron Hart David were each old
enough to run a household even if none was married as yet. Taking care of
the baby was now Catharine's main responsibility. Even so, nearing thirty
years of age, she no longer had the energy she once had. Catharine had to
admit she was somewhat weary in the mornings as well as feeling fatigue

later in the day. Three children in just over three years! Baby Henry's death last December, coming near the end of her latest pregnancy, had made her life even more trying.

Changing the diaper and offering her breast to feed little Monte, she hardly noticed that her husband had gotten out of bed and was dressing for another day at his examining room. Aaron Hart David was not only her husband but also a second cousin, his grandfather, Aaron Hart, being a brother to her grandmother. For the most part it had been a good marriage. Granted that she was a couple of years older than he, but that didn't seem to matter to him.

They never knew much of each other as children. Aaron Hart David was a Montrealer from birth; she, on the other hand, had grown up in the downriver town of Berthier-en-haut, the second oldest of Henry Joseph's offspring. She didn't move to Montreal until she was twenty. When her father and elder brother perished in the 1832 cholera epidemic, she had suddenly become her mother's dependable arm. Nevertheless, a home of her own was a need she could not forsake. Marrying Aaron Hart three and half years ago, she had thought she had that kind of independence. Furthermore, she assumed that she was secure for life. After all, he was a medical doctor; he had just returned from the University of Edinburgh, a licentiate of the Royal College of Physicians and Surgeons. The practice of medicine in Montreal may not earn him the same kind of money that her younger brothers were accumulating in the shipping and tobacco business, but it was a respectable profession. Respectability was important, even if living up to the standards of the Joseph family exceeded the income of a fledgling physician. But she could always go to her mother or brothers when there was a budget crisis in the David establishment.

Aaron Hart had already left the breakfast table by the time Catharine descended the stairs, baby in her arms. Phoebe, the oldest of the three sisters, rushed to take charge of the little boy. Sophia, the youngest, served her sister-in-law coffee and some of the porridge from a pot on the stove. Frances had disappeared into the tiny parlor to practice her piano.

A strong knock on wood could be heard over the music. Abraham Joseph was at the door. He had been in and around Montreal for over a week and wasn't scheduled to return to Quebec until later in April. Catharine guessed that he was not visiting his older sister so much as to be near Frances David. He was clearly smitten with her, although Catharine wondered if her sister-in-law fully appreciated his attention.

Sophia directed Abraham to a seat at the kitchen table. "Don't interrupt Fanny! She is committed to practicing for at least a half hour."

Catharine wondered if Sophia's concern was for her sister or for the guest. But it was not Catharine's place to interfere. Instead she asked more details about his life in the capital. "It must be quiet in Quebec with the Governor spending so much time in Montreal. And the boats from Portsmouth and Bristol have yet to arrive."

"Busy enough though I've been spending more of my time in the Upper Town. I have been staying at the Payne's Hotel on the Esplanade. So much more fashionable than Lemoine's in the Lower Town. Yes, there'll be much to do when I get back to Quebec after *Pesach*." Abraham's eyes were already straying to the open parlor door. The back of Frances' shapely figure, bent over the piano keys, was plainly visible from where he was sitting.

"It is good that you are able to get away from Quebec for so long a time. We'll be seeing you again in just two days." Catharine was looking ahead. On Thursday night the *seder* would be held at the Joseph home. The tradition was to have husband Aaron Hart, his three sisters and the children leave their domicile on Rue Craig to participate in the Passover meal at the family house on Place Près-de-Ville. Usually her brothers-in-law, Eleazar and Moses Samuel, attended as well. There would be a notable difference this year because the new *chassan* from London had promised to be at the table. Catharine had been introduced to David Piza but a few days earlier. He was a Londoner with an odd history. Orphaned in infancy, his early years had been spent in the orphan asylum of the Sephardim community. And now this young man, only twenty-two years old, would be their inspiration during the synagogue services.

* * *

A different Thursday, the one occurring almost a month later on May 14, proved to be the more memorable one. Aaron Hart David brought the news home mid-day: his older brother was throwing away his career, both civil and military. Catharine didn't understand. Not Eleazar? He was widely regarded as a model citizen, a Major in the Montreal Calvary, a professional man who often appeared in court, and once a mother's pet. *How can he be throwing away a future?*

Aaron Hart had the details. Apparently Eleazar David had eloped with the wife of a Captain of the 24th Regiment stationed in Montreal. Seemingly the impulsive couple had no choice but to go into exile. The Captain, a Henry William Harris, would not accept being the cuckold; he was demanding that his colleague be charged and his adulterous wife returned to him.

"Who is this woman?" Catharine had not been told that her brother-in-law was having an illicit affair. True, he was often absent from family gatherings. He had not, for example, been at the family *seder* the previous month.

"She is the former Eliza Locke Walker. Eleazar confided in me about her but swore me to secrecy, Kitty. The relationship has been going on for two years and only last month the woman gave birth to a baby that is Eleazar's."

"And he believes he must do right by her. I suppose that therefore he is not a total cad. But he is giving up so much." Catharine wasn't measuring things only in terms of wealth. Eleazar, 15 months older than Aaron Hart and therefore younger than she, was regarded as a model for Jews in Montreal. Admitted to the bar in 1832 and put in charge of the Calvary during the uprisings, his exploits were legend. Only last October he had been selected as extra assistant to the Adjutant-General. How would the town's citizenry, especially the genteel ones whom the Josephs, Harts and Davids cultivated for so long, react to such disreputable behavior?

By coincidence cousin Aaron Philip Hart called on her husband that very afternoon. More heartache for the Davids: the status of the Congregation was being put in question. A copy of a letter that the lawyer had prepared for his father, the president of Shearith Israel, pointed to irregularities that involved Aaron Hart David, the secretary of the Congregation. "Please, Philip, not now!"

The David household was not the same after that. Neighbors avoided her when she walked to the shop for provisions. And the usual invitations to other homes disappeared. Even Mama Rachel and her brothers Jacob Henry and Jesse clucked their tongues when the subject was raised. The three David sisters were mortified indeed; what had brother Eleazar done to their marriage prospects? Only Tom Judah showed a modicum of empathy for the family. He came around more often than before.

How could they go on? Aaron Hart's medical practice was suffering because of the scandal. Even prior to it they had to concede that they were living beyond their means. Her husband was becoming increasingly bitter. The prospects for an increased practice were negligible in the foreseeable future. If there were aversions in the populace to Jews before, it would intensify for a while at least. And snide remarks from Jacob Henry Joseph suggested that he, the man who controlled the family's business success, resented having to subsidize a physician with a dubious future even if that physician was married to his older sister.

It was Tom Judah who suggested a way out. Why not move to Trois-Rivières, where a nascent Jewish community did exist and where disdain for Jews was much less. He had mentioned other benefits. Home rent was low, wood cheap. Less chance of a big discrepancy between income and expenditures.

*   *   *

Catharine looked about the rented quarters. A little small for a family consisting of one man, four women and two children but *Trifluviens* in general had made the transition to small-town living quite bearable. When she carried the children onto the *Hart* steamer in Montreal three months before, she certainly had qualms. On board, her husband had been kept busy working out the fee with Ira Craig, who had come up from Trois-Rivières for this particular charter. (Ira Craig and Alexander Thomas had transferred their allegiance to this steamboat earlier in the year after having leased out the *Toronto*.) Kid brother Gershom Joseph, however, had agreed to come along on the trip to assist in the onerous task of moving furniture and other household effects.

As it turned out, nothing was broken in transit. She had gotten a little upset when a small toy was stolen after they landed at the wharf. But in retrospect she had agreed that the loss wasn't something to fret about. Tom Judah had been quite right. Aaron Hart's practice was doing better than she could have expected; apparently there wasn't the same level of prejudice against Jews as there had been in Montreal. After all, Moses and Ezekiel Hart, each in his own way, were among the most prominent citizens in the town.

In fact, Esther Elizabeth, Ezekiel's daughter, promptly invited Phoebe and Frances to bunk with her at the big house on Rue des Forges until the new place was properly decorated. Catharine herself had gone with Sophia, the babies and the nurse to stay with Mrs. Judah and son Henry Hage, Tom's younger brother. She had met Henry in Montreal on a couple of occasions. *What a nice young fellow!* She would be sorry to lose him as a neighbor; he was planning to move soon to Montreal to become a partner in Tom's legal practice.

Important for Catharine was that her family hadn't forgotten her. There were separate visits from Jacob Henry in Montreal and Abraham in Quebec. A couple of weeks later Mama Rachel came down to Trois-Rivières for an extended stay. Nobody mentioned Eleazar during these weeks. He could be anywhere in the world with his mistress and bastard but none of the family admitted to being curious about his travels.

In late June most of the relatives gathered at the Rue des Forges salon for a *soirée*. Ezekiel Hart had invited not only the newcomers but also a selected number of residents from the town. It being early summer, the festivities finally spread to the extensive garden that backed onto the house.

It was there where Henry Hage Judah engaged Catharine and Aaron Hart in political chatter. The draft of the union bill was now in circulation and it was being reported that Governor Thomson had given it his blessing. Henry wasn't hiding his disdain. "His Excellency appears determined to imbibe us with English ideas. Did you know that he has chosen Kingston as the capital of the united province? Kingston of all places. It doesn't have a building that can hold a legislature."

By this time Adolphus had joined the group. "I disagree, Henry. Thomson is quite aware of *Canadien* sentiment, though he is hell bent on getting approval of union. At least our Governor did the right thing in releasing Denis-Benjamin Viger from prison in May. And the last edition of the paper from Montreal tells me that he is letting lapse the suspension of *habeas corpus* so that Viger will get his trial if he wants it."

Henry Judah wasn't backing down. "Yes, he is cognizant of the anti-union sentiment in the populace but he is confident that the *Patriote* movement has been crushed for good. Papineau is in Paris and many of the insurrectionists have been transported to Australia. How else can one explain why the Governor was offering La Fontaine the post of Solicitor General? And you may also notice that Caron has been selected as the Mayor in Quebec. That wouldn't happen if he thought Viger and his friends were about to revive serious opposition to his rule."

Catharine seldom ventured political opinions in public and yet she could not avoid commenting on Thomson's intrigues. "Our Governor seems determined to do the bidding of his masters in London even if there is no consensus among the parties involved. They say he has gout. Has he the strength to get that consensus before Parliament acts?"

The men about her were taken by surprise. Finally Adolphus responded. "Well put, Kitty! It will indeed be a busy few months."

With respect to my appointment as a Magistrate, I beg leave
to state, Sir John Colborne was too well aware of my standing
amongst English, Scotch and Irish inhabitants of Montreal to have
removed my name from the Committee of Peace,
and I think I may with all safety refer Your Lordship to
Lord Seaton for the truth of my assertions.
BENJAMIN HART
(letter to Sir John Russell, July 14, 1840)

XLI. And be it enacted, That from and after the said Reunion of the said
Two Provinces all Writs, Proclamations, Instruments for summoning
and calling together the Legislative Council and Legislative Assembly
of the Province of Canada, and for proroguing and dissolving the same
and all Writs of Summons and Election, and all Writs and
public Instruments whatsoever relating to the said
Legislative Council and Legislative Assembly, or either of
them ......shall be in the English Language only
UNION ACT
(ratified by Queen Victoria, July 23, 1840)

Nineteen

The arrangement of tables became more of a misalignment for Aaron Philip Hart. Even the other patrons of the public house were out of focus when he looked about. *Am I not seeing straight?* Without doubt the July heat had been getting to him despite the windows being draped to keep out the sun. He realized just then that he had drunk too much while waiting for William Walker to join him at this establishment on Rue Notre-Dame. *Damn my indulgence!*

He also had to admit being a bit despondent. There was time for an afternoon *tête-à-tête* because his legal practice was in the doldrums. *And whose fault is that? I'm paying the price of my convictions.* Then a hand on his shoulder alerted him to the fact that his friend had just arrived. "You have had your beer, Philip, before I've had a chance to tipple."

Aaron Philip gave him a sheepish grin. "It's a warm afternoon, my friend, and I was parched."

Walker issued a tolerant smile. He was probably aware that young Hart was drinking more than usual but he could empathize. The two lawyers had become even closer in the last year as a result of new circumstances. Aaron Philip had yet to return to his old manner of living; the experiences at the courts martial had so markedly altered his outlook as much as had the attitudes of his old clientele towards him. Walker as editor of the *Canada Times* was also on a different course.

Walker proved to be the bearer of bad news. "I fear the Act of Union is *fait accompli*. The Queen has yet to give royal assent but it should happen before the month is out."

Aaron Philip sighed. He had expected no different a result after reading in the local papers about the debate in Parliament. Lord Gosford, true to his promise, spoke against the legislation, as did Lord Wellington and Colborne. But the Melbourne administration had support from most of the opposition Tories; the troubles in the colonies had gone on too long for these parliamentarians. "I suspect that there is no other outcome unless there is another uprising. The chance of that is almost negligible even though most Canadians will not accept union gladly. Papineau is in Paris; Nelson and Côté have moved elsewhere."

For the next few minutes Aaron Philip waited until Walker limped to the bar to get his glass of ale and then settled into the adjacent chair. The latter was clearly contemplative. "Union without responsible government; a great disappointment. We did have allies in Parliament but they weren't all in accord with Durham on this aspect. With Colborne now in the House of Lords, his voice should have swayed some legislators to oppose the bill as currently written." Walker was referring to the fact that the former Governor upon his return to Britain had been elevated to the peerage as Lord Seaton of Seaton.

"What surprises me is that Colborne chose to speak out at all."

"You recall that Sir John was skeptical of the idea of union from the beginning. He told Durham that it has two drawbacks. The unrest in Lower Canada would spread to the other side of the Ottawa River and the French could only be alarmed further by the prospect of assimilation if the two provinces were united. Where *I* differed with Sir John was his abhorrence of colonial self-government."

Aaron Philip was becoming increasingly agitated. He felt he needed another drink but then restrained himself. *Things are happening too fast.* "Is it true that Durham is on his deathbed? My cousin in Liverpool believes that is the case."

"He is probably right on that account. The future of the province is now in Thomson's hands and he is dedicated to getting *his* plan enacted. And with the Special Council doing his bidding, that may not take too long. Our Chief Justice has already gotten things in motion. Remember that Stuart is not only the Chief Justice and a member of the Special Council but also the president of that Council. When he votes to support the Governor's initiatives it is very hard for the other Councilors to act otherwise. We must live with the certainty that Stuart will back Thomson in everything he does."

"And to think that a couple of years ago James Stuart had been disgraced, removed from his government post. Now he is writing new legislation for a united Canada." Aaron Philip drained his glass.

"You must admit, Philip, that though the man has always been self-serving, even a philistine, he has continually acted for the British interest. Long before he was Chief Justice, he fought to establish English law in the province. Now he is enabling the establishment of registry offices, the abolition of customary dower and separation of more of our citizenry from the *Coutume de Paris*. No wonder he is reviled in the cathedral and in the French press!"

"And encouraged by our people to move even *more* quickly. If men such as Moffatt and McGill have their way, complaints from these former *Patriotes* will be totally ignored."

Walker shook his head. "Thomson doesn't want that. That is why he has been seeking to get men like La Fontaine and Bleury to go along with union. Moffatt only makes things worse for him. It has been reliably told to me that Thomson regards Moffatt as pig-headed and a brute besides."

Aaron Philip was amused but his face then darkened. "Can nothing be done? Is our only option that we make common cause with Neilson, Viger and Lartigue? A united opposition to the Union Act even if Lartigue is as good as dead?"

"That is one reason I wanted to get together with you, Philip. We once worked with Neilson when we had the constitutional associations. Now may be the time to make, as you say, common cause with him. Actually, we need more friends than just Neilson. What about men like Vallières and Parent? Then there is young Drummond. You do have influence with him. Having him on our side would make quite a difference. I'm thinking of his oratorical talents in both English and French."

The mention of Drummond, the young Irishman who was at his side during the trials, had an immediate effect on Aaron Philip. With Lewis Drummond there had been no thought of surrender. *What a time that had been!* And here he was, sulking, drinking too much. *Enough!*

＊　＊　＊

The downstream trip to Trois-Rivières was accomplished in just hours. After the *Hart* steamer nuzzled up to the wharf that evening, Aaron Philip took advantage of the extra daylight to walk to the house on Rue des Forges. Ezekiel Hart and family had been forewarned that he was coming and the reception was most cordial. Nobody in *this* branch of the Hart family held his defense of the rebels against him.

Joining them in a late supper, Aaron Philip was in good spirits. Most of his cousins were on hand. Samuel Bécancour, already into his forties and growing more paunchy than ever, presided over the table. His sisters, Esther, Harriet, Caroline and Miriam, were to Sammy's left. The male contingent, depleted by the fact that Aaron Ezekiel was still in Quebec, sat with Aaron Philip on the right side. The patriarch of the family, Ezekiel, had his place at the end of the table. There were no grandchildren to fit in, none of his progeny being married.

The chatter went on through the first course. But eventually Aaron Philip was plied with questions. There was a general demand for the latest news from Montreal. Was their Uncle Benjamin still a magistrate? What was Wellington doing in Liverpool? How was Aunt Harriot faring? Esther had heard she had been ill. Aaron Philip avoided mentioning that he wasn't as close with his parents and siblings as he once was. Rather, he talked of the impact that the Act of Union was making on his fellow citizenry in Montreal. "Nobody is happy that the Governor prefers Kingston as the capital of the united provinces."

Adolphus spoke up with some emotion. "Incredible! I've been to Kingston. The only building there that would be at all suitable for a Parliament is a vacant hospital building. It may have enough space but there aren't any large rooms in it to bring together a legislative assembly or even a legislative council. This is foolishness!"

"What are the alternatives? The old Bishop's palace in Quebec is also too small for an enlarged Parliament and besides it is too French to satisfy those coming from Upper Canada. Montreal is a better candidate though there would be some of the same objections from our western friends." Aaron Philip's response was a measured one.

"So why is Thomson doing this? He clearly wants cooperation from the *Canadiens*. Selecting Caron as mayor of Quebec is indicative of that." Adolphus was obviously not satisfied with Aaron Philip's response.

"Many of us in Montreal are asking the same kind of questions. The Governor seeks to mollify the different constituencies. Incidentally, Montreal is now an incorporated entity. The Colonial Office thinks it is in good hands; Peter McGill was president of the Constitutional Association and a long-time advocate of union. Had there been an election for the post, Jacques Viger might have gotten his old job back. As it is, Viger is out the picture altogether, deprived of his title as chief surveyor of the city."

"And you are happy with that?" The intonation in Ira Craig's voice suggested his dissent.

"I do think he had to go. Many of us haven't forgiven him for leaving the city roads in such disrepair. And then there is his connection with the Viger-Papineau-Cherrier clan."

Samuel Bécancour also interceded for the first time. "But he did oversee major drainage operations north of Rue Sainte-Catherine. Otherwise we could have seen a repeat of the cholera epidemics. The marshy land up to Sherbrooke Srreet was a menace."

"I give you that, Sammy. Yet there is certainly no uproar over his dismissal. The talk is all about what will happen to *Canadiens* generally. I foresee trouble. Our Governor has succeeded in uniting *Canadiens* against a new constitution that is essentially the abutting of two very different civilizations into a single state. Neilson is getting support for his opposition to these changes from the Church, from Cuvillier as well as from Morin and Vallières. That is one reason why I would like to call on Vallières. It's been said he signed the petition against union even though he still hopes to be reinstated as a judge. Can you facilitate such a meeting?"

There was immediate agreement do so; Adolphus accompanied Aaron Philip to Vallières' house on Rue Notre Dame the very next morning.

*   *   *

Joseph-Rémi Vallières de Saint-Réal proved to be rather standoffish when a hand was extended to him in greeting. It was accepted only with great reluctance. Aaron Philip could hardly blame the man; they had crossed swords on several occasions during the past decade. What struck Aaron Philip most, however, was the frail state of Vallières' body. It had been widely known that the judge previously had to go on temporary leave because of bad health. Obviously his current exclusion from office, which now entailed lost income, was also affecting his wellbeing.

The admission into the residence – Vallières had acquired the Gannes house across the street from the old Récollet monastery – gave Aaron Philip his first opportunity to meet the former Jane Keirman. Vallières, though already in his fifties, had married the widow four years ago after living common law for some time with Esther Elizabeth Hart. The wife was not afraid to ask pointed questions. For example, she enquired as to any responsibilities of Benjamin Hart following the arrival of Governor Thomson in Montreal.

Aaron Philip didn't duck the question. "My father remains disappointed that he is not on the Special Council. I believe he is currently in correspondence with the Colonial Secretary demanding to know why he was excluded from that honor. Needless to say, I don't welcome such an ambition on his part. But he is Tory to the core so what else can one expect?"

Vallières was pleased with this response. "Your attitude has changed indeed. As for me, with Papineau in exile, I am being asked to get back into politics. My old friends tell me I could be chosen Speaker in the new assembly once it has been elected."

The sound of the doorknocker interrupted the conversation. Someone else was calling on Vallières. He was no stranger to Aaron Philip, who recognized him as a fellow lawyer, Édouard-Louis Pacaud.

Pacaud was greeted warmly. "Welcome back, Édouard-Louis! You didn't stay that long in Yamachiche."

Vallières was later to inform Aaron Philip that in late July Pacaud had become engaged to Anne-Hermine Dumoulin, the daughter of a Yamachiche merchant. Pacaud didn't feel he needed to explain why he came back so early. Rather he turned to Jane to respond to questions about the stay in Yamachiche. Apparently Vallières' spouse knew the Dumoulins quite well.

Vallières eventually led Pacaud and Aaron Philip back to the parlor so as to continue discussions on the state of the union. The latter returned to the subject of the new legislation, the final version of which was reportedly now in the hands of Queen Victoria. "Surely there will be continued opposition to union. I have read what John Neilson has stated in the *Gazette* and he has thousands of petitioners to back him up."

Pacaud caught him off guard with a declaration of his own. "You ought to know, Hart, that I no longer oppose the union of the two Canadas. La Fontaine makes a strong case for working within government to make it responsible to its elected members. I have been to see La Fontaine. He is preparing an *adresse* to the electors of Terrebonne along those lines. I've also suggested to him that he write Ludger Duvernay in Burlington to have him return to his native land. Duvernay has publishing experience, something that La Fontaine lacks."

Aaron Philip glanced at Vallières. If La Fontaine and Pacaud were deserting the camp of the anti-unionists, a common front would be difficult to forge. Moreover, if La Fontaine is of that mind, he had to assume that Drummond was also willing to support union. They are, after all, partners.

Aleck will deliver you this letter, and if you mary him it will not only please me, but you may rely that I shall take care of you that you do not want, and shall assist you both, and if you have children, they shall share in my estate as my other grandchildren. Wishing your mother and family health and happiness.
MOSES HART
(letter to Miriam Judah, August 15, 1840)

L' Union est enfin décrétée! Le Canada dans la pensée du Parlement Anglais ne doit, à l'avenir, former qu'une seule Province. Cette grand mesure politique, est-elle dans l'intérêt bien et tendu des populations qu'elle à pour object de soumettre à l'action d'une seule et même Législature? Il fait laisser au temps la solution de ce problème. L'histoire dira que la force l'a imposée aux deux peuples du Bas et du Haut Canada. Pour rendre cette mesure légitime, il faudra le consentement et l'approbation de ces deux mêmes Peuples. Leurs voix ne peut se faire entendre que dans la chambre d'assemblée où cependant, l'acte du Parlement Impérial, avec ses nombreuses injustices, ne permettra qu'à une partis de leurs legitimes Représentants de prendre place, dans la 1è session de la nouvelle Legislature
LOUIS-HIPPOLYTE LA FONTAINE
(L'Adress aux Electeurs de Terrebonne, August 28, 1840)

Twenty

"Who's at the door, Aleck?" Moses Hart had heard the brass knocker strike the carved oak portal but chose to proceed with his correspondence. He had assumed that Alexander Thomas, who returned to Trois-Rivières hours before after his turn on the quarterdeck of the *Hart* steamboat, had gone to deal with the caller at the front entrance. *An unhappy passenger bringing a complaint?* His adopted son finally appeared at the doorway to the study with a visitor in tow; Aaron Philip had finally got around to paying his respects to his uncle.

Moses used his cane to rise from the writing table. Already into his seventies, the oldest surviving member of the clan had to accept limitations to his health. He did manage, however, to cross the room to take an embrace from a nephew with whom he had dealt only sparingly over the years. Their last major interaction occurred soon after Aaron Philip had been called to the bar and Moses had never called on his services since that collaboration. Brother Ezekiel had informed him of Aaron Philip's presence in town but there had been no indication that uncle and nephew would get together. "Tell me, young man, whether your expectations have been satisfied."

Aaron Philip seated himself before replying. "My plan was to go down to the capital to meet with Mr. Neilson but it now appears that the Melbourne government will prevail with its legislation, the Queen having ratified it in July. No matter what the populace thinks, the deed is done."

Moses nodded. "That is the way I see it. Aleck does likewise. I am keenly interested in how this union will work. In fact, I've been preparing different petitions to the Governor giving him advice on what needs to be done."

At this juncture Mary McCarthy Brown entered the room to greet a Hart she hardly knew. Aaron Philip shook her hand and then resumed his seat. His mind was still on the political situation. "What would you have any new legislature do immediately?"

"I've said it before: a change in our judicial system. We require a law that would have as its goal to reduce the cost of justice. Did you know when the French ruled here before I was born, an *Intendant* administered courts? There were no *avocats*, no lawyers to pile expenses on top of judgments. Excuse my bluntness!"

Aaron Philip laughed. "I take no personal offence. But you have always favored British law over the *Coutume de Paris*. Why hearken back to the *Ancien Régime*?

"I have no objections to British principles in jurisprudence so long as the procedures are practical. It is time we stop considering London as the place to hear the last appeal on a court decision. We enact Canadian law, *la loi canadienne*, and then look 3000 miles away for ultimate justice. It's a ludicrous thing!"

"You can't be serious, uncle! Such a measure would imply independence. Wasn't independence the fundamental issue in the two rebellions on this continent?"

Moses ignored his guest's facetiousness; he shifted his gaze to Mary, who appeared intrigued by this verbal sparring. Only the previous night he had reiterated in detail some of the persistent tensions between himself and Benjamin's side of the family. Religion had been only part of the discord; the Deism of Moses and his brood did not sit well with Benjamin's Orthodoxy. But other differences emerged as his brother became more aligned with the Anglo-Scottish merchants in Montreal. Moses was much more concerned with interests of the land-based population, including the remaining *seigneurs* in the province. Mary understood why there was this divide and she chose this moment to ask an impertinent question. "Is the Hart family, which has fought for the civil rights of the Jews in the province, going to be satisfied with being merged with a jurisdiction that has no history of supporting those rights?"

Aaron Philip was obviously taken aback by the question. "You misunderstand me, madam. I am no advocate of union though not out of fear that Jews will suffer because of it. I do, however, argue for the fullest civil rights for minorities. Isn't that true, uncle?"

"Yes and no! I haven't forgotten that not too long ago you and the Attorney General at the time were in accord that Jews could not take the required oath to hold public office. Thank goodness your cousins thought otherwise. They persevered and the upshot was that your father was appointed a magistrate in Montreal." Moses knew that he was treading on treacherous ground; Charles Richard Ogden had given the young Aaron Philip advice that the Hart family had cause to regret. Samuel Bécancour Hart disregarded that advice and his brother Aaron Ezekiel used his influence with the Legislative Assembly to have the law clarified. Moses often wondered whether or not Benjamin and son Aaron Philip had been embarrassed by the initiatives taken by the *Trifluvien* branch of the family. *Certainly they ought not to have any complaint.*

"You are right, uncle. Ogden, who is proving to be no friend of the Jews, took me in. Furthermore, he continues to speak for the royal interest. What do we have now? Ogden countersigning the proclamation of the union of Upper and Lower Canada. If the *Canadiens* despised him for his prosecution of the insurgents the winter before last, they have even more reason to see him as their sworn enemy."

Moses was somewhat gratified by this statement. It was true then that his nephew had had a change of heart. "You have seldom done us the honor of your presence here. This house on Rue Alexandre, as you well remember, protects many of your antecedents. Let Aleck take you outside to show you the tombstones over the graves of your grandparents!"

*   *   *

A month later Moses asked Alexander Thomas to his study to open up a delicate subject. He had become fond of his adopted son in a way so different from his attachment to Areli Blake. Even Orobio, who had died in that tragic accident fifteen years before, had never inspired his total affection. "Aleck" was always more compliant, more committed to him. No wonder that he had become Moses' confidential clerk in all his business dealings. *Why has he outshone his half brothers? Perhaps it is because he came out of another woman.* Sarah Judah Hart raised her offspring to resent their father – especially after two separations that took them into the divorce court.

Alexander seemed to guess that Moses had more than routine business on his mind. It was a warm September night and yet the door had been closed so that servants couldn't eavesdrop. "I've done something, Aleck, that may not meet with your approval. I'm trying to arrange something for you that my father had so much difficulty doing for me: finding a mate for you who can bring you children and the continuation of the fortune we have built up together."

Alexander didn't take Moses seriously. He laughed hilariously but did not otherwise respond.

"All this took place because I believe that you wish to travel to Manhattan shortly. I talked it over with Mary. This may be your opportunity to find a suitable wife since you have shown no preference for the ladies who reside here in Three Rivers."

"And what has New York to offer me?"

"I do have an unmarried niece in New York. Miriam Judah is almost your age. She relies on two of her older brothers to support her, the father, Barnabas, having died nine years ago. I wrote to her on the 14th of last month to enquire as to her willingness to move to Three Rivers if the two of you were to marry."

Alexander showed incredibility. "Would she wed a Canadian whom she has never seen? She can't be that desperate."

"She did show some reluctance to leave New York but undoubtedly the prospect of remaining a spinster weighs heavily on her. She is already well into her thirties. Moreover, I also included a promise of financial support even if the marriage failed for some reason. On demand, I stated, I would pay her at any time if she committed herself to my adopted son."

"And all this without consulting me? I've never met Aunt Catharine or her children. Nor have you showed much admiration for the Judahs even though the Harts and Judahs are so linked by marriage. This is madness!" Alexander was staring into space.

Moses blushed. It was true that the linkages were there. His mother, Dolly, had three brothers, all of them cousins to husband Aaron, who lived in Montreal for many years before migrating to the United States at the end of the American Revolution. Sarah was the daughter of one of those brothers and accepted marriage to Moses at the turn of the century after their relationship had become a bit of a scandal. At the same time sister Catharine, the oldest of Aaron Hart's daughters, had been promised to another of the Judah family, a cousin to Sarah, and had moved to New York. Moses and Catharine were never to sustain the closeness they had as children, in part because Moses had so low an opinion of her husband, Bernard. *Barabas never amounted to much despite his having medical training.* "Madness? Think about it, Aleck! You have often told me you feel an outsider because you had a different mother. Married to a Judah, your position in the family can never be challenged. In any case, you are not yet committed. Go to New York! Meet the woman! She may the right one for you."

*   *   *

The invitation to share the traditional Rosh Hashanah gathering with his brother's family was enough incentive for Moses to endure the walk to the Rue du Forges house. He was not alone; Mary and Alexander Thomas accompanied him from Rue Alexandre. Areli Blake, on the other hand, was out of town and wife Julia begged off bringing their children to the affair.

The weather was reasonably decent for late September. Moses took the walk slowly, having allowed enough time to get to his destination before sundown. He almost never hosted family assemblies related to the Jewish religious holidays – he had broken with Judaism when still a youth – but he seldom declined being present when his brother – or more often lately, Ezekiel's sons and daughters – went to the trouble of inviting him to help celebrate the High Holidays. Esther Elizabeth and Harriet did most of the preparations albeit it would be Samuel Bécancour at the head of the table. On this occasion Aaron Ezekiel had come up from Quebec to be part of the festivities.

Every room was candle lit even though the sun had yet to sink completely beyond the horizon. Moses appreciated that; his eyesight was beginning to fail. But he did notice the dearth of children, none of Ezekiel's sons and daughters being married. *Julia ought to have brought my grandchildren here despite Areli being absent.*

Different this year was the presence of Aaron Hart David and family. Moses had yet to be entertain them at his Rue Alexandre home though they had been in Trois-Rivières for just about all of the summer. While waiting in the parlor for the dinner to be served, he deliberately engaged with the young doctor. The latter's appearance was, after all, a reminder of Moses' affection for the late Sarah Hart David, his baby sister, while he still lived with his parents during the late 1780s. There was a strong resemblance.

At last the guests were called to the dinner table. Moses was surprised to find the head of the David family in the honored seat, Ezekiel evidently having decided that his eldest, Samuel, was not as conversant with the sacred text as was somebody who actually officiated at a synagogue. Samuel showed no sign of being peeved by such a demotion.

An hour later the men at the table retired to Ezekiel's library for cigars and brandy. Moses had his opportunity to ask about what was happening in the capital. He knew that Aaron Ezekiel was thick with many of the functionaries at the *Château Saint-Louis*. Governor Thomson had just returned to his residence in Quebec and Alexander also happened to be there the previous week. He had already told Moses that he had witnessed the arrival of the frigate that brought word of Thomson's elevation to the peerage.

Aaron Ezekiel proved to be quite informative. "The Governor is not in the best of health. He admits that the gout has made life miserable for him. Traveling last month to the Townships and to Upper Canada didn't help. And in July he was in Halifax straightening out government disputes in the three colonies in that region. But being made Baron Sydenham was some compensation for his discomfort."

"It appears to me, gentlemen, that much more discomfort is awaiting our new Baron. I cannot believe that the French party is taking these developments calmly. True, the Governor is counting on his reinstatement of Bédard and Panet to the Bench to mollify public outrage. Talking to Vallières I nevertheless sense a groundswell of opposition. Tell me, brother, what has been the reaction of Neilson, Parent and others to the Union Act as written?" Adolphus had been silent up to this point.

Aaron Ezekiel had an immediate response. "Neilson is most disconcerted by La Fontaine's stance. He had not anticipated the *adresse* that was made to the Terrebonne voters. On the other hand, he believes the anti-unionist position will prevail once there is a test of popular opinion. I plan to meet with Neilson as soon as I get back to Quebec."

Moses got in his opinion. "I read La Fontaine's statement. He insists that the new laws must win the approval of *Canadiens* as well of the British inhabitants if they are to be workable. But he does not pretend that the legislation can be overturned."

Your brother Reformers in Upper Canada will meet you and
your compatriots as Canadians, that no national animosities will be
entertained, that we desire your friendship, esteem, and cooperation
if we can obtain them consistent with our principles.
FRANCIS HINCKS
(letter to La Fontaine, August 23, 1840)

The Priest and the Lawyer return the member now and that without any
Control, or upon any ground except hatred to the English Govt.
and the English name. Establish a field in which the Inhabitants
Can discuss their own interests, and parties will soon be split
in the different parishes and districts, and set there someone
in the confidence of the Govt. who will expose the misrepresentations
which are made, and you will either get different members
or have a good check on them.
CHARLES EDWARD POULETT THOMSON (LORD SYDENHAM)
(letter to Lord Russell, September 14, 1840)

Twenty one

H is footsteps echoed sharply in the second-floor corridor. The courthouse was so much quieter this day, which was after all a weekend. Aaron Ezekiel was reminded of the last time he had interacted with Judge Elzéar Bédard in his chambers. That was before the issue of *habeas corpus* had emerged as a public controversy and resulted in Bédard's dismissal from the Bench. Two years had passed by since then. Aaron Ezekiel wondered for a moment whether he was precipitating another crisis by consulting his former colleague on the current state of the union.

Bédard was more guarded than usual when he greeted Aaron Ezekiel. *Is he also remembering what went on before?* He did rise from his chair to shake hands. "It's somewhat irregular but I've asked Étienne to join us."

"An excellent idea!" Aaron Ezekiel could hardly have been more pleased. *That is prescient of Elzéar! How did he know that I was intending to contact the editor of Le Canadien in a matter of days?*

Seating himself on one of the two unused chairs in Bédard's office, Aaron Ezekiel deliberately chose to engage in chitchat until Parent arrived on the scene. Finally the door was carefully open and on the threshold there he stood. Though not yet forty, Parent was showing signs of physical distress. His once robust shoulders were bent a bit, there was additional gray in the locks of his hair and he cocked his head on occasion because he was obviously partially deaf. He had paid a stiff price for spending those months in a Quebec jail the winter before last.

Aaron Ezekiel explained the purpose of his visit. He had been a staunch support of the *Patriotes* prior to the rebellion. It had been at some cost to his career as a lawyer. Presumably there would be a new legislature as the outgrowth of the Union Act. Could he expect different political alignments as a result? And would changes in the legal system have a bearing on his practice? "I don't mind telling you that as I see events unfolding in the next few months, my willingness to stay in Quebec is diminishing. I still retain connections elsewhere. Montreal, Trois-Rivières, maybe even Canada West, as they are now calling our new sister jurisdiction."

His interlocutors smiled, albeit not altogether sympathetically. Both Bédard and Parent had known real suffering for their convictions. Aaron Ezekiel had to concede that his woes were small in comparison. Parent spoke first. "You ask questions at a time when the answers are not straightforward. I was in Toronto last winter when the assembly of Upper Canada debated the plan of union as proposed by the Governor. It was a revelation. I asked myself whether it will be possible for *Canadiens* to act in concert with so many arrogant bastards. Hincks and several other spoke good sense. But others? How often did they refer to the French-this and the French-that all hating the British and their traditions. The fear of a *Canadien* majority in any combined legislature drove them to demand the limited representation from our province. I came away from listening to those voices convinced that union would never work."

"I can tell from your more recent editorials that your views have shifted."

"*Oui!* When I published La Fontaine's manifesto in *Le Canadien* at the end of August, I was quite aware that I was in the process of shifting my stance once again. La Fontaine thinks deeply. The principle of union need not be rejected, especially if we can collaborate with men such as Hincks and Baldwin to get changes in the law that lead us to ministerial responsibility. The logic of that is a government committed to the popular will. We *Canadiens* are the majority even in a united Canada."

"*Canadiens* may be the majority but they don't speak with one voice. You have only to listen to what your compatriots on the Special Council are saying. And what can we expect from Bishop Bourget, who now represents so many Catholics and who has castigated the *Patriotes* for their recklessness."

Parent sighed. "The new Bishop of Montreal has yet to declare himself on the forthcoming elections though no Catholic cleric can welcome the dominance of *les Anglais* in law or education. Bourget is still adjusting to Lartigue being in his grave."

Bédard had remained silent to this point. Aaron Ezekiel turned to view his impassive face. "Do you see things the same as Étienne does?"

"I would judge, *mon ami*, that most *Canadiens* will show their opposition to the union but, *hélas*, they don't have the chance to vote on the matter directly. Like me, they must follow where the law takes us. The Act of Union is the law."

"But you did stand up to bad law. That was over two years ago. Not a happy Christmas then!"

"If you remember, I spent that Christmas in New York. Left for England the next day to make my case for reinstatement. It was a bad time to be in London, the second outbreak of fighting on everybody's mind. But justice prevailed! It is now just about two months since the Governor stated that both Panet and I deserved to be back on the Bench. Even with a new Judicature Act coming into force and appointments to the courts yet to be announced, I should personally be safeguarded. I leave it to Étienne to help educate the voters in their ultimate responsibilities."

Aaron Ezekiel looked blankly until Parent explained. "I'm working on a new weekly journal that will publish more of the articles appearing in the French press. Up to now I've had to be satisfied with selecting only some of the articles from the Paris newspapers for inclusion in the *Le Canadien*."

"That should be a contribution to our intellectual development – if only you can get enough subscribers."

"We shall see! Look next month for the appearance of *Le Coin du feu!*" Parent grinned.

The conversation petered out after Parent took his leave. Aaron Ezekiel was coming to the conclusion that nobody could predict what would happen in the spring if and when British policy set Canada on a new course. Where did that leave him? As he stood at the window looking out onto Place d'Armes, Aaron Ezekiel could not but believe that this might be the last time he would be part of this cozy arrangement between a jurist, a counselor and a journalist.

* * *

A chance meeting with a *Patriote* counselor served to provide Aaron Ezekiel with more edification regarding the impending political crisis. He was having lunch with his cousin Abraham Joseph at the Union Hotel when they encountered Augustin-Norbert Morin sitting by himself at a separate table.

Aaron Ezekiel had to admit to himself that the man's appearance at the best eating establishment in the Upper Town was quite a shock. Not that Morin didn't deserve dining there. Still, his once prominent position in Quebec society as a Papineau lieutenant had been compromised by the rebellion. A warrant had been issued for his arrest back in November 1837, and he had taken refuge in a heavily wooded parish downstream from Quebec. Two years later he once more crossed the St Lawrence and surrendered to the authorities. Arrested on the charge of high treason, he remained but a short time in prison. The authorities had to admit that they had no case against him. Nevertheless, such tribulations had left Morin both penniless and in ill health. Aaron Ezekiel recalled that he had always been troubled with rheumatism. Now the fellow was obviously less than agile though still in his thirties.

Aaron Ezekiel glanced at Abraham; ought they to invite Morin to their table? It would be awkward, if only because Morin was so much taller than either of them. Nevertheless, here was a man who knew *Canadien* opinion better than did most. A reluctant nod from his cousin helped him make the decision to have Morin join them.

Morin did hesitate when the invitation was made. He knew Aaron Ezekiel only slightly and Abraham not at all. Nevertheless, he rose to his feet and then drew up a chair next to the two of them. He looked intently at Aaron Ezekiel. "I have seen you on occasion at the courthouse. You may not know that I am once more practicing law?"

"I do remember that. Somehow I thought you were back in Montreal. You are living here?"

"Currently I have a small house on Rue Desjardins. I am hoping for a better abode once I develop a clientele."

The food having been served by a waiter and the conversation becoming a little stilted, Aaron Ezekiel decided to open up the subject of politics. He mentioned having talked to Parent about the influence of La Fontaine within the *Canadien* intellectual community with respect to the debate on the right way forward. Was that point of view to prevail?

"As a matter of fact, Hart, I did meet with La Fontaine when he came to Quebec last December. He was very persuasive about the need to support the union of the two Canadas even though most of us thought otherwise.

However, the bill that passed Parliament was not what I could approve of. It did not provide for proportional representation in the Parliament. Nor did it grant ministerial responsibility. Governor Thomson certainly has backed off from what Lord Durham had proposed."

"And yet a new constitution is the reality. I cannot believe, Morin, that you will retire from the field even if the rules are not to your liking."

"You can say that! The terrible time being in hiding and in jail is over. I am ready to get back into politics. In fact, I'm thinking of running for a seat in the new Parliament. It has been suggested that the riding of Nicolet may be open to me."

Aaron Ezekiel glanced at Abraham. They had previously differed on whether *Canadiens* would accept defeat without recourse to political action. Augustin Morin was promising that they would not.

*   *   *

This particular morning in October Aaron Ezekiel carried out one more mission. The day before he had left a note with John Neilson's office on Côte de la Montagne requesting a meeting. An acknowledgement had come to him in return. The downhill walk was accomplished in minutes; the chill in the air kept him from dallying. The clacking sounds of the printshop could be heard once Aaron Ezekiel entered the establishment.

He was not kept waiting long. Ushered into an office to the left – the other closed space had presumably been assigned to Neilson's son, who actually ran the printhouse business – Aaron Ezekiel came face to face with the senior Neilson, the man with a high forehead topping off a thin and bony physiognomy. As editor of the bilingual *Quebec Gazette* and a politican to boot, Neilson had been probably the most prominent citizen in the capital for over forty years. At one time Aaron Ezekiel was somewhat intimidated by him but he did have the advantage of being a son of Ezekiel Hart. Over the years the old Jewish merchant and landlord in Trois-Rivières and the Scotsman on Rue de la Montagne had become both friends and political allies. "I bring greetings from my father. He is reading your editorials with great interest."

"How is Ezekiel? He no longer corresponds with me." Neilson, though in his middle sixties, had the reputation of maintaining contact with many citizens outside of Quebec through letter-writing."

Aaron Ezekiel assured him that Ezekiel's health, though declining in the past few years, was satisfactory. What not said was that the elderly Hart had already been preparing for his demise. In June of the previous year he had dictated a will in his son's presence which would leave his fortune, including all the possessions within the house on Rue du Forges, to his seven surviving children. There were extensive landholdings to distribute as well as the store on Rue du Platon. *I have nothing to reveal about that!* "I regret, sir, that I have not been of greater service to you despite living in the city for so many years."

Neilson chuckled. He obviously recognized that his visitor was not serious. "You know that I have avoided lawyers and judges wherever possible. If legalities are required, I prefer to deal with notaries."

Aaron Ezekiel then declared that he would be leaving the city very shortly. His family could make good use of him in Trois-Rivières. But before the move he was canvassing opinion on how the electorate was reacting to the promise of a different political structure once the new law was enacted. As a member of the Special Council, Neilson would be involved in the transition. Did he anticipate a satisfactory result?

"A good question, Hart! Many of my colleagues on the Special Council believe it is merely a matter of making the *habitants* once more peaceful and obedient. With the rebellion crushed, peace is already being restored in the countryside. I am not totally of that opinion. Our populace will redeem itself if its leaders make political demands that are more reasonable than what the *Patriotes* advocated. I foresee that if forces upriver do not dominate us, we can once again elect our own people to legislate for the province. That is why I oppose union."

"La Fontaine is taking a different tack. Are you therefore more in accord with Viger? You were political enemies prior to the rebellion."

"Politics make strange bedfellows. Denis-Benjamin and I may have been colleagues in the '20s when we were both in London opposing the Dalhousie tyranny but that wasn't the case when the *Patriotes* were set on undermining constitutional government. Today he sees some of the virtues of the old system. It was the bulwark by which *Canadiens* were able to preserve their traditional land ownership, their church and their language, not necessarily in that order. Union threatens those efforts once the bulwark is removed. To argue that point I will therefore seek a seat in the Parliament and will probably have Viger sit next to me."

*A part of the Mighty Empire of England – protected by Her arms –
assisted by Her Treasury, admitted to all the benefits of Trade and
Her citizens – your freedom guaranteed by Her Laws, and your rights
supported by the sympathy of your Fellow-Subjects there – Canada
enjoys a position unsurpassed by any Country in the world.*
CHARLES EDWARD POULETT THOMSON (LORD SYDENHAM)
(proclaiming the Union, February 10, 1841)

*I shall reduce the limits of Montreal & Quebec to the Cities and cut off
the suburbs, which will cause a great clatter with the French and their
Allies, but you might just as well have given no representation at all
to either city as far as the trade and the British Mercantile Interest
is concerned, as not to do so. With the suburbs, these towns are
as much French Counties as the Counties of the same names.*
CHARLES EDWARD POULETT THOMSON (LORD SYDENHAM)
(letter to Lord Russell, February 24, 1841)

Twenty two

Joseph-Rémi Vallières leaned back on his chair. Gazing at the painting on
the office wall, he thought for a minute or so whether there had been
an alteration to the picture carried out during the nearly two years that he
had been exiled from the Trois-Rivières' courthouse. *No, there had been no
defilement. Yet the scene looks different to me.*

Such contemplation was interrupted when he heard a rap at his door.
Vallières, whose torso was quite sensitive to pain, hesitated to comply with
this request for attention. *I will not get out of my chair unless it is an emergency.*
He called out "*entrez*" instead.

One of the intruders turned out to be Adolphus Hart ~ and he had
company, a man more smartly dressed than the counselor from Rue des
Forges. Vallières recognized Aaron Ezekiel at once even though the older
Hart brother had resided in Quebec City for so many years. Both were
bundled up, this February morning being even colder than usual. They were
affable enough albeit Vallières did resent their appearance on the scene.

Adolphus spoke for the both of them. "Our apologies, your Honor, for appearing unannounced. I am showing my brother about the courthouse. He has once again taken up residence in Trois-Rivières. You will soon being seeing him before the bar."

Vallières mustered a smile. *No getting away from the Harts!* The Harts ranked with members of the Kimber and Barnard families as leading citizens of Trois-Rivières. *When Eliza and I were together, the relationship was too close. Things should be more on even keel in the future.* As for her brother, he had come into the legal fraternity in Quebec City while Vallières was at the height of his career there. When the appointment to the court in Trois-Rivières occurred, there had been little contact other than when Aaron Ezekiel came back to Rue des Forges on holiday. "Welcome home, *mon ami!* You will be another addition to the brotherhood. You may not know this, but Barthe will be called to the bar next month. Barnard says he is ready."

Aaron Ezekiel responded quickly. "His imprisonment has obviously not harmed him. I might say, sir, that it was welcome news that the government relented in its persecution of you. I was equally pleased that in Quebec both *Messrs.* Bédard and Panet were back on the Bench at the last assizes."

"Thank you. Nonetheless, loss of salary did deplete my resources. I may need to approach your uncle for an extension of his loan to me. I understand that your cousin has returned from New York. With a wife no less. Will that change Moses Hart's lending policy? "

Aaron Ezekiel ignored the reference to borrowing or to the January marriage of Alexander Thomas and Miriam Judah. "Do you think that the new Judicature Act will alter things now that the Union Act is law?"

"Who knows? Yes, the courts are in transition and a new regime is in place. I read it in the *Gazette* yesterday morning. February the tenth has come and gone and we have a new constitution proclaimed. *Vive la reine!*" Vallières made no attempt to hide his bitterness.

"The Governor styles this Imperial statute as the beginning of a new epoch. He addresses us as inhabitants of the Province of Canada. Not *Bas-Canada* but rather of a united province. Henceforward, he calls on us to be united in sentiment as we are from this day in name. Yet you still oppose the Union?" Aaron Ezekiel asked the obvious question.

Vallières grimaced. "In his declaration Lord Sydenham does concede that many are opposed to the Union. He calls us a faction seeking to subvert the new constitution and regards us as being powerless. When we vote in the spring, I think we can demonstrate to the Governor that we are not powerless. *Hélas,* we don't have a Papineau any more to chair any reconstituted legislature. Believe it or not, Viger asked me last year to get myself elected so that I could be Speaker of the united Parliament."

"I have spoken with Mr. Neilson. He thinks likewise because he wants to save the protections for *Canadiens* embedded in the old constitution."

"Sydenham will have none of that. He refers to the 1791 constitution as an unwise, impolitic and disastrous event that has led to nothing less than a long and painful struggle. He argues that all has been rectified by the new statute. I think it as being nonsense. See here! The act affixes certain conditions over which the provincial legislature can exercise *no* authority. The relations of colony and parent state are within the purview of the Imperial Parliament." Vallières had placed his finger on a line in the *Gazette* report.

Adolphus intervened at this point. "I could not help but notice that the official countersignature to the proclamation is none other than that of our old friend Ogden. It ought not to surprise us. He was an adviser to Colborne even before Thomson arrived on the scene and I am told that he made his presence on the Special Council as a means of fashioning the Union Act to the advantage of his Tory friends."

Vallières laughed sardonically. "Over ten years ago I presided over a royalist dinner here in Trois-Rivières in honor of *Monsieur* Ogden. Much water has passed under the bridge since then. *Canadiens* in the seigneuries are being hemmed in. Land is at a premium. That has been one reason that I have worked with Kimber to have the lease to the ironworks revised in order to open new lands for agriculture."

Adolphus stepped back. "Thank you, your Honor, for seeing us. We still want to visit others in the courthouse."

Before he realized it, Vallières' visitors were gone. Seldom had he been so emotionally charged. Had he been indiscrete? *Should I be so public in my scorn of the new Governor?* And yet he had been badly treated. The decision by Sydenham last August to reinstate him – along with Bédard and Panet – as a judge of the Queen's Bench had been some vindication. The promise of back pay made it even easier to accept what he hopefully interpreted as contrition. *Why did the Governor do it? Was he disarming me because otherwise I would have been seen as a martyr jeopardizing his shaky political compromise?*

* * *

The first hint of spring was in the air when Vallières stepped out of his house onto Rue Notre-Dame to walk the short distance to the residence of Édouard-Louis Pacaud. The distance might not have been much, but Vallières had to negotiate it using a cane. There was purpose to this "expedition." The election to fill the new legislature had been called – the first general contest since 1834. Vallières found his situation this moment somewhat ironic; it was Pacaud who had persuaded him to release Papineau's brother from jail at the height of the first rebellion. That was the beginning of Vallières' falling out with the *Château* over *habeas corpus*. Meanwhile Pacaud rose in prominence as a lawyer for the district of Trois-Rivières and now was in a position to influence the choosing of candidates for the upcoming election.

The sounds of merriment could be heard as Vallières approached the entrance. As expected, several of the *Trifluvien* notables were already in the parlor. Drinks had been distributed, as were various *hors-d'oeuvres*. Pacaud was still a bachelor though it was well known that he would soon marry Anne-Hermine, the daughter of Pierre-Benjamin Dumoulin. It was improper for her, of course, to be on hand to greet the visitors. But the housekeeper made her presence felt as Vallières discarded his outer garments.

Greeting him immediately was young Barthe, who was quite the hero in *Trifluvien* circles because of his incarceration two winters before. Vallières embraced him without reserve. "I didn't have the opportunity to congratulate you when you were called to the bar last week. Barnard is convinced that you will do very well."

Settling onto a chair in the parlor Vallières checked on who else was there. Standing in one corner nursing glasses of rum were René-Joseph Kimber and Edward Barnard, the two *Trifluviens* who had actually had legislative experience. Vallières had seen Barnard often enough in the courtroom; Kimber was a physician.

On the sofa sat another barrister; Joseph-Édouard Turcotte, who was one of the young men who had come to practice in Trois-Rivières while Vallières was exiled from the Bench. He was distinguished by the absence of a right arm, the result of an accident while studying at the *Séminaire de Nicolet*. Vallières had long been impressed with his verbal skills and his willingness to acknowledge that he had been a Papineau supporter during the turbulent times of a few years before.

Notably absent was Dumoulin. Though just over forty years of age, he had graduated from being the Queen's Counselor who once represented Trois-Rivières in the former Legislative Assembly to being part of the magistracy. He spent much of his time at his manor house in Yamachiche but did come into town when his court was in session.

Pacaud, who had left the parlor earlier, returned and signaled that deliberations could commence. Vallières poured himself a glass of rum. *This should be interesting.*

"We do have a serious challenge from the Tories. They have Ogden seeking the one seat in Trois-Rivières and Gugy is going after Saint-Maurice."

Pacaud was indirectly reminding everybody that the ridings in the new Parliament would not have double representation. Barnard and Kimber had been elected the deputies from Trois-Rivières seven years ago. Back in 1834 Ogden as Attorney General under Gosford could not contest the seat despite having a long history of being one of the deputies from Trois-Rivières.

"Hasn't Gugy just been made Adjutant-General of militia for the province? Why would he also want to be in the Parliament? And why choose our district for that purpose?" Turcotte, relatively new to Trois-Rivières, seemed genuinely puzzled.

"You do remember Louis Gugy, the former sheriff of Montreal who died last summer! He has left son Bartholomew not only the seigneury of Beauport but also Yamachiche, Rivière-du-Loup, Grandpré, Grosbois, and Dumontier. Gugy doesn't dare run in Beauport because he would be up against Neilson. Saint-Maurice is obviously his safest bet." Pacaud's explanation was confirmed by a nodding of heads.

After a pause, he continued. "And he could win. So many of the *censitaires* in the county pay him rent. But do we want such a braggart who bashed heads during the uprising being the one representing all these parishes? That is why I am suggesting that you, Joseph-Édouard, give him chase."

"*Bravo!*" There was general support in the room for the suggestion.

Turcotte blushed. "I know not what to say. Going into politics has already entered my mind. But am I ready to take on such a challenge? Gugy is quite a colorful figure."

"Colorful but not beloved by the ordinary *habitant!* And you would also be receiving assistance from all of us. Think about it!" Kimber's voice could be heard over a sudden din.

"And what of young Joseph-Guillaume here? He too needs to be tested." Barnard was speaking up for his *protégé*.

Barthe answered with verve. "I have already been chosen to be a candidate in Yamaska."

To Vallières that made good sense. Yamaska on the south side of the river had long been the domain of the Tonnancours and scion Léonard Godefroy de Tonnancour had been elected in 1834 as one of the deputies. However, he had since abandoned public life. The other former deputy was also out of the picture. He had been none other than Dr. Edmund O'Callahan, Papineau's closest lieutenant and now an exile in the United States. "You do hope that the electors in Yamaska have forgiven O'Callaghan. Didn't they nickname him Doctor *qu'a la gale?*"

Barthe took umbrage at that remark even though he would undoubtedly concede that O'Callaghan was physically an unattractive man. There was a burst of laughter in response to his passionate defense of the exile. Pacaud, his mind on the south shore ridings, made a surprise announcement. "Morin has decided to run in Nicolet. He has become very close to La Fontaine in the past few months."

"Will not Hébert seek reelection?" Vallières had always thought of Nicolet as the bailiwick of Proulx and his son-in-law. Proulx was now dead and perhaps Hébert had been discouraged by having been rounded up by the military and imprisoned for a month in 1838.

"La Fontaine is convinced that Nicolet is Morin's for the taking. "It is important to La Fontaine because he may have to withdraw from the polling in Terrebonne. He aims to have as many friends as possible sitting in the Parliament." Pacaud's statement caught everybody by surprise. He had to explain that a compromise candidate for the riding of Terrebonne, a Dr. Michael McCulloch, was being pushed by both the Governor and the supporters of Viger. Thus La Fontaine might have to back off and depend on surrogates if he seeks to be heard by the legislators.

"I take it, *mon ami,* that La Fontaine still opposes those of us who want to rid ourselves of the union with Upper Canada. My estimate is that he is in the minority on that subject. A voice in the wilderness!"

"Perhaps not for long. I have advised him to contact Ludger Duvernay in Burlington. His *La Minerve* was so influential in the years before '38. He may be persuaded to return to Montreal and revive that publication."

"But will he back La Fontaine? Doesn't he still dream of an independent *Bas-Canada?*" Vallières remembered the Duvernay of yesteryear.

"The *Patriotes* in Vermont and New York are a spent force. I am told Côté has abandoned the fight and is once more practicing medicine in Chazy. Duvernay is too practical to stay with that dream. In my view, he will return to Montreal if he can be assured that there will be no prosecution of him." Pacaud sounded very sure of himself.

"There is still an outstanding quarrel with the Americans that could result in hostilities. I refer to the Aroostook valley. I suspect that our *emigrés* south of the border hope that Van Buren will alter his attitude to their cause if war does break out between Maine and New Brunswick." Barnard's citing of that conflict reminded Vallières that nothing was for certain.

*The honor of being the first representative of our district
is not worth much to you, and the bother and trouble [...] is no small
matter to one so fond of home & so bound to it as
you are. But now you are a public man, doomed
to undergo the labors and to mix in the Stripes of
a Representative Assembly, your best friends can wish you
no better fortune than this — that when you shall see fit to retire,
your enemies may have as little to say against you as at present.*
ANDREW ROBERTSON
(letter to Edward Hale, April 5, 1841))

*Considering that two years ago the people were cutting each
other's throats and in arms against each other while
the French Canadians press and leaders have been doing everything
in their power to excite the passion of the People, I am quite
surprised that they [the elections] went off so well.*
CHARLES EDWARD POULETT THOMSON (LORD SYDENHAM)
(letter to Lord Russell, April 10, 1841)

Twenty three

Theodore Hart was very much looking forward to being a guest at the *seder* meal being prepared by the matriarch of the Joseph family this early April evening. Not only was the former Rachel Solomons likely to bring together several of his cousins to the same table. She was almost certain to invite the nubile David daughters. Phoebe, Fanny and Sophia were but two years apart in age; the youngest was already eighteen. Anyone of them would do nicely and each of them ought to be glad to marry him; he was only twenty-five and well established in his father's business. Nevertheless, he did have a preference.

Walking to Place Près-de-Ville with an eye on the sun setting to the west, Theodore had to admit to himself that the visit was not without some bad feelings. Both father Benjamin and mother Harriot had objected when Theodore declared that he had accepted Rachel Joseph's invitation. Harriot was the most vociferous. "Theo! Think of us! Wellington is in Liverpool; Aaron Philip doesn't come around any more. Where does that leave *our* celebration of *Pesach?*"

For Theodore, however, it wasn't a matter of spoiling his own family's celebration; there were a half dozen of his siblings available to sit down with his parents. Frederick was older than he, and Henry and Benjamin Moses had reached their majority. And then there were the three adolescent girls – Hannah, Dorothea and Elizabeth – who looked forward to being seated for the occasion. *I deserve the right to follow my own inclinations given that I have done so much for papa.* Theodore had been in correspondence with his brother Wellington, who had kept him informed of what was happening during his special trip to London from Liverpool to further family interests. The last letter reported success. Theodore had subsequently conveyed the good news to his father. Minerva Life was giving consideration to appointing Benjamin Hart and Company its Montreal agent. With the current downturn in the economy affecting adversely the company's import business, expansion of the insurance side of its operations would be a godsend.

Rachel Joseph had made a point of meeting him at the door. During their embrace he caught the scent of her perfume, which was a bit too strong. *She greets me as if I've already chosen one of her daughters.* "Dear Theo! I must apologize for not having you lead the *seder.* It would have been an imposition."

Abraham Joseph had been elected to read from the *Hagaddah.* He had come up from Quebec City to be with his family during the Passover. Her son-in-law Aaron Hart David would have been favored for the task but he was still living in Trois-Rivières. Nor was Jacob Henry, Abraham's older brother, versed enough in Hebrew to do a satisfactory job. Needless to say, Eleazar David was absent, having fled to New York with his mistress almost a year before. The David sisters were indeed seated at the table, each in proper rank according to age. Theodore noticed that they had chosen to wear the older white French-style dresses (to wit, loose, draped high-waisted gowns) despite the fact that he had seen them not too long before in three-quarter-length overdresses to keep from being too chilled. They probably couldn't afford the springtime fashion plate no matter that London styles were now readily available in Montreal in time for April wear. The threesome was in a giggly mood and he didn't mind.

His attention, however, was primarily on the in-between young lady, Frances Michaels. *So pretty! So talented! So delicate!* There was but one problem, Abraham Joseph had intimated that he too favored "Fanny" as his future bride. He dared not offend his second cousin, who had become very useful in expediting overseas shipments coming into tidewater Quebec. *Would she be convinced to abandon Montreal and commit herself to life in Quebec City?* The time had come to act with dispatch and do it with finesse.

He would need to wait until the completion of the rituals associated with the Passover meal and the consumption of the various courses being brought in by two female servants. But eventually the diners were able to repair to the parlor and to indulge in chatter not related to divine matters.

Actually Rachel herself initiated a secular comment. "I have a letter from Catharine. It appears that Mr. Gugy will not succeed being elected to the new legislature. A fellow named Turcotte used every trick in the book to win in Saint-Maurice. He even seized a polling booth." Rachel Joseph's grimace was evidence that she didn't approve of such a development.

"But isn't Gugy also running in Sherbrooke, his old constituency?" Theodore wished to show that he was abreast of news on the ongoing election.

Abraham interjected. "He may not make it there either. Edward Hale is a formidable candidate and there is no longer room for two representatives from Sherbrooke."

"But didn't Gugy ask Hale last month not to contest the seat? Knowing Gugy's temperament I would expect him to appeal the vote if Hale wins and it is at all close."

Rachel had moved on. "But it is comforting to know that Mr. Ogden is once more a deputy. I knew that *Trifluviens* would not fail him."

"There is no need to fret, mother. Canada East will probably be safely in the Governor's camp even if the anti-unionists and other French candidates do well in the election. His supporters are bound to triumph in the Townships as well as in Montreal, Three Rivers and Quebec. We can almost be certain that by Thursday the election of Holmes and Moffatt will happen in our ridings!" John Henry was making his contribution to the discussion.

Theodore sighed. Would he be able to segregate Fanny from her sisters and show her his regard? If not this night, he would have to find another excuse after tomorrow's synagogue services to engage her.

* * *

Benjamin Hart insisted that Theodore dress well for the appointment. It being June, a tailored coat and a top hat weren't exactly what Theodore had in mind for the walk to Rue Saint-Jacques. *Too many snickers by fellow young blades at such a display of class.* They were, however, calling on the cashier of the Bank of Montreal. Benjamin Holmes in his role as the bank's general manager had a reputation for expecting a high standard in decorum. Dublin-born Holmes may have been a refugee child at the turn of the century, but he had worked himself up to his current status from a discount clerk with the Bank of Montreal when it was founded almost a quarter century before. Theodore had heard him being described as arbitrary and inflexible and certainly the two suspensions of specie in the past few years must have tested him greatly. Yet he was highly regarded; his stint as a Lieutenant Colonel of the battalion of Montreal Light Infantry during the rebellions had elevated the admiration that Montreal Anglos had for him.

Father and son were treated with deference as they were ushered past the teller cages to the suite of offices in the bank's rear. Holmes called out when they reached the appropriate door and the signal had been given that that the twosome had arrived as scheduled. Benjamin entered without hesitation; as one of the bank's major clients, he relied on his status to eschew any formalities. Theodore held back. True, he had been introduced to Holmes in an informal setting but this was their first encounter at the man's workplace. Holmes, however, got to his feet and proffered a hand in greeting.

There being three of them, the host opted to seat his guests at a sitting area away from the desk. Once settled and top hat in hand, Theodore felt it was incumbent on him to congratulate Holmes on his election as one of the two parliamentarians allocated to the city of Montreal. "Will you be leaving soon for Kingston, sir?"

Holmes was unusually forthcoming. "Not without some displeasure. The town is simply too remote for my liking and the recompense is disgraceful. Talked to Ogden last month. Though winning in Three Rivers, he objects to the fact that he will be paid £1500 in salary compared to the £4000 he was getting as Attorney General. Furthermore, having to spending so much time in Kingston will be at a sacrifice of some of the legal work he does in Montreal. I have the same dilemma."

"One wonders why Lord Sydenham was determined to establish the capital of the new state in Kingston. Is it to distance the administration from its natural economic center? Who in his right mind would expect such an outpost to rival Montreal or Quebec?" Benjamin was repeating what all the merchants along Rue Saint-Paul had been saying for months.

"Talk to Thomas Molson! He spent ten years in that settlement, though he didn't let any grass grow under his feet." Holmes was referring to the one of the Molson brothers who had departed Montreal in 1823 because earlier he had chosen to wed without a marriage settlement. Just about everybody in the community had known that this Molson scion had immediately bought brewing equipment in England and then purchased the Kingston brewery that year, expanded his operations and established various taverns in Upper Canada. It was only seven years ago that Thomas Molson returned to Montreal to go into partnership with his father and brother William.

The mention of a Molson prompted Benjamin to raise a subject that Theodore had heard discussed often in the privacy of their home. The Hart family had been watching with interest the efforts of William Molson to contest the hegemony of the Bank of Montreal by launching his own institution during the currency crisis of the past few years. "It still surprises us to see you, with the approval of John Molson Junior, being so determined to punish William and Thomas for their defiance."

"You are quite aware of our position, Hart. We could not have these bills on sufferance remain outstanding. Nevertheless, Molson's Bank didn't withdraw them from circulation and continued to issue new notes. Together with the Board of Trade we did convince the Special Council to forbid such private currency and we shall prevail. The Molsons have moved over to the Banque du Peuple for the nonce, but they did finally have to withdraw their notes."

Benjamin got around to explaining why he had asked for an appointment. "Son Theodore has dedicated himself to expanding our insurance business. We are looking for support in establishing offices in the new Canada West. Your assistance in this regard would be of great benefit to us."

Holmes turned his gaze on Theodore. "The two of you have certainly done well in insurance. Marine, life and fire I believe."

"Quite right, sir. We represent Equitable Fire Insurance Company of London, the Sun Mutual Life Insurance Company of Montreal, Mercantile Insurance, the Security Insurance Company of New York, Minerva Life of London, and the New York Underwriters." Theodore was able to complete the list despite noticing Holmes' amusement at this recitation. *I must sound like an idiot.*

"The name of Benjamin Hart is well known among our customers, young man. And the reputation of your father is above reproach." Holmes' smile was enigmatic.

"I have said too much."

"On the contrary! I like you, Hart. It seems to me that your talents are not fully appreciated. My advice is that you accompany me to Kingston and sell some of your policies to our new legislators. There is money being made in Canada West. Mining lands north of the Great Lakes are there for the taking. Have you ever traveled the territory above Huron or Superior?"

* * *

This Sunday morning was almost Kingston's last day of summer. For Theodore the several months during which he had stationed himself in the town's only decent hotel had been an edifying experience. Nevertheless, it had been almost a week since the first session of this new Parliament was prorogued and he now had to give thought to securing convenient transportation back to Montreal.

Breakfast was being served downstairs later than usual because of the holiday. Theodore dressed casually for the repast though he knew he would be sitting at a table with one or more of the Parliament's delegates. But after four months of intimate contact with them, he had lost much of his awe at their presence in the hotel. Though much of his intermixing came as a result of his status as an insurance agent, Theodore had come around to the belief that these were very ordinary men in extraordinary circumstances. *Being away from home for so long, their foibles have come to the surface more often than not.*

Most of the windows in the dining hall were ajar; a mid-September breeze was still pleasant enough that no fire was lit in the hearth. Theodore took a serving of bacon and eggs from the sideboard and found space at a table already occupied by Charles Richard Ogden and a couple of gentlemen from Toronto. They were engaged in dissecting the debates in Parliament that had been their preoccupation since the session was opened in June. There was little that Theodore could contribute, but he did listen intently. Yet, the only interesting news was that the Governor's health had come into question. Theodore asked why.

He was informed immediately. "His Excellency is quite indisposed. He had a riding accident but a couple of days ago. I believe the wound has become infected. He is agony."

The second Torontonian interjected. "He has always been a sickly fellow. His gout was so bad in recent months that he submitted his resignation in July."

"Yet he does wish to be honored for his service. I believe the *gcb* he requested has been granted him." Ogden had previously explained to Theodore that this Order of Bath included both military men and high civil servants. It was the fourth most senior of the British Orders of Chivalry. Sydenham would have had to be even more illustrious to earn The Most Noble Order of the Garter or the Most Ancient and Most Noble Order of the Thistle.

The award did make some sense to Theodore. Lord Sydenham, who had moved to Kingston in May to oversee this first meeting of the new legislature, may not have achieved total consensus but he had succeeded in getting most of his agenda accepted even if there was dissent from many of those in attendance. Certainly the Tories from Montreal and elsewhere in Canada East seemed relatively satisfied. Theodore could attest to that from several conversations he had had with Benjamin Holmes. Admittedly, they tended to revolve about the banker's preoccupation with getting a renewal of the charter of the Bank of Montreal. That was understandable; he was on a leave of absence from that institution for that very purpose. Holmes, however, did go beyond pursuing his special interest; during the session he pressed for financial reform. Theodore thought it appropriate to speak favorably of Sydenham's initiatives.

Ogden looked at Theodore with some condescension. "Our Governor did falter on one occasion; he tried to establish a single bank of issue for the colony but we were successful it stopping that measure. He had this fellow Derbishire speaking on his behalf but such a personal friend as he didn't have that kind of influence in the Parliament. The Family Compact is still strong enough to have its way in some matters."

Theodore had to concede that point; he had become accustomed to referring to the members of Family Compact in Canada West as Tories, albeit that was an appellation usually reserved for his compatriots east of the Ottawa River. Similarly he had to remember that the Canada West equivalents of the *Patriotes* were called "Reformists." The few of them present in Kingston were among those dissenters. *I have yet to fully appreciate the various political currents.*

One of gentlemen from Toronto demonstrated that he was also conscious of the divisions to come. "We leave for home still not comfortable with this parliamentary creation by Poulett Thomson. I know from personal experience that those tied most closely to the Family Compact in Toronto speak of him as a most mischievous fellow. And there is no doubting the hostility of the French, who, of course, have no hope of achieving a majority in Parliament."

"And yet they may grow more numerous. At this very moment La Fontaine and Parent are in Toronto campaigning for the one of the York ridings that Baldwin gave up. Can you believe a *Patriote* representing a British constituency?" Ogden's grimace was consistent with the reaction of other Tories who had heard of Robert Baldwin, the leader of the small coterie of Reformers, choosing to hold on to his Hastings seat while relinquishing the one he won in the Toronto area.

"Does that not concern you, sir? You were victorious in Three Rivers, but the *Patriotes* are still a force outside the major towns." Theodore spoke with some strength.

"We thought that we would have Colonel Gugy as part of our bloc, but, alas, he was defeated in April by this fellow Turcotte." Ogden's look of disdain indicated his opinion of the *Trifluvien* lawyer.

But the expression did not last long. Stewart Derbishire was standing at the doorway, his countenance ashen in hue. He finally spoke, loudly enough that all in the room could hear. "His Excellency has died. It was lockjaw."

*What I have seen and what I have had to do during the last
three weeks, fortifies my opinion as to the absolute necessity
of sending as my successor someone having parliamentary
and ministerial experience, someone who will not be afraid
of work and who will govern himself, as I do.*
LORD SYDENHAM
(letter to Lord Russell, June 27, 1841)

*As for the French nothing but time will do anything for them.
They hate British rule – British connexion – British improvement
of all kinds whether in their Laws or their roads. So they sulk, and
will try, that is, their Leaders, to do all the mischief they can.*
LORD SYDENHAM
(letter to Lord Russell, September 27, 1841)

Twenty four

Sleep was not coming easily to Ludger Duvernay. *Is it the brandy? Or perhaps it is because I didn't drink to excess this evening?* At dinner he had sworn not to indulge but there hadn't been the strength of character to resist the temptation to have at least one drink.

Whatever! He had other thoughts. The image of the prelate with his soft blue eyes gazing at him was recurring each passing minute or so. Had *Monsignor* Ignace Bourget come to Burlington deliberately to challenge Duvernay's unsettled behavior in these past few years? *No proof of that!* The Bishop had been asked to send a priest or two to this Vermont community to satisfy the spiritual needs of the expatriate *Canadiens*. But when he did appear in town this morning, Bourget showed suspicion with Duvernay's display of religious orthodoxy. Hadn't the former publisher printed anti-clerical writings prior to the rebellion?

In the darkness of the bedroom Duvernay had to concede having doubts about how he had behaved before and after 1837. His life was not going well albeit he had grown accustomed to living in Burlington. If he must be an exile, better here than when he dwelled in the Vermont villages of Swanton and St Albans or in New York's Rouses Point. From his Burlington residence he had operated a letterpress, even printed a newspaper, *Le Patriote canadien*, for six months. Perhaps the closing of that publication in the winter of 1840 was the cause of his subsequent bitterness. Subscribers in the dwindling exile community were too difficult to recruit, they being so scattered and not well off financially. And he had to give up searching for readers in *Bas-Canada* after Governor Thomson refused to authorize the distribution of his paper by mail to the other side of the border. Finances had been precarious ever since. *Why didn't I take that job with the U.S. Board of Customs at the time?*

Nonetheless, life goes on. He was sober enough most days to escape his occasional abyss in order to organize those *Canadiens* who were living in Burlington into a coherent community. In fact, he was the one who took the initiative in having Bishop Bourget visit the town during the latter's tour of the faithful living in the Border States.

The tour had taken place this spring, about a year after Bishop Lartigue had died and Bourget took charge of the diocese. In 1840 his priority seemed to be the solidification of the Roman Church in British North America. He turned over the training of priests to the Sulpicians in Montreal. Later in the year he helped launch the *Mélanges religieux*, a journal independent of provincial politics.

Yet he was not averse to traveling throughout the see, having visited the north shore of the Ottawa River the previous autumn to set up new missions for the *Canadien* settlers settled in this hinterland. The more southerly trip this May would extend his outreach. Bourget was only a year or so beyond his fortieth birthday though his hair was prematurely gray, (which added to his *gravitas*). Otherwise his vigor - exemplified by a ruddy complexion ~ impressed Duvernay. There remained, however, a lingering fear that ultramontane politics dominated the man's thinking. Wasn't the Bishop enamored with the presence of Bishop Forbin-Janson, the fervent *Legitimist* from France who had come to this continent in 1839 to preach the virtues of the Restoration? Bourget was responding to it by authorizing the building of the world's tallest and most beautiful cross on Mount Saint-Hilaire. Was Duvernay ready for such an ostentatious display of clericalism?

Despite these doubts, he might have to make peace with such a man if he were to be able to resume a place in the political firmament. He was aware of the changing situation in his home province - the British insistence on the union of the two Canadas, the transfer of the government locus to Kingston, the seeming end to the dream of an independent francophone republic. In the previous decade Ludger Duvernay had been a leading spokesman for such a dream, his *La Minerve* testing new ideas from various *Patriote* leaders. Could he renounce everything he had stood for not too many years before?

And then there was the question of a livelihood. Not only was the printing shop of *La Minerve* no longer functioning; it had also been looted. The receivables owing to him had vaporized. With *Le Patriote canadien* also suffering its ignominious fate, he was virtually bankrupt. His wife and five surviving children could only have looked forward to destitution if he failed to recover his standing in the new Canada East. *No, I must think of Burlington as my permanent home. Let Bishop Bourget deal with the new facts of life north of the border!*

The image of the prelate gave way to more incoherent apparitions. Duvernay didn't recover his senses until the morning sun lightened the room.

* * *

The man at the door needed little introduction once he identified himself. Charles-Auguste-Marie-Joseph de Forbin-Janson, draped in a long black overcoat, had already made quite a reputation as the itinerate preacher shaking up the Catholic world from the Mississippi Delta to the St Lawrence Valley. *What brings so eminent a personage to Vermont?*

Duvernay hurried to close the door behind his visitor. It was quite cold; the October wind was still in the process of ripping off the last leaves from the deciduous growth in and about Burlington. The fire in the parlor hearth generated enough heat to make it comfortable enough for his guest provided the room was sealed off from the inclement weather. There was no servant available to put up a kettle so Duvernay had to attend to it himself while giving Forbin-Janson a chance to warm his extremities.

Before pouring the tea Duvernay took the opportunity to scrutinize the man. Forbin-Janson was a descendant of Provence nobility and a lifelong supporter of the royalist cause. Now in his fifties, he had earlier dedicated his life to the re-evangelization of France under the guidance of Pope Gregory XVI. Duvernay wasn't certain whether his appearance this day was a result of his being on his way north or south. Bishop Bourget had already informed Duvernay in May that this French *émigré* had beginning in late 1839 traveled from New York through Philadelphia and St Louis to New Orleans to deliver the Lenten sermons and then to build a church in Louisiana.

Duvernay's first query: "Have you been back to New Orleans in the past year, *sieur?*"

"Not this year. Yet I have had the honor of living among the parishioners of Louisiana, who remain true to their faith in spite of the dominance of godless Masonry in this Modern Babylon.

Duvernay's response was diplomatic. "I grant you that it is a good time for revivalism. You have instilled the Jesuit spirit in the parish missions that have sprung up throughout the United States."

"*Hélas*, this may be my last mission for a while. I am returning to Europe very shortly. Visiting a few select communities on my way to New York. It has truly been a rewarding sojourn in North America. Yet I am most fatigued." Forbin-Janson's continence at that moment confirmed this sudden admission.

Duvernay chose to pick a fight. "Not rewarding enough to form a good opinion of the American republic. I, on the other hand, have chosen to make my way here although I am free to return to my homeland without there being retribution. I once dreamed of being an example for my people as Benjamin Franklin was for his. Even named our youngest son Benjamin in honor of this printer who became a renowned statesman. Unfortunately, the child died before I ever set eyes on him. A bitter fruit of exile. Moreover, I no longer am a printer."

The cleric scowled. "So then you give your allegiance to Martin Van Buren instead of to a British lord. I was present last November when Americans elected Harrison and Tyler. Americans are fickle in their commitments to authority."

"I still have a great admiration for Van Buren. He has been called Martin Van Ruin because of the panic in '37. But he is in the tradition of Jefferson and Jackson. Americans may come back to him once Tyler completes his term. They are proud of their country and, as I have said in the past, they have reason to be." Duvernay was getting argumentative.

"Be that as it may! Your heart should belong to your God and your country. On the sixth of this month I was present at the blessing of the cross on Mont Saint-Hilaire. It is a monument to our *nation*, rising as it does a hundred feet in the air. Candles were lit in all of the openings and proud *Canadiens* perched on top of the structure."

Duvernay smiled. "We have heard stories indeed about its construction. They say the shaft is six feet wide and four feet through. It was being cross-sheathed with tin and ought therefore to be very bright even at night."

"It has a special meaning for me. There once was a cross on what we then called Mont Calvaire before Napoleon confiscated this hill west of Paris. That cross was destroyed. In Mont Saint-Hilaire the carpenters and *censitaires* in and about Beloeil gave their labor to build one just as beautiful.

I called on you, *Monsieur* Duvernay, to appeal for you as a good Catholic to spread the word of Jesus and the Virgin Mary to those who haven't any haven when God seeks them out. Burlington is one of those places deprived of a haven."

Duvernay drained his teacup. How does one argue such a direct challenge? *Once more I'm being reminded of my roots. He knows my weakness.* "I don't exclude the possibility of building a house of worship here in Burlington. You must remember, however, that our people have little coin to spare. I too have very few assets now that *Le Patriote canadien* is defunct. But I shall gather my friends together to see what we can do."

*　*　*

The carriage ride to Napierville took longer than Duvernay had anticipated. There were a couple of stops to be made for additional passengers before reaching the border. And December was not the best time to travel even though the sky was clear. The Richelieu River had yet to freeze over but no watercraft was to be seen on its surface.

The cross-road to Lacolle having been attained, the carriage turned west and up the Chemin Louis-Cyr to Napierville itself. Duvernay could see no signs of the damage wreaked on the town during the confict of a few years before. Actually, the local *auberge* appeared in good shape. Duvernay had not been in Napierville since the insurrection. He remembered meeting with Cyrille Coté at that time but he guessed that it was unlikely that the doctor would once more be living in Lacolle County. The last word he had about Coté was that the latter had settled in Chazy, NY to eke out a living as a physician. Furthermore, Coté's animus towards the Catholic Church had finally pushed him into becoming an apostate. It was already being said that he was preaching Protestantism to expatriate *Canadiens*.

More pertinent for Duvernay on this trip was a secreted letter from Édouard-Louis Pacaud, who had written that he was acting for La Fontaine. They would have to meet incognito; many of the exiles had chanced traveling surreptitiously to their home territory, the Amnesty Act of two years before not releasing everybody from the threat of arrest. Duvernay would be seeking a man with a modish black hat.

Seated at a table at the back of the room was the sole person who fitted the description. Pacaud looked to be in his mid-twenties and very much a prosperous lawyer. They had never met face to face. But they shook hands with alacrity. Duvernay was glad to order a brandy; it was his first drink of the day.

Pacaud got to the point directly. "I'll be frank with you, Duvernay. We want you back in Montreal. I wrote you a year ago February that I was with La Fontaine on his accepting the union of the two Canadas as a *fait-accompli*. As you may have read, La Fontaine is now a member of the new Canadian Parliament. Representing a Toronto riding of all places! He is more than just another legislator. He has been challenging Neilson as the natural leader of *Canadiens* elected from *Canada-Est*. To do that effectively he needs a journal like *La Minerve* to spread his message."

Duvernay's first reaction to this proposal was a negative one. "Do you not see any hope for *Canadiens* escaping British domination? Yet I agree that the Tories are not likely to yield power."

"There is a new administration in London. The summer election has put Robert Peel back in the saddle. Who knows how different the Tories will be from the Whigs? What we do know is that the man replacing Sydenham is one Charles Bagot."

"That name is familiar. Wasn't he a party to the agreement between the Americans and the British to limit naval ships on Lake Champlain? But that was over a quarter century ago."

"Indeed, the very man. Spent some of those years as the British envoy to Washington. Peel must reckon that Bagot knows how to handle colonials. He has yet to arrive in New York but my understanding is that he will be in Kingston by next month."

Duvernay didn't want to be distracted by these political maneuvers. His impatience showed. "Let's get back to *La Minerve*! You realize, of course, that my print shop on Rue Saint-Gabriel was pillaged as soon as I departed Montreal in '37. My friends wrote me people were vying with one another to see who could steal the most. Nor was I able to collect very much on the debt owing me. What a disgrace!"

"*Monsieur* La Fontaine is aware of your losses. He proposes that money be found to set you up in business again. And he has promised to put in a good word for you once Bagot comes through Montreal. There should be no likelihood of prosecution since you were never on the battlefield."

Duvernay was a little tight by the time the carriage destined for Burlington arrived at the *auberge*. Yet his spirits had been lifted by what Pacaud had related to him. *Is it possible that I and my family, Reine and the children, can once more call Montreal home?*

You cannot too early, and too distinctly, give it to be understood that you enter the Province with the determination to know no distinctions of National origin, or Religious Creed; to consult, in your Legislative capacity, the happiness and (so far as may be consistent with your duty to your Sovereign and your responsibility to her Constitutional advisers) the wishes of the mass of the Community; and , in you Executive capacity, to administer the Laws firmly, moderately, and impartially.
COLONIAL SECRETARY LORD STANLEY
(instructions to Sir Charles Bagot, October 8, 1841)

The chief opponents of the Government during the last Session were first the French Canadians – secondly a portion of the (so named) Compact party, and thirdly the ultra popular Section of the Upper Canadians. These parties, though differing entirely on all questions of principle, repeatedly united for the purpose of defeating or obstructing the Government on individual measures.
GOVERNOR SIR CHARLES BAGOT
(letter to Lord Stanley, February 23, 1842)

Twenty five

It was already the fourth day into the New Year and no winter storm had yet to blight Montreal's streets and byways. For Frances Michaels David this was a sign that God was blessing the wedding celebration. She had spent weeks through the autumn haunted by the thought that the marriage would not be performed as scheduled even though there was no reason to believe it so. Theodore had no such doubts and had Reverend David Piza guide her through some wedding rehearsals. With the day already upon them, "Fanny" had to admit to herself that her fears had been nothing but a virgin's fixation on her first sexual encounter.

Meanwhile there had always been Theodore's equanimity despite his admission to being somewhat distracted by the uncertainties emerging since the close of the legislative session in Kingston. Baron Sydenham's rendezvous with lockjaw in September, the advent of Sir Robert Peel's new administration in London, the stalemate in the Kingston Parliament because the cabinet of William Henry Draper could not impose its will, and the persistence of hard times on both sides of the Atlantic were interfering with business as usual for Benjamin Hart & Co. It was once considered expedient that Theodore use the winter months to travel to London. In fact, he had booked passage on the same ship that would be taking Attorney General Ogden to Europe on a year's leave. But Benjamin had second thoughts; son Arthur Wellington had married in mid-October and indicated by letter that this was not the best time to entertain his younger brother. Selena Ezekiel, the bride, had family obligations that could not be postponed. The upshot: Theodore chose to pursue his courtship of Frances David with no worry about a serious physical separation during the approaching winter and spring.

For her, however, looking into the mirror as she fussed with her hair, there were qualms yet not fully alleviated. Though she was reaching the age of twenty-two by October, Frances would be marrying ahead of Phoebe. Her elder sister seemed to be a good sport about it, but there were bound to be hurt feelings. Frances had had two admirers; Abraham Joseph had made no secret of his interest in her though he had never spoken of marriage. *Why couldn't one of the two men have shown his affection for Phoebe instead?* Abraham would be at the synagogue this afternoon (he had come up from Quebec for the occasion) and perhaps he would be more attentive to Frances' sisters.

But no matter, that was the way things had worked out. She and Theo would be under the *chuppah* facing Rabbi Piza this afternoon with Phoebe behind her, a bridesmaid. The ceremony entailed that the *ketuvah* be signed, *lechaims* shouted as the men drank their hard liquor and then the meeting of the bride and groom under the canopy. She was to be addressed formally as Frances Michaels David, a designation she always been shy about. The Michaels part hailed back to a history not fully understood. Her aunt was also a Frances David and this "Fanny" had married Myer Michaels almost fifty years before. She never did fully explain to her niece why the husband's surname should be remembered when she, the younger Fanny, was born to Sarah Hart David.

Fanny had never met Myer Michaels. The old fur trader had died five years before she was born. Her Aunt Fanny did relate stories of a 22-year long marriage that yielded no children. Year after year her husband spent much of his time in Michilimackinac before hurrying to Montreal in early September in order to celebrate the High Holidays with the Davids. Her Uncle David as well as papa Samuel had been closely associated with Michaels in the fur trade prior to their selling the business to the North West Co.

A rap on the bedroom door interrupted her contemplations. Catharine Joseph David stood at the threshold, already dressed for the occasion. Frances hadn't seen her sister-in-law for months, Trois-Rivières being too far away for easy travel. They embraced and it was only then that she recognized the somewhat distended abdomen. Catharine recognized Frances' digression. "I'm pregnant again. Perhaps this time it will be a girl child."

Catharine had previously complained to Frances that having three sons in succession was a mixed blessing. This mention of children had a strange effect on Frances. *Will I be bearing a child by the time of my birthday?* The David, Joseph and Hart families would certainly be expecting it. And yet there were trepidations on her part. It wasn't only that her comfortable routines – light housework, the playing of the piano and singing for visitors – would be compromised. She remembered Catharine going through the agony of childbirth and then losing one of her sons to illness. Her sister-in-law was strong, already over thirty, so she had survived the ordeal. *My body may not be that strong.*

* * *

Though the sun had yet to set, an array of candles throughout the synagogue on Rue Chenneville was lit in anticipation of an early dusk implicit in it being the first week of January. Frances had her place of honor. She was queen for a day, seated on a throne-like chair surrounded by family and friends. She had already been "identified" by Theodore, who was obliged to lower the veil over her face once he had satisfied himself that he had the right woman. The groom, along with Aaron Hart David, acting on behalf of her deceased father, and Benjamin Hart, representing Theodore, had entered the room to do the veiling after having signed the marriage contract and being toasted by all the men assembled in a separate space. Frances could feel her pulse racing; she hadn't seen her Theo for a week, the custom strictly adhered to.

There was no serious thought to holding the ceremony outdoors, January not being conducive to such viewing of "the stars of the heavens" while being ushered into matrimony. Instead, the couple gathered under the canopy in the synagogue itself. Theodore, accompanied by his parents, had already moved under the *chuppah* when Frances was signaled to join him there. She was silently amused at the sight of her intended. He wore a white robe – a *kittel* – to signify that life was commencing anew with a clean slate. *Customs must be respected.* She had to circle the groom seven times in tandem with Catharine and with Harriot Hart while Theodore repeated a prayer. Frances had been told that the seven turns symbolized the days of creation and that they promised a future household in which love and protection would be paramount.

It is all too bizarre! Frances tried to concentrate on the mahogany ark and the Ten Commandments carved in white marble; it was all part of a synagogue done in the Egyptian style. She found it odd that she was but a few feet from a man almost as young as herself. David Piza, officiating this afternoon, had ingratiated himself with the few Jewish families in Montreal. She almost grinned when he began the service.

The rabbi proffered a full cup of wine (*my cup runneth over*) prior to the groom placing a plain gold ring on her finger. Theodore recited the proper words: "Behold you are betrothed to me with this ring, according to the Law of Moses and Israel." The *ketuvah* was read aloud and handed to Frances – her protection against widowhood or desertion.

Piza then recited the seven blessings while the wine was drunk. Theodore was careful to stamp on a glass in a way that the chards caused no damage. They were now free to enter the locked room of privacy (the *cheder yichud*) to demonstrate that chastity was no longer required. They could hear the *mazeltov's* shouted outside the door, the sound of music as the feasting began. Frances was tired, not having eaten all day. Sustenance overruled a lingering of the kissing. There would be time for more of that.

They unlocked the door and were given due notice from the band, the lead musician announcing the arrival of Mr. and Mrs. Hart. Family and friends began dancing and performing around the bride and groom. Frances was almost giddy at this point. For the next couple of hours she had little memory of what was happening about them. Snippets of conversation (Sir Charles Bagot had arrived in Montreal and was leaving any day now for Kingston), embraces from her two sisters, handshakes from her new father-in-law (Benjamin Hart was not the smiling type) and glances from Theodore (was he hinting that they leave early?)

*   *   *

The big house on Rue des Récollets intimidated Frances. Or was it the dominating presence of Harriot Hart, the matron who took her rank very seriously? Hardly had Frances David Hart accommodated herself to being part of a new household when she learned that she was indeed pregnant. Today was the middle of June and she barely was given the opportunity to enjoy the good weather. Harriot had almost ordered her to retire to her bed; no chance must be taken that would endanger the viability of the first possible grandchild to live under her roof. Frances couldn't insist on a different course; the pregnancy was proving to be difficult. Not only the anticipated morning sickness but also painful but unexplained complications. Even having Aaron Hart David brought back from Trois-Rivières to examine his sister brought no peace to the house of Benjamin Hart; the doctor only shook his head to signal his uncertainty. His sister had a delicate constitution.

Harriot hovered over her. The child would not be the first for the grandparents. Another Frances, Benjamin's and Harriot's oldest offspring, had married a Pittsburgh resident, Raphael Schoyer, several years before and had settled in New York City. Unfortunately, she had lost her two sons, Benjamin Hart and David Arthur, while they were in their infancy. This other Frances was also an accomplished musician (as well as a linguist) who had made quite a reputation among the Jewish members of the Spanish and Portuguese congregation in Manhattan. She was undaunted by her misfortunes.

Without doubt mother Harriot had become wary after these mishaps. No grandchildren extant! Aaron Philip Hart had yet to marry. Wellington had written from Liverpool that his Selena was pregnant albeit any imminent child would be an ocean away. Nothing must happen to her newest daughter-in-law.

Frances was also aware that every life was precious when the Jewish community totaled barely over fifty souls altogether. She remembered that in the previous August she had walked behind the Reverend Piza mourning the passing of Mrs. Isaac Valentine, the former Phoebe Hays, as he chanted the traditional prayers while proceeding to the Jewish burying ground. At the time Frances had offered condolences to the husband; Isaac Valentine had served as the spiritual leader of the community prior to the arrival of David Piza. Also visibly distressed was Moses Judah Hays, a justice of the peace and entrepreneur who was especially close to Benjamin Hart. Hays was not only a brother to the deceased but also Isaac Valentine's former business partner.

Theodore did not come home this day until after dusk despite the summer solstice being almost upon them. He apologized for his late arrival; much was happening downtown on Rue Notre-Dame and Rue Saint-Jacques. It wasn't only that the citizenry were still trying to interpret the latest decision by the new Governor. He had announced at the beginning of the month that Michael O'Sullivan, who had died a couple of years ago after being selected Chief Justice of Court of King's Bench for Montreal, was being replaced by none other than Joseph-Rémi Vallières de Saint-Réal, the maverick judge from Trois-Rivières. "Is Sir Charles mad? Papa is convinced that Vallières is a secret rebel pretending to be a legitimate member of the court."

"Aren't you being harsh on our new Governor? You once told me that Vallières is quite qualified as a jurist, being equally versed in French and English laws and languages."

Theodore hadn't counted on this dissent from his wife. "It is not his qualifications we quarrel with; he had made it plain only recently that he opposes the union of Canada East and West. I think I see where Bagot is going: appointing a Canadian to the post should reduce the French opposition to the union. As papa says, however: it may turn out to be a betrayal of the business people who have fought so long to reform our government."

Frances guessed that father and son were increasingly uneasy about the direction of the country despite the expressed commitment of the Governor and the Draper cabinet in Kingston to the Durham policy of "Anglification." Moreover, Theodore was still reacting to the news that the Peel administration had introduced a budget in Parliament in March that involved the imposition of an income tax on British subjects and a reduction in the tariff. *How will that affect trade between the colonies and the mother country?*

Frances, however, didn't want to argue the point. The humid air blowing in from the open window was making her sweat excessively. The pain in her extremities intensified. "Truly Theo, I'm not certain I want to hear again all these complaints about the malevolent French, whether they be in Quebec, Montreal or Three Rivers. I look forward to an early night."

"Actually I have good news from Three Rivers! Catharine gave birth to a daughter two days ago, on the 14th. So we welcome Sarah Matilda David to the family!"

Frances smiled weakly. *So Catharine did have her girl child. Hopefully my brother Aaron Hart David is as pleased as his wife with the result.*

It is on the principle of true equal justice that they intend to live with their brethren of Lower Canada, as the step they officially taken indicates. They elect Mr. Lafontaine to show, they say, their sympathy for the Lower Canadians and their detestation of the ill treatment and the injustices to which we have been exposed.

ÉTIENNE PARENT
(editorial in Le Canadien, September, 1841)

The means which Lord Sydenham had resorted to, in order to carry and complete the measure, may have been absolutely necessary – but they involved a public, and something very like a private quarrel on his part with the whole mass of the French Inhabitants of Lower Canada – and it would have been totally impossible for him ever again to conciliate them, or indeed ever again to have met, with any prospect of success, another Parliament in this Country.

GOVERNOR SIR CHARLES BAGOT
(letter to Lord Stanley, June 12, 1842)

Twenty six

*L*a Maison de Gannes had been unusually silent this evening. It being the beginning of summer, Joseph-Rémi Vallières accepted the fact that wife Jane chose to use the last hours of daylight to visit a neighbor and that the other dependents in the household were also escaping the stuffiness of the dwelling's interior. Actually, Vallières welcomed some solitude; the nearly unprecedented attention being given to him since it became public that he would be filling in as Chief Justice in Montreal had strained his already precarious stamina.

The relative solitude didn't last for too long; Vallières had an unexpected visitor. Étienne Parent first apologized for intruding on a man's privacy after the supper hour but noted that he was taking the early morning steamer to Montreal. "We must consult. I've just come from the celebration of Saint-Jean-Baptiste Day that was quite an experience and I'm on my way to meet with La Fontaine."

This declaration – almost a yell – was made with surprising vehemence until Vallières remembered that Parent had a hearing problem brought on his imprisonment in Quebec during the winter of 1839. His pitch was accordingly elevated. Nevertheless, Parent seemingly hadn't let his partial deafness bother him that much. After standing as a candidate for the riding of Saguenay county, which he won by a majority of three votes in May, 1841, he had spent part of that summer participating in the new Parliament in Kingston.

The guest was directed to a chair in the parlor and Vallières called out for a servant to bring tea. "Tell me why the *Québecois* are marking Saint-Jean-Baptiste Day as a political event after so many years of ignoring its pertinence!"

"The Bishop had a hand in organizing it. *Monsignor* Signay allowed a procession to the cathedral with a civic band in the lead. The *Musique Canadienne* also played songs at the ensuing banquet. Quite a boost to our spirits!"

"And you spoke at the banquet? My guess is that La Fontaine's name got mentioned."

Parent smiled. "As was yours, *mon ami*. You have not been forgotten even though you left the town more than a decade ago. La Fontaine will be pleased that our people are rallying to a symbol of our national identity. Perhaps Lord Stanley will be even more cooperative as a consequence. He is well aware of how disaffected we *Canadiens* are."

"Have you not heard? Bagot will be naming Day to the Court of Queen's Bench tomorrow. The Governor is determined not to offend the Tories by promoting me without also a bow to *les Anglais*. Baldwin and his friends in York will not be happy that it is to be Mr. Day of all people." Vallières smiled wryly; Charles Dewey Day, the deputy judge advocate trying the *Patriote* insurrectionists just three years ago, was Solicitor General in Canada West after having been elected to represent Ottawa County in the Parliament.

Parent shifted his massive head, which served to accent a sturdy neck and ample shoulders. "Notwithstanding that, becoming the first *Canadien* to hold a chief justiceship, your appointment will inevitably have the effect of reducing opposition in *Bas-Canada* to the union. Even Neilson and Viger are applauding the selection. It has been written that you are a man of genius who for twelve years has shone under a bushel. Apparently the powers that be in London want to bring the light upon you."

Vallières had presumed that the Colonial Secretary approved of the Governor bestowing the honor on him. "That may be. Does that not mean Lord Stanley is seeking greater harmony consistent with maintaining the domination of *les Anglais* in policy matters? You once railed against union in the pages of *Le Canadien*. Recently the editorials are more favorable to the concept. So you too seek greater harmony."

"The union, *mon ami*, is a *fait accompli*. Like La Fontaine, I argue that the greatest possible advantage ought to be taken of it. True, there must be equality of the two populations and the two countries, and I spoke to that goal in Kingston. French was not recognized as an official language, a situation I strongly opposed during the session."

Vallières poured the tea. "You are being heard. Furthermore, your replacement on Le Canadien is also being widely noticed. Who is this fellow Cauchon?"

"Joseph-Édouard is not only a law student but also an author. A handbook on science and pedagogy. He likes journalism and I am satisfied that he will keep the faith."

This reply was acceptable, but Vallières did wonder if there was more than a single faith in the ranks of the Patriotes. The suppression of the insurgency had been most traumatic. But it did appear that the La Fontaine position would prevail.

Parent put down his teacup. "Will you be moving to Montreal soon?"

"It may not be easy to do. My leg pains are so severe that I shall need assistance. And yet I must get there eventually if I am to serve on the Bench."

"Any regrets? You have been in Trois-Rivières what is it, a dozen years. A comfortable house, links to the community. Is Montreal that attractive?"

"To be precise, it is thirteen years since I arrived here. I leave Trois-Rivières knowing that Dominique once more presides over our courtroom. At least there will be continuity in the administration of justice here." Vallières had reconciled himself to having Dominique Mondelet substitute for him as the local judge on the Court of Queen's Bench. When the initial appointment was made almost exactly three years before, those sympathizing with the Patriotes cause had been hostile to having a former member of the Special Council and a deputy judge advocate come to Trois-Rivières to provide service to the administration. Once he had been restored to his post, Vallières softened his attitude to the man and had raised no objections to Mondelet's permanent appointment to the court concurrent with Vallières own elevation.

Parent got up to leave. "Let us hope that your health allows you to travel. Incidentally, you may be surprised to find Duvernay in Montreal. With La Fontaine's collaboration, he has returned home from Vermont and is resurrecting La Minerve."

* * *

Ludger Duvernay glanced up to examine Vallières as the latter leaned heavily on a cane while seeking out a chair next to the office desk. The editor of La Minerve had been forewarned that the new Chief Justice was not in the best of health. This inspection was short; he jumped up from his own place to provide some assistance in having Vallières seated.

Vallières now had his first opportunity to gaze intently at his host, who as fate would have it he hadn't seen for many years. Duvernay was still in his early forties but it was evident to Vallières that the gossip was correct: excessive drinking had taken its toll on the man's health. *But I must be circumspect.* "Is Montreal the same as you remembered it before you left the province? Other exiles have commented to me on how difficult it has been to adjust. *Bien sûr,* not all of them have been fortunate in reclaiming citizenship. *Monsieur* Papineau is still in Paris."

"It has not been easy. My old friend Wolfred Nelson is leaving Plattsburgh shortly to set up a medical practice here in Montreal. La Fontaine has been on his case since the expulsions. Even offered to adopt one of his children while Nelson was away in Bermuda. Meanwhile our new Governor grows more lenient. There is no possibility of us exiles fulfilling our original dreams. The Webster-Ashburton Treaty signed last week means that the dispute on the Maine-New Brunswick border will not escalate into hostilities. Meanwhile, we ought to be grateful that the agreement is bringing to an end the slave trade on the high seas. I intend to comment on that subject."

"Your pen will lend weight to those of us who still grieve that there has been no independent voice in the public domain. With Canada East not carrying its proper weight in Parliament, we need *La Minerve* to rally our forces. Our deputies in Kingston should welcome your input. Yet *Monsieur* Draper, who has become Bagot's chief Canadian adviser in Kingston, shows little sympathy for the disproportion of *Canadiens* in the Parliament. Perhaps you too will decide to run for office." Vallières realized that as a jurist he himself could not play a direct role in this struggle, but he could encourage others like Duvernay to participate.

Duvernay smiled but at the same shook his head. "I am out of politics; no thought of campaigning for the chance to go to Kingston. I'll be here at the corner of Rue Sainte-Vincent and Rue Sainte-Thérèse for the foreseeable future. We begin printing next month and I'll be concentrating on making *La Minerve* once again the most important and influential French paper in Montreal. No more printing of books and other materials that only distract me from my mission. Incidentally, my plan is to use the paper to raise funds for the return of the *Patriotes* exiled to Bermuda and Australia."

"I saw Parent in Trois-Rivières at the end of June. He sees great possibilities in promoting Saint-Jean-Baptiste Day as a national holiday. You once had a major role in doing that not too long ago." Vallières recalled Duvernay's initiative in organizing a Saint-Jean-Baptiste banquet on June 24 eight years before.

Duvernay appreciated the compliment. "I did think that I set a precedent, though the subsequent troubles in *Bas-Canada* interrupted the chance to make it an annual event. If you recall, I was inspired by how our Irish compatriots celebrated their St Patrick's Day in '34. They put *Canadiens* to shame parading in March weather without regret. I convinced John McDonnell to lend us his garden for a June banquet commemorating our own holiday. We had about sixty guests – including men such as La Fontaine, Jacques Viger and O'Callaghan. It was the first time that Cartier's song was performed in public."

Vallières did recall the event. George-Étienne Cartier had gotten much attention even in Trois-Rivières for this composition. *O Canada! Mon pays, mes amours* was well on its way becoming folklore during these intervening years even though Cartier himself was no more than a successful lawyer since the end of the insurrection. "The man has a talent with words. I anticipate having him appear before me in the coming years."

"And you should also hear more about the holiday. My intention is to reorganize the Saint-Jean-Baptiste Society. Cartier would make an excellent secretary."

It was Vallières' turn to smile. He had come to call on Duvernay with the hope that the man's misfortunes had not destroyed his will to engage in political combat. Everything Duvernay was saying suggested that was not the case.

* * *

The pain was intensifying despite his decision to rest on the cot in his chambers. *It will be another lost day for me on the Bench.* Vallières was looking forward to finishing the assizes that weren't due to be over until a month or so. He had missed too many court appearances because of his condition. *But enough is enough!*

A knock on the door was accordingly unwelcome. He had advised his clerk that he wished not to be disturbed. But he could hardly ignore this interruption when supposedly on duty.

It was indeed the clerk standing at the threshold. "You have a caller who has just arrived from Kingston. He insists that you will speak to him, my objections notwithstanding."

Before Vallières could reiterate his need for a respite, the visitor pushed the clerk aside and approached the bedside. "Joseph-Rémi, *c'est moi*, Barthe."

"Hello, Joseph-Guillaume. You call at a most embarrassing time. I am not at my best."

"*Excusez-moi de tu déranger*. I should have known better." Vallières could detect the dismay in Barthe's expression. The young man had previously stated publicly that the judge was a shadow of himself when he left Trois-Rivières. *What would he be saying now to others?*

"But you are here, *mon ami*. I thought you would be away for longer."

"I have come straight from Kingston. Did you know that the Governor has asked La Fontaine to form a cabinet in collaboration with Baldwin?"

Vallières almost forgot his pain at that moment. The unexpected had happened. He ought to have guessed that Bagot would be willing to relent in the *de facto* exclusion of *Canadiens* from political power. He had already shown conciliation by appointing Francis Hincks as inspector general of public accounts. This had brought some of the moderate reformers on side albeit the Executive Council was still unpopular not only with the Tories but also with the francophone contingent in the assembly. Apparently the bringing in of La Fontaine to the leadership would change the balance of power. "Are you pleased by this development?"

"It is a trick. Appointing La Fontaine to the post is meant to undermine the influence of Viger and Neilson. And we shall see Drummond, his lieutenant, take full advantage of this promotion."

Vallières thought he understood this counter-intuitive reaction. Barthe was passionate in his loyalties and he was still young. The two men had had an intimate relationship ever since Barthe appeared in Trois-Rivières as a precocious student. Vallières remembered in particular their joint trip to Montreal during the prosecution of several insurgents in the autumn of 1839. Barthe was then basking in popular acclaim because he had served three months in the *Trifluvien* jail during the previous winter. It probably accounted for his subsequent electoral victory in Yamaska. And being in Kingston threw him into the company of his new mentor. Denis-Benjamin Viger had entered the new Parliament as the member for Richelieu. Vallières was subsequently told that Barthe was quick to support Viger whenever the latter clashed horns with La Fontaine and the so-called Reformers representing Canada East. "Now that you are back in Montreal, how will you handle this new situation?"

"I will admit, *mon ami*, that I am here to use my publication to oppose Drummond's bid to control the municipal elections coming later this year. *Monsieur* La Fontaine has chosen the Irishman to handle patronage in Montreal." Barthe was indeed accepting a new challenge. The Montreal's city council, originally appointed by Lord Sydenham, was scheduled to be replaced in December by an elected body. "Is it a battle you can win? For

Thomas Drummond is without doubt an effective orator both in English and in French. It has been mentioned by Cauchon in *Le Canadien* that he combines the Irish richness of imagination with the cold reason of the German."

"I shall have Denis-Benjamin on my side."

"You are thick with Viger." Vallières was stating the obvious.

"Why should I not be? Two years ago he made me editor of *L'Aurore des Canadas*. It will be interesting times. La Fontaine now has *La Minerve* backing him. I do have concerns. Can I be heard when all our people will be praising the man as one who has won a great victory?"

PART FOUR

Impediment
1842-45

I further beg leave to congratulate you and Mr. Baldwin on your recent appointments, which have propped up the drooping spirits of the English Canadians by hopes of seeing better Laws... I have to offer my zealous support if I am called to a seat in either of the Councils.
MOSES HART
(letter to Louis-Hippolyte La Fontaine, October 2, 1842)

I do not mean to blame you for the step you have taken; on the contrary, I believe it to have been inevitable and that sooner or later it would have been found necessary to admit the leaders of the French party to a share in the government.
LORD STANLEY
(letter to Governor Bagot, November 3, 1842)

Twenty seven

The Steamship Hart had eased into Montreal's harbor before Alexander Thomas Hart left the bridge for the Captain's quarters. He required a quick washing and a change of clothes before going on shore. It was mid-September and the day's heat had made him feeling distinctly uncomfortable. The stench of excessive sweat would not do when he joined the celebration.

Tomorrow was the Day of Atonement; although Alexander had never taken the Jewish religion seriously, he felt an obligation to participate in the ritual. In fact, this evening the congregation would be gathering at the synagogue albeit the prayers should be over at half past nine at the latest. His father, being a Deist, had no commitment to celebrating Yom Kippur as the highest of holidays. There had been no mother in the home to insist on orthodoxy. "Aleck" expected to view the gathering with much detachment. But first he must eat because no food would be available during the fasting.

The evening meal, scheduled to be consumed before dusk, brought Aleck to the same table as his Uncle Benjamin and family. Alexander didn't look forward to it. Harriot Hart insisted on needling her *Trifluvien* guest about the lack of religion in his daily life. "Surely Miriam must lament missing this chance to pray with her kin on such an important occasion."

He hadn't brought Miriam to Montreal, she being in her sixth month of pregnancy and not taking travel, even boat travel, very well. Besides, there was their child, Moses Alexander, to consider. Now a toddler, the boy needed a mother's care. He had to admit, however, that his wife, a Judah living for decades in New York, would have welcomed being part of the observances.

Poor Miriam! They had been married for almost two years. Though never absent from New York City until after the wedding, she had come to regret life in Trois-Rivières. Living with old Moses Hart was not always easy but she had made her peace with Mary McCarthy – known elsewhere as Mary Brown – even if Miriam didn't have the independence that would have accrued to being mistress of the house on Rue Alexandre.

The walk to the synagogue was accomplished with minimal loss of time. Even so, the sun was setting behind the mountain as the Hart party arrived at the place of worship. Alexander put on a *kippa* as he stepped through the entrance.

The prayers were finally concluded at about the hour Alexander anticipated and he then had the opportunity to shake hands with members of the congregation. He knew most of the men – Theodore Hart, Isaac Valentine and Abraham Joseph in particular – but it was the first time he met the *chazzan*, David Piza. The Reverend had not done Moses Alexander's circumcision last year.

Walking back to his uncle's place, Alexander encountered his first questioning on secular subjects. Benjamin showed some interest in the shipping business. "How much freight does the *Hart* carry? I realize that it has an engine with a horsepower of 45 and therefore more efficient than your *Toronto* boat. I am told, however, that Munn plans to build a much better steamer in Quebec. Says he is going to call it the *Rowland Hill*."

"Munn is but one of my problems. There are over fifty steamships plying the St Lawrence. Ira Craig and I have more than enough competition." Alexander and his father had often discussed the prospects for the shipping industry and the Scottish-born John Munn was very much on their mind. He had been manufacturing saddle steamboats at Quebec's waterfront for a quarter century and was known as a master craftsman. The *Rowland Hill* would undoubtedly impact negatively on both the passenger and freight traffic the *Hart* could expect.

Benjamin quickly changed the discussion to what was transpiring in Kingston. "You may not have heard that La Fontaine will be called to the Executive Council in a matter of days. Can you believe that as a magistrate I would have arrested that man back in '37 if he had not skipped the country that December? He was more anticlerical and republican than was Papineau at the time. Now we English merchants may be forced to bow to this man as the union's prime minister. If so, we will have failed in everything we fought for."

* * *

A chance meeting with Charles Richard Ogden outside the courthouse in Trois-Rivières confirmed for Alexander what Uncle Benjamin had stated but the month before. Everything the Tories had fought for was being regarded as being in some jeopardy. Ogden had come out of the chambers now occupied by Dominique Mondelet and was in a surly mood. Alexander was not particularly close to the Montreal lawyer and political heavyweight, but they were on speaking terms. (They had consulted when Alexander was in the process of buying woodlots in the south-shore parishes a few years before.) But Ogden could be heard muttering to himself. Obviously his interaction with Trois-Rivières' sole jurist hadn't gone well. Once he focused on Alexander, Ogden did regain his composure. "Hart, isn't it? You catch me at a bad time."

"Is there anything I can do?" Alexander reacted to the man's discomfort in pretended ignorance.

"I've been in Trois-Rivières but a day. Yet already I have heard some disagreeable opinions from men who ought to know better."

"*Trifluviens* are a fickle lot."

"You are perfectly right, young man." Ogden had missed the facetiousness; he must have thought he had a kindred spirit in Alexander; he agreed that they repair to the local inn on Rue du Fleuve for an afternoon libation.

They walked quickly to the riverside; there was a decided nip in the air, which was not unusual for the middle of October. Once there they settled themselves at a corner table, they quaffed some of the ale delivered by a waiter.

Ogden's tale of woe unfolded. He had left the province the previous autumn as the Attorney General of Canada East as well as the sitting member for Trois-Rivières. But having returned from London he had discovered that La Fontaine had displaced him in his cabinet. He had counted on the previous Draper administration to protect his position. Instead he had been ousted in absentia and no government pension was offered as compensation. The £1500 salary he was getting as a member of the Parliament was hardly adequate for his family. He and the former Susan Clarke had four sons and a daughter below the age of puberty. "The union was meant to facilitate the integration of the French into the Empire. Giving government responsibility to ex-insurgents works against that policy."

Alexander grunted. "My father has a less jaundiced view of this matter. He has written to La Fontaine to offer his services. As you are well aware, he has a low opinion of the justice system here. La Fontaine promises reform and that encourages him. My father would like nothing better than to be appointed either to the Legislative Council or, better yet, the Executive Council. He points to his ranking as one of the largest landowners in the St Lawrence valley."

"Moses Hart is dreaming. He has no public support for such an ambition. Has never won an election despite his trying several times." Ogden was almost sneering in his response.

Alexander avoided answering immediately to what he regarded as an insult of his father. *Why am I so quiet? Perhaps I too consider papa's obsession with public acclaim as being foolish?* He drained his glass and then stared at his interlocutor. "So tell me, what are *your* options?"

"I have little choice but to sail again for England. Once there I may win reinstatement. Lord Lyndhurst could use his influence with the Mr. Peel and the Colonial Office." Ogden was referring to the Lord Chancellor who happened to be related to his wife. Alexander had never met her – she almost never accompanied Ogden on his frequent sojourns in Trois-Rivières – but it was well known that there was a connection between the Montreal lawyer and John Copley, the perennial Tory choice for the top legal position in Britain. The barony came with the job.

Alexander was dubious. Governor Bagot had risked much to elevate La Fontaine. Would he be persuaded to reverse course because Lyndhurst wanted a favor for a distant relative? "And if you fail in this effort, can we expect you to be satisfied with rebuilding your legal practice in Montreal?"

Ogden shook his head. "Rebuilding is the right word. I have had great difficulty serving clients because first I was stuck in Kingston for months and then I took that leave to go to England for a year. Many merchants have gone elsewhere. Being in my fifties, I am not inclined to start over again."

Walking back to the house on Rue Alexandre, Alexander was struck by consequences of a single political decision made by the Governor. Ogden had been a fixture in Trois-Rivières politics for almost thirty years. He had won every election held in the riding even after moving his law practice to Montreal. (The one absence from the Assembly occurred in 1824 while he was in London getting married to his first wife.) Eventually he became the province's Attorney General and a confidante of successive Governors. *Who would have thought that he is being forsaken by the powers that be?* In contrast, Moses Hart, his father, has long been an outsider who still dreamed of being acknowledged by the Crown. Undoubtedly, the Harts had to be grateful that they owned land. Alexander could see no future beyond that.

*   *   *

It was during a sailing near the end of the season that Alexander encountered a bearded man on the deck of the *Hart*. Beards were only now coming into fashion though most of the Hart family and associates were clean-shaven. What startled Alexander most, however, was the greeting. "Aleck! Don't you know me? It's Henry."

It was in fact one of Alexander's half-brothers. Hirsute but gaunt. Alexander would never have recognized him at first sight; they hadn't set eyes on each other for almost fifteen years. Henry Hart was but a few years his junior and had migrated to the fur country in the American west in 1829. The separation had not been without rancor but Alexander had long since dismissed from his mind the various quarrels that had occurred during the '20s.

Nevertheless, there was no spontaneous embrace. Alexander excused himself. He was on duty; his presence on the bridge was being anticipated. They could meet again later in the day when he expected to be in the Captain's quarters. "It has been a long time, Henry. Is your wife here as well?"

"No, Aleck. She wanted so much to meet the family but we couldn't afford two fares. Benjamin also sends word; he wishes to be remembered by our papa." Henry retreated, reading Alexander's unwillingness to engage at that moment.

Alexander realized that the encounter had shaken him. He had had a hand in pointing these two offspring of Moses Hart into near exile. Benjamin and Henry had obviously survived their life in the wilds. The very occasional communication with them confirmed that outcome. The last he knew, Henry was living in St Louis and had on occasion spent time as a trader in New Orleans. Benjamin Moses also married and had a son called Henry. His other brother too had ventured over the years into the wilderness --to the Rocky Mountains and the Spanish territory on their perimeter. *A perilous existence but thank God they are alive!*

Henry did arrive below deck as requested. Alexander had already arranged that they would eat alone. He was now much more in control of his emotions. It was not before they had partaken of the prepared supper that he began enquiring about life in the West. "I was shown a letter you wrote when you stopped off at Prairie du Chien in '29 before going down the Mississippi to St Louis. You had signed up with the American Fur Company and submitted to Jacob Astor being your master. I remember you being were very fearful of the savages living up the Missouri."

Henry smiled. "I remember writing that letter. It was not the best of times for me. Traveling day and night, sleeping on the ground for no more than a couple of hours at a time, sick with fever during part of the trip, worrying about the danger from Indian attack when it became necessary to proceed up the Missouri to winter quarters. I certainly did regret being persuaded to sign up for three years at half the pay I was getting at home."

"But you did get beyond Wisconsin without mishap?"

"It so happened that I was in Prairie du Chien at the same time as a delegation from Washington arrived there to sign the treaty with the Council of Three Fires. It got the United States possession of land in northwestern Illinois and southwestern Wisconsin Territory. All the way from the Mississippi river to Chicago."

"The Council of Three Fires?" Alexander was perplexed.

"The united tribes of the Chippewa, Ottawa and Potawatomi Indians. My concern was with the Plains tribes - the Sioux, the Cheyenne, the Arapaho - roaming the shores of the Missouri river and its tributaries."

"And yet you survived the three years."

"The Rocky Mountains are indeed wild and ambushes and other acts of violence were evident all around me. I was very lucky; never was I injured dealing with the Indians. There was much contact with them for after two years I was no longer just a common hand. My education and good behavior resulted in my becoming a clerk and being treated as a gentleman." Henry sounded boastful.

"But you didn't stay with the American Fur Company, did you? Papa received another of your letters from St Louis. You decided to do your own trading. That didn't work out too well, did it?" Alexander couldn't resist pricking Henry's balloon.

Henry's face darkened. "Not as well as it ought to have. I never did have a letter from you, Aleck, even though I sent you greetings on occasion in my letters home. Areli too never took notice of me. You, Aleck, were always on my back. Called me lazy because I hated school. It was true that I preferred playing the pianoforte instead of reading but I did work diligently for papa when given the chance. I don't know why I was talked into leaving Three Rivers to travel almost two thousand leagues into Indian country. My health has not been good lately but I did make a life for myself."

*The Councillors have made no pretensions rendering necessary
a counter exposition of principles, and it can almost be
supposed that the unreasonable declarations previously made
by some of them have been abandoned. I am not sure, however,
and although I see no reason to anticipate an immediate rupture,
I feel that it can happen any date.*
GOVERNOR SIR CHARLES METCALFE
(letter to Lord Stanley, June 25, 1843)

*In a colony subordinate to an Imperial Government, it may happen
that the predominant party is hostile in its feelings to the mother country,
or has ulterior views inconsistent with her interests. In such a case,
to be obliged to cooperate with that party, and to permit party
government to crush those who are best effected, would be a strange
position for the mother country to be placed in, and a strange part
for her to act...It is now, perhaps, too late to remedy the evil.*
GOVERNOR SIR CHARLES METCALFE
(letter to Lord Stanley, August 5, 1843)

Twenty eight

Ludger Duvernay drained the last bit of brandy from the glass on his desk. The time had come to get out of his chair and dress for Montreal's outdoors. Not that he was pleased with the prospect; there was very little light from the window facing Rue Sainte-Thérèse; it had begun snowing. *We have had more than our share of snow this February.* However, he had promised to call on Augustin-Norbert Morin at noon.

It had been a very hectic winter. The aftermath of the December's municipal elections was still having an effect on Duvernay's schedule. Drummond, acting on behalf of La Fontaine, had had a setback in his bid to control the local government. The Reformers had won the overall vote but Drummond himself was defeated at the polls. William Molson, the incumbent city councilor, had rallied enough Anglophones to deprive La Fontaine's party of total victory. All through January Duvernay had to collaborate with the Irish lawyer to help reverse the results of the linguistic divide.

There were other issues; this morning he had finally drafted an editorial for *La Minerve* that praised the progress La Fontaine was making in establishing the principle of ministerial responsibility in the governing of the united Canada. He felt obliged to have Morin review it, La Fontaine's lanky confidant having the authority to act for the Reformers.

Morin had seemingly exempted himself from politics a year before when he resigned from Parliament and became a judge for the districts of Kamorouska, Rimouski and Saint-Thomas. Governor Bagot, however, had prevailed on him to come into the Executive Council. Morin could have been selected as its clerk (Étienne Parent took the post instead) but Morin pressed the La Fontaine-Baldwin government to let him become rather the commissioner of Crown lands.

He did have to procure the Saguenay seat in the legislature to make that possible. Duvernay gave him the support of *La Minerve* for such an endeavor. It was no accident that the journal, which had become the most influential French-language in the province, helped make Morin's election in Saguenay easily accomplished.

The walk to Morin's quarters did not take that long but even so Duvernay had to brush off his cloak and wipe his shoes to rid himself of an accumulation of snow once he arrived. Morin took note of this modicum of distress. "Come over to the fireplace! You'll dry off soon."

"Before I catch a cold."

"It hasn't been a good day for me either, Ludger. My rheumatism always acts up in wet weather. But we couldn't postpone our *tête-à-tête*. I leave tomorrow for Saint-Hyacinthe. As you already know, I am marrying Adèle on the last day of the month." Morin had been courting Adèle Raymond, the daughter of the superior of the seminary in Saint-Hyacinthe.

"La Fontaine lets you take time off for personal business?" Duvernay was being facetious.

"Not for long. You know that I take my new responsibilities seriously. I have already mentioned that my plan is to purchase property north of the city to advance agriculture in Canada East. I'm excited about the prospects. The land can be used to cultivate not only potatoes but also grape vines. There are other possibilities: stock breeding, crop rotation, maple-syrup production. I am counting on you accepting reports on my experiments for publication in *La Minerve*."

Duvernay had let him go on, but now was not the time to expand on the subject. "I won't disappoint you, *mon ami*. But we do have to concentrate on current affairs. Our readers wish to know how the new government will stand up to the onslaught from Molson and the other Tories now that Bagot has resigned and a new Governor is on his way to Kingston."

"Were you at young Molson's funeral?" Morin's question was direct if also a non sequitor.

"I admit I didn't attend. I sent one of my men."

"Worried about catching the pox or being found in a Protestant chapel?" William Molson Junior had died of smallpox in January. The funeral took place at the Episcopalian St Thomas Church that William Molson Senior and his brother Thomas had just constructed.

Duvernay frowned. "You are joking. Be serious! I'm more worried about what is London's response to La Fontaine's current status. Lord Stanley has yet to confirm that there is now a different attitude at Whitehall. The new British Governor may have been instructed not to concede responsible government. Bagot, a dying man, is in no position to argue otherwise. This fellow Metcalfe may have been able to handle antagonisms in Jamaica but Canada's trials may prove to be beyond him."

"And that is why you wrote your editorial, Ludger. Let me see it!"

* * *

The public conveyance hadn't suited Duvernay at all. He could, if he chose, blame the condition of the main road leading into Kingston; there were still remnants of the blackened icy piles that reminded him of the alternating snow and slush characteristic of the recent months. It was already May and the weather had yet to be classified as truly spring-like.

In the last few hours he had begun to fret. An appointment had been arranged with the new Governor of the united Canadas. How would a member of the press be regarded if he failed to show up on time? *I should have allowed an extra day for traveling.* To make matters more complicated, this Englishman he was due to interview was reportedly living not at Alwington House, the relatively new structure rented for the two previous Governors, but rather at a double house on King Street. Sir Charles Theophilus Metcalfe had assumed office at the end of March but his predecessor was still not out of the way. Duvernay couldn't help wondering how much contact there was between the new Governor and Bagot; the latter had remained at Alwington House, too ill to return to England.

Horse traffic along the town's King Street thickened and slowed the carriage's progress. The line of evergreens bordering the lakefront did remind any newcomer to the scene that in normal circumstances this bustling town had its natural attractions. The Kingston General Hospital, converted to function as the parliamentary building, was to his right. But at this moment access to government offices north of the edifice itself was yet to be negotiated. *Patience! Patience!*

In due time Duvernay reached his destination and moved swiftly up the stairs to the Governor's office. He checked his timepiece. He was already an hour late for his appointment. *No wonder there are others in the anteroom!* Indeed, there was the opportunity to inspect the two men already waiting. One was a thick-set, square-jawed man in his forties. Seated next to him was a man in his twenties with abundant red hair and a prominent nose. Duvernay enquired in English whether the two claimed precedence over a visitor from Montreal. The older of the two grunted. He was the town mayor – John Counter – and had no doubt that the Governor would recognize his own presence as soon as possible. "I am a busy man." Duvernay sighed inwardly. *Monsieur Counter is not sympathetic to Canadiens!*

Within fifteen minutes the office door opened, an aide appeared, and Counter was signaled to enter. Then the redhead – his Scottish burr quite pronounced – rose from his seat and introduced himself to Duvernay. "John MacDonald at your service. I was recently elected a city councilor. You have, I would guess, just arrived in Kingston. The weather is without doubt not ideal for such a visit."

Duvernay nodded. "Even with good weather it is an arduous task to travel from Montreal to here. That is but one reason why we *Canadiens* argue for a change of venue for the Parliament. Our merchants and lawyers also object to spending months away from their professional activities when Parliament meets. Kingston is like foreign territory to all of us."

MacDonald smiled knowingly. "The distance is great but Kingston is equally far from Toronto. That has been the price we pay for a united country. Our people have tried to make the hospital more hospitable (pardon the pun) by the renovations they made. Stables and outbuildings were built to house fuel and privies and the security fences were also enhanced. We will be building a new city hall to supplement what we have now. There is already enough space in the old hospital to accommodate the Legislative Assembly and the Legislative Council but we do need room to house more officials and their assistants."

"It's not that simple. Accommodations are only part of problem. Canada East has been shortchanged by the union as it exists today." Duvernay decided to be forthright speaking to this Scotsman.

"You are on dangerous ground, sir! I will admit that Bagot relieved the concern of the French that they were being excluded from office. But the distribution of patronage that has followed goes beyond what was intended. Metcalfe is the representative of the Crown and charged with strengthening the ties between the Canadas and the Empire – not accepting more independence for the French element. Let me be frank! We have in fact been most displeased with our previous Governor. We have called him

Granny Bagot, one who dared to bow to the likes of La Fontaine, Hincks and their cohort. Our fear was that Bagot would have acceded to moving the capital to Montreal had he remained in office."

"And you believe that Metcalfe will ignore what the Parliament ultimately decides? For so young a man, you speak with much confidence. Am I right to suspect that are a member of the bar? But you have yet to hold public office." *I don't know how seriously to take this fellow.*

"Take it from me, sir, that I shall be heard in Parliament, whether here in Kingston or in Montreal. The voters in this district know me as a barrister who speaks for the public interest – even if I was born outside the country. I was in Scotland a year ago, my father having died is September '41 and I having family business to attend to there. This town's population has doubled in that time frame, which convinces me that Kingston will rival Toronto as a population center in Canada West."

Duvernay would have continued the conversation had not the aide reappeared in the anteroom. This time he explained that the Governor apologized for keeping the journalist from Montreal waiting. "He can give you a half hour of his time."

The introductions were limited to handshakes and a few pleasantries. Metcalfe was quite short in stature and certainly lacked a handsome face. Outdoors living had roughened the skin texture. Duvernay detected a sore on the man's right cheek. The disfigurement was not easily ignored. *Too much soldiering in India and other sub-tropic regions? The sun can be deadly!*

There had been no pre-agreement on the nature of the interview. Duvernay wanted most of all to get some indication from the new Governor what instructions he had received from Lord Stanley, the Colonial Minister. Would the new La Fontaine-Baldwin coalition gain support from London?

Metcalfe didn't hold back. "The members of the Executive Council seem dedicated to Mr. La Fontaine and Mr. Baldwin. They have used patronage to install what is essentially a cabinet loyal to the so-called Reformers rather than to the Crown. I have come to the conclusion that the Executive Council as currently constituted is hostile to my plans for good government."

"Does that mean that the Council's support for forsaking Kingston does not meet with your approval?"

"It is not that I oppose moving the capital of the union to Montreal. But I cannot agree that ignoring the wishes of the inhabitants of Canada West will result in the harmony we all desire."

"In other words, Your Excellency, you are departing from the policies put in place by your predecessor."

"I am, if anything, very persistent. You will not see me back down when I have determined what my duty is. You may not know that I shall be laying the cornerstone for the new city hall in Kingston within a week or two. Moreover, Lord Stanley has indicated that the reasons Baron Sydenham chose Kingston over Toronto and Montreal are still valid."

"May I say, Your Excellency, that your views will not be well received in Montreal and Quebec!" Duvernay could not hold back his dismay with what he was hearing.

"You must not forget, *Monsieur* Duvernay, that all citizens of Montreal and Quebec are subordinate to an Imperial authority. And I will exercise that authority for some time to come. I am not yet sixty and I will be moving into Alwington House within days."

Duvernay rose from his chair to indicate that he considered the interview over. There was much to think about. *Is Metcalfe declaring war on Canada East? Are we going back to the aftermath of the rebellion? Did I return to my native home too soon?*

Metcalfe had also gotten to his feet. "I wish to inform you that Sir Charles died this morning."

Duvernay realized that learning of Bagot's death would only increase his speculations.

*   *   *

The subdued rays of the June sun illuminating the Place d'Youville also revealed to Duvernay the men crowding the entrance to the trading hall of the Marché Sainte-Anne. He had decided to walk to the conference room rented for the occasion. He ought to have been there earlier; after all, he had organized this meeting, which he was counting on leading to the setting up of the Association Saint-Jean-Baptiste. But he had been at deadline for the current issue of *La Minerve*. The printer was demanding the last corrections to the proofs.

Morin had spotted his approach and advanced towards him. The greeting was tinged with some anxiety. Duvernay guessed that Morin was worried that he had been drinking. "Sorry for being late. It couldn't be helped. But it does look like a good turnout."

"An excellent response, Ludger. You have done your work well."

"Montreal is indeed the natural place to celebrate our distinctive identity." Duvernay issued a reflective smile. The *société* that he had championed for months would be the culmination of his efforts to reorganize *Canadien* sentiment for a national holiday.

It took some time for the conference room to fill up. Most of the audience was in shirtsleeves, the weather having warmed considerably though official summer was a couple of weeks away. There was much gaiety, much shuffling of chairs, much spontaneous singing. Duvernay worked his way to the head of the long table that lined one of the walls. *And to think that I was resigned to living out the rest of my life in Vermont!*

He had prepared his remarks carefully; there would be allusion to the impending meeting of the Parliament in September. Would the popular pressure for transferring governance from Kingston to Montreal succeed in overcoming the reluctance of the British overlords to act otherwise? When he was in Kingston the previous month, Duvernay had touted the virtues of the Marché Sainte-Anne as the alternative site. He repeated the proposal for the benefit of his audience. "If Governor Metcalfe wants *Canadien* acceptance of the fledgling union, he must abide by the will of the people." The audience greeted that argument with unrestrained enthusiasm. (As for Duvernay, there was no mention of the Governor's animus towards the Reformers in the Executive Council.)

The sun had set by the time Duvernay emerged from the meeting. The gas lamps on Place d'Youville had been lit for the night.

*I regret extremely to be compelled to call the attention of the President
and trustees of the Congregation of Shearith Israel of Montreal to the
singular and most extraordinary course of conduct adopted relative
to the legal proceedings which at times have been necessarily connected
with the existence of the Congregation of Israelites in this City.*
AARON PHILIP HART
(letter to Benjamin Hart, May 14, 1840)

*It is with deep regret that I have to communicate to you
the sad intelligence of the death of my father, Ezekiel Hart, Esquire,
seignor of Bécancour, aged seventy-three who departed
his life on Saturday last (16th). I take the liberty of mentioning
this to you, as I believe you were one of my father's dearest friends,
as I may judge from the many times he has mentioned
your name as of his earliest acquaintances in Canada.*
AARON EZEKIEL HART
(letter to John Neilson, September 18, 1843)

Twenty nine

A aron Ezekiel Hart glanced about the room he had rented in one of
the downtown inns in Montreal. *This will have to do!* As a barrister he
occasionally had reason to travel upriver from Trois-Rivières to represent a
client. This day would be unusual in that it had a different purpose: legal
practitioners had picked this weekend in June to gather for the purpose of
organizing a bar association. For Aaron Ezekiel the day was also different in
that it marked his fortieth birthday anniversary. Facing a mirror set over a
side table, he mused at his reflection; the years had taken their toll.

There was no time to tarry. The meeting at the Marché Sainte-Anne was
scheduled for two o'clock. Once he changed into his best attire, Aaron Ezekiel
proceeded along Rue Saint-Pierre to the Place d'Youville with dispatch.
Entering the conference room earmarked for the meeting, he realized that
very few vacant seats were available to him. Nevertheless, he was pleased to
note that some of the city's most prominent attorneys-at-law were on the dais,
Louis-Hippolyte La Fontaine and George-Étienne Cartier among them.

All eyes were on La Fontaine, who, after all, was a leader in the Executive Council. He didn't speak until near the end of the session but there was no equivocation. "What is needed is legislation to incorporate the Bar so as to give us autonomy from the Crown. We should be seeking complete control over admission to the study and practice of law."

The applause was vigorous albeit Aaron Ezekiel wondered about the practicality of getting the state and the judiciary to accede to surrendering their freedom of action. In fact, there was as yet no motion to accept such a measure.

Once a strike of the gavel brought an end to the proceedings, the lawyers broke off into groups still discussing what the various speakers had offered. Aaron Ezekiel had an immediate purpose; he had earlier spotted his cousin sitting in the front row. *I must pay my respects.*

Aaron Philip was engaged in heated conversation with a fellow counselor when Aaron Ezekiel put his hand on his cousin's shoulder. The response was gratifying. Though they had not been corresponding for some time, the eldest son of Benjamin Hart greeted the intrusion with some alacrity. He quickly broke off his involvement with a fellow lawyer and proposed that the two cousins repair to a nearby *auberge*. "I can use a drink right now."

Not until they were seated in the drinking establishment did Aaron Ezekiel recognize that his near namesake, albeit the younger man by eight years, showed signs of dissipation. *Has alcohol become his curse?*

"You haven't called on me, Eze, for ages. No more reasons to visit our fair city?"

"The last time I came up to Montreal it was to use the advocates' library. Without it what would I do to access the proper law books?" Aaron Ezekiel had been relying on the pooled resources of judges and lawyers that had been established five years before.

"You aren't fooling me, Eze. As you already know, I have not been on good terms with my immediate family for some time. It wasn't only my defense of the rebels, my taking a brief that so offended my papa; I also pursued in court the legality of his behavior along with that of the other trustees when the synagogue was incorporated. That was three years ago and we have barely been on speaking terms since. My kin in Three Rivers must be quite aware of the breach."

Aaron Ezekiel blushed. The relationship with his cousin had been marked for years by serious disagreements. Just over ten years before Aaron Philip had advised his father Benjamin and Moses Judah Hays to decline the office of magistrate because of some ambiguities about taking the oath of abjuration. Meanwhile Aaron Ezekiel had felt obliged to defend his brother Samuel's commitment to being a justice of the peace in Trois-Rivières.

There were contentious words uttered in the Legislature soon thereafter. "What has been said in the past, Phil, is now history. We *Trifluviens* hold no grudge. In any case we were on the same side when it came to how we reacted to the rebellion."

Aaron Philip sighed. "It was so different a decade before. I was so secure in my profession. Remember when I owned a horse that was entered in the first running of the King's Plate! That was but seven years ago."

"I am not likely to forget." Aaron Ezekiel had come up from Quebec for the event in Trois-Rivières. The race was for a purse of 100 guineas and was restricted to horses bred in Lower Canada. Soon it would become known as the Queen's Plate, recognition of there being a female monarch. *Alas, his cousin Philip didn't get the prize.*

"Today I have a paltry number of clients and have few prospects for doing better." Aaron Philip swallowed the last of his drink.

"You are too pessimistic, Phil. You did, however, cause quite a stir when acting as the counsel for Henry William Harris you prayed to be heard at the Bar of the House.

"It was certainly unusual. The petition was in support of a divorce. Harris deserved to be free of his obligations to this woman after she deserted him for Eleazar. And I accepted the brief even though I would take harsh criticism for it." Aaron Philip had not endeared himself to the Hart-David clan by representing the cuckold and thereby drawing more attention to the disgrace of Eleazar David, the onetime hero of Montreal's Anglophone community.

"Have you ever heard from cousin Eleazar?"

"He still lives with that woman. Eliza Lock Walker has already given him a couple of children."

"You have had your share of escapades, Phil. I seek to avoid such entanglements."

Aaron Philip's laugh was bitter. "We lawyers can't seem to escape dueling, verbal or otherwise. How else but resort to pistols to settle a dispute or atone for an offense if an argument goes too far? I've been at the wrong end of a gun three times and survived. I can't say that for my old friend Sweeny. But then I didn't let a quarrel result in a fatality."

"Things will look up, cousin."

"Do you think so, Eze? My doctor says I may not live out the year."

* * *

For Aaron Ezekiel the sprawling house on Rue des Forges never seemed so somber. It being a Saturday and just a week away from Rosh Hashanah, the daily routine of its inhabitants would have in any case been rather subdued. But this morning the family patriarch had closed his eyes for the last time. Ezekiel Hart would be receiving the mourner's *Kaddish*. *B'rikh hu.*

Like his siblings, Aaron Ezekiel had dreaded this day for some time. Who could not but notice the deteriorating health of his father? Frances Hart, the mother of thirteen children, had died twenty-two years ago but her place was partially filled by two of her eldest daughters. Esther Elizabeth in particular had opted to care for her father rather than to begin her own family.

Ezekiel Hart's corpse, dressed in linens, was laid out in the salon. There would be visitors from the extended family. Aaron Hart David had already viewed the body, his presence having been dictated by the fact that he was the physician called upon to issue a death certificate. Wife Catharine, probably without the children, could be expected to come later in the afternoon. Furthermore, Aaron Ezekiel was counting on Moses Hart and at least some of his progeny paying their respects. The two brothers had maintained a lasting relationship over seventy-three years in spite of their different temperaments.

Elsewhere in the house Aaron Ezekiel's sisters were probably busy preparing to welcome their kin by preparing appropriate appetizers. Esther could be the exception; he wouldn't be surprised if she had gone to her room grief-stricken. Harriet, Caroline and Miriam were made of sterner stuff.

As for the male side of the family, Samuel Bécancour as the oldest son was already making arrangements for the funeral. Ira Craig, on the other hand, had to be on duty running the family steamboat. Adolphus Mordecai had traveled to Montreal in the previous week and would presumably return as soon as possible. Aaron Ezekiel sighed; Abraham and Henry, two other sons of Ezekiel Hart, had not outlived their father.

Included in Samuel's task was alerting the *Trifluviens* of the passing of one of their leading citizens. Born and bred in this river community, Ezekiel Hart had once been a deputy in Quebec's Legislative Assembly. Thirty-five years before, other legislators may have spurned him because of his ancestry, but his status in Trois-Rivières had without doubt been solidified in the intervening decades. Samuel had already reported to Aaron Ezekiel that most of the town's shops were planning to close during the funeral to show their respect. Moreover, Dominque Mondelet, who was in the midst of overseeing the current session of the Court of Queen's Bench, had announced that the proceedings at the courthouse would be suspended in order to allow the legal fraternity to join the cortege. Officers of the 81st Foot were planning to attend in full dress.

"I have already indicated to the townspeople that the family will be sitting *shiva* at our place. There will be enough room to accommodate as many guests as will show up." Samuel did have a 16-room house on Rue du Platon. As a town magistrate, he was bound to attract the *notables* of Trois-Rivières, men such as Judge Mondelet, as well as luminaries like Pacaud, Barthe, Dumoulin, Heney, Turcotte, Polette and Dorion. It was even possible that Chief Justice Vallières would come down from Montreal in spite of his disabilities.

"What about the eulogy?"

Samuel had responded affirmatively. "We shall all speak. I'm also expecting Reverend Piza to arrive from Montreal by tomorrow. It will be only fitting that he comes here on the *Hart* steamboat. Ira Craig will see to that."

With some reluctance Aaron Ezekiel mounted the stairs to the salon. Death was still a mystery to him. True, his mother had been lost to him while he was in his teens. But that memory was clouded by the sibling rivalries of the time as well as by the inattention of his parents then coping with a public persona and a dysfunctional family. In later years it had become a meaningful association that death had now disrupted.

In the declining light of late afternoon the father's face in repose revealed little of that history. Aaron Ezekiel recalled how papa took pride in the career of what he proudly boasted was the first Jew in the province to be admitted to the Bar. When Aaron Ezekiel eventually opted to leave the city of Quebec to practice in Trois-Rivières, the father overtly showed his appreciation.

*   *   *

The parlor on Rue du Platon was already crowded when Aaron Ezekiel entered the room and began shaking hands with the guests. *Sammy has obviously spread the word far and wide.*

His brother finally cornered him at the entrance to the corridor. "Turcotte sends his regrets. Parliament is meeting a week Thursday in Kingston. Given what is at stake, he believes that the district must be represented when our deputies respond to Governor Metcalfe's address to the first session."

Aaron Ezekiel accepted the excuse. Joseph-Édouard Turcotte had been elected to the Legislative Parliament as the member for Saint-Maurice in 1841 despite his opposition to the union of the Canadas. It hadn't been easy going for him; he was soon forced to resign because he had accepted two government posts. Gugy, the defeated candidate in 1841, wouldn't let that go by. Nevertheless, a by-election returned Turcotte to office a year later. Aaron Ezekiel regarded him as a Reformer who didn't let the absence of his right arm interfere with their wrangling when both appeared before the Bar. His absence at the funeral would be noticed.

There was at least one deputy visiting the Harts this day. Dr. René-Joseph Kimber made an appearance, albeit of short duration. Aaron Ezekiel had it on good authority that the former surgeon was also in physical decline. Considerably younger than the deceased, Kimber showed a fragile frame and an ashen mein. Also opposed to the union, he had been elected to the Assemby for Champlain, the riding just east of Saint-Maurice. However, he had but a month ago been elevated to the Legislative Council. *Was that promotion alone recognition that he wasn't a well man?*

Most of the guests had brought their respective wives. In the case of Joseph-Guillaume Barthe, it was a fiancé. The mercurial lawyer, editor and poet would be marrying Louise-Adélaïde Pacaud in January. It was Aaron Ezekiel's first opportunity to congratulate the two of them on their pending nuptials.

Barthe used the encounter to comment on the political crisis brewing in Kingston. As editor of *L'Aurore des Canadas* he had become the mouthpiece of the anti-unionists in the Parliament. Denis-Benjamin Viger, who owned the journal, remained a critic of La Fontaine's reforms being proposed in the upcoming session. "*Messieurs* Neilson and Viger predict that all his plans will come to naught."

Aaron Ezekiel chose not to engage in a political debate in this environment. Actually he had no strong feelings in this matter. Earlier in the day he had written a short letter to John Neilson in recognition of the fact that his father had been a personal friend of the Quebec statesman. Neilson's opposition to the union had not hindered his reputation in the new Parliament.

There was a stir in the room when Moses Hart was spotted standing at the entrance, his body twisted by an arthritic skeletal frame, his eyesight obviously impaired. Aaron Ezekiel had wondered if his uncle would avoid appearing at such a gathering given his physical condition. *He's a very proud man who cares how he shows himself in public.*

Aaron Ezekiel and his siblings advanced quickly to greet the family elder. They were quite aware that Moses Hart had a mixed reputation in the community. Though one of the richest men in the province, he had offended so many *Trifluviens* because of his personal behavior. A Jew, a Deist and a libertine in a Catholic milieu could not but rouse disdain. Yet Aaron Ezekiel felt he need not apologize for acting as his uncle's counsel for so many years. He offered his arm to lead him into the room. "All by yourself, uncle?"

Moses showed an impish grin. "All alone! My Mary is with child once more. She may give birth in a matter of weeks. Tell me, my faithful nephews, how will you proceed now that Ezekiel is no more? There is a big estate to share."

Samuel could barely be heard over the cacophony. "We will abide by the will. Nonetheless, I don't look forward to the formal inventory of his estate. I have seen some of what he has collected. Broken glass, cracked china, worn mirrors. Nothing got thrown out.

It was almost midnight. Eventually the room cleared. Aaron Ezekiel turned to the one remaining guest. The young *chazzan* had said little during the evening - this was not his kind of crowd - but he did have an important piece of information. "I fear that you may shortly be seeing more of me. Your cousin Aaron Philip is very near death."

*My chief annoyance at present proceeds from the discontent of what
may be fairly be called the British party in distinction from the others.
It is the only party in the colony with which I can sympathize. I have
no sympathy with the anti-British rancour of the French party, or
the selfish indifference towards our country of the Republican party.
Yet these are the parties with which I have to cooperate; and because
I do not cast them off, the other party will not see that I cannot,
and contrive all my acts as if they were the result
of adhesion to anti-British policy.*
GOVERNOR SIR CHARLES METCALFE
(letter to Lord Stanley, June 25, 1843)

*On Friday Mr. Lafontaine and M. Baldwin came to the Government House,
and after some irrelevant matters of business and preliminary remarks
as to the course of their proceedings, demanded of the
Governor-General
that he should agree to make no appointments, and no offer
of an appointment, without previously taking the advice of the Council;
that the lists of candidates should in every instance be laid before
the Council, that they should recommend any other at discretion;
and that the Governor-General in deciding, after taking their advice,
should not make any appointment prejudicial to their influence*
GOVERNOR SIR CHARLES METCALFE
(letter to Lord Stanley, November 25, 1843)

Thirty

The distinctive clang of the doorknocker diverted Theodore Hart from his task of cutting some bread to serve his wife. She hadn't eaten since morning and he was responding to her whispered request. *Fanny will have to wait; Henry has arrived.*

It took no more than a minute for the distressed husband to receive his visitor. Henry Judah entered the hallway without saying much; he undoubtedly understood that Theodore, a second cousin, had not invited him for social reasons. It was widely known that Frances David Hart led a precarious existence. She had been a semi-invalid ever since their marriage almost two years before. Their first child, Sarah Harline, had died in infancy and Frances was once again pregnant. Henry Judah wasn't the only one who feared trouble with the prospective childbearing, due to happen in the middle of winter.

Seating his guest in the parlor, Theodore finished preparing the food for his wife. Her comfort came first. He felt a little guilty sending this particular note to the lawyer he so often consulted. The subject would not be business-related; no talk about land purchases or insurance deals. There were some very personal questions to ask.

Henry Judah was eight years older than Theodore. Born in London, he had come to Trois-Rivières as a child. He studied law there and along with his older brother, Thomas, became another of the lawyers who emerged from the Hart-Judah-David clan. Unlike Aaron Ezekiel and Aaron Philip, however, the two Judahs had grown up as Anglicans. Indeed, Henry had in 1834 married Harline Kimber, the daughter of one of the leading gentiles in Trois-Rivières. Dr. René-Joseph Kimber, physician and politician combined, had been Henry's *entrée* into the province's elite especially after the thirty-something counselor moved his practice to Montreal three years ago. He had succeeded in this endeavor even more so than his elder brother; Tom Judah, also practicing in Montreal, fraternized more often with the Hart-David clan than did Henry. Theodore, leaving the bedroom, finally entered the parlor and shook hands with his visitor.

"I know you have been busy, Henry. First, let me congratulate you on your election to the Parliament! My guess is that you will be off to Kingston very shortly." The by-election had been three weeks ago, the 22nd of September to be exact, and the outcome had been as expected. Henry Judah was voted in as the deputy from Champlain, thereby replacing his father-in-law, who had been elevated to the Legislative Council in August.

"I depart for the capital next week. I hope that I am not leaving you in the lurch, what with your personal circumstance."

Theodore sighed. "Sickness and death have been with me for much too long. My wife was particularly mortified by the loss of our daughter. As for me, not only must I deal with Fanny's condition. Brother Phil was buried a few days ago and Uncle Ezekiel died last month."

"My condolences, Theo. I didn't even learn of Phil's demise until after he was interred on Friday. Were you there?"

"One of the few in attendance. Reverend Piza did pray over his grave and Myer Solomon and Moses Binley kept vigil. But there was no family present other than myself. I did make note of it in my bible." The rift in his immediate family had sorely troubled Theodore. It put into question his very allegiance to the synagogue.

"At least Myer will look after his client's interests. He's a good lawyer."

"Enough said. I need your advice, Henry. You are aware, of course, that we are expecting another child. Is there a way of ending the pregnancy? I fear for Fanny's life."

Judah's expression gave Theodore the answer he expected. "You put me in a difficult position. You don't have to be told how the public views abortion. The churches dictate how the state regards it. I would not be surprised if it is not soon ruled as a criminal act. One of my colleagues contends that the punishment will be life imprisonment. Do you want to take that risk? In any case it may not come to that. Your Fanny does have a good doctor."

"You are saying that I have no choice but to accept what is fated. What if the child outlives the mother? How will I cope?"

"There is always insurance. After all, you and your father hold the agency for Sun Life. Would the company not write you a policy?" Judah was reminding Theodore that Benjamin Hart and Company was deeply involved in insurance. Not only Sun Mutual Life Insurance Co. of Montreal but also Equitable Fire Insurance Co of London, the Mercantile Insurance Co, the Security Insurance Co of New York, Minerva Life of London, and the New York Underwriters.

Theodore didn't reply. He got to his feet and moved to the open window. Though it was early October, the breeze was warm enough to invigorate him somewhat. "What can I say, Henry? It is not the money that I really worry about."

* * *

"**Come in, Theo! We have to talk**." Benjamin Hart had looked up from his desk to recognize his son standing at the office door.

"Can it wait, papa? I was just checking the sailing ships docked at Pointe-à-Callière. Our cargo has been unloaded on schedule, an achievement, I suppose, that is advantageous for our import business this time of the year. I shall have to get back to the wharf to supervise the transfer of the goods to the warehouse. One cannot be too careful!"

"Good for you, Theo! You may yet be worthy of becoming a full partner in the firm. But give me a few minutes."

Benjamin's rare expression of delight caught Theodore unprepared. *Why can't papa show his softer side more often?* "I suppose, papa, you regret not having more of the family involved in the business."

"It is true that my sons have found other things to do. I won't mention Phil, but I have also been disappointed that Wellington chose to remain in Birmingham and that Henry opted for studying law."

"Ten years ago Henry seemed destined for business. I remember him acting for Uncle Moses ten years ago." Theodore recalled Henry when he was but fifteen years old – Theodore was sixteen at the time – and charged with the responsibility of handling his uncle's business interests in Montreal. There were goods to buy (tea, potash kettles, beam scales and the like), premises to rent and debtors to pursue. Henry was subsequently encouraged to join Arthur Wellington and Theodore in York to operate a branch office there. But it didn't last; in May, 1834 Henry got it into his head to study law in Upper Canada. He even asked for a £100 loan from both his father and uncle in order underwrite his new career. Eventually he moved to St Louis and married there.

At one time the house on Rue des Récollets was filled with Theodore's siblings –mother Harriot had gone through fifteen pregnancies in just under a quarter century ~ but now there were only a handful of those who had survived over the years living in the upstairs rooms there. Frederick and Benjamin Moses had yet to marry and daughters Hannah Constance and Dorothea Catharine were still in their teens. Papa Benjamin did have two sons-in-law albeit they were a mixed blessing. Raphael Schoyer, who had married his oldest daughter, was doing well in New York City but Samuel Hort, who had wedded Emily Abigail but a few years ago, proved to be a bankrupt and a forger who had brought shame to the congregation that was Benjamin's pride and joy. In fact, The Shearith Israel had long been his father's handiwork. Theodore had accepted being an active participant in the congregation. Unlike Aaron Philip, he had had no reservations about serving the governing board.

Benjamin had suddenly become silent. Theodore commiserated: "Perhaps Hannah or Dorothea will find husbands with business acumen."

"At least my daughters have fared better than some of their cousins. Ezekiel's offspring are still unmarried. And look what has become of Louisa. She is a mad freak, eloping with a married man. She has been utterly ruined and I blame your uncle Moses for the way he raised her." Benjamin's outburst didn't surprise Theodore; the bitterness had been growing over the past while. Being a magistrate in Montreal was offset in part by the refusal of the government to recognize his contribution to defeating the Papineau "republicans". And now men such as La Fontaine were once more dictating policy in Lower Canada.

"That may be, papa. But did you not want to talk to me about something else?"

"Actually, I have good news. A crisis is brewing in Kingston. I've talked to some of the travelers from there. One of them, Luther Holton, informed me that our Governor General is standing firm against La Fontaine and his followers. Many in the British party, including those in Upper Canada as well as in Montreal, have pressed Sir Charles to resist what we regard as hostility to the Crown. Until now they did not understand why he hadn't been more forceful in safeguarding the royal prerogative. Perhaps we underestimated his resolve?"

"Interesting! I've know this fellow Holton well. He persists in advocating my membership in the Unitarian Society, which he helped found last year. Yet he is an astute observer of politics." Theodore could have said more about Holton, who happened to be a year younger than he was. They had been acquainted for some years, Holton having been employed in the firm of Henderson and Hooker as a clerk before he reached his majority. Every once in a while they had frequented the same drinking establishment. It now appeared that Holton had even gotten Benjamin's attention, the young man being involved in transporting goods and passengers up the St Lawrence into the Great Lakes.

Benjamin's spirits had obviously been improved by what was going on in Kingston. "Things will get better when the seat of government comes here to Montreal. Our people will be able to exert more influence on the makeup of the Executive Council."

Theodore left the courtyard through the curved iron gate that opened onto Place d'Youville. The Marché Sainte-Anne was its usual busy scene, it being not yet mid-day. He wondered how much busier it would be if and when it became the site of the Canadian Parliament. Father and son may be destined to witness almost first hand history in the making.

* * *

The snow that had accumulated earlier in the week had been cleared from the main thoroughfare as Theodore proceeded along Rue Notre-Dame. Nevertheless, it was a cold day and he walked with deliberate speed to reach the Bank of Montreal building at the northeast corner of Rue Saint-Jacques and Rue Saint-François-Xavier.

There was an unplanned distraction; at the edge of the Place d'Armes a group of pedestrians had gathered around a gentleman Theodore immediately recognized him as being Benjamin Holmes, the banker who had won election to the Parliament but two years before. *He has returned from Kingston. Has the House been prorogued after all?*

The crowd was breaking up as Theodore approached it; Holmes was explaining that he was bound for the Bank and could be delayed no more. Theodore interjected that he was also on his way to that destination. "May I accompany you, sir?"

Holmes smiled gratefully. They had not seen each other since that first summer in Kingston but the middle-aged banker had developed a fondness for the young Hart at the time. As they strolled across the street to enter the banking institution, Holmes confirmed that the Governor had prorogued the Parliament. "I'm back in time to celebrate Christmas with my family."

Theodore could not refrain from questioning him about the current crisis in Kingston. Interestingly enough, Holmes obliged him, slowing his pace as a result. "Let me relate what did transpire last month! The rupture began when our Governor refused to dismiss the Speaker of the Legislative Council, who is a Tory. When the fellow finally did resign on his own accord, Metcalfe took it upon himself to look for a replacement without first consulting the Executive Councilors. With the parliamentary session already into its third month, La Fontaine and Baldwin went to Alwington House to demand such consultation be in force now and in the future. Metcalfe stood fast: the royal prerogative must prevail."

Theodore nodded. "And so the Executive Councilors resigned en bloc. That we have been told."

"Not all of the Councilors. The provincial secretary stayed put. And Metcalfe tried to scrounge up other Councilors to allow him to govern. Believe it or not, our friend Viger agreed to join Draper in heading up a new administration. I spoke to Denis-Benjamin; he reckons that he can trust Metcalfe, whom he regards as an enlightened Governor, more so than Baldwin and his colleagues. It doesn't matter; the House rejected the Viger-Draper alliance and Metcalfe had no choice but to prorogue."

"Am I to assume that you voted against a change in the composition of the Executive Council? Your views have changed drastically from what you stated when the Parliament first met. As I understand it, you have stood with the French faction even if that has made you less than popular with Montreal's merchants. I must admit that I didn't expect this from the cashier of the Bank of Montreal."

"I admit that I had an epiphany last year while talking at length to La Fontaine and Baldwin in Kingston; the veil fell from my eyes and I was ready to act cordially with gentlemen of French origin. Thus La Fontaine's new ministry gained my full support when Governor Bagot approved it. True, I am regarded as a traitor by the editors of the Herald and Gazette. Most of the Executive Council resigned in November and they are being pilloried in the Tory press. Consequently I am certainly much in the minority dealing with my compatriots in the West Ward."

"Is that what you were hearing before we left the Place d'Armes?"

Holmes grinned. "It is just a year ago that I was returned as councilor from the West Ward. I shall be serving as one of the city aldermen for at least another two years. Meanwhile, Viger is not totally isolated in his cooperation with the Governor. Denis-Benjamin Papineau stands with him, as does Turcotte."

Theodore had one final question. "Can our colony manage without stability in government?"

"At least for a while. The economy has revived in the last year or so. We are visibly prospering. Look up Beaver Hall Hill! The St Patrick church will soon supersede the Frobisher mansion as the high point in the city." Holmes was alluding to the new place of worship for Irish Catholics as if he, Irish born, had a hand in its construction. Theodore knew better. On the other hand, he did not dispute the fact that Montreal was in its ascendancy. There would soon be fifty thousand citizens in the city and railway access to the west was just beginning. "I would guess, sir, that you will be crossing swords with William and Thomas Molson, especially with William still a city councilor."

The two were only now entering the portal of the Bank. Holmes did not hesitate to reply. "The Molson brothers have never forgiven me for the Bank of Montreal refusing to take deposits from their private bank. They think they have outsmarted me by investing in the Banque du Peuple and using its banking authority to handle transactions with their suppliers and customers."

Theodore decided to suspend what had become a debate. Holmes too showed some sensitivity. "My wife tells me you will soon be a father."

"Indeed, my Fanny is due to give birth in a couple of months."

Jacob drove me with his paid horses (tandem) round the Mountain stopping at Hayes. I called at 4 on Miss Sophia David – had an hour's chatting found her very gay & lively – would have no objections to drive down with me "but people would talk"..
ABRAHAM JOSEPH
(diary, January 21, 1844)

I have as yet received no further particulars – Poor Fanny was a great favorite of mine –one I used to look forward to as my intended wife. These hopes I declared to poor Fanny at Three Rivers in October 1841 when she pleaded a prior engagement and censored my tardiness.- I was present at the wedding on Tuesday Jany 1842 and sad indeed has been her fate. Mrs Theo Hart has scarcely known what it is to be in health – she was an invalid from her marriage to her decease. Peace be to thy name! She leaves an infant daughter.
ABRAHAM JOSEPH
(diary, February 28, 1844)

Thirty one

Abraham Joseph noticed the lettering on the office door as he mounted the stairs. His youthful brother Gershom made a point of fingering it; he had wasted no time in declaring to the public that he was now a full-fledged advocate, he having just been admitted to the bar late in the previous year. And who were to be among his first clients? Abraham had traveled from Quebec City to join his brother Jacob Henry in Montreal in sorting out how their business partnership was to continue. For five years Abraham had been a partner with a one-fifth interest in Jacob Henry Joseph and Company. Now the family firm, wholesale manufacturers and importers of tobacco, was due for reorganization.

This being a typical Monday in January, Montreal's Rue Notre-Dame had taken on the character he would have expected for a winter week; overcast, a threat of snow. How different from yesterday! Abraham had had his chance to visit not only with his mother's household on Près-de-Ville Place but also with the David family not too far away.

The latter opportunity was of great importance. Abraham had not hidden his assertive posture when confronting the David sisters. He had once failed in his bid to marry Frances because, as she claimed, he had spoken up too late. It so happened that "Fanny" had since given birth to Theodore Hart's second child in mid-January. Phoebe, the elder sister (who would be turning 26 at the end of the summer), should be more amenable to his advances, although the recent death of her aunt had made her the titular mistress of the David establishment. Then there was Sophia, who had the advantage of youth (she had just reached her majority last year) and whom he regarded as the prettier of the two. Undoubtedly both the David and Joseph families would be happier if he settled for Phoebe; her options were diminishing with time. He was determined, however, that it be Sophia.

Sophia had been rather coy when it came to his overt courting. She did agree to have him come for Sunday tea in the afternoon. On the other hand, she balked at his suggestion that they share a carriage ride. (Jacob had given him permission to use his two-horse vehicle while staying in Montreal.) She had demurred: "What would people think?" Nevertheless, the visit went pleasantly. As he wrote in his diary that night: "– had an hour's chatting found her very gay & lively."

Earlier in that day he had made use of the horse and carriage tandem to travel beyond the town limits. On an impulse he drove to the new mountain home (which was still under construction) of Moses Judah Hays, an uncle of the David sisters. Hays had bought an extensive piece of land on the lower slopes of Mount Royal. He could well afford to. He owned the city's waterworks and acted as a director of the Montreal Provident and Savings Bank. Along with Benjamin Hart, Hays was recognized as a leader of the Jewish community. A magistrate since before the uprisings and one of the founders of the synagogue on Rue Chenneville, his eventual move to the "Mountain" seemed so fitting.

This morning's meeting at the offices of Gershom Joseph had come at Abraham's urging. On the Sunday he had written Jacob Henry to insist that their meeting of the previous Friday required further negotiations. "Your refusal to have any notarial agreement between us for a future partnership has given me to understand that our concession in trade will cease on 1 April next. It would be well therefore that we come to some arrangements (before my departure) as to the manner of disposing from stock in its time (as you remarked Friday). The partnership does not cease until 1 April but I hope you do not wish to retard to that period the arrangements I will be compelled to make particularly as I must write to Jesse on the subject today or tomorrow. If we can make any arrangements for a future partnership let us do so at once. I am willing provided you give me a fair proportion of the profits – and if we cannot then let us arrange finally for the closing of the presents."

Thus the first piece of business was to draft a partnership agreement that he knew would be altered and re-altered. He could be taking several visits to the office to get a finished document. But he was determined to call on Sophia later in the afternoon and to have dinner at his mother's at six. Though it would be dark for hours after that, there was also an intention to visit Moses Eleazar David and to express his condolences for the death of the young man's mother. There was also the matter of ordering a conveyance for his trip back to Quebec assuming that all the signatures were in place to make the new agreement legal.

Abraham had had some qualms about using Gershom for the negotiations. There was no dearth of Jewish advocates in Montreal. Gershom could, if he so chose, consult with Moses Samuel Hart David, Sophia's brother, or with Moses Binley, both of who incidentally had been present along with Gershom during the last rites for Charlotte David.

Abraham had not been in Montreal to bury Charlotte David, Phoebe's aunt, who had passed away two weeks earlier. He had never gotten to know her well. Arriving in Montreal from Berthier when he was already fifteen, he remembered her as the mother of Moses Eleazar David, a fatherless adolescent a year or so older than he. Auntie Charlotte, as she was referred to by the children born of Samuel and Sarah David, was always in the background, usually morose in continence. Yet she had taken great pride in being a daughter of Aaron Hart, the legendary founder of the clan. Husband Moses David had lived long enough to give her a child but he was gone before Abraham was born.

There was some frustration as Jacob quibbled about the wording of the document. At one point they decided to break for lunch. It required the donning of cloaks to withstand a wind that had been whipped up outdoors but there was no serious complaint about postponing the wrangling for a bit. *There were other things to wrangle about.*

Abraham, living in Quebec, was eager to get the insight of somebody closer to the new political center. "I'm told that Benjamin Holmes is on the verge of resigning his seat in the Parliament. I suspect that the banker feels he's lost his influence now that Parliament has been prorogued and La Fontaine is out of the Council. What can the Governor do without a Parliament to vote funds for any of his initiatives?"

"My guess is that he will try to survive until he finds more legislators to replace the executive councilors who resigned. Without doubt, Metcalfe has strong support in Upper Canada. Coming from Toronto, I can vouch for that sentiment." Thus Gershom, sounding very authoritative, had a different perspective on the political crisis that had gripped just everybody residing in Montreal's business quarters. Abraham marveled at how quickly he had grown up. The family had insisted that he get his education in York and at the University of Toronto and he earned their confidence by doing so well in his schooling.

Their meal consumed, Jacob insisted that they get back to the office. But not before he gave his kid brother a compliment. "You should make a great success with your practice, Gersh. Just handling the business of our enterprises alone should be rewarding."

Gershom grinned but he added a caveat. "Don't count on me staying in Montreal. My time in Toronto has broadened my vistas. I'm giving thought to traveling in Europe."

* * *

Abraham left his desk to stand at the window facing the river. Casting his eye on the wintry scene, the harbor bereft of sailing vessels, Abraham's mind flashed back to the day but a month or so earlier when he had driven to the slope of Montreal's "mountain". The weather at home had not been as cooperative since then despite it being the initial day of March. *Is it true that being downstream in Quebec has a bearing on how Mother Nature treats the inhabitants along the St Lawrence?*

Nevertheless, his mood had improved somewhat over what it had been a week before. Last Thursday he had been so exasperated with his brother Jacob that he let his temper get the better of him. His family was in the midst of a quarrel about money, which wasn't so surprising when he thought about it. Brother Jesse had intimated that Jacob was using his control of the purse strings of the Josephs to bully him into paying more for boarding at the family home on Près-de-Ville. When Abraham agreed to intervene, he was greeted with a letter from Jacob to the effect that there was no reason to do so. There was *no* dispute; mother and sons were of one mind on the subject.

Abraham grunted. *Not true! Jesse will not be fool enough to pay anything like what was demanded of him.*

As he wrote Jacob on the 22nd of February, Jesse could not be expected to do more than living up to an earlier agreement with his mother to pay at a rate of £84 per annum. To be certain that Mrs. Joseph did not lose income, he, Abraham, would advance £15.2.6 to bring the sum up to £84 level. *I shall take my chances of being repaid by Jesse!*

Abraham retreated from the window. Enough! This was a new month. *Tonight the Sabbath and a time to devote myself to higher thoughts.*

And then came the day's mail. A letter addressed in the handwriting of Alexander Thomas Hart was on the top of the pile. *What could Aleck possibly want from him with boat traffic at a standstill until the thaw?* In any case, his cousin's partner, Ira Craig Hart, was supposedly on his way from Trois-Rivières to spend the weekend in Quebec. *Is the message intended for Ira Craig?*

Indeed the letter was not about steamboats; Alex was announcing that Fanny Michaels David Hart had died on Wednesday. Abraham wasn't totally shocked; Fanny's health had been delicate since her marriage to Theo. But for him it was the end of a longstanding fantasy. A secret obsession with this woman was being rudely dashed. Moreover, newborn Fanny Augusta had lost a mother. *Poor Theo!* He had an offspring and yet no helpmate to raise the infant to adulthood. For the next hour or so Abraham periodically re-examined the letter. *God help us all!*

He did not eat well at lunch when he repaired to the local *auberge*. But by luck he encountered a couple of business acquaintances who distracted him from brooding on the matter. Back in his office, he made an entry in his diary.

It was already three in the afternoon. Business would soon be suspended for the weekend. But Abraham's day was not finished. Standing at the office door was Ira Craig Hart, who had indeed just arrived from Trois-Rivières. "I have sad news for you, Ira. Aleck just informed me that our cousin Fanny Hart has passed away."

Ira Craig was appropriately sad, albeit the age differential of eleven years and his residence in Trois-Rivières had minimized the interaction of the two cousins. His immediate concern was whether Catharine David had yet learned of the demise of her sister-in-law. "I suppose Alex will have talked to her. She must have been devastated."

Abraham sighed. "I must write to Theo. He is, I understand, caught up in dealings with the Bank of Montreal now that Benjamin Holmes has returned there as cashier. A difficult time with the by-elections coming up."

"At least Theo is not *caught up*, as you say, in political strife. Drummond is contesting Holmes' old seat even though William Molson is expected to win it. Old Benjamin is in the thick of things but Theo is determined to stay out of the fray. Unlike his father, Theo isn't that determined to support the Governor. He prefers to grieve in peace."

Abraham had no interest at the moment in thinking about politics. "Is it true, cousin, that Catharine and Aaron are giving thought to returning to Montreal? I understand he felt guilty about living in Three Rivers while Fanny was in such a state. He will probably do very well if he reestablishes a practice in Montreal."

*   *   *

A package was waiting for Abraham once he reached the office in mid-morning. He tore off the wrapping, which was formidable. He quickly understood why: the contents were fragile – eight *matzoh* and a cake. *How thoughtful! This is Manna indeed!* Was it compensation for his decision not to join his mother in Montreal nor sister Catharine in Trois-Rivières to celebrate the Passover? *Mama obviously forgives me for my planned absence at the seder table; she is giving me a taste of the holiday flatbread during my sojourn in the cultural desert that is Quebec City.*

The gift might have soon been overshadowed because April was so busy at his Lower Town facility. The economy had certainly recovered from those tough years since 1837. Furthermore, the ships crossing the ocean from Portsmouth and Bristol would be adding to activity at the port within weeks. In the meanwhile Ira Craig was returning this day from a trip to Montreal. *Surely my cousin will have much to report.*

The by-elections there may not yet have occurred but Abraham had been forewarned that there could be trouble. One contest had Lewis Drummond pitted against William Molson, the leading spokesman of the city's Anglophone Tories. The other Montreal riding was also expected to bring on the fireworks. In February Benjamin Holmes had unexpectedly resigned his seat in order to return to the Bank of Montreal. George Moffatt had his chance to stage a comeback in politics. Abraham reckoned that he regretted having resigned his seat last October. *Wanted to make a point even though he has long supported union.* Moving the capital from Kingston to Montreal, Moffatt argued then, was unfair to Canada West. Now he doesn't want to leave the scene; he hopes to get back the seat he relinquished.

Ira Craig Hart showed up in late afternoon. Nevertheless, he didn't disappoint; he didn't even wait until he sat down. "You may not like it, Abe, but Drummond has taken physical control of the polls. The *Patriotes* could well come out a victor in at least one of the contests."

"You mean the battle between Drummond and Molson? I was expecting that. The Canadians are dedicated to La Fontaine's efforts to hand the Governor a political defeat."

Ira Craig then elaborated on the violence perpetrated by the Irish dockworkers allied with the *Canadien* faction. "The magistrates could do little about it. I did talk to my uncle in Montreal. Nevertheless, he is still sanguine about events. In Upper Canada the support for the Governor grows stronger. Metcalfe has won over the majority of those living in Kingston and Toronto. Even in Montreal his people did well in the municipal elections last January. Needless to say, he has a powerful spokesman in the form of Molson. And Viger is able to attract some Canadians to Metcalfe's way of thinking. Nevertheless, Drummond is contesting Holmes' old seat even though William Molson is expecting to win it. And of course old Benjamin is in the thick of things,"

"What about Theo? The last I heard he is behind the publishing of the *Pilot*. That makes him a friend of La Fontaine. Uncle Benjamin must be very unhappy." Abraham had received a letter from Sophia in which she had reported that Theodore had invited none other than Francis Hincks, the Irish colleague of Robert Baldwin living in Toronto, to take over as editor of the Montreal *Times and Commercial Advertiser*. The aim was to make the publication an organ of the Reform party in the same way as Duvernay operated his French-language journal. Unfortunately the proprietor of the English paper, which relied so much on advertising from the Montreal merchant community, didn't see it the same way. Theodore had very quickly to convince Hincks to launch the *Pilot*, which by the way would be available to the public that very week.

"You are right, Abe. Uncle Benjamin will be heard from."

Abraham changed the subject. "You didn't by any chance stop over in Three Rivers? I've heard nothing from there. Just a parcel from my mother in Montreal."

Ira Craig's expression was one of surprise. "Will you not be going to celebrate with your family?"

"I've been invited to stay in Three Rivers but it will be after *Pesach*. Catharine does want me to see the children before they pack up to return to Montreal. This is one holiday season that I'm stuck here in Quebec."

"Business obligations coming first? Not like you, Abe."

Abraham didn't wish to answer. "I have news for you. Ogden is back in Canada. Saw him in the *Place Royale* yesterday. But he won't be staying long. Says he is here to settle his affairs. Did you know that he was just admitted to the English bar at Lincoln's Inn and that he will be acting as Attorney General for the Isle of Man? Our cousins in Three Rivers will be pleased. They have crossed swords with him for at least thirty years."

In the meanwhile the affairs of the Government proceed
as regularly and efficaciously as if the Council were
complete. The country is tranquil. Business is active. The people
are prospering, and there is little political agitation,
other some of the members and partisans of
the late Council endeavour to excite it.
GOVERNOR SIR CHARLES METCALFE
(letter to Lord Stanley, February 27, 1844)

I regard the approaching election as a very important crisis,
The result of which will demonstrate whether the majority
of Her Majesty's Canadian subjects are disposed to have
responsible government in union with British connection
and supremacy, or will struggle for a sort of goal that
is impracticable consistently with either
GOVERNOR SIR CHARLES METCALFE
(letter to Lord Stanley, September 26, 1844)

Thirty two

The meeting to be held in one of the rooms in the renovated *Marché Sainte-Anne* had been called for eight in the morning. Hardly a word was spoken as leaders of the La Fontaine election committee assembled in twos and threes. Ludger Duvernay, one of them, was in a tremulous mood. The appearance of soldiers in the street had as yet an undetermined effect on the balance of power electorally. But *Patriote* control of the polling stations was definitely in jeopardy.

Nobody was in shirt sleeves; the sunlight had yet to warm sufficiently the mid-April atmosphere and clouds were gathering in the west. Lewis Thomas Drummond was already on hand and he was flanked by another Irishman, Francis Hincks. Duvernay had yet to adjust to the presence of this eloquent Toronto politician in the ranks of the Canada East *Patriotes*. Hincks had been invited in early winter to help Drummond organize the Reformers in Montreal, a city where the citizenry normally bent to the will of the Tory merchants doing business on Rue Saint-Paul. Duvernay conceded that Hincks had not held back in using his editorship of the *Pilot* to rally the Irish laborers, who were applying their brawn to occupy the polling stations in the impending by-elections. But would he be as effective as say, Cauchon and Cartier in bringing *Canadiens* to the polls and countering the influence of Viger and his allies?

There were other new faces seen within the gathering; Duvernay recognized Henry Judah, who was in earnest conversation with Drummond. *Ought he to interrupt?*

It was a moot point. Drummond beckoned Duvernay to join them. The latter wondered if the two lawyers needed an outsider's opinion on the legalities of what was transpiring in the streets outside. And indeed, the subject was the clashes between the workers on the Lachine Canal and the soldiers of the garrison.

Drummond looked every bit the barrister despite the rumpled state of his morning dress. A couple of years before he had married the eldest daughter of the late Pierre-Dominique Debartzch, a *seigneur* and former Legislative and Executive Councilor. Deportment had become even more important to him. Drummond's reputation had been made when he defended some of the defendants in the treason trials of 1839. "Judah here believes we can be in trouble with the law even if we prevail at the polls."

"Yes, *if* we prevail. Molson has been doing everything he can to have the sheriff and the army secure control of the polling stations. He did get a postponement of the election from the 11ᵗʰ. Six days have gone by and Delisle has yet to declare a victor." Judah spoke up before Duvernay could respond. He was referring to Alexandre-Maurice Delisle, the returning officer.

Drummond looked rather crestfallen. "If they take the seat away from me, will I be able to challenge the results in court?"

Judah nodded. "That is the question. But don't forget that we do have a friend in court. I dropped in to see Vallières the other day."

"At home on Lagauchetière?" Duvernay had been given advice that Vallières was incapacitated.

"Indeed. You wouldn't believe that he was in constant pain. As lively and gay as ever."

"What a pity! He may be Chief Justice, but his infirmity will soon be the death of him." Duvernay too had remembered his visit to Vallières not too long before.

"It must be the court of public opinion vindicating us; I'm convinced of that." Drummond didn't look that confident.

"We'll have Barthe assailing you in public." Duvernay was reminding both of them that Joseph-Guillaume, the publisher of *L'Aurore des Canadas*, would not spare his abuse of the La Fontaine party no matter what.

"Not if Viger stills Barthe's hand." Drummond's interjection was almost a mutter.

At that moment La Fontaine made his appearance at the door. He was flanked by George Cartier and Augustin Morin, the two most prominent of his party's lieutenants. There was a respectful silence as the committee members waited for La Fontaine's reaction to events.

He was surprisingly ebullient. "Cheer up, gentlemen! I have just spoken to Delisle. He is declaring our friend Drummond as duly elected. We have stood firm and victory is ours."

"And we have given Denis-Benjamin a black eye." Morin's contribution came after the gleeful responses.

La Fontaine chose to explicate the assault on Viger's political stance. "Denis-Benjamin has been most unwise. He fails to understand that there must be unity of purpose. Without it, we cannot regain power. I've always believed that we ought not to compromise on the important things. Avoid demagogy and violence if we can, but never close the door to responsible government. We shall not survive as a nation otherwise. Beware of the *vendus* who would divide us!"

Duvernay didn't know what to think. Was Viger, the man whom he had followed all those years, deserving of the label of *vendu*? The Papineaus and the Vigers had long been heroes in the cause of *Canadien* advancement. *Could the habitants in Lower Canada be convinced that the people were being betrayed by them?*

* * *

Duvernay wasn't altogether surprised when Reine showed little sympathy as he, her husband, launched a series of expletives. She had learned from almost twenty years of marriage that despite his usual affability, her Ludger could be quite belligerent when somebody, including her, crossed him. But then he usually calmed down and marital peace was restored. And on this day there was reason to be upset; Joseph-Guillaume Barthe had wangled a government contract to run official notices in his journal – a contract that Duvernay had sought ever since he had revived *La Minerve*.

The announcement in *L'Aurore des Canadas* had caught Duvernay unprepared. Sir Charles Metcalfe was showing his true colors despite the continuing negotiations with La Fontaine and his colleagues on reversing their decision to withdraw from the Executive Council. Reine was in a position to say "I told you so". It was already mid-July and her husband, like other "Reformers" had little to show for their obstinacy. Ever since he had relocated to Montreal, the Governor reiterated his contention that he would meet the *Canadiens* half way so long as patronage was kept in the hands of the Crown. "Don't despair, Reine! We still have the summer to convince the Governor that he can't prevail if he won't listen to La Fontaine."

"I know it is summer, Ludger; and you did promise the children that you would take them to the riverfront before sundown." It had never been easy for the former Reine Harnois to keep house and raise a family for her controversial husband. Four of the nine children had died in infancy and she had to endure the many months of abandonment while he was in exile south of the border. Indeed, one of the offspring was born and died while Ludger was living in Vermont. Typical of his passions Ludger asked her to name the male child Franklin in honor of Benjamin Franklin, one of his political heroes. There were other sons, however, who doted on their father. Louis-Napoleon was already eleven years old and Ludger-Denis only a little younger. Furthermore, Reine was pleased that her husband seemed determined to give their two daughters a good education. He listened paternally when they took turns playing the pianoforte.

At the moment Duvernay was paying no attention to such familial obligations. His livelihood could be at stake. *What bad luck! La Minerve* once counted on financial assistance from men like Viger and Fabre. Ten years ago its circulation was as high as 1,300 and he could boast that he owned *the* "national" newspaper. *Hélas,* that was before the rebellion and when Viger and he were on the same side. Now it was La Fontaine who helped pay the bills. *Will he and his advisers be willing to contribute more?*

The question was still on his mind the next morning when he entered his office to find Morin paying a visit. The latter was fully aware of Duvernay's dismay. "The Governor is getting his revenge."

Duvernay unconsciously fingered one of his sideburns. "It is a blow. You realize, *bien sûr,* that I must compete with Barthe for advertising if *La Minerve* is to survive. He now had the advantage of the government purse. It being the Wednesday deadline and business slowing down for the summer, it will be hard to put out a decent issue."

"I will speak to Louis-Hippolyte this very day. But don't lose heart. This cannot go on for much longer. Parliament must be called into session within a few months and the Executive Council is still bereft of members. Not only have I refused to accept an appointment. Cherrier, Quesnel and Caron have also declined." Morin could be going to La Fontaine with the promise of a modicum of unity in the ranks of the *Canadien* intelligentsia.

"But Metcalfe does have Viger and Papineau in his pocket. How do we counter that?"

Morin responded with a grin. "The church may prove to be a decisive factor. As founder of the Association Saint-Jean-Baptiste you can appreciate that. We are all Catholic, be we *Canadiens* or Irish. Support from the Bishop can only be to our benefit. Bourget is no longer as committed to doing the bidding of the British throne as were previous *monseignors*."

Morin bid *adieu* before Duvernay could formulate a response. He wasn't certain how he would have responded. Not everyone in his Society was willing to accept the hand of the clerics. But his attention was diverted by what he saw looking out the window at the street outside. None other than Joseph-Guillaume Barthe was standing on the sidewalk in conversation with two other men.

"*Merde!*" Duvernay rose from his chair and strode to the entrance. By the time he was able to encounter Barthe, the latter had turned away from his interlocutors. A look of triumph on the man's face was unmistakable.

Duvernay deliberately put his hand on Barthe's shoulder. "Your schemes will not succeed in the end, *monsieur*. You are a *vendu*, indeed!"

"And you are a sore loser, Duvernay. You and your friends are heading for an ignominious defeat. So take your hand off me."

"Take my hand off? You deserve a thrashing."

"Are you ready to settle this with pistols?" In retrospect Duvernay wished his anger had been under better control; he remembered another time when he did engage in a duel. *Will I escape with my life this time?*

*　　*　　*

The courtroom was well occupied -- much to Duvernay's chagrin. Not often in recent years did a newspaper publisher have to face a magistrate. True, he had been jailed four times in his career and eight years before he was wounded in the leg when he accepted a challenge from Sabrevois de Bleury to exchange shots when they met behind Mount Royal. This day he was standing in court, Barthe's suit against him stipulating that dueling was no longer permissible in these times and that Duvernay ought to be punished for such a threat.

Duvernay had the sense to engage Côme-Séraphin Cherrier to defend him. Cherrier may be a cousin of Viger. Nevertheless, they had known each other for years. On the other hand, the sitting justice of the peace was Moses Judah Hay, no friend of *La Minerve*.

Already seated in the chamber were associates of Barthe who weren't paying proper attention to the sound of the gavel. Cherrier had warned Duvernay that despite the latter's popularity among *Canadiens*, some of them judged, probably correctly, that the publisher of *La Minerve* was much too impulsive in personal relationships. He had been advised to be quite contrite; Hays was not likely to forget how they had clashed in those momentous days in November, 1837. Hays, along with Benjamin Hart, had accepted being a magistrate that same year and had not held back from enforcing orders received from the Governor to suppress the *Patriote* agitators.

Cherrier explained the course of events that had occurred this particular July day in 1844. "A mistake in judgment, yes. But no harm has befallen the plaintiff."

Hays seemed to be satisfied. There would be no penalty. "The defendant must give me assurances that he will keep the peace."

"My client has behaved quite correctly since then. How long will his assurances be in effect?" Cherrier wanted the judge to be definitive.

"At least for another six months."

Cherrier shook Duvernay's hand. "Let's repair to the tavern! I think it has worked out for the best."

Duvernay conceded as much. In point of fact, there had been no duel, the adversaries being distracted within days by the announcement that the Governor had finally put together an administration planning to engage with the Parliament in the fall. Duvernay had to reconcile himself to the news that Denis-Benjamin Viger would become President of the Council and thus a partner in a cabinet headed by William Henry Draper, the Toronto Conservative that had been pushed out of Parliament by the La Fontaine/Baldwin alliance during Bagot's time as Governor.

Of equal import was the news that Denis-Benjamin Papineau, Viger's cousin, had agreed to become the commissioner of Crown lands. For the Attorney General for Canada East the Governor had been forced to go to a Montreal Tory, James Smith. A Viger-Draper ministry, though a makeshift arrangement, would indeed face the people this autumn.

*I am the oldest English Canadian in Canada
and the largest landholder in this district.*
MOSES HART
(letter to Governor Metcalfe, December 6, 1843)

*The results showed that loyalty and British feeling
prevailed in Upper Canada and in the eastern townships
of Lower Canada, and that disaffection is predominant
among the French-Canadian constituencies.
By disaffection I mean an anti-British feeling, by whatever
name it ought to be called, or whatever be the foundation,
which induces a readiness to oppose Her Majesty's Government.*
GOVERNOR SIR CHARLES METCALFE
(letter to Lord Stanley, November 23, 1844)

Thirty three

A lexander Thomas Hart led the walk up Rue des Forges with first born
Moses Alexander clinging to his left hand. Miriam was encumbered
with baby David Alexander, whom she had to carry given the fact that
he was less than three months old. The decision to proceed by foot to
Alexander's late uncle's home had been the product of proximity (the house
was not more than a few hundred feet from where he and family lived)
and weather (though late morning, the temperature was quite moderate
for mid-September). Miriam would have preferred to use the carriage, but
it seemed to Alexander that this would have been an indulgence under the
circumstances.

The invitation to join his cousins to celebrate *Rosh Hashanah* had come
some time before. Esther Elizabeth Hart, who ran the household on Rue des
Forges with no interference ever since her papa Ezekiel had died, guessed
that her uncle Moses and his sons were loath to recognize the High Holidays
in view of their Deist outlook. And yet Miriam would welcome the chance

to honor the Jewish New Year in much the same way she undoubtedly did while growing up in New York. An afternoon get-together in the garden could accomplish that.

Because of the relatively warm weather, Esther had insisted that the dining be picnic-style in the garden rather than indoors. Her two sisters, Harriet and Caroline, had already supervised the setting up of a long table under the largest of the deciduous trees overlooking what was a 16-room house. They made the time to coo over their two little nephews whom they had seldom had the occasion to embrace. The male members of the household seemed satisfied to engage Alexander in small talk.

When they got to the seating, Samuel Bécancour had pride of place at the head of the table. He was flanked by the two barristers in the family. Aaron Ezekiel was on his left and Adolphus Mordecai, who had traveled from Montreal for the occasion, was on his right. Alexander sat farther down with wife Miriam and took responsibility for overseeing the children in their high chairs. By purpose Ira Craig would be across the table from him despite the *Hart* steamboat being scheduled to sail the St Lawrence for another two months. Alexander had arranged for a co-worker to act as the ship master for this particular run.

Miriam drew attention to the fact that there was space for children, her two sons not having to share it with other minors. "If Catharine were still here, we now would have had to accommodate five others, the Davids having had another child this year."

Esther agreed. "There is more room at the table with the Davids back again in Montreal. By the way, our good doctor writes that his practice is coming along well. And did you know that Catharine received a salmon from her brother Abe almost as soon as they made their move home?"

"The salmon, I know, was intended to make up for Abe's absence at the Joseph *seder* in April. He felt guilty not making the trip to Montreal last spring." This contribution was from Ira Craig, who knew Abraham Joseph better than did everybody else at the table.

They were interrupted by an outburst of tears emanating from one of the high chairs. Moses Alexander was obviously rebelling against being confined without as yet having any food to show for it. Miriam apologized. "It is Mo's birthday tomorrow. Three years old and a bundle of energy."

Alexander thought he caught a hint of bravado. Little Moses was healthy enough even if persisted in dragging a leg. Miriam didn't mention the absence of her second offspring. Augustus, born in the winter of '43, had died seven months later. Nevertheless, there was a dearth of children at the table. "None of you is married as yet. We bring the only children to the party." Alexander hoped the remark didn't offend but it was odd that even with Adolphus Mordecai coming down from Montreal, the seven surviving children of Ezekiel Hart were all unwed. Alexander was due for a surprise. "I bring you news, brothers, sisters and cousins. I am betrothed and will marry in December." Adolphus could tell that everybody at the table looked astonished. Adolphus, the youngest in the family at thirty years of age, would be the only one of Ezekiel's offspring to go so far as to choose a bride.

Esther Elizabeth was the first to react. "Do we know her?"

"In a sense it is a family affair. I'm marrying Hannah."

Alexander joined in the chorus of congratulations, albeit he had been told of that possibility when on his last trip to Montreal. At that time, Adolphus had cautiously admitted that he was courting his cousin, Hannah Constance, one of the last two unmarried daughters of Benjamin Hart.

Servants appeared on the scene to dispense the edibles. Soon thereafter the men at the table couldn't resist speculating on the political situation in the province. The summer had been quiet but the more astute of those present had strong opinions about the new cabinet that the Governor had put in place. Aaron Ezekiel was the most vocal. "The Executive Council as now constituted will probably not fare well at the hands of the Parliament even if the sessions will be in Montreal rather than Kingston."

Samuel wasn't as certain. "There are four Lower Canadians on it. Out of a total of six, that should sit well with some members."

"I wouldn't regard Daly and Smith as being much help to Viger and Papineau even if they do reside in Canada East. Daly has been damned by siding with Metcalfe when the resignations took place; Smith is a Scot and without a parliamentary seat."

* * *

The ferry crossed the St Lawrence in good time despite the sky's first hint of inclement weather. Alexander loosened the reins on the two horses that had to remain stationary during the water crossing. The carriage moved forward onto the Nicolet dock. "Where do you want me to take you first, papa?"

The question was asked with some impatience. Moses Hart had previously shocked his adopted son when he declared that he intended to contest the electoral riding of Nicolet in the upcoming election. Alexander was certain that his father would have no success standing as a candidate for the seat even though more than one of the seigneuries on the south shore were the property of the family and the name of Moses Hart was known for more than half a century throughout the parishes that bordered the river. *Half a century! That's the point.* His father would be seventy nine in the following month and yet was never able to be elected to any office in the district of Trois-Rivières or beyond it. Besides, it was generally understood that Antoine-Prosper Méthot had become the favorite to win Nicolet; he resided not too far downstream in Saint-Pierre-les-Becquets and would have been elected to the Parliament in 1841 had he not backed off at the last minute to let Morin take the seat.

The election call had come as bit of surprise; the Governor had spent so much time putting an Executive Council in place to face the existing Parliament. Alexander had no doubt that in the forthcoming contest the La Fontaine party would do well in Canada East, the francophone vote favoring any opposition to those who were beholden to Metcalfe and the new administration he had assembled. The British element living in the south-shore ridings was too sparse to make any difference to the results. He felt that even at this late date it was an obligation to dissuade Moses Hart from so fruitless a course. "It is almost noon, papa, let us stop at the *auberge* for lunch before doing anything."

Though Alexander had reluctantly acceded to Moses' request to cross the river, he did have some interest in paying visits to the Godefroy, Dutort and Courval seigneuries, properties that were in the name of Moses Hart and therefore made him eligible for seigniorial rights. Well timbered, the land could the basis for a thriving business in wood products. True, Alexander had his investment in shipping, an enterprise that had been launched by the family eleven years before when the *Lady Aylmer* was acquired by his father in partnership with John Miller. Two years later the Harts had purchased the steamship *Toronto* and then had the 45-hp *Hart* built for them. But competition for traffic revenue was stiff – there were more than fifty commercial steamers plying the St Lawrence – and Alexander had begun wondering if the shipping business ought not to be left to the Molsons and other corporate interests.

The first priority, however, was to convince his father that the candidacy was doomed to failure. The battle was between the coalition of forces linked to the Governor and those Reformers – La Fontaine and Baldwin in particular – set on getting "responsible" government. Moses Hart was not likely to get judicial changes to the system put on the public agenda.

Moses wasn't paying attention. He had lost so much personal wealth because the courts as constituted failed to mete out "proper" justice. That had to change. "There is no greater curse than law. I've been sorely troubled all my life with bad laws. I have lost several thousand pounds by bad laws.

There is no country that laws are so badly administered and so expensive as this."

Alexander tried once more. "The issue this autumn is whether La Fontaine or Viger will prevail in Lower Canada. I think Viger is a spent force. He himself may be beaten at the polls. He faces formidable competition in Richelieu from Wolfred Nelson."

"Nelson! I thought he had vowed to stay out of politics." Moses seemed confused. Formerly exiled to Bermuda after the 1837 rebellion, Nelson had returned to practicing medicine, first in Plattsburgh and then in Montreal. His return to the province had been facilitated by La Fontaine, who in his capacity as Attorney General for Canada East in 1842 had entered a *nolle prosequi* in Nelson's case. Apparently La Fontaine had prevailed on him to forget his resolution to stick to medicine. Nelson had previously lived in the Richelieu Valley and was bound to have popular support in that district in view of his leadership during the fighting.

Moses pondered a minute. "You don't think, then, that Barthe's pen will see Viger through to victory in the election?"

"Barthe himself is in danger of not being reelected. Yamaska voters aren't too different from other south-shore parishioners"

"You are so sure, Aleck. Nevertheless, I've been told that even Drummond is in trouble in his campaign."

Alexander took the rebuke gracefully. It was true that Drummond might not hold on to his seat in Montreal; the Tories were working hard to outbid him in winning the support of the Irish canal workers. "I'm not saying that the Reformers will succeed everywhere. Metcalfe has great support in Upper Canada. But there won't be the double majority that Viger and his friends are hoping for."

Moses retreated; he repeated his whole rationale. Legal reform must come.

"You needn't depend on being elected in our district, papa. It is possible to secure an appointment to either the Executive or the Legislative Council. You have already written to the Governor offering your services to the province. My only concern is your health."

* * *

The interior of the synagogue on Rue Chenneville was reasonably warm enough in view of the temperature outdoors. The Reverend Piza had agreed to have the reception inside following the ceremony that would join Adolphus Mordecai and Hannah Constance in matrimony. Torches illuminated every nook of the Shearith Israel, which made it possible for Alexander to distinguish all the guests. The bulk of them he knew because Montreal's Jewish community was a tight knit group. All the Harts, of course, plus the Davids, the Josephs, the Hays, the Judahs, the Benjamins.

The *Trifluviens* were well represented. Miriam had remained at home to care for the children but Alexander had brought Areli and Louisa with him by using the family carriage rather than a *calèche* to travel the distance. Needless to say, none of Adolphus' siblings were absent.

Piza, still in his twenties, seemed to Alexander a bit too tender in years to be standing in front of Adolphus, who was already thirty years of age. But most eyes were on Hannah Constance, a bride with all her regalia. *If only Miriam were so young and delectable.*

The alcohol was freely available during the subsequent reception and inhibitions were reduced as a result. Alexander was able to engage with many of the other guests and the conversations were often enlightening,

Thus, there was much discussion of the election results even though a month had passed since the voting was completed. Most of the guests, being Anglophone and in business, were biased in favor of the Tories. The Draper-Viger combination would control the legislature even though candidates committed to La Fontaine won the majority of seats in Lower Canada. In Montreal, the victory of George Moffatt and Sabrevois de Bleury over the La Fontaine candidates was welcomed. Still, note was taken of the fact that Dr. Wolfred Nelson had beaten Viger in Richelieu. A by-election to find another seat for the latter would be necessary. Moses Judah Hays, one of the founders of the synagogue, was the most vocal on the subject. "With the Governor having the full support of the Colonial Office and willing to speak for Draper and Viger, he has a majority to work with in the next Parliament. It is a pity, however, that his sight is so impaired by the treatment of the growth on his face. We all pray for him."

Alexander's longest conversation was with Theodore Hart, a cousin much more sympathetic to the Reformers than were his brethren. Moreover, Theodore indicated that there was another purpose to this encounter; he steered Alexander to a nearby corner in the room to introduce him to a gentleman standing alone against the wall. "Aleck, I want you to meet Mr. Holton. He's in the same business as you, albeit his field of action is between Montreal and Kingston."

Actually Alexander had heard of Luther Hamilton Holton, a junior partner in the forwarding firm of Henderson & Hooker. Though the steamboats, schooners and barges he supervised dealt with freight rather than passengers, their success in traversing the rapids on the western side of Lachine was legend in shipping lore. But he had never before talked to the man in person. Here he was, erect and over six feet tall, heavy black eyebrows and hair parted in the middle, a stylish beard at his chin and a countenance that suggested assurance, energy and sagacity even though he had to be fifteen years younger than Alexander. "Your reputation precedes you, sir. Welcome to our synagogue."

Theodore hastened to explain that Holton's presence was at his instigation. "Luther is a Unitarian. In fact, he helped organize the Unitarian Society of Montreal a couple of years back. Like you, Aleck, he is closer to the Deists than to the orthodox religions. This is a wedding, however, so let all men of good cheer eat, drink and be merry!"

Justice pour nous, justice pour tous; Raison et liberté
pour nous, raison et liberté pour tous
INSTITUT CANADIEN DE MONTRÉAL
(founding motto, December 17, 1844)

The man must be either in his dotage or is a consummate hypocrite.
He is or rather pretends to be my best friend to my face while behind
my back he is my greatest enemy – suing us to recover an amount
we do not owe but which taking advantage of an error in our sales,
he is endeavouring to recover – calling me a 'rascal' & I know not
what to some of my friends – with such in my memory
I cannot look upon the old man with that respect his age would
demand. I left Mr. B.H. & hurried to Mother's for dinner which I had
very little time to demolish. Mr & Mrs Piza dined there.
ABRAHAM JOSEPH
(diary entry, April 19, 1845)

Thirty four

A braham Joseph cursed himself for being late arriving at the coffeehouse on Rue Notre-Dame. He had promised Cousin Theodore to meet him first thing in the morning, the mutual assumption being that the junior partner in Benjamin Hart & Company had other business to attend to later this Friday. Nevertheless, Abraham had been delayed at the Chenneville synagogue. April flooding had made walking the streets hazardous and he had fallen. *I ought not to have gone to shul this morning knowing that contingencies can occur. Theo may not linger at the tavern.*

Normally Abraham would have corresponded with Theodore by letter; he had been doing business with Benjamin Hart and Company for some years if only because the latter's mercantile business overlapped with the general wholesale and retail trade Abraham was conducting in Quebec. The prospect of a lawsuit being launched by the Montreal branch of the family called for face-to-face contact.

Theodore had not given up on his cousin; rather, he had busied himself examining some documents he had evidently extracted from a briefcase at his feet. Nor was there any indication of animus. The two young men (they were less than a year apart in age) embraced.

"Your trip from Quebec was without incident? I'm told there was much flooding on the Queen's road west of Three Rivers." Theodore's tone seemed natural enough.

Abraham in turn enquired as to his cousin's plan to walk down to the Parliament building to hear the debate later in the morning.

"I've decided against it. The deputies have already authorized the deepening of the channel through the Lachine rapids. Nevertheless, we are still trying to decide what are the implications of the passing of James Henderson. It has been but a few weeks since he succumbed to a bout of gout. Where does that leave his forwarding and commission business?"

Abraham had had occasion to deal with Henderson & Hooker, although his main contact was with Luther Hamilton Holton, a junior partner. "I suppose all depends on whether the City Bank will continue to finance the firm."

"Because Henderson is gone as a director of the bank? The shipping season opens in May and prospects are good for all of '45. It is true that there is competition from New York using the Erie Canal whereas we must struggle with rapids to move up and down the St Lawrence or the Ottawa. Yet I wouldn't be surprised if the tonnage coming through Montreal will be much higher than it was in the last couple of years."

"You may be right, Theo. My brother is also convinced that things are looking up and is investing accordingly."

Theodore nodded. "Like Jacob Henry, I'm intent on acquiring more real estate. You may not realize that the Sulpicians are commited to selling off their Montreal properties in order to raise money for their good works. I'm seeking to own the Le Closse fief. It runs up Saint-Laurent to the north river."

Abraham had already learned from his brother that the Sulpicians had settled on this policy a few years before, the British government having confirmed their ownership of lots running from the banks of the Lachine Canal to the Montreal eastern suburbs. It appeared that both the Hart and Joseph families were destined to be major landlords in the city. "As for me, Theo, I've decided to restrict my capital to improving my position in Quebec."

"You are missing a good bet, Abe. I've been putting money into mining shares and the projects look very promising."

"You're talking about those ore deposits north of Lake Huron, are you not?" Actually, Abraham had been advised to invest in some of the key acreage near that lakeshore as well as a site off the St Mary's River separating

Huron and Superior. If a mineshaft were sunk east of Sault Ste-Marie as planned, it would be the first recovery of copper in the province.

"Yes, indeed, those very discoveries in Upper Canada. Papa agrees that I'm risking my money wisely."

The mention of Benjamin Hart gave Abraham the opportunity to question his cousin about the lawsuit. "You realize, Theo, that I was deeply hurt by your father's decision to make an issue of an accounting mistake regarding last autumn's deliveries. I understand that he called me a rascal. Surely you cannot be serious about taking me to court?"

"Believe me, Abe, that I had nothing to do with any such legal action. If I were you, I would visit my father as soon as possible to straighten things out. We are family. I am not likely to ever forget your condolences last spring when my Fanny left us." Theodore looked sorrowful enough that Abraham could not continue demanding an explanation. A year has passed since Theodore was widowed. Abraham had taken the death of Fanny Hart particularly hard because he too had courted her when she was still a David. His affections had since shifted to Sophia David although he had yet to commit to a marriage.

*   *   *

Benjamin Hart was at home when on the Saturday afternoon Abraham called on him at the house on Rue des Récollets. A servant led the visitor to a room off the library. The host was hunched over a small table shuffling papers. A stooped man despite his being only sixty-six years of age. Abraham hadn't seen him personally for over two years and he could not but be appalled by the deterioration in the man's physical fitness. And yet he seemed in control of his senses. "Abraham Joseph, is it not? My eyesight is not the best. It is so good of you to visit."

Abraham was determined to be blunt. The usual courtesies were kept to a minimum. "I had the pleasure of having breakfast with Theo yesterday morning. He suggested I come to see you. You can imagine that I was taken aback by the notification that I am being sued for non-payment of a bill. Certainly you are aware that it was an unfortunate miscalculation and that currently there is no outstanding balance."

Benjamin's face showed no recognition of what was being talked about. He smiled weakly and lowered his head. Abraham was confused. *Is he in his dotage?*

Finally there was a response. "Thank you for coming, young man. You being in Quebec, we don't see enough of you. There was a time when having the Governor resident in the *Château* made living there so critical. But times have changed. Perhaps now is the time to relocate."

Abraham tried to conceal his impatience. "I have no regrets settling in Quebec. It is, after all, the link to the Empire. Even Hart & Company maintains a ship there to move merchandise to England and back."

"And yet Montreal has outgrown the old capital. We are a thriving city. Our population must be close to sixty thousand. When I first moved to Montreal back in '18 it was less than half of that number. Now there are foundries and factories on either side of the Lachine Canal. Our trade with Upper Canada has become vital. And isn't the Parliament located here at the Marché Ste-Anne? The old quarrels may eventually come to an end. I think that as a magistrate I have contributed to that possibility."

"You sound more positive, sir, than when we spoke last. My guess is that with the Governor and Mr. Draper in full charge, you are in a better frame of mind. Nonetheless, *Monsieur* La Fontaine is a force to be reckoned with even though he is in the opposition. Draper is not having everything his way, especially with Viger not yet in Parliament."

"Our French citizens do have their own disagreements. You undoubtedly have read that there is now an *Institut Canadien* in Montreal. Last December a group of 200 or so liberal professionals broke away from the Société Saint-Jean-Baptiste to promote this new literary and scientific group. They object to the Church dominating Duvernay's organization. Many of them have had connections with the old rebels."

"That doesn't worry you, does it?"

"As long as Mr. Peel stands firmly with Metcalfe and the economy improves, I believe we are safe. Yet we ought to be vigilant. The French still aim to undo what we accomplished with the Act of Union. When Viger returns to the Parliament, he will probably be leading the charge to allow French to be used in the chamber. Some partner for Draper!"

Abraham was revising his estimate of Benjamin's acuity. *He may be feeble, but the old man is as dedicated a Tory as he always was.* "Thank you for seeing me, sir. I trust that all our current differences will be resolved satisfactorily. I shall visit my mother this evening with that in mind."

*   *   *

The Passover festival actually began on the Monday evening. Abraham had dutifully attended synagogue on both the Friday and Saturday before but that didn't discourage him from joining the other congregants at the

Shearith Israel for the holy day evening service and then again on Tuesday morning.

Exiting the synagogue at eleven, he had to decide what to do with a limited amount of free time. There would be an afternoon service at 2:30 and the Reverend David Piza was scheduled to give a sermon. He could hardly avoid being there even if he had already dined with the *chazzan* and his wife at the Joseph house on the Saturday evening. But he was also mindful of the fact that the Davids were invited to Place Près-de-Ville an hour later. He didn't want to miss interacting with Sophia this afternoon.

In the event, Abraham was at the door when the David clan arrived. The doctor, Aaron Hart David, led four of the five children into the foyer with a minimum of fuss. The fifth, Moses Edmund, was not yet walking and had to be carried in by Catharine. Abraham relieved his sister of this burden. It didn't escape his notice that Catharine was showing the strain of trying to produce a big family while she was already in her mid-forties. *Six births in the space of seven years. Aaron should be warning her of the risks.*

The two David females, Phoebe and Sophia, were the last to come through the entrance. Abraham, still holding the child, was in no position to embrace them but he offer his broadest grin. Rachel Joseph in her capacity as hostess led the procession to the main salon. Once everybody was settled there and Catharine had retrieved her baby, Abraham dared to take Sophia's hand.

Sophia reciprocated. "How wonderful of you, Abe, to travel here for *Pesach*. We missed you last year."

"A most unfortunate situation, albeit I had visited Montreal that January. April is undoubtedly a more convenient month. It so happens that tomorrow I'm borrowing a mare from my brother Jacob so that I can ride out to the Hays property on Côte Saint-Antoine. I offered to drive you to the Hays place last January but you declined."

Sophia frowned as if trying to recall the incident. "Remember, Abe. It was under construction at the time and not fit for viewing."

"That certainly is not the case now. There are now four stone houses on the site and Moses Judah has moved all six of his children to Côte Saint-Antoine.

"Including Esther?"

Aaron Hart had been listening to the conversation. "Yes, Esther is there. The big news is that Hays has sold the waterworks to the city. He has finally escaped that burden."

Abraham's eyes widened. He had long been a critic of the Hays investment in a public utility that had brought esteem but also grief to him for so many years. "How much did he get for the waterworks? I hope that he didn't lose too much."

"Apparently the final price was 50,000 pounds. He can now concentrate on running the Provident, which can also cause him financial embarrassment." Aaron Hart was referring to the fact that Hays had been chosen managing director of the Montreal Provident & Savings Bank in February. Saving banks were relatively new to Canada although they did follow closely the British pattern. The Montreal Savings Bank, formed in 1819, was a creature of the Bank of Montreal and opened for business for only three hours a day once a week. The Montreal and Provident Savings Bank, emerging in 1841, was more ambitious. But would its directors, including Hays, succeed in making it profitable, the economy being in such disarray over the past few years?

Rachel Joseph took exception to what her son-in-law was implying. "I've known Moses Judah since he was a child. He is a true entrepreneur and a credit to our people. Look what he is doing with the hotel and theatre he is having built on Dalhousie Square! It's the most splendid place in the city. And badly needed now that the Molson Theatre is being demolished."

Abraham quietly seconded his mother's comments. The venture of Moses Judah Hays would be enhancing the reputation of Montreal as an oasis of English culture in Canada East. Abraham had already been informed by Theodore that the new four-story stone structure, dubbed Hays House, would be the most elegant address in town. In the theatre adjoining it, according to what Hays had told Theodore, the plan during the long winter season was to have a German orchestra playing Viennese waltzes. *I would miss that living in Quebec.* "It ought to be a great success. I have heard that Mr. Hays intends to hire George Pope to run the place. Pope has demonstrated what he can do managing Donegana's Hotel on Notre-Dame."

The testimonials from mother and son hadn't satisfied Aaron Hart David. "Hays House may do well once it is built. Still, our friend Moses Judah does take risks and personally I wouldn't put my money into the Provident. Tell me, Abe! Have you decided to open an account at the *Banque du Peuple.* Louis-Michel Viger and De Witt are eager to bring in your family as clients of their institution."

Abraham opted for discretion. He too had qualms about involving himself in the Provident especially after learning that Hays had borrowed heavily from this savings bank to underwrite his investment at Dorchester Square. He had also been advised that a new benefits society under the patronage of *Monseigneur* Bourget was in the making. Having the Catholic Bishop sponsor a savings bank could only mean that the Provident might be limiting its reach to the Protestant portion of the Montreal population. Would that be enough to sustain the institution? He was expecting to ask Hays that very question once he got out to Côte-Saint-Antoine on the morrow.

*The established churches of England, Scotland, and Ireland
are avowedly Trinitarian. In the liturgy of the Church of
England divine worship is perpetually paid to Jesus Christ,
so that no serious consistent Unitarian can join in it; and as
to the Dissenters, there are few of their societies that are
clearly and professedly Unitarian.*
JOSEPH PRIESTLEY
(forms of prayer for Unitarian societies, 1783)

*I learn with very great and sincere concern how much
you are still suffering; and I anxiously hope, both on public
and private grounds, that the anticipation of your medical
attendant may be realized, and the affection of your sight
may prove to be but temporary*
COLONIAL SECRETARY LORD STANLEY
(letter to Sir Charles Metcalfe, November 17, 1845)

Thirty five

"I've invited you to our place, Theo, because I want to introduce you to a visitor from Boston. Mary Kent Bradbury is spending the summer in Montreal to help us expand our church activities." Luther Hamilton Holton stood outside his house on Queen St as he informed Theodore Hart that he was springing this surprise. Theodore wasn't certain how to respond. He guessed that his business friend had another agenda. Holton had frequently clucked his tongue when Theodore mentioned that he now lived alone. Theodore had avoided female company for well over a year, the wounded psyche following Fanny's demise not having healed by any means.

Nonetheless, the timing was right for overcoming his reluctance to such socializing. The night was pleasantly cool, a consequence of the two men being in close proximity to the wharves on the St Lawrence and catching the breeze from the southwest. A female connection being proposed: *What a setting for romance!*

A voice from the house interior interrupted Holton's hurried explanation. Theodore realized that the mistress of their dwelling brooked no delay in having the guest admitted inside. She probably had a dinner prepared and had arranged for serving at a certain time. Holton led the way indoors.

The two women in the parlor rose to their feet to facilitate the introductions. Theodore already knew Eliza Holton as a result of an earlier visit to this house in the *faubourg* Sainte-Anne and was acquainted with her altered religious views. Holton had married his cousin Eliza in 1839 in a Presbyterian ceremony. But once the Holtons' connection to the Church of Messiah was established in 1842, she had embraced the new allegiance willingly.

The other female, however, proved to be more fascinating. Somewhat older and taller than Eliza, she seemed quite self-possessed ~ even more assertive than most women. His Fanny had been the model of femininity: delicate and sweet and so dependent on him as a male protector. This Mary Kent Bradbury was a different woman indeed.

The first opportunity Theodore had to relate to her came after they had been seated in the small dining room next to the parlor. A range of comestibles had already been laid out albeit there was no servant to apportion them. Holton might have moved ahead in March to partner Alfred Hooker in the renamed forwarding firm, but his lifestyle had to date shown to no evidence of change.

Theodore took the initiative. "I have been told that you are visiting our fair city in order to provide service to the Church of Messiah. I am long aware that Luther calls himself a Unitarian but I am ignorant of the various distinctions in the Christian creed. You are looking at a Jew who swears by his Torah and almost never enters a church."

"We are open to all faiths, Mr. Hart. Faith combined with reason: that is our creed."

Theodore was wary. *Is she proselytizing?* "It so happens that I have family in Three Rivers, some of whom are committed to Deism. And yet they adhere to no religious institution."

"They are not organized that way. We, on the other hand, have a church. Unitarians do share common beliefs with Deists in that we all cherish freedom in matters of faith."

"You will be returning to Boston in the fall? We shall miss your presence in Montreal.'

"I'm a Bostonian through and through. Been living there since we Americans were at war with Britain in 1812. Not that we approved of the war. Most New Englanders didn't share the widespread passion for extending our boundaries. My grandfather was a judge who met Joseph Priestley when he came to America before the turn of the century. He was most impressed with the man's outlook. I've recently given a talk on Priestley, who has, of course, been dead for over forty years."

"I have read of a Priestley, though isn't his reputation that of a scientist? Dephlogisticated air and all that."

"The same man! Not only the one who discovered oxygen but also an expert on optics, vision and colors. But his science only reinforced his belief in humanity. In England he paid dearly for that belief. Rioters encouraged to violence against the French Revolution destroyed Priestley's house, laboratory and library in Birmingham. He finally departed for America and settled in Pennsylvania. For ten years he was what you might call the spiritual leader of Unitarians on this continent."

"Not the religious leader?"

"We're spiritual, not religious."

Holton chose to put an end to this *tête-à-tête*. "Don't you need more credit, Theo, with business so brisk? Given any thought to switching to *La Banque du peuple*? Since getting its charter last year, it has raised its capital to £200,000."

"My father has had a longstanding relationship with the Bank of Montreal. He will be in no hurry to make changes." Theodore was a bit annoyed being dragged into a discussion of finances.

"Speaking of the Bank of Montreal, you probably know that Hays is in serious trouble. The Board of Works is close to bankruptcy and Holmes once more as bank cashier threatens suspension of payments to it. Surprisingly, Holmes is blamed; though the cashier, he is not well regarded by the Tory press given his past political activity."

"But you don't have that kind of problem, do you, Luther?"

"It is true that James Henderson now resides in the Old Burying Grounds on Dorchester. Yet I've associated myself with City Bank even before Henderson succumbed to gout. You have merely to ask Mr. Castle, the current cashier."

"I raise the matter because one does need money to buy good insurance, my friend. Moving cargo over the Lachine rapids and through the channel leading into the Ottawa is always a gamble. I recall the accidents of a few years ago." Theodore didn't need to add that his own firm could offer the appropriate insurance policies. They had talked about it in the past.

* * *

The grapevine was never more active. Word of the deterioration of the health of the recently ennobled Metcalfe had spread throughout the business community populating downtown Montreal. The office of Benjamin Hart and Company was no exception to this rumor mongering. Benjamin was especially disturbed when it was learned that the Governor had actually resigned and that he would be returning to England within weeks. "We may be witnessing, Theo, the end of the Draper-Viger administration with Sir Charles no longer in command. It couldn't come at a worse time."

This opinion was delivered after Theodore had been called into his father's business office off Rue d'Youville on a raw October morning. Theodore couldn't say he was surprised by this assessment; it was undoubtedly shared by most of the Tory merchants who had committed to Metcalfe's side in anticipation of a second session of Parliament at the Marché Ste-Anne. *But surely papa knows I have been no friend of the Governor.* "What do *you* regard as being the worst thing that will happen?"

"I fear for the future of our union. Even with Metcalfe still here, Whitehall has already accepted the general amnesty and has allowed the use of French in official documents. Anglicization of Lower Canada as envisaged by Lord Durham has seemingly been abandoned." Benjamin was never more indignant.

"Has not Metcalfe been stubborn on the question of patronage? Lord Stanley supports that position." Theodore regarded the issue as the crucial one.

"At least that! The Governor has relied more than ever on the advice of Draper and Higginson, the civil secretary. Viger has finally been elected in Three Rivers but his future as co-leader of the government is most uncertain. Don't you agree to at least that?"

"Draper does have all but a dozen of the ridings in Upper Canada as well the foothold in the Eastern Townships and in Montreal. La Fontaine may have close to thirty seats here in Lower Canada but not enough votes to defeat Draper in the legislature. Nevertheless, with Viger and Neilson no longer so effective, the administration is not that stable and Metcalfe will be sorely missed." Theodore remembered that Denis-Benjamin Viger and John Neilson once formed a most powerful coalition. Now Neilson has gone to the Legislative Council and Viger was a beleaguered man in Parliament.

Benjamin Hart sighed. "He will indeed. It is sad. I understand that Pollock, this London doctor sent out by Lord Stanley to treat the growth on the Governor's cheek, has made things worse by applying a chemical that has affected the man's eyesight."

"Cousin Aaron says it was caustic chloride of zinc. He contends that what was a tumor of the flesh has been transformed into a hole in his face."

"Who do you think will replace him as Governor?" Benjamin was obviously perplexed.

"The logical person is Earl Cathcart. He has just taken over command of the forces in British North America and with the boundary dispute unresolved, the Peel government could see some advantage in combining the military post with that of civil administrator." Theodore was referring to the latest diplomatic crisis that currently engaged the United States and Britain. Stalled negotiations between London and Washington over how to divide Oregon had been worrying the Peel government, which was preoccupied with the emergence of a strong Bonapartist movement in France. Meanwhile, the Democrats in the USA, which had campaigned throughout the 1844 presidential election in favor of "Fifty-Four Forty or Fight", had put James Polk, the recently elected head of state, in an awkward position. The compromise of dividing the territory along the 49th parallel appeared out of reach.

"Fair enough! While I have you here, Theo, I should mention that people are talking about your public appearances with an American woman. I heard of it when attending *shul* on *Yom Kippur*. You have not said anything to me directly. I hope that this isn't leading anywhere."

Theodore, whose squiring of Mary Kent to a local fall festival had roused gossip, was undoubtedly leading to a confrontation that could not be avoided. "On the contrary, papa, it is leading in a direction that cannot but cause you pain. You may have noticed that I haven't been at *shul* in recent weeks. I have been accepted in the Church of the Messiah. I intend to marry Mary Kent Bradbury."

Benjamin Hart was thunderstruck. He had almost single-handedly resurrected the congregation that now gathered routinely at the Rue Chenneville synagogue. Theodore had prayed there from the day its doors were opened. The father finally regained his voice, a voice so unnatural that it prompted Theodore to shudder. "You have, Theo, dishonored the Hart family by this act. Your mother will be heartbroken when she hears of it. First it was Philip who betrayed me, then your brother Henry married outside the faith and now it is you. Can I expect Wellington in Liverpool to do likewise?"

Theodore didn't remain in the office to hear more. Instead he retrieved his overcoat and stepped onto the street. *I must talk again to Mary about what to do next.* He had already discussed marriage with her but the assumption had been that the nuptials would happen in Montreal even if they would not take place on Rue Chenneville. Now that option looked dubious and Mary Kent might yet get her way. He resigned himself to the conclusion that Boston should be a more agreeable place for newlyweds.

Nevertheless, there were many regrets. He walked swiftly. The October chill was even more intense than in the morning.

*   *   *

The carriage ride to Boston was endured without complaint. The couple didn't relish traveling in November weather. Yet there was some urgency. Mary Kent had missed her period. Waiting for the spring to wed was no longer an acceptable alternative. Theodore took some comfort in the fact that the rift in his family would likely be alleviated by the likely emergence of a grandchild.

Charles Bradbury proved to be a most gracious man albeit Theodore did wonder whether he was genuinely pleased having his daughter betrothed to a foreigner and a Jew to boot. *Not a sign of regret.* The mother was the more inquisitive of the two. Would any member of the Hart family be attending the ceremony? She had already written to her parents in Maine to brave traveling the snow-covered highway to Boston to be present at the nuptials.

Bradbury shushed his wife. "Montreal is much farther away than is Portland, Eleonora. It is not that easy for the parents of Mr. Hart as it is for the Cummings. Moreover, there may not be enough time. It is my understanding that Mary Kent has booked passage to England for the honeymoon. It may not be the prudent thing to do, however. Who knows what foolish things our government in Washington is capable of?"

Theodore recognized what Bradbury was getting at. "I did read in the newspaper this morning that majority opinion is in favor of claiming the entire Oregon territory for the United States. There is talk of 'manifest destiny' as justification for such a claim. The Peel government will not abide such an outcome."

"Our president has not committed himself but Mr. Polk has already shown his temper with regard to Texas. It may not be wise to sail to England in such circumstances."

Mary Kent interceded. "Please, father! Don't believe everything you read. Neither side is in a position to undertake war."

Nothing more was said on the subject. Theodore devoted himself walking the streets of Boston with his fiancé as guide despite the imminence of winter. Meanwhile Mary Kent wanted him to confer with Ezra Stiles Gannett, who would be performing the ceremony at the Federal Street Church in Boston. "He's the Unitarian pastor who defends our principles against Transcendentalism."

Needless to say, Theodore was bemused by this citing of a theological quarrel within the Unitarian movement. Mary Kent explained. Theodore Parker, it seemed, was preaching in Boston despite being ostracized by many of the church officials, including Gannett. Nevertheless, Parker had friends such as Louisa May Alcott, William Lloyd Garrison, Julia Ward Howe and Elizabeth

Cady Stanton, who were in the process of installing him as a minister in a new house of worship in suburban West Roxbury.

The conference with the pastor came off quite nicely and the couple departed the church without much ado. They were about to cross over to the corner of Milk and Congress from Federal when Mary Kent chose to apologize for the sorry state of the neighborhood. Industry and commerce had come to the area; machine and carpentry shops lined Federal and made the green surrounding this oasis of spirituality seem so incongruous. More noteworthy for Theodore was the gathering of indigent men, women and children outside the entrance to this church. He was genuinely puzzled and sought an explanation.

"Have you not heard? These Irish peasants are in great peril. A blight destroyed the potato crop and starvation has driven hundreds if not thousands onto ships destined for Boston. Let me show you!" Without waiting for Theodore to object, she began marching to the Long Lane bounding the harbor.

The dock area was more crowded than Theodore could have anticipated. Bedraggled passengers were emerging from the sailing boats straddling Long Wharf. He had never seen such a piteous sight. The men were gaunt, the women more so and yet they hung on to their children. All were being herded into renovated warehouses to provide them with some relief from the cold.

It occurred to him that the ships returning to the British Isles would be empty in comparison. He and his bride would be traveling at a tragic time.

If they ask me what are my propositions for relief of the distress,
I answer, first, Tenant-Right. I would propose a law giving to every man
his own. I would give the landlord his land, and a fair rent for it;
but I would give the tenant compensation for every shilling
he might have laid out on the land in permanent improvements.
And what next do I propose? Repeal of the Union.
DANIEL O'CONNELL
(address to the Repeal Association, December 8, 1845)

In reference to our proposing these measures, I have no wish
to rob any person of the credit which is justly due to him for them.
But I may say that neither the gentlemen sitting on the benches opposite,
nor myself, nor the gentlemen sitting round me....Sir, the name which
ought to be, and which will be associated with the success of
these measures is the name of a man who, acting, I believe,
from pure and disinterested motives, has advocated their cause
with untiring energy, and by appeals to reason, expressed
by an eloquence, the more to be admired because it was unaffected
and unadorned—the name which ought to be and will be associated
with the success of these measures is the name of Richard Cobden.
SIR ROBERT PEEL
(Speaking to the Commons, June 29, 1846)

Thirty six

A rthur Wellington Hart could feel the draught emanating from the open door; he realized that Selena was returning from her afternoon outing albeit somewhat behind schedule. But letting in a December breeze for too long would offset the good work of the house's fireplaces. He would have to leave his writing desk to reprimand her.

When he reached the vestibule, Wellington found his wife in some disarray. Packages were strewn on the floor and her headdress was askew. "What has happened to you, dear? You appear most distressed."

"Liverpool can be so trying at this time of year and the city in such chaos. It was so busy in and about the dock area that the carriage couldn't get through the streets. The worst of it is that we had to protect ourselves from being overrun as those doomed refugees disembarked the ships in the harbor. They are desperate people and who knows what molestations could have occurred."

Wellington understood the point. But there was little that could be done about it. Liverpool, long the artery to and from Ireland, had become a way station for an exodus. It has been like this since September at which time the famine happening on the other side of the Irish Sea became public knowledge. "Unfortunately, I fear it will get worse before it gets better. It may be time for you to visit your family in Exeter, where such unpleasantness may not be so evident."

"Intolerable! Can nothing else be done by our government?" Selena wasn't taking his suggestion seriously.

"The Prime Minister does propose to repeal the Corn Laws so as to reduce the price of bread. He has even tendered his resignation to the Queen on this matter because his Cabinet is not with him. It is a fact, however, that half the potato crop in Ireland has been destroyed. Action must be taken though the ministers in Parliament are so divided. Come Selena! Be seated while I pick up your shopping from the floor. I'm certain you want to check on Harriet, who is with the nurse upstairs."

Selena was calmer once seated. "I did learn from our driver that Daniel O'Connell is in town this very minute. Came from Dublin in the morning. He'll be speaking tonight from the balcony of the Adelphi Hotel. To think that but a year ago he was a convicted felon. Now we will be paying rapt attention to how he is reacting to the famine."

Wellington had followed O'Connell's career closely since arriving seven years earlier in England. The man had yet to be elected mayor of Dublin at that time but already he was celebrated as the major public figure who mobilized British opinion in favor of Catholic Emancipation. His current cause was the repeal of the 1801 Act of Union and to that end had drawn huge crowds throughout Ireland. At Tara a reported 750,000 citizens cheered him on during one "monster" rally. Nevertheless, in early 1844 the Peel government chose to prosecute O'Connell for sedition and convinced a jury to jail him. Though released in September of that year, this parliamentarian returned to civil life a hero to the Irish citizenry albeit not as a healthy man. "Will he still be demanding repeal in the current circumstances? I admit that the man is a master organizer. His campaign for Catholic emancipation showed what an appeal to public opinion can accomplish. Yet I am convinced that most Englishmen are not in favor of giving the Irish their own legislature. News of the famine will not likely improve their willingness to support repeal. I think I might walk down to the Adelphi later today to see if O'Connell is still committed to that cause."

They were interrupted by the appearance of their three-year old daughter. Harriet Blanche had been trained to control her exuberances but on this afternoon she proved to be unusually demonstrative in the affections for her mother. The nurse sought to restrain the child but Selena waved her away.

Meanwhile Wellington decided to keep to his intention of hearing what O'Connell had to say. There was time enough before dinner was served to walk down to the public square outside the hotel. He donned his heaviest cloak to withstand the chill of the December outdoors, adjusted his top hat and stepped into the street. The walk was a short one and he soon could hear the tumult. Irish bricklayers and dock workers were already crowding the square in front of the Adelphia to hear the "Great Liberator" give his oration. The influx of such immigrants had brought the population of Liverpool to beyond 300,000 in recent years. O'Connell had passed through the city many times on his way to London's Parliament. Curiously, Wellington had previously thought seriously about going over to Paradise Street on the occasional Sunday that such a visit occurred to listen to O'Connell speak at Repeal Hall. But he never did.

Today he was being treated to the sight of this aging agitator, resplendent in a long cloak but daringly showing his shock of hair unadorned, speaking extemporarily. O'Connell did not hesitate to damn equally the Whigs (Lord John Russell and the 3rd Earl Grey) and the Tories (Peel and Wellington) for their inadequate responses to the distress in Ireland. Now, he was saying, was the time to press ahead with repeal of the union – in effect, a dramatic shift in the relationship between Catholic Ireland and Protestant Britain.

Arthur Wellington was contemplative. *O'Connell is indeed a threat to law and order. The anger in the crowd is palpable and the man is not holding back in his rhetoric.*

* * *

London was still the dirty metropolis Wellington had escaped when he first came from the other side of the Atlantic. Even the advent of May and the initial signs of summer weather didn't alter this assessment. But there was business to conclude for Benjamin Hart and Company and it could be done only in the big city. The latest letter from Montreal reminded him of a variety of tasks previously enumerated by his father. By coincidence that letter came only days before he received a note from his younger brother; Theodore had been spending a few months in London accompanied by a new wife. Wellington was forewarned of this latest attachment: Papa had declared that Theo had taken a reckless course, marrying outside the faith and committing himself to one with strange ideas.

Wellington could hardly reject a visit from a sibling despite parental censure but it did disturb him that another family rift had developed. First, it had been Aaron Philip that had defied Benjamin. Wellington had taken his father's side and had actually benefited from the estrangement. He had been more ambiguous about the choices made by the other male offspring and their effect on him. Henry Naphthali remained for a while within the family fold, worked for his Uncle Moses, but eventually followed Wellington to Toronto, took up law and settled in St Louis. Furthermore, he too wed outside the faith. Jane Elizabeth Church, born in Connecticut, had already given him five children. Also Baruch Frederick was no longer under the Union Jack but rather in New Orleans (the American hinterland was attracting immigrants as never before). Benjamin Moses, the youngest of the sons, was off in New Jersey. Unmarried, he had not yet offended the rules of conduct insisted upon by the parents. Only Theodore had agreed to serve with his father, and now his future was in some doubt.

Theodore appeared content enough when two days later they faced each other in a fashionable restaurant near the hotel. Wellington had to decide whether he would confront his brother on his life decisions. But at least he would do some probing. "Your note mentioned you being in Boston for a marriage. I take it that your stay in London is in the way of a honeymoon. None of our correspondents here cited any business contact on your part."

"I had no instructions from papa to intercede in your dealings with our British clientele. Mary Kent, whom you have yet to meet, was satisfied with us just touring London – the landmarks, the theatre and like institutions. Yet we must return to Montreal immediately. Mary Kent is with child and we do not want to be trapped here in England when she gives birth."

"When is she due?"

"Probably in August. By then we ought to be nicely settled in our quarters at home."

Arthur showed some pique. "You did not invite me to your wedding, not that I would have sailed to Boston even in the best circumstances. But it is another example of a family growing apart. None of my brothers and sisters stood with me at the altar when I married in Exeter. At least Raphael traveled to Montreal to wed Harriet ten years ago even if the Schoyers live in New York."

Theodore shrugged. "We seem fated to wander away from home. Benjamin Moses in New Jersey, Emily married in California. Yet I have every intention of living out my days in Montreal. At least two sisters remain there although Constance is no longer in the house. And I think papa is content with how his progeny have managed."

The waiter brought the coffee and a generous portion of a rice pudding. Wellington dipped into the dessert before he remembered something else. "Papa writes that he has had a new will drawn up. It was dated on February

23 and leaves most of his estate to our mother. Three of the family advocates are the executors."

"Who specifically?"

"Henry Judah, Sam David and Adolphus Hart. Adolphus has apparently moved his whole practice from Three Rivers to Montreal now that he's married to our sister." Arthur smiled knowingly; he had had a letter from Hannah Constance just after the ceremony in December, 1844. She had set her cap for her cousin in Trois-Rivières ever since those stormy days of 1837-38 though she had to wait until she was in her twenties before the knot was tied. *What a determined girl!*

"Why do you enquire about the executors? Do you foresee mama not looking out for her children when she inherits? I ask this, brother, because one ought not to forget that the old will stipulated that mama renounce any claim she might have by virtue of the marriage contract back forty years ago. Did he insist on that in this latest testament?"

"No, the document makes no mention of that old proviso. Papa probably forgot all about it. He was then worried, of course, that his mother-in-law would become a burden on the family. As it so happens, the widow did live with us in papa's house in Montreal before she died three years ago. She had my old bedroom." Wellington chuckled at this reminisce.

Theodore sipped his coffee. "It was so different from when we were growing up, all sitting around the old dining room table competing for the attention of the elders. We were very much a family. I would not have believed then that papa and mama would choose not to be in Boston for my wedding. They took such great pride in the ceremony before Reverend Piza when I took Fanny under the *chuppah*."

"Don't be disingenuous, Theo! You know why they weren't there. They are set in their ways. To tell the truth, I favor theirs over yours."

* * *

There was still enough time during his London trip for Wellington to consult with Selena's cousin living in Westminster. Was it true that the Irish crisis was undermining the Peel administration? And what consequences for business would come out of the uproar in Parliament? Wellington had heard rumors that the Prime Minister was preparing to resign. There was no certainty that the crop failure in Ireland would not be repeated in the coming months. Summer was already upon the country and parliamentarians were eager to depart Westminster if only there could be a resolution of the matter. An invitation to the office of barrister Francis Henry Goldsmid ensued.

The clerk ushered Wellington and his friend into a windowed room at the Lincoln's Inn. Goldsmid, the son of the renowned Sir Isaac, member of the banking family of that name, was reputed to be the first Jew to be admitted to the English bar. He undoubtedly looked the part of a seasoned barrister despite the fact that he was still in his thirties. *And he has connections!*

Goldsmid spoke frankly enough. "My guess is that the Whig opposition will go along with Peel on repealing the Corn Laws but that the Tories, still divided, will desert their Prime Minister at the first opportunity."

"May I say, sir, that all this sounds like a repeat of what happened last December." Yet Wellington was suitably deferential.

There was a wry smile on Goldsmid's face. "At that time Peel dared Sir John Russell to accomplish what he couldn't do. The Whigs are as uncertain as the Tories on the Irish famine. You did know that Howick – I mean the new Earl Grey – refused to join Russell in a new coalition last December. Claimed it was because he wouldn't serve with Palmerston also being in the cabinet but I suspect he wasn't eager to take on the fight against the Corn Laws. It will take somebody like Cobden to show some leadership in that regard."

"Will it be O'Connell who benefits from this squabbling? He still insists on pressing for taking the Irish members out of the Commons and into a local legislature." Wellington's tone was tenuous.

Goldsmid shook his head. "The idea of abolishing the union does not sit well with most Englishmen. For O'Connell it is a lost cause and he will falter as a result. Even the blight gets more attention. But there is a connection. Did you see the cartoon in *Punch* last week? A drawing of O'Connell as a potato! The banner: O'Connell, the real potato blight."

Wellington joined in on the round of laughter. But was he satisfied with the man's easy dismissal of the "Great Liberator"? He wondered if the troubles in Ireland could be overcome by a change of government in London.

*I beg to acknowledge the receipt of your communication concerning
my election as Hazan to your congregation. For the confidence thus
evinced towards me I have to return my warmest thanks, and beg
most emphatically to assure you that my most earnest exertions
will be directed towards securing your esteem by a proper
and zealous discharge of my duties.*
ABRAHAM DE SOLA
(letter to the Shearith Israel, September 17, 1846)

*The usual quantity of kissing and rejoicing followed the ceremony –
the company then departed. - My wife and I then changed our dresses
for traveling and at half past four we made our way to
the Steamer Queen for Quebec. Numbers called on board & bid us adieu
with many many kind wishes. I should here mention that our friends
bestowed on my bride numerous & valuable presents. Sophia & I slept
in the same stateroom but I kept to my promise to her which was that
we should occupy different berths until we reached our house. Arrived
at Quebec at 6 am – a cab drove us home – we were fatigued –
at least my bride was – we retired- breakfasted at 2.*
ABRAHAM JOSEPH
(diary, November 15, 1846)

Thirty seven

For Abraham Joseph it was quite an honor to have Antoine-Charles Taschereau come up to his rooms in Lemoine's. As he confided to Ira Craig Hart earlier in the day, the presence of the renowned patrician to celebrate the first night of Pentecost constituted quite a coup. Taschereau had explained that on the morrow he would be off to Mass at the cathedral to honor Whitsunday, which coincided with the Jewish harvest festival of Shavuot. Both came fifty days after the Passover-Easter holidays. (Abraham had at one time wondered on reading the *Exodus* story why a harvest could occur in May.) This evening, however, Taschereau was free to pray at a place of his own choosing.

The invitation originated with Ira Craig, who fraternized with the elite of Quebec City even more diligently than did Abraham. This Hart cousin had initially made the city his base of operation whereas Alexander Thomas ran the *Hart* steamer service out of Trois-Rivières. Despite the eventual sale of that boat, he had elected to remain in Quebec City. A chance remark that

Taschereau's wife Adélaïne was spending the forthcoming weekend together with most of their children at the manor house some distance away on the other side of the river prompted Ira Craig to urge Abraham to make his place at Lemoine's available for an evening's gathering. At the time the two of them hadn't thought seriously of offering a religious setting. Taschereau saw it otherwise. "I honor the Lord's Day of our Christian calendar but at the same time I realize that the Jewish Pentecost, which you call the Feast of the Weeks, tells me that the seven weeks after Easter apply to both religions. The languages may be different; I cannot comprehend your Hebrew although I know the text to be holy. Let my Latin mix with your prayers."

It was a chilly evening, cold enough to activate the fireplace and the stove as well. Abraham boiled some water on the cast-iron stove top and made tea. He suspected that before the evening was over, a bottle or two of port would be opened. This could be the last socializing before he moved to his new abode and it warranted some imbibing.

Taschereau had the bearing of an aristocrat, and for good reason. He was a son of the late Gabriel-Elzéar Taschereau, the *seigneur* of Sainte-Marie in the Beauce area south of the Quebec City, and once a judge of the Court of Common Pleas and the *grand voyer* for the district of Quebec. Antoine-Charles himself had been elected to the legislature for Beauce (subsequently Dorchester) in 1830, 1834 and 1841. His nephew, Joseph-André, was currently the member from Dorchester and acting for the Draper-Viger government as the Solicitor-General of Canada East.

Earlier in the week both Taschereau and Abraham had been in attendance when the leading citizens of Quebec City gathered in a room at the Union Hotel to debate whether it was time for the community to have it own district savings bank. Montreal already had two, the Provident and the Montreal City, vying for the savings of its citizenry. At the meeting there wasn't unanimity; Provident had a reputation of lending its money much too freely and at the same time favoring the Protestant element in the city. Should a Quebec City institution rely primarily on the francophone community for its customers even if the timber industry was controlled by *les Anglais*? Abraham spoke forcefully against sectarianism albeit he recognized it would take some doing to reach a consensus at this point in time.

Eventually the port was dispensed from a decanter and the conversation ranged from assessing the outlook for Canadian governance now that Earl Cathcart had been ensconced as Metcalfe's successor to the likelihood of the border dispute with the United States being settled amicably. The banking matter got scant attention.

Ira Craig was less diplomatic than Abraham when it came to the political issues. He didn't believe that Draper could win every vote in Parliament despite Cathcart having been confirmed officially the month before and presumably backing the coalition to the hilt. The La Fontaine-led opposition was growing in public approval. "What surprises us is that a Taschereau votes with the government."

"Joseph-André and I do not see things the same way. Our family is noted for being on the side of reform. Joseph-André still supports what Draper is doing. I suspect, however, that if he lost his post my nephew would be more inclined to join ranks of the *groupe canadien-français.*"

Taschereau's frankness didn't surprise Abraham. The latter had it on good authority that Denis-Benjamin Viger was on the verge of resigning. Even the *L'Aurore des Canadas*, the newspaper which supported him, was hinting at this being the end of an era.

The same sense of changing times occupied the minds of the threesome. Apparently the Oregon Border Treaty would be signed in the next thirty days and Cathcart's advice on military affairs was no longer demanded in London. The Peel government was preoccupied with the Irish famine. But that could be all the more reason to make a change in the Canadas now that the risk of war had been removed.

The speculation as well as the banter went on for hours and another bottle of port was brought out. Taschereau resisted. It was already half past one. Both Taschereau and Ira Craig agreed that it was time to call it a night.

*　*　*

Abraham didn't sleep well despite having the most comfortable cabin on the steamboat *Queen.* He had planned for this trip to Montreal for almost a year. Traveling to his mother's place on Place Près-de-Ville for the High Holidays could be accomplished in less than 24 hours but it did mean an overnight passage. His mind was on what would be the reaction to an enterprise initiated almost a year ago. He had kept it a surprise for Sophie; worrying him was that all his planning might come to naught.

A single candle provided enough light to allow him to view himself in the small mirror supplied to the cabin. He had begun growing a beard, an increasingly common vanity among men of his age. Now over thirty, a hirsute bachelor may or may not appeal to Sophie. At the same time she ought to be impressed by his new status as an owner of a full-fledged home.

The acquisition of the house on Clapham Terrace had its origin when Abraham noticed a foreclosure notice almost a year before. The house and a lot immediately to its rear were located on Grand Allée, the extension of the

Saint-Louis road outside the city wall. When first built fifteen years before, it had been part of six uniquely designed but structurally joined residences that were attracting the attention of the more prosperous citizens in town. One of them was John Greaves Clapham who had rented his home while on military duty elsewhere. His fortunes, however, had deteriorated and Abraham gained the property as the highest bidder in a foreclosure sale.

Once the deed was signed Abraham had to wait out the winter until the tenant moved out and carpenters, masons and painters could be brought in to do the renovations. Through the early days in the month of June he had had to travel to the Upper Town every day to consult with the crew. Impatience overcame him; on the tenth instant he had decided to sleep in one of the bedrooms while the carpenters and painters finished their tasks. On that Wednesday morning he was accompanied by a young lad named Ambroise who would be helping him with the transfer of furnishings from Lemoine's. It did cost him $4 a month plus board and lodgings for the boy.

The steamer docked in Montreal as scheduled just before dawn. The city was alive with morning activity. He hailed a *calèche* to take him to Place Près-de-Ville. Rachel Joseph greeted him warmly; Jesse had already left for the day but had promised to see his brother at dinner. Abraham carried his traveling bag to his old bedroom and then joined his mother for breakfast. *There is much to talk about.*

"You can congratulate me, mama. I am to become a magistrate for the district of Quebec. Received a letter from Dr. Daly this very week saying that the appointment will come very shortly." Abraham hadn't had the chance to thank formally the secretary of the province or the Governor himself though he had expected that he would be so honored. Taschereau had intimated that his name was before Earl Cathcart. Abraham reckoned that he had been fully embraced by the people who counted in Quebec City.

Abraham also elaborated on the features of his new dwelling on Clapham Terrace. "I can barely wait to describe it to our friends. Indeed, I hope to visit the Davids this very afternoon and give them the good news. We have much to rejoice even as we say our Yom Kippur prayers tomorrow. I look forward to seeing our *chazzan* again."

Rachel Joseph grimaced. "Reverend Piza is quite distracted. He will be sailing back to England before the year is out."

"Piza leaving us? What will happen to our *shul?*" Abraham was truly ruffled.

"You must not upset yourself, Abe. He is being replaced by someone else from the Bevis Marks. We expect the new *chazzan* in January." Rachel Joseph went on to explain that one Abraham De Sola would soon be the designated cleric for the Shearith Israel.

"Is everybody happy with the situation? What are De Sola's qualifications?"

"He is quite the scholar, the son of the senior *chazzan* at Bevis Marks. We are told that one of the cantors there recently died and David Piza offered himself as a candidate for the position. After all, though an orphan he grew up a member in that synagogue. The chief rabbi recommended that we be satisfied with Abraham De Sola, who is six years younger than Reverend Piza but has all the credentials to be a good *chazzan*. What is more we recently received a letter from the young man showing his willingness to come to Montreal. Unfortunately he can't do so until mid-winter."

Abraham waited till after lunch to inform his mother that he would be visiting the Davids. *She must know why I am determined to call on Sophie. Yet she has promised not to interfere in my courtship.*

"Don't forget, Abe! Dinner will be early today. We must eat before dark."

The walk to Rue Craig was with much trepidation. Would he fail with Sophia as he had with her sister some years before? Theodore had preempted his interest in Frances David albeit he now realized it would have been a marriage fraught with trouble. Yet there was no denying that he had not showed enough initiative at that time. Would it happen again? He had been told that Moses Eleazar David, Sophia's cousin, had already declared his affections for her. She hadn't yet committed herself to such an attachment but there was always the possibility that she could change her mind.

Sophia was at home helping with the holiday preparations. So was Phoebe, who insisted that all of them have tea in the drawing room. Abraham had come to the realization that the sisters were very conscious of the fact that they were unmarried though Phoebe was already twenty eight and Sophia but four years younger.

Abraham's praise of his prospects – the house on Clapham Terrace, the appointment as a Justice of the Peace – had the purpose of advancing his suit even if he couldn't be explicit in that purpose. Phoebe demonstrated more enthusiasm for his good fortune than did her sister. Abraham watched Sophia intently for signs of approbation, which, if there, were only reluctantly given. *Is she comparing me to Moses Eleazar?*

She had a strange question: did Abraham intend to call on the Benjamin Hart household before the day was out? It took him a few minutes to decode the message. She was suggesting that his main interest was in Dora Hart, the one unmarried daughter living on Rue des Récollets. *Does she actually believe that Dora is my intended bride?*

Phoebe finally withdrew from the room; there was more to do in the kitchen. It was now necessary to disabuse her of the notion that Dorothea Catharine Hart was the object of his affections. He had met Dora on the various occasions he came to Montreal and she had now reached the age of eighteen. She might have been quite accomplished in many of the arts – she always showed her poetry to her acquaintances – but he had never considered her seriously as a possible wife. Abraham was frustrated; he had spent three hours at the David house and yet he had not convinced this young woman that it was she he desired. He had to return to his mother's for dinner and was expected to pay a courtesy call on the Harts, but he would not give up pressing his suit. *It will not be like the last time!*

*   *   *

The image of Sophia baring her breasts dissipated only slowly as Abraham fell asleep in his cabin on the steamboat. Another trip to Montreal but for a very happy purpose. This was Monday and he would be married on the Wednesday. His nightwear had already been donned. This time he was dressed more warmly than during his September trip; mid November, which was near the end of the navigation season, called for greater protection from the elements.

He was indeed content. Things couldn't have worked out better. He had gone back to the David home on the eve of Yom Kippur and had confronted Sophia as never before. She agreed to walk with him back to the Joseph place to pick up his prayer book. Nobody accompanied them even though Abraham suggested that perhaps Phoebe or a member of Aaron David's family join them. She had made up her mind; they should be united in marriage. She was ready to yield all. They walked back arm-in-arm to the David house.

Needless to say, the Joseph household was thrilled by their engagement. The nuptials would not be delayed despite the absence of Reverend Piza. Rabbi Jacques Judah Lyons was prevailed upon to travel from New York City to do the officiating. Brother Jesse Joseph came down to Quebec City, insisting that he had business to do downriver, and spent almost a week helping Abraham host a bachelor's party and to set up the house for an added occupant. He was even there for Abraham's 31st birthday, which they celebrated on the Sabbath just prior to walking down to the Lower Town so that Jesse could catch the *Queen* to return to Montreal. Subsequently Abraham went up Rue Côte de la Montagne to Rue Saint-Louis and then to his house in the Upper Town. There was still time to write his last letter to Sophia. *No need to maintain this daily correspondence come Wednesday.*

It was on the Monday night that he himself settled in his berth on the steamer. The erotic dream finally ended with deep sleep. He was ready for a major change in his life.

On the Tuesday morning he spent the day and evening with Sophia. In the afternoon the contract of marriage was executed before a Montreal notary. Wednesday did finally dawn. In the morning Abraham had breakfast with his mother and family, then went out and paid off all his accounts. Subsequently he went back to his mother's at noon to dress. Next Abraham made his way to Rue Saint-Jacques. The ceremony at 2:30 was being held at the home of Dr. Aaron Hart David. The Reverend Lyons of New York officiated, and a large gathering was in attendance.

The following day he wrote in his diary. "All was fun until the last moment when I was rather nervous and began to feel for the nervousness of my darling intended wife – but she behaved beautifully – was firm and altho' her little hand trembled when I put on the ring – one could not have behaved better had she been twice as old (she was actually 24) or twice her size."

There was no time to waste. The new couple had to be on board the *Queen* for the return trip to Quebec City. It was not till the next day that Abraham lived his fantasy – Sophia's bare breasts and much more.

I am getting very weak and scarcely can do any business.
I cannot read not with spectacles at my advanced age 77
the 28th nov. last. Aleck is in bad health and Sarah this sometime past.
I have never heard anything of Orobio. I do not speak to Areli
he is so passionate impudent and foolish.
He has three boys and a girl. Aleck has two boys one a cripple.
Louisa stays over the river, at an Irish family.
MOSES HART
(letter to Henry Hart, September, 1846)

alors et au dit cas sa part retournera à l'autre survivante et dans
le cas ou la survivante descenderoit aussi sans enfans, alors
et au dit cas ceux fiefs retourneront en toute proprieté aux autres enfans
et petits enfans du dit testateur, nommes Moses Ezechiel Hart,
son fils naturel, et à Moses Alexander Hart et David Alexander Hart,
enfans issue du mariage du dit Alexander Thomas Hart et de Mariann
Judah, … et à Edward Hart, et Moses Aaron Hart, enfans issue
du mariage de Aaron M. Hart et Marguerite McCarthey et à
Henry Moses Hart, enfant de Benjamin Moses Hart fils du dit
testateur, actuellement dans les Etats Unis
MOSES HART
(his will and testament, April 1, 1847)

Thirty eight

M oses Hart could barely reply dispassionately to the barbs coming from the mouths of his two "legitimate" children as the trio had arranged for a private talk at his abode on Rue Alexandre. They were revealing grievances he had only suspected they shared since they reached adulthood. Areli Blake's main target was half-brother Alexander Thomas, who resided with their father and who had succeeded so well as an independent businessman. Louisa was revealing a love-hate relationship with Mary McCarthy Brown, the titular mistress of the house on Rue Alexandre. His daughter could hardly be comforted by the fact that the entrenched "wife", several years younger than she, was her father's confidant on matters going beyond just management of a household.

The study in which they sat was darkening; the autumnal sun had begun disappearing beyond horizon. Areli rose from his chair and indicated that he had to leave for home. Moses determined to get in the last word.

"Are you suggesting, son, that Aleck owes his success in timber because I favored him over you? You have been given every opportunity to take the initiative in business. Aleck had the sense to extricate himself from running the steamboat when he saw it wasn't going to stay profitable. Now he is gathering wood from our seigneuries on the south shore and I applaud him for doing so."

"Damn you, papa! Whatever I've done has never satisfied you. Let's leave it that!" Areli stormed out of the room.

Moses shifted his gaze to Louisa, who had remained silent during the latest exchange. "You too want to damn me. Take pity on an old man who has trouble seeing! But what will you do about your complaints?"

"I'm ready to do something, papa. Julia has invited me to stay in Saint-Célestin. I've decided to accept."

Moses frowned. His eldest daughter had lived on Rue Alexandre for most of her adult life. She had spurned marriage these twenty years or so and never found a vocation. How would she fare living on the other side of the river? Saint-Célestin wasn't that far from Nicolet and the ferry that crossed the St Lawrence, but he guessed that she wasn't too willing to be an integral part of the family in Trois-Rivières. In addition, Julia McCarthy could be a disturbing influence on Louisa. Though both sisters were Irish Catholic, they had very much a different outlook on religion. "You are being rather hasty, Louisa. Not that we can be together forever. I'll be seventy-eight next month. But what future can you foresee living on the other side of the river? You have also relied on me to care for you."

"Papa, I wasn't always able to rely on you in the past. You separated me from my mama when I was but a child of six. I will never forgive you for that."

"Never forgive! It was for your own good. She and I were not on speaking terms. Your grandmother in Montreal offered you a haven." Moses had at times regretted having tried to resolve a domestic affair by using Dolly Hart for that purpose. In the end his wife Sarah retreated to her father's home in Verchères for a couple of years. Even when the parents reconciled, Louisa had to remain in Montreal, where she was enrolled in a girl's school.

"Haven? You abandoned me. Wouldn't answer my letters! Grandma kept telling me that I ought not to go home because not all was well with you and mama. And then I'm told that mama has sued for divorce." Louisa's anger was palpable. She wasn't forgetting the shame that had befallen her during this period up to 1815. She had quit Miss Gambell's School the previous year.

"You had your chance to marry. Matthias Gomez agreed to wed you when you were staying with your aunt in New York. I would not have opposed you being part of the Gomez family." Moses wasn't ready to admit that he had mixed feelings about the proposed match. The Gomez brothers, the last of a generation of Sephardic Jews, had been well known to Aaron and Dolly Hart and could claim being one of the most prominent families in Manhattan. Moses remembered visiting Benjamin Gomez, the bookseller located at 32 Maiden Lane, while attending Ezekiel's New York nuptials back in 1794. Matthias was Benjamin's only son and was widely known for both his verve and his haughtiness. In the end Moses was relieved when Louisa spurned Matthias' advances, this Gomez ending the line of male descendants when he was killed in a duel in New Orleans in 1833.

"Be honest, papa. You have been too busy over the years accumulating wealth and fathering children to worry about my happiness. It's about time I removed myself from the picture. Let Mary Brown take care of you!"

*   *   *

Mary had done all she could to make Moses Hart's 78th birthday a success. Of course, Alexander and Miriam did their part, they being resident at the house on Rue Alexandre. Even Areli and his brood consented to attend despite the fact that father and son were barely on speaking terms. Louisa, on the other hand, had left town and Moses couldn't be certain that she would deign to honor her elderly father with her presence in the big drawing room this coming evening. *Maybe it would be for the best; her hostility towards me is so transparent.*

Moses took pride in reaching yet another birthday; Every November 28 was a milestone. (Brother Ezekiel had failed to make it past seventy-three anniversaries.) Not that he, the oldest of the Hart clan, felt in the best of health. His ability to read was limited and he no longer could roam without a cane about the common on the other side of Rue des Forges. Moreover, living with a relatively young woman wasn't the pleasure it once was. Thankfully his common-law mate paid due respect for his age.

Actually Mary McCarthy Brown wasn't quite as supportive as before; she had become quite exercised by what was happening about her. Born in Ireland and in contact with her Erin relatives, she kept up to date on what was transpiring there. The news from her place of birth was most disheartening.

Moses knew very little of the tragedy. He found it hard to read the *Nation*, the newspaper founded by *Young Ireland*, the intellectuals associated with the repeal campaign of Daniel O'Connell. Mary did subscribe, and she was alarmed by the recent schism in the movement. The militants had broken with O'Connell, who eschewed violence in support of mass protest.

Mary was particularly entranced by a poem written by somebody appearing under the pseudonym of Speranza. It caught the sense of rage that was gripping most Catholic Irish, including expatriates like her. Moses had chided her in the past for overt nationalism. She had once applauded an editorial position taken by Thomas D'Arcy McGee in a Boston publication. It had advocated that the Irish in Canada support Baldwin and La Fontaine because responsible government north of the USA border was the same cause as O'Connell's call for repeal of the British union act. Moses had been less enthusiastic about the stance of the political opposition in Canada albeit the fall of the Peel government in Britain was quite worrisome to him.

But Mary had promised him that political differences would not mar their celebration. If anything would upset the festivities, it would be the weather; the first snowstorm of the season was in progress. Would his nieces and nephews, having to struggle through snowdrifts to come over from Rue des Forges, find the experience too distressing? Moses kept checking the scene outside the window in hope that the snow would abate.

In the event most of Ezekiel's offspring were in attendance by the time there was total darkness. None brought children, the bulk of Ezekiel's progeny never marrying. Furthermore, Adolphus Mordecai, living in Montreal, had already written that he couldn't make it to Trois-Rivières. He had a valid excuse; Constance had to care for her first-born, George Ezekiel, who was in a sickly state. Moses regretted the absence; he liked Adolphus, who was more venturesome than his brother, Aaron Ezekiel. As for the newborn George Ezekiel, he was the first grandchild of his late brother and yet unavailable for display.

Not that Moses could boast of that much larger a collection of grandchildren in spite of having sired so many sons and daughters over the decades. Areli Blake, his eldest, did have four youngsters but wife Julia had decided to keep some of them at home. Louisa, in her forties, was a spinster. Other sons and daughters who were now adults had long since departed Trois-Rivières for other locales. In fact, he had just received a letter from the one living in St Louis; Henry had left for the Wild West almost twenty years before and had a family of his own. He had seldom undertaken to correspond, distances being so forbidding.

Grandchildren? Miriam and Alexander had brought their five-year-old, Moses Alexander, downstairs, dressing him in the latest finery although not able to hide his limp. Their other son, David Alexander, was still upstairs in bed; just over two years old and currently bedridden with cold.

Settled in the most comfortable chair in the room, Moses let himself ponder on the make-up of this gathering. The younger generation in the drawing room was represented primarily by Moses' "natural" children, including those borne by Mary. Aaron Moses was already in his teens. Sarah Dorothea, Charlotte Matilda, Samuel Judah and Andrew had congregated in a corner of the room and were engaged in the hilarity common with being young.

The chatter about him didn't distract Moses from reviewing in his own mind a life that had spread over seven decades, spawned countless children (he had known many women during the years) and taken him to various locations in Lower Canada, upstate New York and Great Britain. In the process he had made himself a rich man, a landowner that even his father Aaron would envy if he were alive this day, an investor in other industries, a man willing to interact with the electorate in several districts. *I may be failing in health and betrayed by bad government, but I regret very little.*

The ruminations of Moses Hart were suddenly interrupted by a procession emerging from the kitchen. Mary carried a large cake decorated with a plethora of candles. The applause seemed genuine enough after he blew out the candles. Another year on Rue Alexandre had gone by and he was satisfied.

*   *   *

Aaron Ezekiel Hart had made the proposal that brought Moses this afternoon to the inn on the *Rue du Fleuve*. The latter had frequented the establishment many times over his lifetime. It was once the *auberge Sills* and Sam Sills was probably his father's best friend in Trois-Rivières, but many of the Sills were long since buried.

Using his cane with care, Moses managed to navigate the few streets to the inn without mishap although he did worry about the ice accumulation that was normal in early winter. His nephew kept next to him in case he fell. *Why am I doing this?* In all those years Moses had never consorted with Mathew Bell here or anywhere else. But Aaron Ezekiel thought it was time for such a meeting. Though the two men, unquestionably the two most prominent Anglophones in Trois-Rivières, were almost the same age, they had not crossed paths except during the by-election of 1807 when Ezekiel defeated Bell for a seat in Lower Canada's National Assembly. Perhaps it was inevitable; Bell was living in Trois-Rivières proper as of early autumn after having been based at the distant ironworks for 47 years.

In the past Moses had coveted the lease to the Saint-Maurice ironworks but the *Forges* as they were known for over a century, had eluded his grasp. *It could have been so different.* Money lent by his father to Laterrière, once the works manager, with the object of sharing in the management of the operation, came to naught when Laterrière was imprisoned in 1779. Mathew Bell appeared on the scene fourteen years later and by hook or by crook had held onto the lease for so long.

Not too many patrons were in the dining area when Moses extended his hand to greet Bell and then took a seat opposite to him. Aaron Ezekiel sat between them. Bell may have been in his late seventies and obviously infirm but he had retained the haughty bearing that had been his mark over so many decades. He was British to the core even if he had chosen to settle in the isolated community that constituted the *Forges*. In fact, he had succeeded in recreating the lifestyle of an English gentleman. Moses was aware of Bell's pretensions to being an aristocrat. His house at the ironworks was reputed to be spacious and well furnished. It contained a ballroom in which guests could be entertained in style. Moreover, stables quartering thoroughbreds were on his estate. Even several of the past Governors of the colony were impressed when they visited the property.

Nevertheless, pressure from *Trifluviens* who had long demanded some of Bell's domain be released for cultivation and expansion of the town northward eventually caused the government's Crowns Land Department to put the ironworks up for auction. Last August Bell offered £5,450 to retain the assets but he was outbid.

Aaron Ezekiel opened the dialogue. "Gentlemen, I arranged this meeting after you, Mr. Bell, indicated that you might need financing for your latest venture. I have represented my uncle for many years. He believes in straight talk."

"Straight talk, you will get. I have the opportunity of buying acreage in Durham Township. Alas, no longer have I the resources that were available to me when I was at the Forges. Nor do I have my old partners to turn to. Monro is dead and Stewart is too busy with his government posts. I am well aware that you are the largest landowner in the province."

Moses waited a few minutes before replying. *Does Bell take him for fool?* "David Monro may not be alive any longer, but my understanding that his son is suing you. Claims that you have refused to give a statement of accounts required as part of his father's will."

"It's a ludicrous claim. Says he wants £60, 000 in compensation. The court will never grant that."

Moses realized he was being disputatious. "I mean no disrespect, sir. Your reputation is without question. Why else would you have been invited to sit on the Special Council in '38?"

"You are indeed correct. I am held in high regard by most people. I declined that specific honor even though I was on the barricades defending the Crown with all my might while at the Forges. I administered the oath of allegiance to the Saint-Maurice militiamen and formed two companies of volunteers to maintain order in the region. I reckoned later that Colborne had things under control and didn't need my advice. As you know, Hart, I have involved myself in the life of this town for many years though much of my stay in this district was at the *Forges*. My wife has been dead almost ten years. I feel I'm at loose ends. Investing in land should make life meaningful again."

Moses felt pity for the man despite their long history of mutual distrust. But backing him was another matter. "I thank my nephew for getting us together after all this time. Unfortunately, my health prevents me from exploring new possibilities. If it were otherwise, I would be investing in the timber industry."

That was the end of it. Aaron Ezekiel helped Moses lift himself off his chair and the two patriarchs shook hands. Walking back to Rue Alexandre, Moses commented on the audacity of Bell coming to him for money. He then spat into a nearby snow bank.

His nephew was philosophical. "Bell thinks he is still living in the time when British gentlemen could count on the Governor and his bureaucracy supporting those who have good connections with London. Bell and his friends benefitted from sleeping partnerships and the use of personal credit to get their way and there was no accountability until now. I wonder if the British Empire will be run the same way in the future. The repeal of the Corn Laws indicates that times are changing."

Moses wasn't paying that much attention. The sight of Mathew Bell having fallen off his perch metaphorically had given him a sudden chill. "Ezekiel, I believe it is time for me to write a new will. You were present at my birthday party. It may be the last one I shall have. My progeny multiply in number. I wish to protect them – especially the daughters born to my natural offspring. Can you come to my house next week so that we can discuss how to change things so that all are satisfied?"

I take the liberty in appealing to you as I have got myself into difficulty with my land lord, Francis Deshotel for my rent, which amounts to £15, the times have been so much against me as a new beginner this last winter that I have not made sufficient to pay for my bread, he threatens me with a seizure on my goods. I believe he is in your debt if you would make some arrangement with him I should pay you within three months. I have wished him to come and pick out the amount of his money which I owe him in goods out of my store but he refuses to do so... I have asked Papa but he says he has not it to lend me, therefore I appeal to you and hope you will prevent my little stock from being sold on the first of May.
BENJAMIN MOSES HART
(letter to Moses Hart, April 23, 1847)

I have not a bed to lay [the invalids] on... I never contemplated the possibility of every vessel arriving with fever as they do now.
DR GEORGE M. DOUGLAS
(report from Grosse Isle on May 17, 1847)

Thirty nine

The walk to Rue Saint-Jacques had to be conducted with an umbrella protecting his top hat from a light spring rain. Adolphus Hart had hoped the cloud cover would dissipate by the time he was scheduled to appear at the offices of the City & District Savings Bank. His presence there had been required because Cousin Theodore was determined to ascertain the performance of the new banking institution. The bank's first annual report dated March 31 had already been distributed. Both Theodore and Benjamin Hart, Adolphus' father-in-law, were becoming alarmed by what was being said about the rival Provident and Savings. Was their money safe or ought they to be giving their business to the City & District? Perhaps some clues to the differences in lending practices of the two banks could be discerned by the interaction between a management and its shareholders.

Adolphus was certainly not looking forward to this assignment. The request had originally come from his Uncle Benjamin just after the Passover celebration at the beginning of April. Constance (she insisted on being called by her middle name, Hannah being too old fashioned) concurred with her father. Adolphus had resisted "spying" on men who were business clients potential or real. He sought out Theodore, who was not in the good graces of the other Harts, Davids or Josephs. Theodore too thought there was benefit to be achieved attending the meeting on Rue Saint-Jacques.

The assemblage there was impressive. Scanning the room Adolphus recognized that Henry Judah, his second cousin, was seated as part of the executive group and very much engaged in conversation even though the chairman had yet to call the meeting to order. Henry and his brother Thomas were in a sense competition to him for legal work in the city but Henry, the younger of the two, was very active as one of the bank's administrators – and politically engaged as well. Adolphus explained to himself that Henry had the advantage of being an avowed Anglican whereas he, Adolphus, prayed at the synagogue. *I shall always be the outsider.*

There was a distinct Irish tinge to the persona of the managing directors sitting on stage. Of the fifteen men, five of them were Irish by birth and included Hincks and Drummond. Adolphus perceived that as being a deliberate strategy of the bank's founders. Moreover, a Catholic connection was established during its founding the previous year. Bishop Bourget agreed to be the patron of the institution for the very purpose of attracting his flock to deposit their savings other than in the Provident and Savings, which was run by mostly diehard Protestants (Moses Judah Hays being an exception.)

Listening to the cashier outline his triumphant comments on the financial results, Adolphus was indeed impressed; the bank was reporting that it had 647 depositors who had entrusted it with the surprising sum of over £47,000. *The economy has been strong in the past couple of years, but even so!*

As soon as the meeting concluded, Adolphus crossed the room to engage Henry Judah in conversation despite the surrounding hubbub. Was his cousin satisfied with the running of City & District?

Judah stroked his graying side-whiskers – his age was not yet forty years old but he looked much more mature than Adolphus– and admitted that the good times might not last. "We must prepare for a mass immigration of indigent Irish beginning in the next few months. We can't accommodate all of them in Griffintown or Pointe-Saint-Charles. Moreover, they bring disease. I've been to the fever sheds. The conditions I found there are incredible."

He wasn't questioned further until they had exited the building. Once on Rue Saint-Jacques (or Greater St James Street in the parlance of Montreal Anglophones), Adolphus enquired whether Judah had any indication from the new Governor on his stance regarding policy matters.

"I have spoken to Lord Elgin. He may be a Tory by inclination, but he accepts Lord Russell's outlook. The impasse in the Canadian Parliament must yield to compromise. Metcalfe was too much of a partisan to achieve a reconciliation of the two camps. Whether our new man can bring compromise and also cope with the immigration crisis is another matter." Judah's face was set in a frown.

Adolphus had much to think about as he retraced his steps to reach home. The sun had finally come out from behind the remaining clouds so he had no need for the umbrella. His concern, however, was with how he would report to the family on his mission to Rue Saint-Jacques. Except for his encounter with Henry Judah, there had been no effort on his part to test the financial results reported at the meeting. Even Constance would not be satisfied with his scrutiny of them.

He needn't have worried. Constance didn't even ask about the outing. Rather, she was showing the strains of confinement. The baby was due in June. Her anxieties, he believed, were groundless. Fortunately their only son, George Ezekiel, gave no indication that the ailments during his early infancy had any lasting effect. She did, however, insist that Dr. Aaron David attend her every week or so. The doctor acceded even if it caused him some inconvenience; he had committed himself to providing assistance to poor and needy immigrants. Reverend Abraham de Sola, newly arrived in Montreal, had recruited him to participate in the Hebrew Philanthropic Society that he had just founded. Moses Judah Hays was its president. *Does even cousin Aaron fully appreciate what may be in store for him in the coming months?*

*   *   *

Dr. Aaron David emerged from Constance's room after a perfunctory check on her condition. Adolphus wasn't expecting any new developments. The delivery wouldn't be coming for another six weeks or more. But his cousin had something on his mind. "I have a favor to ask you, Dolph. I've been asked to go to Grosse Isle to assist in the treatment of Irish immigrants quarantined there. Typhus is rife and the number of doctors on the island is inadequate to cope with the outbreak. You've been there before whereas I never got beyond Three Rivers even when I lived downstream. I would feel more comfortable if you were with me."

Adolphus had in fact visited Grosse Isle, one of the islands in an archipelago in the St. Lawrence just east of the Quebec City area. It was the site of an immigration depot set up by the former government in Lower Canada in response to the cholera epidemic fifteen years before. He had not forgotten the rows of graves that marked the burial of the Irish who had brought the disease to British North America and yet never set foot in the new land. "Is that wise, Aaron? Constance will need both of us here in not too many weeks."

"My doctor's sister Phoebe has agreed to care for her in my absence. The pregnancy is coming along nicely and the likelihood is that my presence will not be required until next month at the earliest."

The journey to Quebec City on the *Queen* was undertaken the next day. Adolphus found his cousin good company. A dozen or more years before the doctor had studied in Edinburgh so that he had insights denied to a younger and less traveled lawyer. Aaron also described the tribulations associated with setting up a practice in Montreal. Once in the capital the twosome chose to spend a night with the newlyweds Abraham and Sophia. Aaron retired early while Adolphus chatted for a couple of hours with his sister and brother-in-law.

In the morning a small boat took the two travelers to their ultimate destination. They cleared Île Orléans and docked on Grosse Isle within the hour. The long string of ocean-going vessels waiting to disembark could not but catch their attention.

Dr. George Douglas proved to be the medical officer in charge of the quarantine station. He looked in desperate straits. "My wards are dying like flies."

Adolphus was indignant. "This should not be happening."

Dr. Douglas shrugged. "We certainly knew there would be an influx of emigrants but we weren't ready for a deluge. In February I asked for £3000 to handle the spring arrivals. Can you believe that I was granted £300, a small steamer and permission to hire a sailing vessel for no more than £50?"

"And look what we have! This is inexcusable!"

"I concede that we should have been better prepared. Based on what had already happened in Boston and elsewhere, it was no surprise when we were told that beginning in April over 10,000 emigrants had left Britain for Quebec. Nevertheless I was given funds for only one fever shed that could house 200 invalids should the circumstances dictate. The first vessel arrived two weeks ago with over 400 fever cases! And within a week seventeen more vessels appeared at Grosse Isle. They are still coming. One of the ship captains predicts that there will be forty ships to unload before the spring is over. I am desperate." The doctor's countenance confirmed his dismay.

The following week Adolphus accompanied Aaron as patients in pitiful condition were being treated. There wasn't enough space to deal with both ill and healthy bodies and Dr. Douglas had demanded that those passengers that had not come down with typhus stay on ship for fifteen days whereas the sick were carried off to be quarantined on land. Yet the infection on board did not cease to spread. Thousands would be dead even if more medical help was on the way. More volunteers did come but the number was still insufficient. Nevertheless, Adolphus was troubled. *Are we to abandon Constance in order to bring relief to strangers?*

Eventually Aaron had to declare that he was returning to Montreal. Adolphus arranged for a boat to take them back to Quebec's harbor and the following day they departed for home on the *Queen*.

They didn't arrive in Montreal 24 hours too soon. A boy was born on June 11. Later in the latter day Constance berated Adolphus for his travels but listened soberly to the account of what was occurring on Grosse Isle. Her first concern, however, was with the newborn.

"The Reverend will be here on Friday to name the baby. My doctor and my papa will bear witness." Constance had insisted that Benjamin Hart participate, he having complained often enough that so many of his grandchildren were born elsewhere.

"You are certain you want that name you suggested?"

"Yes. I think Abraham Emile is just right for this boy. Abraham is a bow to tradition and Emile will remind us all of Rousseau's great novel on education."

*   *   *

The summer months began peacefully enough but in late July Adolphus had a communication from his brother Aaron Ezekiel in Trois- Rivières. The household of their Uncle Moses was in turmoil; the will and testament of the patriarch had been put in jeopardy. Constance grumbled that this was not the time for her husband to travel again. But the urgency that Aaron Ezekiel made implicit in the message could not be ignored.

The *Queen* docked in Trois-Rivières the next day and Adolphus recognized his brother waiting for the steamship to be brought to shore. They repaired to the inn on Rue Fleuve for glasses of beer so that Aaron Ezekiel could elaborate on the nature of the crisis. Their uncle and his favorite son had quarreled violently and the latter, his family included, were driven from the house on Rue Alexandre. On Tuesday he had me draft a codicil to his will that revoked Alexander Thomas' inheritance.

Aaron Ezekiel explained that Alexander Thomas had been well taken care of in the will when written and dated April 1. His father Moses had stipulated that his oldest "natural" son, who had established a flourishing wood business in the parishes on the south side of the river, be left the seigneury of Courval, which happened to be about six leagues square in the heart of this territory. "It only confirmed a previous formal donation of Courval made *inter vivos* to Aleck for life. Uncle Moses had also promised him one ninth of the residue of the estate."

"Incredible! We all knew that the old man had little patience with Areli and Louisa, who have been disappointments. But Aleck! His right hand man! Went out of his way to get Miriam to marry Aleck and for them to live together in his house. What went wrong?" Adolphus remembered his own interventions when Moses Hart corresponded with the then Miriam Judah in New York. Cousins tended to marry cousins in the Hart clan but Adolphus thought his uncle was going too far with his commitments to have a daughter of Aunt Catharine give up New York for Trois-Rivières.

Aaron Ezekiel drained his glass. "It all began with this Irish thing. Mary was dead set on bringing a couple of her relatives stationed at Grosse Isle to Rue Alexandre. Aleck balked. Miriam had just given birth to their third son. Would the life of little Lewis Alexander be threatened by proximity of ailing immigrants. He spoke things he ought not to have uttered."

Adolphus could imagine the scene. The loyalty of Moses Hart to Mary McCarthy Brown had intensified in the last decade. She was the mother of his younger children and very much his confidant. *Why did Aleck so misspeak?* "What can I do, Eze?"

"I realize that our uncle has a high regard for you. I may be his legal counselor but you are much more admired. Perhaps you can persuade him not to cast out a devoted son. Aleck is not a strong man. His heart is giving him trouble and there are three little boys to consider. I've brought a hand copy of the will for you to peruse so that you know what's at stake."

There was enough sunlight filtering into the room for Adolphus to read the script. Scanning the terms of the will, he noted that Moses Hart had been very kind to almost all of his illegitimate children. Aaron Moses, only now in his early twenties, was slated to receive a three-story brick house on Rue du Platon; Sarah-Dorothée and Charlotte, still minors, would have a lifetime interest in the Godefroy fief; Samuel-Judah and Reuben-Moses, even younger, were promised the seigneuries of Bélair and Gaspé when their father was gone. *He is generous enough in giving to his offspring so that each will have a good start.*

The walk to Rue Alexandre was accomplished with dispatch despite the July heat. A servant meeting Adolphus at the door recognized him as a nephew. Would Mr. Hart be at home? Answered in the affirmative, the visitor was escorted to the study he knew so well. The two men embraced.

They hadn't seen each other for well over a year, Adolphus not having participated in the birthday celebration the previous November.

"I have come about Aleck and Miriam. Ought I be talking to both you and Mary?"

"Mary is in Saint-Célestin today so that you have to reckon with me alone. I suspect that you have spoken to Aaron Ezekiel. He believes I have been too hasty in this matter. He may be right."

Adolphus was flabbergasted. *Have I come all this way for no good reason?* "Are you saying that you do not intend to register the codicil?"

Moses didn't answer directly. "You remember, young man, that I have made rash decisions in the past though in the end I do the right thing. It shall be the same in this case."

Can I validate such an observation? Moses Hart was for his nephew such a contradiction. Shrewd but undisciplined. How else to explain a man who has had countless liaisons and takes on the responsibility for his behavior? Or one who scoffs at established religions and still contributes to church and synagogue? "You do, uncle, seem to win in the end."

"I regard myself as a man who knows how to use money. At present much of it is in land. Yet I have been a brewer, traded in potash and invested in banks. Now it is a question of donating to family, including kin in Montreal. My body is weakening." Moses giggled.

"Are you saying that you are giving up on business?"

"If I were a little younger, I would be investing in companies buying water wheels to exploit the falls upriver. The *Chutes* Shawinigan could supply the power for at least a few sawmills and flour mills along the shores of the Saint-Maurice. Oh well! You were wise, Adolphus, to leave Three Rivers for Montreal. We may yet have a thriving timber industry here but the future is in railroads."

"But you haven't put any money into the St Lawrence and Atlantic despite its promise." Adolphus had once been intrigued by his uncle's hesitation in this matter. This international project made sense on paper. Montreal, Sherbrooke and other Quebec towns would get access to Portland, the ice-free port on the Atlantic. And businessmen in New England should be able to reach markets in the St Lawrence Valley and beyond. Construction of the broad-gauge railway had begun in the previous year and the section from Longueuil to the Richelieu River should be ready by autumn. Nevertheless, as Adolphus learned from talking to Henry Judah, the capital base was thin and not likely to be augmented easily given the repeal of the Corn Laws and its effect on the Canadian economy. Share subscriptions from Montreal business had totaled £100,000 but only 10% of it had been paid up. The chief promoter of the railroad in Canada was

Alexander Galt, who happened to be in England this very summer trying to sell stock on the London exchange.

It was already dusk when Adolphus departed Rue Alexandre. He would bunk with his siblings on Rue des Forges for the night and catch the next steamer to Montreal in the morning. *Enough rescuing others for a while!*

*I believe that the problem of how to govern Canada would be solved
if the French would split into a Liberal and a Conservative Party
and join the Upper Canadian parties bearing the corresponding names –
The great difficulty hitherto has been that a Conservative Government
has meant Government of Upper Canadians which is intolerable to
the French – and a Radical Government a Government of the French
which is no less hateful to the British.*
GOVERNOR LORD ELGIN
(letter to Colonial Secretary Grey, March 27, 1847)

*Since my last, the wind has been blowing fresh from the northeast,
and several vessels have arrived in port, the names of which you
will find enclosed. Four have just arrived, but are not yet boarded.
I make out the names of three, viz:-Bark Covenanter, Bark Royal
Adelaide, and Schooner Maria, of Limerick. ...The accounts from
Grosse Isle since my last, are not of a favorable nature,
and the number of deaths is much the same.*
QUEBEC CORRESPONDENCE OF THE MONTREAL HERALD
(written Monday afternoon, August 9, 1847)

Forty

Dalhousie Square looked quite different to Theodore Hart as he and wife Mary Kent approached the theatre this opening Saturday night. He had been paying very little attention to the progress being made on the redevelopment of the buildings that had lined one side of the area between Rue Saint-Paul to the west, Rue Sainte-Marie to the east. Now the full extent of the make-over could be appreciated. Moses Judah Hay had made good on his boast that he would transform the square into the most fashionable spot in Montreal. A hotel, designated as Hays House, was every bit as grand as the Donegana on Rue Notre-Dame and as utilitarian as the Ottawa on Rue Saint-Jacques. The latter establishment, completed but two years previously, had the advantage of being the last stop in the carriage route between Montreal and Ottawa, but its austere arcades and Tuscan pilasters were no more fanciful than the greystone architecture of Hays House.

But this night the centre of attraction was the new theatre, the salute to the Royal Theatre on Rue Saint-Paul that beginning twenty years before provided musical and theatrical entertainment similar to the music halls of France and England,. But the older building, also know as Royal-Molson, had recently been demolished to make way for the Bonsecour market. A substitute had been the Royal Olympic on Place Jacques-Cartier, which featured musical events. But that site was being closed now that the Royal-Hays was opening.

It being ten days into July, there was no need to employ horse transport to get to the Royal-Hays. Even the evening air was warm. Theodore and Mary-Kent joined the line of patrons waiting to enter the foyer. Once in, they could view the stage beyond, a stage said to be 110 feet wide and 76 feet deep. The ceiling was four stories high. All indeed was on a grand scale, which seemed quite appropriate for an audience that could number as high as 2400. Would that many citizens of Montreal be ready for the Shakespeare play to be presented that night? George Skerrett, the manager of the London company brought to Montreal, was confident that it would.

Many of those just ahead of them surrounded Hays himself, who was stationed in the foyer and beaming in response to the adulation. In the past he had had his share of criticism that culminated in his exit from ownership of the waterworks (selling it to the city for £50,000 two years before) but he was irrepressible. Hotel and theatre were only part of the commercial project at Dalhousie Square; a series of elegant shops had also emerged. Who else but Moses Judah Hay could be that enterprising?

The crowd, of course, included a host of acquaintances. Theodore had already spotted members of his extended family milling about. On Friday Benjamin Hart had mentioned that he and his wife had tickets for the event and Theodore noticed that members of the David and Joseph families were in attendance. Would they ignore him if and when they saw Mary Kent at his side? They still disapproved of the marriage and the birth of a child, Charles Theodore, the previous August didn't mollify them.

Perhaps it won't be that bad. Yet if he could judge from his father's unsolicited comments the previous day, his bitterness was probably infecting others. *Papa was like that.* Earlier in the year Theodore's brother Benjamin Moses had been denied the £15 he needed to pay his landlord. Granted that the lad was proving to be a bit of a wastrel, but to argue that Benjamin Hart, one of the most affluent citizens in Montreal, didn't have the funds to come to the support of his family didn't meet the test of credibility. Theodore's younger brother rubbed it in by appealing to his Uncle Moses in Trois-Rivières for him to intervene in the dispute.

"Look, Theo!" Mary Kent was pointing at the familiar profile of a national hero. Theodore was thus distracted by the appearance of the celebrated Louis-Joseph Papineau in the midst of a Francophone cluster of gentlemen. He had yet to encounter the iconic Papineau in the many months since his return from France whereas the man's younger brother, Denis-Benjamin, was an integral part of the Draper administration and seemingly at odds with majority opinion in the *Canadien* population.

Perhaps the lack of interaction was because the elder Papineau was spending more time in his Ottawa Valley seigneury. And for years before that he had been in exile in the USA and then in Paris. Theodore had been told that he had lived overseas in poverty despite having visited liberals, socialists and nationalists not only in France but also in Italy and Switzerland. His wife Julie had gone to Paris for a period but had returned to Montreal in 1843 and pushed the government to include him in the amnesties granted. There was no indication, however, that he would return to the political landscape although it was everybody's guess that he still opposed the union of the two Canadas. *Now is not the time to think about politics.* Theodore and Mary Kent found their seats and waited patiently for the curtain to rise.

*   *   *

Mary Kent organized a party on the first anniversary of the birth of their son, which was exactly thirty days later than the theatre engagement. Charles Theodore, whose first name honored the maternal grandfather, had grown normally over the twelve months. However, the choice of whether to have the child circumcised or baptized was still unsettled. Theodore invited many of his friends and colleagues who might still be in town in early August. Most of them were hirsute, which reflected the new style for gentlemen in the city. A few, including Luther Hamilton Holton and Tom Judah, were from the Church of Messiah. Others were political allies associated with Theodore's support of the *Pilot*, the journal launched by Francis Hincks.

Francis Hincks himself, however, had sailed off to Ireland earlier in the year and might not be back in Montreal for some time. Ironically Theodore had much to do with this sojourn. During the spring months Hincks, investing in the Echo Lake Mining and Lake Huron Silver & Copper Mining companies, netted $4500 by selling the stocks at a premium. (Theodore chose to retain his investments in Upper Canada mining.) The Irishman had certainly enough money to satisfy his creditors. He might have had more if he agreed to sell the *Pilot*. Theodore convinced him, however, to remain a journalist. He even accepted a £450 loan from Hincks, business having slowed in the past few months. Hincks still had enough liquidity to pay for the trip to his homeland, the first visit there since he immigrated to the Canadas.

Once the drinks had been served, Mary Kent satisfied all by bringing out the child to show off his initiation into walking. There were cheers when Charles Theodore did take some tentative steps before collapsing. The result was the boy's squall that could only be stilled by Mary Kent leaving the room. The score of guests delved into the appetizers on a table set alongside the parlor wall and soon forgot about the toddler.

Several of the guests approached Adolphus Hart, who had already been made known because of his presence on Grosse Isle in May. In fact, the group could not avoid debating the significance of the Irish migration to American shores. All seemed to concur with the prediction that as many as 100,000 Irish would be entering the country before the end of 1847. Many of these migrants were already in graves, one of every five dying from disease and malnutrition. Adolphus vividly described to them the scene at Grosse Isle. Thousands perished either on the "coffin ships" or on the island itself.

Mary Kent, who had just returned to the parlor (but without the baby), gave her own take on what was happening. "Many of these immigrants are just passing through. One wonders what will be the impact of Toronto's population tripling in a period of a single year. Our friends in Upper Canada must be saying 'enough' but what can they do when our ports, part of the Empire, cannot legally be closed to British citizens? Furthermore, being indigent doesn't prevent the Irish from fleeing the famine. Those tenants evicted are being given free passage on boats heading west. With so many vessels carrying lumber to Britain, there is space for hundreds at a time when they sail back to Quebec."

"*Madame* knows of what she speaks. Our country will never be the same with so many Irish here." The interjection came from the youngest man in the room, one in his twenties whose English was quite accented. Everyone there knew of Antoine Gérin-Lajoie. He was the talk of the town, writing as he did in the *La Minerve*, acting as secretary of the Association Saint-Jean-Baptiste and founding the *Institut Canadien*. Mary Kent had cultivated his friendship and repeated many of the political comments he had made orally as well as on paper.

Eventually the conversion did shift to other political issues. Gérin-Lajoie pontificated. "We are in a new situation, Draper going to the Bench and Sherwood taking over as cabinet head. Draper hadn't given up trying to seduce *Canadiens* to cooperate with his administration. Even tried to drag our Chief Justice into being president of the Executive Council. Vallières was very vocal in his rejection of the offer. Nevertheless, his bad legs make him unable to function as a member of the Bench. His frequent absences are going to make it easier for his enemies to force him into retirement."

Holton made his own contribution. "La Fontaine is unbending when it comes to responsible government. When the key figures in colonial policy were Peel, Stanley and Metcalfe, he had to be very pessimistic about reform. But with Russell heading the ministry in Whitehall and with Elgin showing more realism here, the cause is not hopeless."

Theodore agreed but added a caveat. "My prime concern is with La Fontaine's health. Only last November he had to undergo an operation to relieve his rheumatism. He's in Newport this summer to recuperate. One wonders if at this time of year the climate in Rhode Island is any better than in Montreal."

A renewed crying of the infant from the bedroom finally did interfere with the festivities. Several guests announced their need to depart and within a half hour the parlor was empty.

*   *   *

The invitation caught Theodore and Mary Kent by surprise. They were being asked to attend a house warming at #1 Près-de-Ville Place and the note was signed by no other than Abraham De Sola. Theodore had withdrawn from the synagogue even before the Reverend had arrived in Montreal the previous January. Was this an olive branch?

The cleric had now a permanent residence, the house having been built as an extension of the terrace on Près-de-Ville Place. It was on land next to the Rue Chenneville *shul* itself. Furthermore, it gave him close proximity to most members of the Joseph family. The late Henry Joseph had purchased the property twenty years before. Wife Rachel and three of her sons –Jacob Henry, Jesse and Gershom – were once again residing in the terrace (at #8) after a three-year absence. The move to 44 Saint-Urbain had been temporary in order to facilitate an extensive renovation of the house on Près-de-Ville Place.

Mary Kent did not receive the invitation kindly. Her in-laws had pointedly snubbed her ever since she had returned from Boston the wife of one of their most prestigious members. In addition, she had just taken the step of having Charles Theodore baptized three week before in late September. That reality was bound to make her uncomfortable if and when she attended such a function just next to a synagogue. "I cannot see myself in such a situation."

"It would be awkward. I suspect De Sola has learned about the baptism." Theodore was showing suitable empathy. He too had some qualms about bringing the child to the front of the sanctuary on that Sunday even though the Unitarian congregation did not go for Christian-style baptisms.

"You ought to go, Theo. There must be a reason for such an overture."

The designated Sunday finally arrived. Theodore donned an overcoat, the October weather having a distinct autumnal aspect. Dead leaves rustled under his feet as he entered Rue Chenneville. He could hear the echoes of conviviality as he reached the entrance to #1 Près-de-Ville Place. De Sola met him at the door and explained that not everything was in order, the house just being completed for residency. Theodore, looking over his shoulder, recognized just about everybody in the room. The Davids, the Josephs, the Benjamins – and, of course, a few of his own siblings. Most members of the congregation were participating in the celebration. All were courteous, but there was no rush to engage.

Dr. Aaron David did approach him and Theodore took the opportunity to congratulate him on the birth of an eighth child (a sixth son), which supposedly had happened in mid-July. "I do not notice Catharine being here. Extend my best wishes to her as well. What is the boy's name?"

"Robert Sullivan David. I think Kitty is running out of boys' names. But this may be the last of our breed. She is in her late thirties."

"Your practice is going well? My information is that you are being much noticed in the profession now that you have published."

"Yes, that was two years ago. My treatise on Concussion of the Brain."

"I remember reading it! Wasn't a patient's death erroneously attributed to trauma? Yet you were able demonstrate through postmortem examination that there was no evidence of fracture or hemorrhage."

"You remember correctly. More recently I published a document on Acute Pericarditis. Noticed the frequency of inflammation of the pericardium in rheumatism." Aaron couldn't resist citing his triumphs.

Theodore remembered something else. "It has been said that you are treating our former Chief Justice for problems relating to his leg disabilities."

"I have indeed been to the Donegana Hotel to look in on Vallières. A sad case. Between you and me, he is not likely to recover."

"I gathered that from talking to Gérin-Lajoie. Apparently Vallières is preparing mentally for his imminent demise. His wife has had to accept that likelihood." Theodore had met with Gérin-Lajoie the previous week. The young journalist had also visited Vallières, who was a leading light in the *Institut* Canadian despite his physical condition. He had gone on to say that it was regrettable that the jurist was almost out of the picture just at a time when it was likely that within weeks Draper would be resigning and leaving the government in the hands of the faction in the Parliament headed by Henry Sherwood. Gérin-Lajoie opined that a Sherwood ministry could not survive a confidence vote.

Theodore had taken heart at that possibility, but he still wasn't certain that the new Governor was ready for elections. *I'll wait and see.* Meanwhile he partook of the edibles still remaining after the guests had their fill. Yet he found it difficult to engage in another conversation of substance. Nor did Reverend De Sola seek him out. If there was any ulterior motive for the invitation, it was not immediately apparent.

PART FIVE

Confrontment
1848–1850

In the name of the French people: A reactionary and oligarchical
government has just been overthrown by the heroism of
the people of Paris. That government has fled, leaving
behind it a trail of blood that forbids it ever to retrace its steps.
The blood of the people has flowed as in July; but this time this noble
people shall not be deceived. It has won a national and popular
government in accord with the rights, the progress, and the
will of this great and generous nation.
PROCLAMATION OF THE 1848 REVOLUTIONARIES
(following skirmish at the Tuilières, February 24, 1848)

Our clergy is from the people, lives in it and for it; is all for it, is nothing
without it. Here is an insoluble alliance. Here is the union which makes
the strength; because it is free and indigenous; not founded nor
of importation. Here is a pledge of indestructibility for a nationality,
which is guided by the enlightened and virtuous pastors of virtuous
people and trustful of them, withdrawn all and sundry from the
influence of authorities, for such a long time hostile to their nationality.
LOUIS-JOSEPH PAPINEAU
(speech at Bonsecours Hall, April 5, 1848)

Forty one

Ludger Duvernay could be pardoned for regarding this assembly of the many thousand *Canadiens* in the grand room of the Bonsecours Market as the epitome of a political revolution. As early as February it was clear that the general election results would give the *Patriotes* and the La Fontaine Reformers a combined total of 32 deputies for Canada East. Only eight Conservative and Independent winners were left east of the Ottawa River to support the Sherwood administration. On this Wednesday night in early April Duvernay would get a better picture of how the landslide victory might translate into a new direction in the province, the Reformers in Canada West also having triumphed.

Prior to entering this forum Duvernay sought out Augustin-Norbert Morin, who was easy enough to spot standing near the entrance given his unusual height as well as his attire. There was bit of a struggle getting to each other because of the intervening crowd. Duvernay noticed immediately that Morin's limp was quite pronounced, the man's chronic rheumatism

275

taking more and more of a toll. He guessed that Morin's electioneering in Bellechasse County had not been easy for him.

The voting there as elsewhere had commenced before Christmas and had been extended into January and beyond. *La Minerve* thus reported polling victories for several of Duvernay's old comrades. Louis-Joseph Papineau entered the electoral fray and defeated Joseph-Édouard Turcotte in Saint-Maurice; Wolfred Nelson got himself reelected in Richelieu; Louis-Michel Viger, Thomas Boutillier, André Jobin and Étienne-Paschal Taché were other *Patriotes* who had paid a price for participating in the rebellion and yet prevailed in these contests. Nevertheless, several of them had followed Duvernay into the Reformist camp headed by La Fontaine, a development that suggested that forming a unified "French" bloc in the upcoming parliamentary session would be difficult to achieve. Much depended on what stance Papineau intended to take now that he was back in the political arena.

The meeting room was large enough to handle more than 12,000 people and already it was full. Within minutes it was evident that thousands were pressing to get through the entrance but were probably being forced to return home disappointed. "Can you believe this, Ludger?" Morin was indeed impressed.

Some of the early speakers could not be heard. Moreover, Papineau's approach of the lectern was delayed as a result. He acknowledged that they hadn't gotten off to a good start. "We have before us all that Montreal has of individuals distinguished by their virtues, their lights, their talents. They represent the very whole of the *Canadien* nationality. I regret that some of seats reserved for the ladies were surrendered because they were not properly protected."

His voice rose as he paid tribute to the *Messrs* of the *Institut canadien* and *Messrs* of the *Association canadienne des townships*, who had organized the mass meeting. Settlement of the Townships east of the St Lawrence had become a major political issue in recent years. For the past three decades immigrants, primarily from Britain but also from the United States, had populated much of the Townships. *Canadiens* had had to be satisfied with land they had inherited in the seigneuries along the river or leave the valley altogether for other climes. Papineau underlined that point. "It is this nationality being compromised by the loss of a quantity of its members who would be able to give it energy, richness and strength were they not leaving to be lost and to disappear in a nationality foreign and enemy. That is why we are here."

Then he took note of the presence on the stage of *Monseigneur* Ignace Bourget and other members of the clergy. "Our worthy bishop is so justly loved and venerated by all his people and all the virtuous pastors, who following his example and under his direction, educate and edify the people. I see the superior of the Saint-Sulpice house, under whose auspices this city was founded, this island cleared, at the price of the blood of its priests, spilled and mingled with that of the first colonists, our worthy ancestors."

Duvernay recognized that Papineau was laying it on thick; as a Deist who had crossed swords with the clergy over the past quarter century, the former leader of the *Patriotes* was deliberating equating religion with nationality in order to create a united front against assimilation. *Is he actually seeking an alliance with Bourget in the new Parliament?*

Papineau then switched the subject to the Irish question, which was now more acute then ever. The audience was receptive to the idea that the British government and the Church of England had brought Ireland to ruin. The speaker expanded on that idea. "Only one year of food shortage literally killed a tenth of its population, despite all the efforts and the goodwill of a State and an aristocratic Church, too overwhelmed and necessitous by their needs for luxury, which are limitless, to give effective assistance to the most pressing needs of nature which are so limited. And yet Ireland is not short of lands. A quarter of its surface is uncultivated, because it never had a national government."

"Here comes an appeal for a national liberator in Lower Canada." Morin's whisper could still be heard over the cacophony of voices that surrounded them. Duvernay made no attempt to reply.

Papineau chose at that moment to cite his choice as the "Liberator" of Ireland. "Since Moses, no other mortal, inspired as Daniel O'Connell was, powerful in works and in words, had the consolation to lead his people, from the land of servitude, so far towards the land of peace and freedom that he promised to them; where they are about to enter, though, once again, the driver could only see it from atop the mountain, located in the wild desert, at the border of the country where oil and honey will flow; where strength and abundance will be installed, when tomorrow Ireland governs herself; to dig his people out of a state of legal inferiority, as iniquitous as that which arise from several centuries of oppression, to raise first in theory, and soon in practice, the most oppressed and humiliated of nationalities, that of Ireland, to a level of perfect equality with the one which, a few years back, was the proudest and most superb of the globe, the British nationality."

The speech did not end without Papineau repeating his admiration of the American republic. "One looks at the flag of the United States with its 29 stars, with its magistracies and institutions superior to ours and then reproaches oneself for not understanding that *Canadiens* ought to have preserved their *pied-à-terre* when there was a chance to do so in 1775."

Once free of the crowd, Duvernay and Morin sought refuge in a nearby tavern. Even after quaffing some ale, the two men had yet to sort out their reactions to what they heard. Morin was tentative. "Well, Ludger, we shall soon have some big challenges. The Governor has already signaled that London finally accepts responsible government and that the majority will be allowed to form the next administration."

Duvernay smiled. "Let's drink more to a new world! I believe you are on the verge of being one of the province's major leaders."

"You may be right, Ludger. I expect to be a very busy man when the new Parliament meets. The party wants me to take over the Speaker's chair from MacNab. Given our pending majority in the House, that outcome seems almost certain. We can anticipate me sparring with MacNab in future debates for the next few years."

"Something to look forward to." Duvernay drained his glass.

"I still have some worries."

"They are?"

"Louis-Hippolyte is once again ill. With his Adèle also doing so poorly, it is a bad time for him to think of putting together a cabinet assuming Lord Elgin will ask him to do so. *Hélas*, we are all mortal. I'm told Vallières has been given last rites. There will never be a jurist as learned as he and he will soon be no more.'" Morin had kept close to the La Fontaine family throughout these years in the political wilderness and had also known the former Chief Justice quite well.

"Surely our leader will let Baldwin take the lead. I would guess that his problem is here in Lower Canada. How do you think he will handle Louis-Joseph now that he is a Member of Parliament? Do you actually believe that our old friend will not utilize the Papineau good name to his advantage? His brother Denis-Benjamin tried to do so although he is now out of the picture." Duvernay had chosen to articulate what had been bothering him ever since Papineau, his former mentor, reappeared as a political force.

"You are saying what others are thinking. Louis-Joseph is still not reconciled to the union despite it being in effect for so many years. Nor will he be comfortable being overshadowed by La Fontaine. The big difference, however, may be over his admiration of the governing principles of the United States."

Duvernay dropped his gaze. "To be frank, Augustin, I have long admired the American republic and cannot dismiss Papineau's arguments out of hand. Having lived in Vermont during my exile years, I had come to appreciate why Americans have so high a regard for their institutions. Let us hope that the issue doesn't divide our people."

* * *

The lecture hall at the *Institut Canadien* was virtually full when Ludger Duvernay began looking for an empty seat. He was in luck; George-Étienne Cartier, the Montreal lawyer most committed to Duvernay's Société Saint-Jean-Baptiste, waved to him. He had saved Duvernay a place. Cartier was in good humor. He had just won the parliamentary seat of Verchères in a by-election a few weeks before.

Duvernay was not surprised by the turnout; Louis-Joseph Papineau as the featured speaker was bound to draw a crowd. Besides, it was a balmy night for early May. Many of Montreal's citizens were in a giddy mood; the revolutionary activities in Paris that commenced in late January had only now been made known to them.

The call for order came from Antoine-Aimé Dorion, who had been elected second vice-president of the *Institut Canadien* six months earlier. Cartier took the opportunity to mutter that Dorion had but days ago decided to give up his job as a store clerk to concentrate on running *L'Avenir*, the organ of the *Institut Canadien*. Duvernay shrugged. He had never regarded *L'Avenir* as serious competition to *La Minerve*. At best it had about 700 subscribers.

The task of introducing Papineau to the audience had been left to Louis-Antoine Dessaulles, the son of the *seigneur* of Saint-Hyacinthe and of Rosalie, Papineau's sister. His heavy black moustache moving vigorously, he spoke bluntly about the need to repeal the Union of the Canadas, a position that his uncle had adopted despite his election in Saint-Maurice. "You will understand, *messieurs*, that there are certain principles that we in the *Institut Canadien, les rouges*, will strive to reaffirm in this parliamentary session."

There was a hush when Papineau confirmed some of the provocative statements already made by his nephew. "The *bleues* regard themselves as reformists, but in effect they have betrayed the great cause of independence in order to have a seat at the table of *les Anglais*." Most of the audience shouted their approval. Nevertheless, these barbs had in Duvernay's view the intent of splitting the alliance of anti-Tory *Canadiens. How dare Papineau impugn the reputation of La Fontaine in this way?*

The vocal response to Papineau, however, came from another source. Everyone turned to gaze on another hero of the rebellion stepping into the aisle. He was his usual majestic self, a rugged face with sideburns coming down below the tip of his nose and sporting a black cravat. Dr. Wolfred Nelson was now practicing his medicine in Montreal albeit he would be sitting again as the deputy from Richelieu in the new Parliament. "I will not be silent, Louis-Joseph. You impugn the integrity of *Monsieur* La Fontaine, who is not here to defend himself. And you suggest that it was the *Patriotes* of the Richelieu who failed our cause in '37. Better you look in the mirror; it was you who withdrew from the field at a most critical moment."

Duvernay was well aware of what transpired that first December day in 1837. Nelson commanded the *Patriotes* at Saint-Denis in the Richelieu valley. A victory over the British regulars a week earlier was negated when the British brought up reinforcements, Papineau disappeared from the scene and Nelson's sharpshooters abandoned their positions for the safety of the woods. Nelson also had to flee and spent ten days without food until being captured and imprisoned in the *Pied-du-Courant*.

Papineau refused to ignore the interruption. "You would say that now, *mon ami*, having as you do a personal allegiance to our new Attorney General. You need not, however, insult those brave *camarades* who risked their lives for national independence."

Nelson was ready with a reply. "I am proud to say that I regard *Monsieur* La Fontaine as a good friend and an honorable man. He offered to adopt one of my children just before I was exiled to Bermuda in '42. And I owe my return to the province to his refusal as Attorney General for Canada East to prosecute me in absentia. This does not detract from the fact that your premature disappearance from the front lines contributed to the ultimate defeat of the rebellion and the miseries that resulted. It was perhaps a favor for which we should thank God that your projects failed, persuaded as I am at present that you would have governed with a rod of iron."

The lecture had come to a virtual end. The audience had never before witnessed such a clash between two icons of the *Patriote* movement. Such words had seldom been used in public. All attempts by Dorion to bring order to the proceedings failed. Probably the early exit of the hall by Nelson avoided a riot. Duvernay and Cartier, known spokesmen for the *Bleues*, were immediately surrounded by Dorion, Dessaulles and others to register their protests. How could Nelson talk as he did? Duvernay had seldom been in such a confrontation. Except for Dessaulles, these were young men of a different generation, deeply loyal to the Papineau mystique and offended by its denigration. Duvernay recognized that Joseph Doutre, a contributor to *L'Avenir*, had only weeks before had boasted that he and his friends had helped La Fontaine get elected. The young man was forthright. "I favored the Reform party until now, but I cannot abide what Nelson said."

Forty two

The hospital corridor was empty as Aaron Hart David briskly made his way to the next ward. Sunlight streamed in from the windows lining the outer wall of the building. It was late May; a harbinger of summer was evident this Wednesday morning. Aaron took little notice. The Montreal General Hospital had been in operation for over twenty five years, the institution on Rue Dorchester running 72 beds on two floors and it was familiar territory for Aaron. Moreover, his mind was elsewhere.

Without warning a nurse in a white smock and matching cap stepped into the corridor and signaled Aaron that she had a message: Dr. Arnoldi wished his appearance in the first-floor office at his earliest convenience.

"Does that mean at once?" The question was rhetorical but he did have more patients to see before returning to his own office outside the hospital. *Was the senior doctor questioning a diagnosis?* One doesn't like to argue with Daniel Arnoldi. Aaron long ago realized that the dapper physician, now in his mid-seventies, was the most prominent medical man in the province.

The president of the College of Physicians and Surgeons, a justice of the peace and the father-in-law of such worthy citizens of Montreal as Benjamin Holmes, William King McCord and Robert Gillespie, Dr. Arnoldi's opinions had to be taken into account if not immediately accepted.

In the event Aaron curtailed his rounds in order to comply with the request. There were two men in the office. Sitting across from Dr. Arnoldi was none other than Dr. Wolfred Nelson, whose facial features, a prominent nose underlining heavy eyebrows, were as austere as the cut of his jacket and the starkness of his black cravat. (There was no concession to the day's summer-like weather.) Aaron did not find his presence totally unusual, Nelson never having given up medicine despite his political activities over these many years.

"The new Parliament is not in session today so Doctor Nelson is paying us a visit. He is increasingly worried about further contagion associated with the influx of immigrants this spring. Fewer boats are landing in Quebec this year than in '47 but there is still disease. A cholera outbreak is not his only concern. You, David, have some experience with ship fever as a result of your trip to Grosse Isle last year. Moreover, you have some authority to act."

"True! I am now Secretary to the Central Board of Health." Aaron smiled somewhat smugly.

"This is a deserving post even for a man so young." Arnoldi was a bit condescending.

"So young? It's been twelve years since I earned my medical degree in Edinburgh. In my mid-thirties now, I have been diligent in undertaking new techniques for the treatment of my patients. My hope is that they will be successful."

"Indeed, we pride ourselves in conducting clinical teaching at the patient's bedside. As you know, we were the first hospital on the continent to do so."

Nelson had kept silent during this exchange. Aaron wondered if the legislator was letting past history influence his reluctance to speak. To begin with, Dr. Arnoldi had been a medical examiner for the district over the past couple of decades and so could rule against one practicing his profession in Montreal. Subsequently politics had interfered with their relationship, the older doctor having a reputation of showing his bias during the imprisonment of captured *Patriotes* during the uprising. Nelson, of course, was one of those captives.

Nevertheless, the silence was broken when Nelson reminded the others in the room that he had been tending to dying immigrants at

Montreal's waterfront the previous summer. "It was almost like being on a battlefield."

Nelson knew of what he spoke. He had been dealing with people in distress as long ago as in the war of 1812-14. A minor at the time (Aaron knew him to be currently sixty years old), Nelson had been licensed as a surgeon in the fifth battalion of the embodied militia. "

"I concur, Dr. Nelson. Like a battlefield. Desperate measures are normal."

If I remember, Doctor David, you have had experience in a more recent conflict."

Aaron frowned. "We happened to be on opposite sides, but I never did get to the Richelieu in '37. I was assistant-surgeon in the Montreal Rifle Brigade and participated in the battle at Saint-Eustache."

"I meant no disrespect. Have known your family for generations. My father, a teacher, had a Hart as a pupil in Trois-Rivières when he lived there. My brother operated on your uncle many years ago. In his own home, as you probably have been told!" In 1822 David David was the center of attention for members of the Montreal medical profession who gathered at the house on Rue Notre-Dame to watch young Robert Nelson perform an operation on him.

Dr. Arnoldi intervened at this point. "Enough history! I am recommending that the two of you form a committee to deal with a possible pandemic in our jurisdiction. Will that satisfy our new administration, Nelson?"

* * *

Catharine roused Aaron, who had fallen asleep while sitting erect in the parlor's one easy chair. "Cousin Adolphus is calling on us. Constance has sent over a big watermelon to make this heat wave just a bit more bearable."

Aaron was on his feet before his guest entered the room. He was fond of Adolphus, their sharing of living quarters on Grosse Isle the previous year having made the cousins closer than ever. Moreover, the man's intimate connections with the leading citizens of Montreal had redounded to Aaron's advantage on several occasions. "What brings you out on such a hot day? I for one have cancelled my rounds at the hospital until tomorrow."

Adolphus chuckled. "A difficult day for us all! This morning I visited my father in law. Benjamin Hart is not in the best of moods. It's not just the weather. Business has become precarious. The repeal of the Corn Laws has finally struck havoc with our British trade."

A female greeting from up high interrupted them. Aaron looked up to see his sister descending the stairs. Phoebe David, the last of the siblings living with him, was underdressed in an obvious response to the temperature in the house. She didn't seem at all embarrassed. Catharine, however, showed her chagrin. Aaron guessed that his wife was growing increasingly impatient with her spinster sister-in-law. Nevertheless, she was indirect in her discourse. "Jacob Henry has returned from Philadelphia and looks no worse for his undertaking of the journey in the heat of summer. Having a new bride, of course, made the trip very worthwhile."

Jacob Henry, the eldest of the Joseph brothers and the one most committed to the tobacco trade, had finally duplicated what Abraham had done less than two years before; he married well, the Gratz family in Philadelphia being into philanthropy. Catharine had but one comment about her new sister-in-law. "Remember, Sara Gratz Moses is an orphan. Thank God her aunt Rebecca has raised her to be a proper young woman."

"And where are they now?" Adolphus, not invited to the wedding, was a little put out being out of the loop.

"The newly weds are ensconced in a private hotel apartment until their renovated quarters at #7 are ready." Aaron was reminding Adolphus that prior to the marriage Jacob Henry had been living with his mother, brothers and sisters at #8 Près-de-Ville Place. He was determined, however, to leave the family nest now that he had a wife of his own.

Aaron continued the discourse. "Jacob Henry had to be sad that two of his brothers were out of the country. Jesse writes from London that he accomplished much during the winter months. He even had time to meet with Reverend Piza and the De Sola family. Abraham was pleased at the fact that his mother wrote of Jesse's visit to her home. And then there is Gershom. Though called to the bar, he decided to travel extensively in Europe. I don't think he is eager to settle in Montreal, the competition from his kin for clients being a disincentive."

Catharine was still remembering the courtship. "You know, of course, that had not Sara visited Montreal a couple of years back, the two would never have met."

Aaron amended the observation. "It may not have happened if John Henry hadn't visited Boston. He saw his opportunity when he stayed with friends at Cape May last summer. Sara was there at the same time."

A sigh emitted by Phoebe reminded the group that talk of romance wasn't sitting well with at least one in the room. Aaron appreciated Phoebe's dismay. She would be thirty years old this summer; both of her younger sisters had been married relatively early even if Fanny was never equipped for bearing children; Phoebe never had a serious suitor.

Adolphus had also noticed Phoebe's disheartenment but he had a different take. "Phoebe, you ought to turn your attention to my bachelor brothers in Three Rivers. Sammy ranks very high in that community now that he is a *seigneur* and a magistrate. And Aaron Ezekiel is a barrister of some note."

Aaron decided to change the subject. "Everybody is following the news from Paris. We read that in early May a national assembly was elected. Most of the 900 deputies are monarchists but there are many committed republicans or socialists determined to make the national workshops there a success. We shall hear more from the likes of Louis Blanc and that is why Bourget and his fellow clerics are so exercised. They fear that Papineau will follow their example."

"A real possibility! *La Minerve* was right to accuse Papineau of being a great agitator. Coming from Duvernay, who has always admired republican elective institutions, it was a condemnation that rings true to many educated *Canadiens*. Like Duvernay, they may be unhappy with the Union, but nevertheless prefer it to devastation." Adolphus had obviously been following the matter rather closely.

"Does your friend Holmes agree?" Aaron suspected that Adolphus had discussed the matter with the former banker, who was again a Member of Parliament as of the 1848 election.

"I do speak to Holmes, though we don't always see eye to eye. He is, of course, disappointed at not being part of the La Fontaine ministry. Though a supporter of reform, he is linked too closely with men like Holton and De Witt to get La Fontaine's approval. Leans to the *Rouge* rather than to the *Bleu*."

Aaron had no patience with *rouge* versus *bleu*. Too much politics!

* * *

The short impromptu conference had come to an end by mid-afternoon but Aaron hoped to hold the attention of Dr. Wolfred Nelson for another half hour at least. The usual hospital hubbub would not subside for a while and, in any event, Aaron's rounds had been completed in the morning. He had questions for Nelson that were not medical in nature.

His first objective was to clarify what had become the talk of the town this first week in September. "I've been told that there's a pamphlet out defending Papineau's conduct during the '37 rebellion. It's titled *Papineau et Nelson: Blanc et noir* and those who have read it see the hand of Dessaulles in its writing. To me that interpretation appears reasonable; who else is as close to Papineau as his nephew? I understand that you have responded to that event."

Nelson's reaction was deliberate. "I was clear enough. As you probably read in Monday's *La Minerve*, I have spoken out on Papineau's conduct at Saint-Denis over ten years ago."

"As I remember it, much of the criticism was directed not only at Papineau but also at George Cartier."

"Indeed, among other things Dessaulles maligned George Cartier. As I attested in the journal, when the second expedition of troops moved against St. Denis; resistance then having become impossible, I sent Cartier, towards two o'clock in the afternoon, to Saint-Antoine for some stores, and he promptly returned with succour, after about an hour's absence. And contrary to what was written in the pamphlet, Cartier did not wear *a tuque bleu* on the day of the battle."

"You do believe, then, that Dessaulles was responsible for this public *contretemps?*"

"I don't doubt it was he. Unfortunately, Dessaulles is back on his Saint-Hyacinthe seigneury. Says he is planning to run for election as the town mayor. We must wait to see if Papineau has anything to say."

"You have just returned from visiting Quebec. Was there any reaction by Cauchon and his friends to the controversy?" Aaron's question was pertinent because Cauchon was editor of the *Le Journal de Québec*, the successor to the *Quebec Gazette.*

"Cauchon had yet to be aware of what was happening. I did call there on Dr James Douglas, who is now the superintendent of the Beauport Lunatic Asylum as of two years ago."

Aaron's eyes lit up. "I have become keenly interested in how the insane are being treated in Beauport. Tell me what you discovered!"

"The asylum is a model for humane procedures. To start with, its wards are capacious, lofty and well ventilated. The clean hot air circulated throughout the building encourages the patients to perform their daily functions, be they washing, sewing, writing, playing the violin or whatever."

Nelson rose to his feet. Aaron, however, had another question. "Have you seen the *New York Herald?* It reports that there is gold in the foothills of California and that towns on the Pacific coast are being deserted as everybody is now engaged in panning for nuggets in the American River."

"It so happens that my brother Robert has written on the subject from the United States. He is set on trying his luck in California to overcome the debts he has accumulated in the last while. I know not how to advise him since he has refused to return to Canada despite the pardon granted him." Nelson's candor astonished Aaron.

Meanwhile Nelson began making his excuses. "I must depart. Théophile Hamel has promised to begin painting my portrait beginning this evening. They say it is important to spread my influence here in Montreal albeit I don't know whether with my notoriety, it needs spreading."

Aaron was aware of the presence of Théophile Hamel in Montreal, the young painter having moved away from his Quebec studio the previous year to settle in town. His reputation had preceded him; he had studied in Rome and was widely acclaimed for his technical mastery of the brush. It had occurred to him that perhaps Dr. Aaron Hart David could benefit from having his portrait painted. *Or am I being too ambitious? Is it consistent with me adhering to the philosophy that man's service to humanity should be the yardstick by which we are measured?"*

But Canadiens are so much an unusual people on this continent, that it is painful to think of the necessity of a dispersal in which they would not recover the combination of circumstances that has given them their moral and religious habits, their language, their laws, and a nature as happy, gay and sociable as theirs is. There is no Englishman who does not derive the greatest advantage from settling in any part of independent America, or who has not the most legitimate reasons for doing so. For such people emigration leaves no true cause for regrets.
LOUIS-JOSEPH PAPINEAU
(letter to his wife, May 1848)

For we are all children of the same Father who is in Heaven; we all live under the same government, which has no other end but the welfare of its subjects, and which must take its glory from ruling peoples speaking all languages of the world; we all have the same rights; we are all members of the great family of the mighty British Empire; and finally we are summoned to possess together the same land of the living, after we shall have finished our pilgrimage in this land of exile.
BISHOP BOURGET
(pastoral letter, June 17, 1848)

Forty three

Son Louis-Napoléon knocked softly on Duvernay's office door. Duvernay's response was gruff enough; he had the weekly edition of *La Minerve* to check out before it went to the press and the noon deadline was almost upon him. His eldest, who had committed himself to learning the publishing business, was acting as the personal secretary but he had yet not enough experience on when to divert Ludger Duvernay from his major responsibilities. Louis-Napoléon, however, was not intimidated by his father's show of temper. Augustin-Norbert Morin had entered the premises from Rue Saint-Vincent and was insisting that he see Duvernay. How does one deny the Speaker of the House, perhaps the second most important *Canadien* in government, a requested entry to Duvernay's lair?

To offset the first cold spell for early autumn, Morin had donned a cloak to cover his long frame. The usual greeting was absent. "I've come from breakfast with Louis-Hippolyte. He has come around to the view that we must act with determination on the rebellion-losses issue. Parliament is not in session but it isn't too early to engage the public in this matter."

So La Fontaine is ready for political battle! Compensation for the *habitants* whose property was destroyed during the military onslaught carried out by the British troops putting down the two rebellions a decade before became a real possibility when the Parliament of Upper Canada set a precedent: a few years ago it passed an act of indemnity for the victims of the parallel uprising west of the Ottawa River. The Draper-Viger government then set up a commission to examine the claims made by citizens in Lower Canada although nothing had come of the effort. With La Fontaine and Baldwin in power, the strong sentiment for this correction of a wrong imposed on the populace could not be ignored. "What happens next, *mon ami?*"

"Once the House is back in session, our first minister will move to have a committee formed to establish the amount of losses incurred during the rebellion. We can anticipate the opposition members in Parliament to resist since they will maintain that we are paying the rebels. They may take it to the streets."

Duvernay frowned. "How serious can that be? Our British Tories are not like the *sans-culotte* in Paris. Our biggest concern would be to get the new Governor General to accept the will of Parliament. That won't happen till after January but I suppose there is no option other than to argue it through."

"We are counting on you, Ludger. You can imagine what will be written in *The Gazette, Herald, Courier* and other English-language journals once the motion is tabled. Hincks will be using the *Pilot* to reach fair-minded *Anglais*–if they exist." Morin's grimaced at his own reference to the Tories.

Duvernay opened a drawer to take out a bottle of brandy. *Let the print deadline slide! This could be more important.* "*La Minerve* will do its part."

At first they drank in silence and then the publisher referred to something that had been bothering him in past few weeks. "Speaking of urban violence, I am still shaken by the Paris uprising in June. I know that the street fighting between workers and the army lasted but three days, but it illustrates the discontent of the masses throughout Europe. The reforms promised by the new republican government don't seem to satisfy the *sans-culottes*. They want bread, not just universal suffrage. On the other hand, outside Paris they are voting for the same politicians that supported the monarchy prior to the February revolt. I have the feeling that the winners in all this will be the Bonapartists. Louis-Napoleon is back in France and appealing to those so fearful of the *sans-culottes*."

Morin nodded. "I'm reminded of this time of the year in '37. A storm was on the horizon then. In Europe we have chaos not only in France but also in Germany, the Hapsburg Empire and the Italian states. I don't know what is going to happen to our Pope."

"Pius IX may regret having been so liberal in his attitudes. Without Austrian protection, his authority may be superseded by men such as Garibaldi and his revolutionaries. I wonder if Papineau welcomes such a threat to our institutions." Duvernay was being reflective.

"What of Papineau? How *will* he behave?"

"That remains to be seen. We did publish Dr. Nelson's critique of our friend Louis-Joseph's record during the rebellion. I am of the opinion that it has tarnished the Papineau image somewhat. In any case, I doubt whether he will object to action on reparations."

Morin sipped his drink. "There is more unity in our ranks than you may think. Thus I believe it to be quite an accomplishment to bring Taché into the Executive Council."

Étienne-Paschal Taché had a reputation as a soldier, monarchist and conservative who had accepted an appointment in the Draper-Viger government as deputy adjutant-general of the militia for Canada East. Nonetheless, his nationalist credentials were such that he had no qualms about supporting La Fontaine once the Reformers took power earlier in the year.

You must be pleased, Augustin, that this has happened."

"There is a history to this. I'm grateful to Taché for giving me asylum when I was a fugitive at the end of '37. He risked much because Colborne was suspicious of his involvement with us. Ordered a search of his home after the '38 skirmishes. Fortunately there were no firearms discovered and no arrest ensued."

Louis-Napoléon was once more at the door and somewhat mystified by the scene in the office. No proofs approved, no indication that his father was doing what he had said must be done. Duvernay offered a smile for his son. The eponym could be making history and there might be reflected glory for his offspring, one who would likely be running the business in future years.

* * *

It was a short walk to the intersection of Rue Saint-Denis and Sainte-Catharine, where the Bishop resided proximate to the *Cathédrale Saint-Jacques*. Bourget had sent a note to Duvernay's office on Rue Saint-Vincent inviting the publisher for a *tête-à-tête*. It wasn't that pleasant a day and the carpet of dead leaves characteristic of October, soggy because of an overnight rain, made walking the route just a bit more uncomfortable.

Duvernay was not about to forget another conversation with Bourget that took place in Vermont seven years before. Did the Bishop help turn his life around? Or could he attribute his reversal of fortune to other circumstances? As it turned out, his association with the clergy was very much on a different basis. Part of the Reformist movement, he had accepted its new alliance with the church.

Entering the Bishop's palace, Duvernay was quickly informed that Bourget had gone over to the cathedral itself for prayers and would meet him there. Duvernay complied. He had been inside the cathedral often enough not to take special notice of how the columns were designed. He remembered being originally impressed by the main altar, which was surmounted by a canopy, the semi-circle of which was linked to columns supporting two floors of chapels with their own altars.

Bourget himself had supervised the construction of the Bishop's palace and the Saint-Jacques Cathedral over twenty years before. At the time he was secretary to Bishop Lartigue and already demonstrating that he was an energetic and tireless aide.

Duvernay wondered if this arrangement would stand once the grandest of Catholic superstructures became fully accessible to the public. The *Basilique Notre-Dame de Montréal*, located on Rue Notre-Dame at the corner of Saint-Sulpice, was already known as the largest church in North America. The sanctuary itself had been completed in 1830 and the first tower was ready five years ago. There was much to do in the interior.

This Bishop's church he had entered was modest by comparison. About 160 feet long and 66 feet wide, it had walls 36 feet high. The narrow tower rose high enough that Duvernay could barely distinguish the cross atop the spire, the low cloud cover reducing visibility.

The prelate wasn't too hard to locate; he could be seen at the other end of the nave conversing with a couple of priests. The usual mitre crowning his prematurely white hair was not to be seen. Otherwise, Bourget was very much the same man who had visited Burlington years before, one quick to engage with everybody willing to accept his authority and to do so in a dignified manner. He crossed the open floor to grasp Duvernay's hand as if the latter were yet another acolyte. "You have not disappointed me, young man." (Actually they had been born in the same year at the tail end of the previous century.) Once again Duvernay was transfixed by Bourget's bright blue eyes and intense countenance. They repaired to a room off the nave.

"You asked to talk to me, *monseigneur?*"

"Yes, a talk we must have in very troubling times. Let me begin. When I visited the Vatican two years ago, Romans were celebrating the election of Giovanni Maria Mastai-Ferretti to the papacy. Pius IX was and is much more popular than the late Pope Gregory and his reforms in the next several months made the Papal States seem a model of enlightened government to the world. But giving amnesty to political prisoners has been his undoing. Riots are more frequent and he can count on little or no help from the Austrian army. I fear for his safety."

"And you believe that his fate will have a bearing on the state of things in Canada?"

"The fate of our Church is at stake. Much has been accomplished since the dark days of the rebellions. Christianization of our *Canadien* brethren has proceeded despite the insidious machinations of Dessailles, Dorion and their fellow members in the *Institut Canadien*.To think that last April on Dorion's request I became chairman of the central committee for the *Association des établissements canadiens des townships* with Papineau as the vice-chairman. We may have agreed on opening the Townships to *Canadien* settlement but certainly not on anything else. The June uprising in Paris demonstrated our profound differences. I resigned the post last month."

Duvernay was listening with willing ears. He had had his crisis of faith back in Burlington and it had been the Bishop who had showed him the way forward. On the other hand, the old allegiance to Papineau and his republicanism had not stood the test of time. The man's fiery words enunciated at the Bonsecours Market in April, though reiterated by nephew Dessaulles, were proving dangerous in the current period of world revolt. "You may be correct, *monseigneur*. Men such as Dessaulles are not true believers. I see it in his writings in *L'Avenir*. I sense an implicit rejection of our faith. Moreover, he is most open in his denunciation of the Union. I quote him: 'the Union is the most infamous outrage upon our natural and political rights that could be perpetrated.' *La Minerve* takes the opposite view. That is why I no longer support Papineau and his ilk."

"I agree! Many of the articles in *L'Avenir* are revolutionary. I, on the other hand, have no other message to the faithful than that we must side with God and all legitimately constituted authority. Such is the will of the Lord. I advise you not to listen to those who address seditious remarks to you for they cannot be your true friends." Bourget's blue eyes were now very fierce.

The walk back to Rue Saint-Vincent would be hard for Duvernay to recall in later times. He had declared himself before a witness who was impeachable and there could be no going back. He must face men such as Papineau and Dessaulles in public forums on many occasions. What he would be writing in *La Minerve* could not be easily retracted. But he was determined; he would accuse Dessaulles of being an atheist. *The man practices no religion and if he says otherwise he will be a perjurer!*

Louis-Napoléon Duvernay found his father at his desk scribbling a message that was obviously intended for the print shop. What surprised him was the passion that seemed to be driving this usually affable man of letters. At that moment Ludger Duvernay wheeled about in his chair and berated the son for not recognizing the importance of getting text to the typesetters with dispatch. Louis-Napoléon was understandably peeved and finally said so. "You may be cheerful and good-natured by disposition, father, but you do have a temper."

*If we refuse to afford all the facilities we can for commercial intercourse
between Canada and her powerful neighbour we must certainly
create discontent with our retention of the Colony – if on the other hand
we encourage that intercourse there is every probability that Canada
ere long will be Americanized by the influx of Yankees – between
the two I have no hesitation in preferring the latter, and if
ultimately it should lead to the separation of these Provinces
from the British Empire let us hope that this may take place
by amicable arrangement instead of war*
LORD GREY
(letter to Governor Lord Elgin, July 27, 1848)

*There is something in the mission of the Rabbi which calls for
a more than usual exercise of generosity, for in the words of the
Herald of yesterday morning, we may say: after centuries of changes,
one of the people most stable in their faith, comes from Persia,
a land most stable in its manners, to a country inhabited by the most
restless nations in the world'…We hope the plea will be responded.*
MONTREAL TRANSCRIPT
(editorial, October 26, 1848)

Forty four

B enjamin Hart made certain he was well protected from the elements
while he dressed for the evening's lecture. He had celebrated his
seventieth birthday in August and was aware that a cold October evening
could give him no end of trouble if he were not careful. Harriot had made
that point to him *ad nauseam.* Indeed, he had spoken sharply to his wife
after the last of her repetitions. His cloak, he deemed, was adequate and he
already had his walking stick in hand.

The lecture had been anticipated for more than a couple of weeks. On
the day before Yom Kippur evening a Persian rabbi arrived in Montreal
on a mission of mercy. Nissim ben Shelomoh spoke to the congregation
on Rue Chenneville the following night but the worshippers, despite
a most passionate plea from Reverend de Sola to come to the aid of the
unfortunate Jews of Hamadan, could raise no more than seventy dollars.
Benjamin agreed with De Sola that the cost of the trip from the Middle East
exceeded the sum raised in this small Congregation. The audience had to

be much broader. De Sola, a resident of Montreal for less than two years, would appeal to the whole populace. The Benjamin brothers, no relations of Benjamin Hart, concurred.

The strategy was seemingly quite successful. In fact, the support of the Montreal community leaders was such that the venue for the lecture, announced as being held at the old News Room in Rue Saint-Joseph, had since been shifted to the Temperance Hall. The various religious denominations mentioned the event in their Sunday sermons and the newspapers editorialized on the plight of Jews in Persia. Benjamin had heard that La Fontaine, the Attorney-General, Morin, the Speaker of the House, and other leading citizens would be in the audience.

Benjamin was confident that the *chazzan* would be up to the task. He had given a course of lectures before the Mercantile Library Association the previous winter and demonstrated his eloquence and his erudition. The subjects of his dissertations had been the long history of Jewish persecution in Great Britain and other nations in Europe and the moderation of anti-Semitic attitudes in more recent times. *How pleasing to have this young Sephardic Jew, London bred, get the attention of so many Gentiles!*

The Temperance Hall was indeed filled to capacity. Benjamin had never before seen such a public response to promotion of the lecture and he was a Montreal resident for thirty years. De Sola was at his best; though still in his early twenties, his command of the English language, his pedigree as the scion of accomplished rabbinical scholars and his fearless approach to community work won him admiration. He was not particularly handsome, yet his spectacles, heavy eyebrows and fringe beard made him look very much the intellectual.

After the dissertation ended and the bearded Samuel Benjamin took the stage to make his appeal for funds, the meeting broke up. The Harts, Benjamin and Harriot, moved onto the dais to confer with the other members of the Congregation who had organized the affair. Congratulations were bestowed everywhere. Benjamin made a point of getting confirmation that all went as planned. Samuel Benjamin obliged. "Successful also from a financial point of view! I believe we raised about two hundred dollars for the relief fund, more than enough to send the Rabbi home a happy man."

Benjamin Hart, however, was not overjoyed despite the success. When he and Moses Judah Hays had created the synagogue but a few years back, he had been hailed as being its inspiration. Things had changed in so short a time. The Benjamin brothers, Samuel, Goodman and William, now dominated the Congregation. One was treasurer and another secretary of its governing body. There was little doubt that Samuel too, the most prominent of the trio, would be chosen president of the Congregation when the next election came around. Indeed, there was every possibility that Samuel Benjamin would run for a seat on the city council. Never before had a Jew appealed to the general electorate to be selected as an alderman. Benjamin Hart had mixed feelings on the matter: the three brothers weren't born in the province and had on occasion expressed a willingness to return to Britain if the circumstances were right. *I've spent my seventy years here and what I get are frequent curses walking the streets of Montreal. I may be a magistrate but my actions during the rebellion have not been forgotten.*

* * *

The servant brought him a calling card. Son Theodore was at the door. Benjamin had been brooding over his account books at that moment and a social visit from Theodore, infrequent as they had become in the last couple of years, was not particularly welcome. But how was he to turn away his own business partner? Besides, a glance at the window reminded him that it was snowing and that it being Sunday, he could not be that discourteous. He would *not*, however, alert Harriot to her son's presence in the house; she had not yet forgiven him for his marriage to a Unitarian.

"I have looked at the books, papa, sales are dismal and our liabilities are piling up. Even the insurance accounts I supervise are showing the effect of the downturn in business."

"Are you surprised? The railway boom in Britain has come to an inglorious end. The economy of the home country is in great trouble and Lord Russell has little stomach for maintaining the protections we merchants in Canada have come to expect. Let's face it! There is almost no overseas demand for my potash. It is no better for our friend Hays. The Bank of Montreal is onto him regarding the non-payment of loans he has endorsed."

"I would not worry too much about Mr. Hays. His place in Dalhousie Square is doing very nicely. We will again be entertained this winter by a German orchestra and Viennese dances. All you say may be true, and if that is the case, I think we must find a way out. My interests, papa, go beyond the insurance agency and the mercantile business we run together. I intend to involve myself in railways and other modes of transportation. And you know of my land purchases not only in Montreal but also in the mining areas north of the Great Lakes. That is why I invested personally in the railway terminal on Saint-Bonaventure. The short link to the other side of the Lachine Canal is already making a difference in business activity." Theodore's involvement in the Montreal and Lachine Railroad, which started up the previous year along Victoria Street to supplement canal transportation, had received Benjamin's approbation and he had to accede that point.

"That is all well and good, Theo, but you know what the problem is: current British trade policies are destroying our economy. You need only to talk to the merchants on Saint-Paul Street or elsewhere to get agreement on that point. And with conditions as they are, peace and stability are at stake." Benjamin had realized for some time that the repeal of the Corn Laws and the Irish emigration to America had undermined the old colonial system. Would the discontented Irish element in Montreal organize a threat to the legitimacy of British rule in North America as had the *Patriotes* a decade before? And will the Americans let us be?"

"You must admit, papa, that we cannot persist in limiting our trade with the Americans. The very existence of British rule in Canada would be in jeopardy if the people continue to suffer economic dislocation. I think that even the Colonial Office reckons that such a result could occur. It is said that Lord Elgin is of that opinion and will not stand in the way of trade reciprocity. What we need is greater access to the American market and therefore agreement on the St Lawrence and Atlantic Railroad. Subscriptions to it are below par. Hincks is pressing for legislation that will ensure completion of the line to Portland by guaranteeing bonds for that purpose. I think that Baldwin and La Fontaine will go along with such a bill when Parliament meets in the spring."

Benjamin's laugh was sardonic. "Good luck on that. You can guess that I hold no brief for *Monsieur* La Fontaine despite the fact that he is gravitating towards ties with the church. His government is still ill-disposed toward the English interest and now he has the audacity to show sympathy to the pardoned rebels by rewarding their followers financially for their misdeeds."

"Papa, you haven't changed. The French can do no right in your opinion. I have long thought differently in this matter. That is why I'm not a Tory."

* * *

The meeting in the office of Adolphus Mordecai Hart had been arranged with little notice. Benjamin was in a panic that he had scarcely experienced in his lifetime. Creditors were at his establishment demanding payment though most of his assets were not liquid. Lawsuits were being threatened. Was there any way to escape bankruptcy? *Who else better to turn to than one's son-in-law and legal advisor?*

Adolphus listened patiently as Benjamin enumerated the difficulties he was facing. And that took some time. Benjamin went into detail describing the complexities of the import/export business he had developed over the years. And then there was his representation of the different insurance companies, which accounted for much of the company's income. ("Theo handles much of that segment of the business but ultimately I am responsible to the principals.") The changes in the commercial policy of Great Britain coupled with the decline in world trade were causing him much grief. Should he be worried that the connection with England will soon be sundered? "And can I survive in the meanwhile? I'm an old man and my offspring have scattered in all directions."

"How is your wife responding to all this?"

"Harriot is certainly exercised by these events. She reminds me that my good fortune beginning in 1825 was owing in large part to the inheritance she received when her father died. She has never since contemplated the thought of being destitute. Sixteen children she has had and so few of them left at home to give her comfort."

"You do have extensive holdings in land. The acreage you hold in the Townships has undoubtedly increased in worth. And your progeny is well fixed financially. I do not hear of Theo complaining. Frances is happy enough in New York. Soon Wellington will be joining the Schoyers there. And what about the Horts in California? Right in the middle of the Gold Rush!"

Benjamin had not been looking at extended family in the same way. True, Raphael Schoyer and wife Frances were well established in New York. She had recently boasted of how she was charming her social circle with her accomplishments in music. Both Emily and Dora had traveled with the Hort brothers to the west coast to make their fortune. Arthur Wellington had married well in England and had brought his family back to America following an unfortunate bankruptcy. But his other sons? Henry had ended up in St Louis, Frederick in New Orleans and Benjamin Moses in New Jersey. None of them was able to fit into the Hart import/export business. Only Theo had stood by his side though the two of them were on separate tracks philosophically.

Adolphus was still lecturing his father-in-law. "Have you thought out the consequences of declaring yourself a bankrupt? Your assets would be at risk and your wife has reason to be concerned how she would fare in such a circumstance. At least she is the main beneficiary of your will and testament. If you remember, your latest will was dated three years ago on February 23. Most of your estate is scheduled to go to your wife. I'm an executor along with Henry Judah and Sam David."

"She does have property in her own name in Manhattan. Can that be touched by my creditors?"

"I wouldn't think so although I would have to look at the land registrations. Perhaps Raphael could help in this regard."

"Which leads to another question: If she sues me, will that qualify her as a creditor?"

Adolphus chuckled. "You are being devious. Let's wait until we know what will transpire! Meanwhile, I suggest we adjourn. Constance is in her last week of her pregnancy. We wonder if it's going to be a girl. We already have two boys."

"I'm so glad you married my Hannah. To think that she survived after I had just lost three children in infancy." Benjamin had worried at the time – this was in the mid-twenties – whether Harriot should avoid another pregnancy. She, however, had insisted it was God's will that she bear children as long as she could.

"I don't call her Hannah any longer. It's Constance from now on and that is what all our children will hear. Little George has never heard the word Hannah escape her lips. Meanwhile, Abraham Emile will be two years old in late March, thus one week before *Pesach*."

Benjamin nodded his head slowly. "Life does go on even while my woes increase."

"Woes felt by many. We are still recovering from the failure of the Provident.." Adolphus was referring to the bankruptcy of the Montreal Provident and Savings Bank the previous year. The depreciation in value of stocks, securities and real estate had magnified the assumed mismanagement by its Board of Directors. Depositors were out by over £160,000, i.e. more than three quarters of a million dollars. Benjamin reckoned that the bank would eventually compensate the victims at about eighteen shillings a pound, but the reputations of the managers (including the cashier himself) were badly stained. Benjamin had special regard for Moses Judah Hay, who had been managing director of that institution from February 1845 to April 1846 and had borrowed from it extensively. Knowing his old friend so well, Benjamin shared the man's humiliation even if the latter would suffer no lasting damage to his public stature.

*Those who call me and my friends rebels I tell them that they lie in
their throats.... I tell those gentlemen to their teeth, that it is they
and such as they, who cause revolutions, who pull down thrones,
trample crowns into the dust and annihilate dynasties.*
WOLFRED NELSON
(parliamentary debate, March, 1849)

*Let the parliament pass the bill, let the Government sanction
it if he pleases, but while there is an axe and rifle on
the frontier, and Saxon hands to wield them, these
losses will not be paid.*
MONTREAL COURIER
(editorial, April, 1849)

Forty five

The weather was reasonably mild given it being the end of January.
Theodore Hart was grateful; he had agreed to have lunch with
Benjamin Holmes and Luther Hamilton Holton at their favorite eating spot
near the Place d'Armes. There would be talk about railway construction
and other business issues but Theodore could expect that the subject of
Habitant reparations to dominate their conversation. On Monday but a few
blocks away in the relatively new home of the United Province of Canada,
La Fontaine, the Attorney General, had moved to form a committee of
the whole House on February 9; its purpose: to "take into consideration
the necessity of establishing the amount of Losses incurred by certain
inhabitants in Lower Canada during the political troubles of 1837 and
1838, and of providing for the payment thereof."

Theodore had no illusion about how most of Montreal's Anglophones
would react to this government action; Tory sentiment prevailed, buttressed
as it was by the fear that the resorting to violence by the *Patriotes* would

endanger the lives and properties of the "British" minority. Undoubtedly, papa Benjamin epitomized that sentiment. He had personally read the riot act back in the autumn of 1837 when the outbreak occurred in Montreal. *But would men such as Holmes and Holton be as indignant?*

The snow pushed up alongside the sidewalk of Rue Notre-Dame was diminishing somewhat because of the thaw that had persisted for several days but that meant some slush that had to be avoided as he hurried to his destination. Theodore had to balance such caution with some consideration of how much time should be allocated to reviewing the economic malaise and how badly it was affecting their ambitious plans to get financial backing for the St Lawrence & Atlantic railroad scheme. Furthermore, any public quarrel over reparations could be an unwelcome diversion.

Benjamin Holmes was already seated when Theodore followed the waiter to a table in the back of the dining room. Holton, however, had yet to arrive. Theodore extended his hand and Holmes grasped it with alacrity; there was genuine affection in the gesture. The age difference didn't matter.

The Irishman, now into his fifties, had befriended Theodore during their joint stay in Kingston several years before. Out of banking for three years, Holmes had formed a partnership with John Young to do merchandising and railway promotion. His influence with the Reform movement, however, was what made him of particular interest to Theodore. Holmes had cast his lot with the Reformers while in Kingston. *Did he really believe then that La Fontaine and his cohort could stand up to the Tory consensus?*

They had barely engaged in civilities before Holton made his appearance. He did not immediately take a seat. The atmosphere changed. Unlike Theodore's spare frame, Holton was well built. Standing six feet the man's stature and his inherent energy and intelligence made him a dominating personality.

Holton looked excited. "You may not have been told that our friend Hincks is selling the *Pilot* and joining the administration as Inspector General."

Theodore and Holmes exchanged glances. This announcement called for a response. Holmes was the first to react. "Does he want that responsibility? Cayley was in deep trouble with his expenditures on public works. His loan of £140,000 is in jeopardy, neither the interest or the principal having been paid down during the three years since he floated it. He will have to do some unpopular things to solve that problem."

Holton smiled. He had other news. "I've spoken to Hincks. He is already planning to sponsor a bill that will create a sinking fund for the eventual retirement of the provincial debt. He is conscious of the need to improve the financial reputation and credit of the province, especially if the government chooses to guarantee loans aimed at getting the St Lawrence and Atlantic financed properly."

Theodore was pleased with this information. William Cayley was to him an example of what was wrong with the previous administration. He had failed to act on the establishment of a sinking fund during his term as Inspector General. Hincks, on the other hand, was a breath of fresh air in the merchant community. "Neither he or you will get the thanks of our colleagues running the banking industry. They have been openly hostile to the new administration."

Holton had a rejoinder. "I'm cautiously optimistic. I'm well regarded in those circles despite my divergent views. On the Board of Trade for more than two years now. And I do support reciprocity in trade with the USA. My relationships, however, may be affected if political strife gets out of hand."

Holmes interjected at this point. "We are in for a very stormy period, gentlemen. Elizabeth and I were at a dinner party at the Arnoldi house last weekend. Even the rumor that this latest measure would be introduced had everybody at the table enraged. My father in law, who is a justice of the peace as well as a surgeon, reckons that he will be spending less time at the hospital and more in carrying out his political duties. You can imagine what the younger Tories are thinking. They haven't forgotten their days in the Doric Club, their opportunity to take clubs to the *Patriotes*."

* * *

The walk to the Place d'Youville needed no forethought on the part of Theodore, who had often traversed the route when he visited his father's office in one of the warehouses near by. This time, however, he had to deal with unusual crowding on Rue Saint-Pierre all the way to the Parliament itself. Debate on the Rebellion Losses Bill was at its most intense point.

The February 9 date for voting on La Fontaine's initial motion had not been held to. The opposition Tories, in high dudgeon ("we mustn't pay the rebels"), had proposed amendments to the government initiative in order to delay its consideration. The first counterattack involved arguing that the members deserved an extra ten days time to test the feelings of the country. By the 20th of the month a second amendment declared that the House had "no authority to entertain any such proposition", the Governor General not having alluded to the subject in his Speech from the Throne the month before. The amendments were rejected and the committee was eventually formed on Tuesday, February 20. But the House was adjourned until early March.

The *Marché Sainte-Anne,* home to the capital of the Canadas for the past five years, was remembered by Theodore as primarily the city's marketplace and therefore a hive of activity each day of the week. The limestone building was rather new (built in the early 1830s) and large enough (350 feet long and 50 feet wide) to accommodate both branches of government in the upper storey. The Legislative Council was in the east wing, a House of Assembly in the west wing. Today the legislators gathered in the halls were augmented by a host of onlookers.

Theodore was one of them; he could not resist witnessing the debate once he had been apprised of the physical violence accompanying the arguments that went on prior to the February creation of the legislative committee. At that time leaders of the old regime, Henry Sherwood and Allan MacNab, had predictably challenged the legitimacy of the bill because it would reward the "rebels" of yesterday and insult the "loyal" subjects who had defeated them in battle. Hincks and others had responded by accusing the Tories of being the true rebels. They had violated the British constitution during the run up to the political crisis in 1837 and were therefore responsible for the civil war that followed. A fight broke out in the galleries and the Sergeant at Arms had to intervene.

The following day the action shifted to the floor itself. The member from Kingston, John A. MacDonald, kept interrupting a pro-government speaker and the upshot was MacDonald being challenged to a duel. The duel never happened but tempers were not assuaged by the arguments offered prior to the February 20 vote. The bill itself, introduced by La Fontaine seven days later, authorized total payments of £90,000.

Second reading was scheduled for this morning, the second of March. Those offering amendments would undoubtedly display with great passion their dismay given what Theodore had listened to in every contact he had with the Tories from his social circle.

Speaking for the government was Dr. Wolfred Nelson, who maintained that his constituents in the Richelieu Valley deserved redress given the brutality of the soldiery rampaging through Saint-Denis and other riverside communities. Cries of "traitor" and "rebel" could be heard as he spoke. Theodore wondered whether it had been wise for La Fontaine to put up Nelson front and center; he had led the Patriotes in battle with the army marching up the Richelieu. *This is waving a red flag in front of a bull.* After fifteen minutes or so the taunts drew an unexpected response. His voice rose to a level that overwhelmed the hecklers. "To those who call me and my friends rebels, I tell them that they lie in their throats." Theodore was hearing the reiteration of the *Canadien* basic complaint against British rule at an emotional level comparable to the passion of most English citizens opposing the bill. *And to think that Nelson himself is of British stock!*

*   *   *

The furor in Parliament could not be ignored even when family business had to be discussed. Benjamin Hart had already made the decision to declare bankruptcy but that didn't prevent him from considering his duty as a magistrate dedicated to uphold the authority of the Crown. And entertaining his son in his study gave him the chance to give advice on where his son should be standing while his peers were on their collective feet.

Theodore was not about to be lectured to. "Many are convinced that the Parliament is acting within its rights. Papa, I do agree that the Governor General may not assent to the bill. He is, after all, partial to English sentiment. If the protests become too violent, he may declare that social peace is too important and not let the conflict escalate. On the other hand, Lord Elgin has said he recognizes the principle of ministerial responsibility. The new administration does have the majority of the people behind it."

Benjamin grunted. He obviously didn't want to hear such a defense of La Fontaine and his allies. "Don't underestimate the volume of protest. Not only is the English-language press opposing the indemnification measure most strenuously. The public meeting last month brought together all our leading citizens. George Moffat, MacNab, Gugy, Molson and others have staked their reputations on supporting the petition to dissolve Parliament and have new elections."

Theodore wasn't certain how to respond. Looking at his father, who was so much in despair because the world had turned against him, he felt some compassion. But he had realized for some time that the bitterness consuming Benjamin Hart was distorting good sense. The dutiful son had an obligation to set his father on a better course. "This province doesn't need another election if it means a return to Sherwood and Viger."

"I would be satisfied with Moffatt and MacNab."

"Papa, accept reality! The fact is that the bill is now law. The House of Assembly passed it by a vote of 47 to 18 with even the English members from Upper Canada favoring it in their majority. You expected the Legislative Council to vote otherwise, but it too approved the measure. And what surprised me is that they did so despite Viger's opposition." Theodore had indeed been caught off guard by the intervention of Denis-Benjamin Viger on the side of the naysayers. Appointed a Legislative Councilor in the

304

winter of 1848 following the defeat of the government in which he was a co-leader, Viger had seemingly lost interest in politics. Those who knew him personally had noted that he seemed content living in his two-storey stone house on Rue Bonsecours without engaging with his former colleagues in the Marché Sainte-Anne. But last week he did attend a Council meeting in which damned the Rebellion Losses Bill on the grounds that the province was already too burdened with debt to undertake so extensive a compensation package.

Benjamin said no more. He was obviously at the end of his tether. The face never looked so pale. His distinctive nose twitched. His eyes seemed unfocused. Theodore reckoned that this was not the time to talk about settlement of accounts.

It is evident, from the known character of our race, that patient submission to any ascendancy founded on feelings of nationality alone, and not actuated by any generous or progressive principle, never has been, and never will be for any length of time, endured by Britons.
BRITISH AMERICAN LEAGUE
(Manifesto, April 19, 1849)

A Mass Meeting will be held on the Place d'Armes this evening at 8 o'clock. Anglo-Saxons to the struggle, now is your time.
MONTREAL GAZETTE
("Extra" of April 25, 1849)

Forty six

Adolphus Hart hadn't been forewarned that his mother-in-law would be calling on the family this afternoon. But Harriot Judith Hart often didn't believe in niceties. Constance was her daughter and she had the right to learn first-hand how the new grandchild, Gerald Ephriam, was faring. The infant, born to Constance and Adolphus but three weeks earlier, was one of a very few offspring of her several children that she had easy access to. Frances' brood in New York City had yet to be visited even though her eldest daughter had resided there for so many years. Also in New York was her namesake, Harriet Blanche, because her parent, Arthur Wellington, had departed England for America. Henry, living in St Louis, had already fathered six children but Harriot's relationship with his wife, Elizabeth, was not the best and there was no possibility that she would travel to the Wild West. Two of her youngest daughters were even farther away in California. Frederick and Benjamin were bachelors. Theodore's son by his second marriage was, of course, closed to her since she had so disapproved of Theo as an apostate. Constance's three boys were her only consolation.

Adolphus was properly solicitous of his mother-in-law but he found the first excuse to retreat to his study. Hardly had he settled in a chair when there was a knock at the door. Harriot looked a bit sheepish. "Can we talk, Adolphus? You are close to my husband but you seldom take me into your confidence."

Adolphus offered her a seat and ordered a servant to bring tea. Harriot made a few remarks about the resemblance of little Gerald Ephraim to his maternal grandfather, the late Ephraim Hart. Once the tea had been served, she revealed the real purpose of her visit. "My husband is at wit's end. Not only is our personal fortune in jeopardy; the situation in Montreal reminds him of a dozen years ago. It is a tinder box. Whereas before he was strong enough to declare himself, to assert his authority in the streets, today he feels himself inadequate for the task. He has no peace of mind."

Harriot herself was showing the effects of this confusion. Adolphus had never before seriously examined the ravages of time that had affected her countenance. Sagging flesh, drooping eyelids, a bent back and an obvious loss of weight. It should have been no surprise to him. A woman in her sixties who had borne eighteen children was not likely to be a paragon of a healthy female. "Alas, my dear woman, I cannot give him peace of mind. Only legal advice in a very difficult situation. But remember this: It has been a month since Parliament passed by bill. Lord Elgin has yet to give his assent to it and most of my friends think that he dare not do so given the depth of feeling in our community."

"But what if he does?"

"There would be consequences. You may have read in the *Gazette* this morning of the new British American League. Its purpose goes beyond opposition to the Rebellion Losses Bill. The sudden disappearance of a protected Imperial market for our exports has created consternation for many of those supporting the Empire's architecture."

"That is so, and Benjamin is of a like mind. He believes he has been ruined by this change in British policy."

"Is he ready for the consequences? I shall gladly discuss the options when the time comes."

Harriot seemed satisfied with that. She got to her feet and mentioned that she wanted to get back to Constance and the baby. Adolphus was left to ponder on the matter. He himself was yet uncertain how this British American League would alter thinking in the merchant community. More and more of his clients were becoming friendly to the idea of free trade, but that meant to them that they had to consider the prospect of annexation to the United States.

Looking at the list of manifesto sponsors, Adolphus could not but notice that the leading exponents were well placed in the Conservative opposition. George Moffatt had accepted the post of president of the Association's Montreal branch. He was describing the group as "children of a monarchy, too magnanimous to prescribe, too great to be unjust."

Too much wishful thinking! Adolphus was becoming convinced that many Conservatives and Tories, no matter their basic outlook, were more impressed than before with the arguments of Papineau and his cohort. The British connection was not inviolate. On the other hand, the *Rouges* were out-and-out Annexationists because of their anti-monarchial bias. *Very much a dilemma!*

*   *   *

A brisk wind was blowing from upriver throughout the Wednesday but Adolphus didn't at first understand it as being a portent. He had walked down to Place d'Youville in the late afternoon to be present in the gallery following word that the Governor General intended to visit Parliament this day. Ostensibly Lord Elgin had been summoned from Monklands, his residence northwest of Montreal, to sign an authorization that would permit the authority to apply cargo duties, the first boat of the season having reached the port of Quebec the day before. There could be yet another reason that he was making an appearance: he might be ready to act on the Rebellion Losses Bill.

Adolphus was not disappointed in his surmise; Lord Elgin's carriage had drawn to a halt before the west wing of the building and he and his aide-de-camp moved with minimal ceremony up the stairs to the Parliament chamber. After putting his signature to several bills requiring attention, he then declared that he was giving the royal assent to the more controversial measure. The majority of the legislators applauded but Adolphus suspected that the reception in the streets would be very different than in the chamber. He excused himself and went downstairs. News of the royal assent had passed from mouth to mouth and reached the onlookers milling about the market area on Place d'Youville. Rue Saint-Pierre was now fully occupied with pedestrians and more people were on the horizon despite the approach of dusk.

A substantial number in the crowd were not restraining themselves. Profanities abounded. Cries of outrage could not but be noticed. The incendiary editorials in the *Montreal Gazette* and other English-language journals were certainly having their effect. When Lord Elgin and his retinue appeared at the entrance to let him return to his own establishment, the carriage was assaulted with stones. Adolphus thought he saw eggs retrieved from the marketplace being thrown at the representative of the Queen. The saffron color now conspicuous not only on the garments of Lord Elgin and his party but also on the sides of the carriage attested to that likelihood. The driver began driving furiously up McGill Street bound for Monklands, which was west of the mountain.

The sight of the head of state fleeing the scene stimulated new disrespect of authority among the citizenry. A Tory hothead, posting himself atop a cab and furiously ringing a bell as he was being driven down Rue Saint-Jacques, shouted for all the hear. "To the Champs de Mars, to the Champs de Mars." The mob was growing larger. Many of the new arrivals were unsteady on their feet. They had seemingly reinforced their courage by frequenting their favorite public house prior to joining the fray.

Adolphus recognized that the anger would be channeled into action once the opposition could be gathered at an open-air rally. Hurrying east on Rue Notre-Dame he became part of the throng that were waiting for Moffatt, Gugy and other dissenters to speak their piece. When they did address the crowd, their repetition of the argument for petitioning London appeared too tame given the current mood. There were yells of "Fire" and the sounding of the alarm, which provoked the firemen in the crowd to rush back to the Marché Saint Anne. Again Adolphus followed this surge, although he could see no evidence of a conflagration. But the firemen at the door of the Parliament were not deterred by a barred entrance. It was almost inevitable that in this atmosphere any restraint would be ignored. The main portal yielded to the axes and a battering ram and the same weapons were undoubtedly being employed upstairs even though the popular Assembly was still in session. It already being evening, many in the invading party were also equipped with torches. Several thousand spectators had by now assembled on Place d'Youville. Most cheered lustily when one of the Tory stalwarts came out of the building carrying the mace that would normally have been in place before the Speaker of the House. Adolphus groaned. *There must be a massacre upstairs.*

As if to confirm that conclusion, the night was being illuminated by the flames showing through the windows. Everything was being destroyed. Adolphus was to learn later that all that was saved from the fire was the legislative mace and a portrait of Queen Victoria.

But that *was* much later. The protesters were still on the rampage, seeking targets for their wrath. The homes of Reform politicians were under assault even as an inadequate police force sought to restrain the rabble rousers. It was indeed going to be a long night.

Seeking refuge in his own house after relative silence had at last descended on the city, Adolphus spent some time briefing Constance. She was appalled as was he. Rather than retiring for the night, he took refuge in his study, where he reviewed in his mind the day's events. Lord Elgin certainly knew the scope of the Tory opposition to legislation. He probably considered the likelihood that he was being tested. The rules for responsible government had yet to be fully demonstrated to men such as MacNab and others from the old establishment. Moreover, George Moffatt was no longer in the chamber as a voice of moderation (He hadn't run for reelection last November.)

For their part, MacNab, Moffatt and their like must have been convinced that a Reform ministry with *Canadien* support would solidify their control of the government if the bill was allowed to stand. Adolphus could not believe that they intended all this violence but for them it was convenient not to intervene.

Their appeal to Elgin to use the power he still retained in the transition to responsible government must have been considerable. Adolphus reckoned, however, that if the Governor had reserved the bill, the Imperial suzerainty would at once be challenged by men like Papineau and there would be a replay of 1837 or a resort to Annexation. Moreover, dissolving Parliament was not likely to result in any major realignment of membership in the House.

*   *   *

Calm had not returned with the rising of the sun over the St Lawrence. Though he had slept in till noon, Adolphus, sensing that there was to be more trouble ahead, opted to walk to the house on Rue des Récollets to confer with his father-in-law. Benjamin Hart, after all, was still a justice of the peace.

He was pleased to see that his host was no longer lethargic. Actually, Benjamin had already been visited by Moses Judah Hays, who was also a magistrate. Adolphus appreciated their discomfort. They were as hostile to government policy as were the rioters; they conceded to Adolphus that their commitment to law and order was being tested by their own constituency.

"The Mayor is calling the municipal council into session. He will, of course, ask permission to suppress the riots." Benjamin was no admirer of Édouard-Raymond Fabre, the bookseller and *Patriote* recently elected to the post, but the situation was desperate.

"It will be important to see how a man like Badgley responds. After all, he was Attorney General under Sherwood before the election and he has taught at McGill's Faculty of Law. I think it will be hard for him not to support Fabre." Adolphus' comment was probably superfluous. William Badgley was certainly a conservative who had help found the Constitutional Association during the years prior to the 1837 rebellion. Nevertheless, he too must be outraged by the failure of law and order in the city.

Adolphus was invited to stay for supper. Harriot, though under the weather, actually insisted on his sharing a repast. Her downcast mien suggested that the upset in the outdoors was adding to an existing malaise. She had lived all her life in a well-to-do household and now she was faced with economic circumstances threatening her very livelihood. The bits of dialogue between husband and wife indicated that she would rather not be left alone with Benjamin when the candles were lit in the dining room.

The conversation at the table did match the mood to a certain extent. Adolphus sought to be non-controversial but the dominant sentiment was that of blame. The Ministry in London had taken a disastrous course; the men at Government House on Rue Notre-Dame were advising Lord Elgin badly; the city councilors led by Fabre were cowards. Benjamin's voice was higher pitched than usual.

While he was reporting on the reaction of officialdom, Benjamin was interrupted by the appearance of son Theodore, who looked quite harried. He chose to ignore his father. "Glad I found you here, Dolph. Mobs are back on the street. One of them is heading to the Holmes residence. I need people to help defend him and his family. Aaron is also outside waiting for us."

The three cousins wasted no time; they began running along Rue Notre-Dame. One scene did catch their attention. Standing next to a lamp post on the Champs de Mars the oversized figure of a man in a stylish hat could be seen trying to shout down the rioters who were surrounding him. It was Colonel Bartholomew Gugy. Adolphus found it instructive that Gugy, one of La Fontaine's sharpest critics, was bewailing the outcome of his fierce rhetoric during the parliamentary sessions. Men in the very mob he was facing were repeating phrases that Gugy had himself employed while sitting in what was once a sanctuary for free speech.

In the event, the crowd outside the Holmes dwelling was rather small and the appearance of those obviously intent on protecting a public servant from harm had a sobering effect on the attackers. The front door opened to admit these reinforcements. Benjamin Holmes had retreated to a bedroom, where he had been comforting wife Elizabeth. He finally emerged in the parlor, no doubt because he probably felt safe for the first time. His grown-up sons were also in the room.

The Irishman's face was quite pallid. "One fright after another! This is madness! Last night I escaped perishing in the House while doing my duty as a legislator. And now this!"

Holmes went on to describe what happened inside the Parliament at the very time Adolphus was witnessing its attack from the street outside. The description was vivid. After the torches had been thrown onto the roof of the building, the cry of fire could be heard in the vestibule. Smoke was creeping into the main hall from various orifices and some flames had already reached the curtains in the chamber itself. The deputies commenced a stampede towards the exits. Morin began banging his gavel. He was asking for a formal motion of adjournment as if he could expect good order in such circumstances. "We were not expecting the entry of a mob into the chamber and the destruction they were intent on inflicting."

Aaron David commiserated. "I know what they have in mind! If I were La Fontaine or Hincks, I would be looking for a way to escape their vengeance by finding safe houses. Their dwellings are in danger."

One of Holmes' sons spoke up. "They have already invaded La Fontaine's house. I was there. It's incredible; the mob broke in, smashed woodwork and broke the furniture, even period pieces that must have cost him a pretty penny. You should have seen the mess; window sills and shutters pulled away, floors ripped up, china and glass shattered. The stables were set on fire and several coaches were burned. They even pulled up saplings from the orchard. A rage you could not believe!"

Holmes sighed. "It was probably inevitable this would happen. This day, April the twenty-sixth, is not likely to be forgotten soon."

The whole row is the work of the Orange Societies backed
by the commercial men who desire annexation and
the political leaders who want place.
GOVERNOR LORD ELGIN
(letter to Lord Grey, April 30, 1849)

You find in this city I believe the most Anti-British specimens
of each class of which our community consists –
The Montreal French are the most Yankeefied French in
the Province – the British, though furiously anti-Gallican, are,
with some exceptions, the least loyal – and the commercial men
the most zealous annexationalists which Canada furnishes.
GOVERNOR LORD ELGIN
(letter to Earl Gray, September 3, 1849)

Forty seven

The tale told by his son-in-law disturbed Benjamin Hart no end. The vandalizing of the residences of so many of the Reformist leaders during the previous night could only embarrass the municipal authorities to which he was intricately associated. And yet his sympathies were with the rioters. The same thought kept being repeated in his mind during the Friday morning: *Why has the Crown forsaken us?*

The full extent of the rampage was only made known to him after breakfast when Adolphus summarized all the gossip. Rioters had not only gone to Beaver Hall Hill (aka *Place du Castor*) to invade the homes of Hincks, Wilson and Holmes. They had then proceeded to the La Fontaine residence in the *faubourg* Saint-Antoine. If a detachment of soldiers had not arrived on the scene on Rue de l'Aqueduc, the fire would have consumed the Attorney General's domicile as well as the stable. Meanwhile, the mob had returned downtown to break windows on the boarding house where Baldwin and Price were staying during their Montreal sojourn. Next came damage to the homes of Solicitor General Lewis Thomas Drummond on Craig Street and of Dr. Wolfred Nelson at the corner of Saint-Laurent and Petite Saint-Jacques. Vengeance spread wide!

Benjamin had time to ponder on the subject because he had committed himself to walking east on Rue Notre-Dame to get more insight on the tragedy that was unfolding. At noontime the Champ-de-Mars was usually quiet ~ but not on this Friday. A public meeting had been organized by Moffatt and Gugy for the avowed purpose of calming tempers. Advertising themselves as "Friends of Peace", they appeared to Benjamin as talking out of both sides of their mouth. It was soon evident that they had no answer to the crisis other than to repeat previous political slogans. They asked support for a petition to the Queen that would have her relieve Lord Elgin from office and disavow the *Rebellion Losses Act*.

It was a pleasant spring day and the crowd turnout more or less what he expected. The sunlight was glaring enough that at first he didn't recognize the presence of Moses Judah Hays standing next to the rostrum. His old friend looked as distraught as he did; it had been a bad two days for both of them.

The rally having come to an end, most of the onlookers faded away. *Was this just calm before another storm?* Hays seemed to think so. "Let's face it, Ben! We British haven't been so humbled since we have had representative government in '91. And to think that we had given our blood to conquer the republicans less than a dozen years ago!

"I must admit that if business were not so bad, I could live with this humiliation. Now I feel out of control. What do I do next?" Benjamin was not hiding his dismay.

He could think of a no more useful task than to appear that afternoon at the Bonsecours Market, where the Canadian Parliament had been transferred following the Wednesday fire that had gutted its home at the Marchée Sainte-Anne. The space was there because the civil administration, cognizant of the burgeoning growth of industry and population in Montreal, had agreed in its wisdom to design the top floors of both the Sainte-Anne market and the Bonsecours to accommodate large audiences – not only for legislators but also for public reading sessions, theatre, music and other purposes. The Governor had initially rented the Place d'Youville site as the location of the new Parliament but the Mayor could now have the stranded legislators squeezed into Bonsecours – at least on a temporary basis. It was obviously not an ideal location given its existing commercial commitments. But it did belong to the municipality and civil government had to act. Nevertheless, troops from the 71st Regiment equipped with fixed bayonets patrolled the eastern end of Rue Saint-Paul in anticipation of rioters emerging at the market gates later in the day.

The Speaker set the tone; Morin appealed to Moffatt to aid in restoring order in the city. The latter conceded that he had a responsibility in that regard but drew attention to the arrests already made – five men were incarcerated in the *Pied du Courant* gaol – and to the prospect of further government retribution. During the morning La Fontaine's office had informed the citizenry that at six in the afternoon it would be handing out arms to volunteers who showed up in front of the *dépôt de l'ordonnance* on Rue du Bord-de-l'Eau. The government was determined to create a special police force loyal to the administration. The safety of citizens and the preservation of private property were at stake.

Moffatt was objecting. "There will be trouble. We cannot accept having hundreds of armed constables threatening the people. The recruits will almost certainly be Canadians and Irishmen seeking to get even for what happened last night. Don't be surprised if there is resistance to this measure when the arms are actually distributed. Only the intervention of the regular army can forestall confrontation."

La Fontaine was not relenting; the new force would be under the orders of Montreal's justices of the peace to act if law and order were threatened again. Benjamin blanched. Was he expected to authorize what would be the launching of civil war? He had done that once – in November, 1837 and had never been forgiven by so many for such action.

Moffatt spoke up again. "I am calling for a public meeting this evening at the square on Beaver Hall Hill. We shall see whether the people accept such tyranny!" And with that he walked out of the chamber.

*   *   *

The imbroglio slated for that Friday night was not witnessed by Benjamin. The advent of the *Sabbath* dictated that as dusk descended on the city he be lighting candles in honor of his God. He subsequently learned that regimental commander Colonel Gore did not use the two cannons he had brought to dissuade the rioters from engaging with the new constables. Furthermore, he defused the crisis by appearing at the meeting on Place du Castor to promise that these 500-600 newly created policemen were being *demobilized*; the army itself would indeed maintain order.

On the Saturday Benjamin did venture out – but to the synagogue rather than to any public affair. There were such events; the Thistle Society met to strike Governor's name from its list of benefactors and the Saint Andrew

Society decided that it no longer recognized Lord Elgin as a member. But at least for the weekend there was peace in the city.

Not so on Monday. The Governor agreed to travel from Monklands to the *Château Ramezay* to publicly receive that afternoon the Friday address of the House of Parliament giving its support to his public demand for peace and order. (The favorable vote had been 36 to 16, which reflected the split in the political spectrum.) But when he had gotten to Rue Notre-Dame he ran into further protests. Rocks, eggs and other projectiles hit his carriage and the Governor and escort were forced to detour to the Bonsecours Market to meet with the deputies. On the return trip to Monklands, which began by going north on Rue Saint-Denis rather than on McGill, the rioters intercepted the Governor at the corner of Saint-Laurent and Sherbrooke. More rock throwing that resulted in injuries to the Governor's brother, the police commissioner and an army captain.

Where was there safety? Moses Hays had a proposal: use his theatre on Place Dalhousie as the meeting place until the end of the session. The following Monday a nervous body of legislators did walk to the square north of Rue Notre-Dame. Much more genteel! Who would smash windows there?

At the end of May another crisis loomed. The Parliament was due to meet on the 30th to receive an address from the Governor, who intended to prorogue the body. The interval of five weeks did not quell the discontent in Tory ranks. Once again the Governor's carriage was the target of a rock barrage. (One recovered missile weighed two pounds.)

Benjamin discussed the impasse with Adolphus. Could Lord Elgin continue as the Crown's representative in Canada under such circumstances? His son-in-law opined that the authority of the British government was at stake; it would fear that the resignation of the chief executive in Canada might be regarded as an unacceptable weakness on the part of the Russell administration.

Windows at the lower level of the Rue des Récollets house were open that night to catch the cooling early June breeze. Benjamin could not keep himself from wandering to the opening in order to restore some measure of comfort in his feverish mind. His lifelong commitment to conservative principles was being tested as never before. "I ask you, Adolphus, whether there is a chance Whitehall will reject the Act. MacNab and Cayley have already left for London to petition Parliament."

Adolphus shook his head.

Benjamin himself was dubious that with both the Whig Russell and the former Tory leader Peel agreed on its current policy towards Canada, any lobbying with the Colonial Office would be ineffective. Hincks had also departed for London to support the La Fontaine-Baldwin majority coalition and to counter the arguments of any of the Tories in the British Parliament showing sympathy with the cause of their brethren in the Canadas. "To be honest, Adolphus, I do not know where to turn. I seem to have lost everything. What a pity! Just when railway development is on the verge of success. The Torrances, the Molsons and Galt may not be ruined by British government policy, but I am doomed. What is more, my wife barely speaks to me."

* * *

The summer was no kinder to Benjamin than had been the spring. One would have thought that political fratricide was less likely now that Parliament was not to meet for the rest of the year. Furthermore, Lord Elgin had declared that when the legislators did reconvene, they would do so in Toronto for the next two years. (After that, Quebec and not Montreal would be the seat of government for yet another two years.) And to avoid further insults to the representative of the Crown, Lord Elgin intended to remain cocooned in his Monkland residence outside of Montreal proper. It didn't work out that way and the upshot for Benjamin was more grief.

To begin with, Harriot Hart spent more and more of her time in bed. Dr. Aaron David was having difficulty making a diagnosis but he did conclude that her ailment was serious. The sultry weather didn't help in this regard. Aaron David, moreover, was very much distracted by an outbreak of cholera in the city. His superior, Dr. Arnoldi, perished in July from the infection, which was accounting for hundreds of deaths in the province as diseased immigrants came off the boats. (Judge Eleazar Bédard in Quebec was one of the victims.)

Press reports from Britain, where the incoming immigrants were originating, confirmed that cholera was rife throughout the mother country. There was more bad news from abroad. Benjamin had learned from reading the press that in mid-June the House of Commons rejected decisively a motion to disavow the Rebellion Losses Act. A second initiative by Lord Brougham, which would have ensured that no person who participated in the rebellion of the '30s be compensated, was also defeated, albeit by a closer vote.

The La Fontaine-Baldwin administration could now act with greater impunity. On the morning of August 15 five men were charged with the arson that had occurred in April. The arrest order, though signed by the police commissioner, the top military officer in the region and a justice of the court, was not accepted by the Tories. A mob returned to the home of La Fontaine with the intention of torching the place. What they did not know was that a group of the Attorney General's friends waited in the dark. Pistol shots were exchanged, six of the combatants were wounded and one rioter, William Mason, killed. The inquest into Mason's death, held at the Hôtel Cyrus, had to be moved because the building was set ablaze.

Once again Benjamin avoided involvement in these events. A priority for him was regaining some stability in his own life as he watched Harriot's health deteriorate. After consulting with son Theodore, he summoned the courage to call on Jacob Henry Joseph, a cousin once removed. The latter had but a month before split his merchant and tobacconist business so as to give his brother Abraham free rein in the district of Quebec and Jacob more independence in Montreal.

A visit to the residence at #7 Place Près-de-Ville was arranged. Jacob appeared willing to listen to his pleadings. First, Benjamin made mention of the reorganization of Jacob Henry Joseph & Company. "Will you and Abraham be in competition?"

"In a sense. My brother was once satisfied with working under my supervision but Sophie pushed him to demanding a full partnership. What he will do with that freedom I cannot say."

"Your Rebecca is doing well?" Benjamin had been so preoccupied with the encounters beginning with Place d'Youville to neglect congratulating Jacob Henry and wife Sara on their late April return from Philadelphia after a two-week visit to Rebecca Gratz, Sara's aunt. Rebecca Gratz Joseph was but an infant at the time.

Finally Benjamin got to the point. "You are aware of the fact that I am in bankruptcy. I cannot continue in my business without eliminating my debts and that will require a substantial loan. My understanding is that your sales have held up despite the slow economy. I would pay the prevailing rate of interest."

Jacob's expression was quizzical. "Why haven't you gone to your own son? Theo had done rather well in real estate. His resources are no less than mine."

"You probably know that Theo and I have been operating at arms-length for some time. I wish a true business relationship with a lender rather than a favor from an offspring."

"A true business relationship? How sound *is* your business these days? You must remember that I am now thirty five and a father who must protect a family in these troubled days."

Benjamin could not restrain his resentment at being rebuffed. "I have overcome great challenges over the years, young man. My older brothers were fortunate in acquiring seigneuries downriver and deserved everything they accomplished. I had to struggle to establish myself in Montreal. And success was mine until the British lords in their infinite wisdom abandoned Canada in their quest for free trade."

If we are desirous 'to give of the fruit of her hands' to a 'virtuous woman,'
like of whom Solomon speaks; if we would duly observe this injunction
of the wise king: then we cannot but sorrowfully remark that
'a virtuous woman' has indeed departed from us;
ABRAHAM DE SOLA
(sermon upon death of Harriot Hart, October 12, 1849)

...the wretched selfishness of the Montrealers ... caused the removal
of the Seat of Government from Western Canada; from amid an Anglo-
Saxon race, to place it within the control of French Oligarchists and
their Helots. Had the Government remained at Kingston, or any
place within the limits of the upper province, the Franco-Canadians
never would have attained and exercised that arbitrary power which
has been the exciting cause of all the late political troubles and riots.
A war of races might have existed, as it now does, but it would
have been a defensive war on the part of the Eastern Canadians
DAILY BRITISH WHIG
(editorial, October 26, 1849)

Forty eight

Mary Kent fussed more than usual in supervising the servants in their preparation of the dining room table. In part it was because she wanted the small dinner party to come off without possible embarrassment to any of its participants. And then there was the specter of the cholera epidemic, which had Montreal in its thrall in the past couple of weeks. Hygienic practices were more important than ever.

Theodore had proposed that they entertain both Benjamin Holmes and Luther Holton. She, of course, had insisted that these guests be accompanied by their spouses. Mary Kent had developed a close friendship with the former Eliza Forbes, whom Holton had married ten years earlier, the two women being part of the Unitarian congregation in town. Elizabeth Holmes, however, was the daughter of Dr. Arnoldi and had married the banker thirty years before. Mary Kent had worried that she would be unavailable, Dr. Arnoldi having died during the cholera outbreak. But she put on a brave face. Prolonged mourning was not for her.

In the event the affair went smoothly enough. Theodore proffered a wide selection of alcoholic drinks to go with *hors-d'oeuvres* prior to the meal. The women did not isolate themselves when the conversation turned to politics—as it was bound to do given the makeup of the group. Mary Kent, in fact, made reference to the latest bits of vituperation in the daily press. The raw sentiments evidenced during the rioting had seemingly not abated. "These appeals to the Anglo-Saxon race and the antipathy to anything French undoubtedly plays into the hand of the British American League, which still hopes to keep Tories faithful to the Monarchy."

Holmes guffawed. "George Moffatt probably welcomes such views if it helps to bring about unity of the British American provinces and leads to more protection for home industry. He apparently was saying as much at the League's convention in Kingston last week. Remember, Hart, that we experienced the same kind of anti-Gallic commentary when we were both in Kingston back in '42."

Theodore nodded his acknowledgement. It was that summer that Holmes converted from being a typical Tory into a partisan of those seeking reconciliation with the *Canadiens* at that first parliamentary session. "There is much debate in the press on Canada's loyalty to the British Empire. Surely it is difficult to be neutral in this matter in today's climate."

The subject didn't come up again until after desserts were served. Holton raised it without any preamble. "We are in the midst of drafting a manifesto that would call for our annexation to the United States. It should be ready before the summer is over."

The statement roused an immediate reaction from just everybody at the table. Theodore asked the obvious question: Was there any solid support for what all agree would constitute a dramatic shift in public policy? The many thousands of British immigrants in Montreal, though not yet a majority in the city, were still imbued with monarchist traditions. The Doric Club, that had spearheaded the recent rioting, was not noted for republican sympathies.

Holton responded without hesitation. "To begin with, we have had positive responses from Montreal's leading business heads. Men such as John Torrance, the Molson brothers, Galt, Redpath, et cetera. And, needless to say, we know where the *Rouges* stand. No matter what we think of Papineau, he has long favored the American system of government."

Theodore wasn't convinced. "Which means we could not expect support from La Fontaine, Drummond, etc, who feel that everything is going their way. I ask myself whether even our friend Francis Hincks will be at our side. He is currently in London to argue for the Rebellion Losses Bill. And to him, raising British money for railroad construction here is paramount."

"The same ambivalence could be applied to Duvernay at *La Minerve*. I know him to be an admirer of the republican form of government. But he is so intertwined with the *Bleus* that I seriously doubt that he would go against whatever La Fontaine wants. Last week he retracted *La Minerve*'s opinion that annexation never frightened his publication. In a matter of days it had to state the paper is *not* an apostle of annexation. Either La Fontaine or the Bishop got to him." Holmes had obviously been monitoring how the French-language journals were treating the debate.

Holton responded after some hesitation. "You are right about Duvernay's dilemma. After all, his suit against Dessaulles for perjury is still in the courts so that he has a stake in opposing whatever position Papineau takes."

The table talk eventually swung to other topics. Eliza Holton enquired whether it was true that Holmes would be a candidate for city council in next March's municipal elections. She had heard that he was interested once again in representing the West Ward (his first term as city councilor had ended in 1846) and also that he might make a bid to replace Fabre as city Mayor.

Holmes chuckled. "This is not for public consumption, but it is true that I'm interested in local politics. My advocacy of annexation may be a complicating factor. As for the mayoralty, Fabre says he doesn't want another term and I have to believe him."

* * *

The bedroom was unlighted but for a single candle on an end table casting flickering shadows. Theodore had to adjust his pupils to distinguish his mother's ashen face. For some time he had not been invited to pay his respects but apparently there had been a change of heart. He could not know the reason. *Perhaps because she realizes that she is at death's door?*

"Hello, mama! I am so glad that I can visit. It has been a while."

Her whisper was quite audible. "But you are here. At least I can make out your features. My mind still functions, Theo, even if my eyes are failing."

"You cannot see well?"

"That is not altogether true. When the curtain is raised, I see red and golden colors at the window. That tells me that we must be into October. Alas, I am fated not to watch the leaves change color ever again."

"I doubt if your doctor is ready to confirm that." Theodore was going along with the white lie.

Harriot said nothing for a minute or two and then spoke firmly. "I go satisfied that I have always kept virtue as my watchword. Over two decades seventeen children came out of my womb. I have been a dutiful wife and mother for over those twenty odd years. It was God's will that I devote myself to bearing sons and daughters. If I had not been so fertile, would I have had progeny who have survived the ravages of time? Still alive are Wellington, Frederick, Benjamin, Constance and you."

"You have not mentioned Henry in St Louis, Emily and Dora in California. They would be here now if the distances from there weren't so forbidding." Theodore smiled sadly. He did remember that as a child his mother spoke sweetly of her children. *Was it ever directed particularly at him?*

"But only you and Constance are here in the flesh. I have but one message to my children. Your father needs you."

Withdrawing from the room, Theodore encountered cousin Aaron. The doctor had rushed to Rue des Récollets from the hospital to be at Harriot's bedside. Theodore did wonder how he was able to maintain his composure given the pressures on him. Harriot was not his only patient – especially once he had become attending official at the Montreal General as of the last May. He had met the test of the cholera epidemic and seemed no worse for the strain it had been for him. The doctor closed the bedroom door behind him.

Theodore paid a courtesy call on his father, who was sitting in his study in a virtual stupor. Benjamin barely acknowledged the presence of his son. The imminent loss of his wife had obviously been too much for him.

Aaron David joined them in the study just as Theodore was preparing to depart for home. The doctor must have realized that Benjamin was in no condition for a consultation. He put his hand on the man's shoulder and then engaged with Theodore. "It has been a long day. I need a drink."

Ignoring Benjamin, he went to the sideboard to pour a whisky and raised his glass to Theodore. The latter enquired as to the health of Catharine.

"She is well, albeit somewhat concerned about the whereabouts of her brother Gershom. There has been no letter from him since he left for California in the summer." Gershom Joseph had decided to try his luck joining the Gold Rush that was exciting so many since the discoveries along the American River the previous year. Theodore hadn't agreed that it had been a wise decision; Gershom had been admitted to the bar in Montreal over five years ago and had traveled extensively in Europe since then. *He ought to be settling down.* Aaron signaled that he felt the same way. His youngest brother-in-law was not emulating the older members of the family. Jacob Henry, Abraham and Jesse were making quite a success in business.

*   *   *

Mary Kent accompanied Theodore to the Mount Royal cemetery on the Friday despite a light drizzle that had begun at dawn. Harriot Judith Hart, aged sixty-three, had died on the Wednesday.

Regardless of the weather, the local members of the Hart, David and Joseph families surrounded the grave site. A few others not otherwise committed to some occupation were present as well. Also in the circle was Aaron Ezekiel Hart, who happened to be in Montreal when Dr. David pronounced Harriot Hart dead. Theodore had conferred with the Trois-Rivières lawyer earlier that day. Unbeknownst to him Aaron Ezekiel had been calling on his cousin Phoebe David for some time. In fact, he had proposed marriage to her that very day. She had reportedly given him her hand but any rejoicing had to be put off until the mourning was over.

The sound of shovel hitting dirt was a counterpoint to the Hebrew prayer emanating for the Reverend De Sola. Theodore's mind wandered; he noticed that the gravestone next to the new pit displayed the name of Aaron Philip Hart. Theodore felt guilty that he had not visited the cemetery over the years to pay tribute to his elder brother. But then, Philip, who had died in 1843, was not then in the good graces of his mother. Or of his father, who in the current circumstance stood next to the grave supported by Constance. Benjamin Hart demanded loyalty from his offspring.

De Sola had delivered the eulogy at the synagogue earlier in the morning. Theodore had not been present for that part of the ritual but he suspected that the young *chazzan* had been fulsome in his praise of a departed member of his congregation. He would hardly risk offending Benjamin Hart, one of the pillars of the synagogue.

Dr. Aaron David had been selected to officially witness the burial. One other with that task was Isaac Aaron, an auctioneer who was part of the congregation. Theodore kept a respectful distance from the others, many of which he had known intimately when he was a founding member of the synagogue.

Needless to say, Theodore and Mary Kent passed up a visit to the *shiva* already organized for his old home on Rue des Récollets. Mary Kent prepared a light supper before Theodore retired to his study. He had neglected his business during the past few days but there was time to prepare an agenda for the following week. What he did regret was missing the public reaction to the publication of the Annexation Manifesto, which had published the previous day. He and Mary Kent had decided even before the Thursday date to sign the declaration. The die had been cast. What the consequences would be had yet to be determined.

Before seeking refuge in sleep, he opened his bible. The death of Harriot Judith Hart on October 10, 1849 was recorded in his handwriting.

To the People of Canada.
The number and magnitude of the evils that afflict our country, and
the universal and increasing depression of its material interests, call
upon all persons animated by a sincere desire for its welfare to combine
for the purposes of inquiry and preparation with a view to the adoption
of such remedies as a mature and dispassionate
investigation may suggest.
MONTREAL ANNEXATION MANIFESTO
(October 11, 1849)

Canada cannot be saved unless you force the selfish scheming
Yankees to concede reciprocity.
GOVERNOR LORD ELGIN
(letter to Colonial Secretary Earl Grey III, October 25, 1849)

Forty nine

The parlor at the Hart residence on Rue des Récollets was relatively deserted on this fifth day of the *shiva*. Adolphus, however, did feel satisfied that at least one of his cousins was seated on the large sofa in the room; Theodore had seemingly been in attendance for some time. Any serious conversation, however, had to await interaction with other direct members of Benjamin's family. Adolphus in particular was conscience of the presence of Constance, who was dispensing food and drink. He addressed her directly. "I'm sorry I came late, dear!"

The opportunity finally arrived for thoughtful talk and Adolphus took it. "I have been reading, Theo, this Annexation Manifesto with much care. It does offer a persuasive argument but I fear that it asks too much. I see your signature on it so perhaps you can explain what is to come of this piece of political ambition."

"The intent is quite clear. It is indeed a response to the reversal of the established policy of Great Britain. The colonies have lost their protected market and the effects on Canada are disastrous. We must seek other options. The most desirable remedy? You note that it calls for a friendly and peaceful separation from the British connection and a union upon equitable terms with the North American confederacy of sovereign states."

Adolphus interrupted with some impatience. "All this is predicated on the willingness of Americans to welcome us into their fold. Until now they have rebuffed measures leading to trade reciprocity. Annexation is an even bolder step. In addition, the southerners in Congress must worry about more free states in the union when the slave states maintain so delicate a balance of power. With General Taylor, a hero of the South, in the White House as president, their attitudes may not change that much. If we do ask for admittance to the republic, they will oppose it."

Constance, within hearing distance of the dialogue, raised objections to its continuation. "Not here, dear!"

Theo wasn't listening to his sister. "And yet, Adolphus, we ought not to remain obedient to an Empire in which we have no voice or in which we share none of its honors or emoluments. As citizens of the United States the public services of that nation would be open to us."

"I am thinking of the practical problems. The Governor is not about to abdicate royal authority. And having the *Rouges* ally themselves with us may be a mixed blessing. Certainly we know where the *Bleus* stand. You saw the pledge of loyalty just published in *La Minerve*. You know what Bourget thinks of those who argue for the abolition of tithes, the secularization of education and the separation of church and state. True, *La Minerve* has yet to mobilize those not committed to the *Institut Canadien* to act *against* annexation. But from what we are hearing from La Fontaine and Drummond, Duvernay will be forced to take a stronger stand than he has to date." Adolphus had become convinced that the alliance between the clergy and the La Fontaine-Baldwin party would make it a bulwark of political and social order.

"Certainly *L'Avenir* is with us. Needless to say, all the anti-unionists in Quebec City have signed. Soulard, Aubin, Plamondon and Bardy included. I've been told that Bardy will chair a public meeting there a week Saturday in support of the manifesto."

Adolphus suddenly became very thoughtful. "I'm very interested in what Moffatt will do. The Tories are not of one voice despite the setting up of the British American League. The League met in Kingston in July and supported protection for home industry. In the next week or so Moffatt is due to receive a report from a committee regarding the union of Canada with other colonies. Annexation is one of the issues to be considered. And whichever way Moffatt goes, so will men such as Sabrevois de Bleury. A most interesting time!"

Theodore laughed. "You have been playing the devil's advocate. Both you and I agree with the aims of the Annexationists. My fear, of course, is that fighting the *status quo* will be very painful."

*   *   *

It was an *ad hoc* meeting in the downtown office of Adolphus but he thought it a necessary one. Father-in-law Benjamin was still in his grief-stricken period and his future had to be considered by cooler heads. Henry Judah and Moses Samuel David were the other executors of Benjamin's last will and testament and they had some responsibility in advising the old man on his options.

"Most of Benjamin's estate was supposed to go his widow. But with him in bankruptcy and Harriot in her grave, we must pursue alternatives." Adolphus spoke forcefully. He had been one of three family lawyers who in February, 1846 had convinced Benjamin to accept a less complicated will that would benefit his widow. He had seen a copy of the will Ephraim Hart, Harriot's father, signed in July 1825, in which the New York landowner left everything to his wife Frances and didn't provide for any disposition of his assets to any surviving children. (In the end Harriot did inherit, most of her siblings having died early.) *Perhaps some thought should have been given to the possibility Benjamin would outlive his spouse!*

The three cousins were congenial enough. Adolphus enquired as to the health of Moses David's wife. "Gertrude's pregnancy is progressing well, I trust? Constance tells me that she is kept busy with Augustus, who is rather sickly."

Moses, who had married Gertrude Virginia Joseph in New York three years before, acknowledged the enquiry. "Yes, she is managing but caring for two children and expecting a third has not been easy for us with our limited income. My practice is not as well established as it is for the two of you. Without help from my brother Aaron, we would be in difficult straits."

This was an irony that didn't escape the attention of Adolphus. He recalled the doctor's sojourn in Trois-Rivières earlier in the decade. *To think that not too long ago he had to move to Three Rivers to make a decent living! Now he is one of the mainstays at the Montreal General.*

Adolphus sought to give the discussion direction. He commented on the fact that a revised wording of the Annexation Manifesto had made its way to the public domain. The chances of previous trade connections with the mother country ever being repaired seemed more remote than ever. Benjamin Hart will no longer be what he has been in the past. All of them had to take seriously the consequences of a break with Great Britain.

"I beg to differ. As a director of the City Bank I have a big stake in the economy as threatened as it may be. I'll wait for Hincks to return from London before I do anything foolish. He may have rounded up the capital to make railway building a practicality. I'm especially intrigued by the possibility of linking Montreal with Bytown on the Ottawa River." Henry Judah was indicating that there was not yet consensus in the Anglo community on the benefits of annexation.

There was agreement, however, that the future of Benjamin Hart and his few remaining dependents needed to be addressed. He would not likely be able to afford maintaining living quarters on Rue des Récollets. Should they contact his son Arthur Wellington, who now lived in New York? Perhaps he could ascertain what properties Harriot had title to as a consequence of her father's death in 1825. Could they provide the means to allow Benjamin to live in New York? Benjamin would have to be willing to emigrate. It struck all of them that it was ironic that the "patriot" of the family might have to accede to such a move.

Adolphus accepted the assignment. He got into his heavy cloak in anticipation of facing the freezing temperatures of late December. The walk to Rue des Récollets was accomplished in spite of the inclement weather. He took time to gather himself before seeking out his father-in-law. *What a time of year to face so many different crises national and family!*

Benjamin had been nodding off while sitting in his big study chair when Adolphus entered the room. He did not object when his son-in-law put a hand to his shoulder. The gesture seemed appreciated.

Summarizing what had been said by the three meeting in Adolphus' office, he explained why he was paying Benjamin this visit. "Your future is in the hands of outside forces. A new draft of the Manifesto has now been published. It so happens that is a document I could endorse. The loyalists have no good arguments to reject it."

Benjamin remained slumped in his chair. *No immediate response.* Adolphus looked for signs that the old man was still of sound mind.

To his relief, there was finally a reaction – and a cogent one at that. "I too have read the document. You need not have to convince me, Adolphus. My allegiance to the Crown is at an end. The colony is being abandoned in the interests of the free traders in England. It shouldn't be that way. We possess much water power and cheap labor and yet there is no domestic manufactures. As the Manifesto says, the Canadian market is too limited to tempt the foreign capitalist so that our economy will remain undeveloped for years to come."

"You are quite right, sir! Where is the network of railways that already exist south of the border? Canada has but three lines which, as the Manifesto points out, barely exceed 50 miles of working track." Adolphus was now relieved of the fear that he was dealing with a ghost.

* * *

Theodore had agreed to meet him in the foyer of Government House on Rue Notre-Dame. Adolphus often visited the old *Château Ramezay*, the bureaucrats ensconced there frequently demanding his presence if his clients required government action on some matter. This day, however, he would be attending to family business. He and Theodore had arranged to meet with Francis Hincks, the Inspector-General who not only handled much of commercial policy for the La Fontaine-Baldwin coalition but was also a long-time friend of Theodore.

The cousins took seats in the anteroom until they were given the signal that Hincks was ready to receive them. They did fear that this meeting was an exercise in futility. It was widely reported that Hincks had been instrumental in getting Lord Elgin to have avowed Annexationists, be they public officials or other servants of the Crown, struck off the official lists. Thus Benjamin Hart was removed from the Commission of Peace and lost his rank as a Lieutenant-Colonel of the 1ˢᵗ Battalion in the Montreal militia. *Would the government reverse its position and make an exception for this former magistrate?*

Hincks stood up and came around his desk to shake hands with Theodore. "We haven't talked, Theo, since before I sailed for England. It is good to see that you show no signs of fatigue given what has been happening in the interval."

"Nor do you look any worse for wear but events have not gone as one would expect. I'm here on behalf of my father. You are of course aware that Benjamin Hart was stripped of his office and lost his military rank. He is an old man recently widowed and doesn't deserve such treatment after so many years of service to the Crown. Incidentally, I have with me my brother-in-law who practices law in Montreal. Francis Hincks meet Adolphus Hart."

The two men also shook hands and Hincks resumed his seat. He had seemingly anticipated the complaint coming from members of the Hart family and wasted no time stating where he stood. "It has been six years since I settled in Montreal, ostensibly as editor of the *Times and Commercial Advertiser*. It was in part your initiative that turned me into a journalist as well as a politician. For this I will be eternally grateful. But I have now sold the *Pilot* and have new priorities. I returned from London most discouraged by the agitation here for annexation. Canadian bonds were not well received when British investors heard of such talk. I wrote both Baldwin and La Fontaine that they were failing to come down hard enough on those who threatened Canada's future. I have to be pleased that they took my advice. The economy is rebounding somewhat, which makes the outlook for loyalists less bleak."

"You will admit, my friend, that it will remain bleak unless the Americans open their market to us. Annexation would allow for that possibility." Theodore was repeating what he been saying to his business associates and had been finding little disagreement.

Hincks, however, was quick to disagree. "Are the Americans taking notice of what some of us wish? With the new territories being organized in the west without slavery being authorized there, the South is once more talking secession from the union. There is currently deadlock in Congress regarding election of a Speaker and little regard for debating what to do with the Annexationists in Canada. The Whigs are more concerned with finding a compromise on the slave issue. Even the New York *Herald* in its editorializing writes that Canadian advances cannot be considered unless this colony has the express permission of the British Parliament to surrender sovereignty. I think that's another way of the USA saying that it is neutral at best on the issue."

Adolphus had remained silent during this interchange but he found it hard to argue with Hincks' reasoning. The long-time Reformer was pointing to the prime weakness of the case for annexation. He had a strong motive: there would be very little railway building in Canada East or West without British capital, the Americans already committed to expanding their railroad network throughout the territory they controlled. Adolphus said as much to Theodore as they exited the *Château* and proceeded west along Rue Notre-Dame. "Unless the sentiment for America's 'manifest destiny' translates into more support from across the border for Annexation, we are in for much disappointment. In addition, domestic support for so drastic a measure has yet to solidify. Men like Duvernay cannot equivocate as much as they do."

Theodore's face, buried as it was under a winter hood drawn over his head, looked squarely at his cousin. "You mention Duvernay. *La Minerve* is also a prisoner of its political patrons. La Fontaine and Bishop Bourget would need to shift their positions before Duvernay can say what he probably feels. Besides, he is preoccupied with his quarrel with Papineau and the *Rouges* in general."

Adolphus had a ready answer. It so happened that on the previous day Duvernay suffered a defeat. He failed to convince the court that Dessaulles had to prove that he practiced one religion or another. Otherwise according to the plaintiff's counsel, Papineau's son-in-law would be guilty of perjury. The upshot is that Duvernay has to pay Dessaulles £100 in damages."

I do not think that time is yet approaching. But let us make them, as far as possible, fit to govern themselves – let us give them, as far as we can, the capacity of ruling their own affairs – let them increase in wealth and population, and whatever may happen, we have the consolation of saying we have contributed to the happiness of the world.
LORD JOHN RUSSELL
(speech in British Parliament, February 8, 1850))

Here for instance, where the vicinity of the U.S. exercises so great an influence, it is, I think, possible, that the time may come when it may be expedient to allow the Colonists to elect their own Governors, to reduce their civil lists to the starvation point, &c, England withdrawing all her forces except 2,000 men at Quebec and being herself represented in the Colony by an Agent – something like a Resident in India.
GOVERNOR GENERAL LORD ELGIN
(letter to Colonial Secretary Earl Grey III, May 23, 1850)

Fifty

Mary McCarthy Brown looked up from her book. The head servant had been seeking to catch her attention. "Mr. Alexander is at the door. He wishes to speak to the master."

She had become accustomed to hearing the servants refer to Alexander Thomas Hart, who once resided at this house on Rue Alexandre, as Mr. Alexander. They knew, of course, that Moses Hart's son as well as his family had moved to the village of Saint-Zephirin in the seigneury of Courval not too long after Miriam had given birth to her fourth son, Lewis Alexander. The family seldom crossed the St. Lawrence River to visit Trois-Rivières since then. It being January, he must have come by sledge over the frozen river. There was no hint of his mission although he did look rather pale. Mary immediately speculated. *Something important must have happened to bring Aleck here.*

Relations between Mary and Alexander had been strained for more than two years despite the two having the same mother. The Hart family had called on Adolphus to return from Montreal to mediate a crisis and in the end

Moses did not follow through on his threat to disinherit his "natural" son. Nevertheless, Alexander and wife Miriam thought it best for all concerned if they moved themselves and their children to the seigneury of Courval. Alexander had a flourishing wood business in the parishes on the south side of the St Lawrence and would eventually become Courval's *seigneur*.

Mary was gracious enough. She enquired as to the health of Aleck's family. Miriam was now over forty and not likely to have more babies. Her three sons were six years apart in age, the biggest gap being between the eldest, Moses Alexander, who soon would be nine, and David Alexander, three years younger. (Augustus, the child coming between them, had died in infancy.)

"I am here, Mary, to pay my respects to papa. I know that he is in his eighties and in poor health so that the time for true reconciliation is short. I also know that he will not see me if you don't consent."

"Why would I not give my consent? Your father truly loves you. Has he not treated you as well as - if not better than - Areli and Louisa? He was napping the last time I saw him. I shall look in on him immediately. You will not go away disappointed."

Alexander sat down on a nearby chair as if he had been instructed to do so. This house on Rue Alexandre has been his home for decades. "This was always my favorite chair. Incidentally, I do not see your two sons Samuel and Andrew about. They are well? It is winter after all."

"They are in good health. Samuel, who is soon eleven, is in Catholic school. So is Andrew, who we now call Reuben. Reuben Moses. Your father is insisting on that. He is the same age as your Moses. It is unfortunate that distance keeps cousins apart."

"Yes, Mary, unfortunate!" Alexander's face betrayed regret.

"You still blame me, Aleck. Our quarrel can be traced to how we ought to have treated my Irish relatives. Things could have been worked out."

"The famine did upset all of us. And it still brings emigrants to America."

"That is true. You cannot deny that Britain's Poor Law has led to a disaster in Ireland. The landlords there, denied adequate food and relief by the Whig government in London, continue to evict their tenants." It grieved her that a clause in the Poor Law prohibited anyone holding at least a quarter of an acre from receiving relief. The British public appeared to agree with the principle that Irish poverty was the responsibility of Irish landowners. Her aunt quipped that the process of tenants being ejected from the land was equivalent to an Irish male going into the workhouse as a man and coming out a pauper.

Mary excused herself to check whether her aged partner could be wakened.

* * *

Areli Blake also wanted access to his father and it was up to Mary to accommodate him. She had determined beforehand to show proper respect for the eldest son of Moses Hart. Now a man approaching fifty, he was increasingly involved in running the family's business affairs.

Areli had not brought Julia with him. Mary wasn't sorry. She and the former Julia Seaton had little in common. Areli had wed this daughter of a distinguished English soldier whereas Mary was merely an Irish immigrant who still had a deep-seated hostility towards the Anglo-Saxon rulers of her homeland. Mary had often wondered why Julia had distanced herself from her roots to raise children for Areli in semi-rural Canada. Her ancestors had apparently served under several kings and presumably could have extended privileges to her if she had married more appropriately.

Mary made some comment on the weather, which was turning milder, it being well into March. Areli grunted. "Not that easy to cross the river with the ice cover so treacherous. My *censitaires* are thus often delinquent in paying their rents."

"You father does appreciate your diligence in collecting what is owed him. Having so many seigneuries to administer, you have indeed a laborious task." Mary was being careful how she phrased the matter since she didn't have that much sympathy for those who had to extract money from impoverished peasants. She had read too much about how it was ruining the tenants of Ireland.

"And to think that La Fontaine wants to abolish the seigneurial system! What are we to do if that happens?"

Mary said nothing. Instead, she led Areli to the master bedroom. Moses was engaged in adjusting spectacles in order to decipher a book at his side. Propped up by several pillows, he surveyed his visitors. "That is you, Areli? You now live by yourself, do you not?"

"Not by myself, papa. I have a wife and five children. Do you not remember Henry Thomas? He's the lad who pestered you about the travels you undertook before even I was born. You spent a whole afternoon describing them." Areli's patronizing tone annoyed Mary.

Moses showed no sign of being offended. "Some day, Areli, this will be the home for you, Julia and your five children. The family cemetery is on the property and will quite rightfully be part of your legacy. My dream is that you will be as influential as your father. The Harts are highly regarded by *Trifluviens*. You ought not to forget that. Make your mark in this district!"

"Have you forgotten, papa, that I ran as a candidate in the '37 election? That was four years before you tried to win in Nicolet and a time when the riding was still called Buckinghamshire."

"True. You have settled down since your adventures in Europe. You gave me a hard time then." Moses was referring to years Areli had spent in France and Italy twenty years ago. The young scion of the Hart family had gotten embroiled with a Florentine beauty. Moses had to pay handsomely to extricate his son from an imprudent marriage. In fact, the annulment didn't happen until after Areli was back in Canada and already involved with Julia.

Mary knew all the details because by that time her mother and she had moved into Rue Alexandre. Areli was more than a prodigal son; he was like an older brother. Moreover, she had been exposed to a lifestyle that was so romantic that she could not get herself to disprove of Areli. *Like father, like son!* She had been the recipient of many of the tales Moses told of his own flamboyant youth. The travels to Albany and New York subsequent to the American Revolution, the sojourn in London just after the French Revolution, the escapades when he ran a store outside Fort William Henry on the Richelieu, the venture into operating a brewery and potashery, the building of sloops and steamboats to ply the St Lawrence.

Mary was even informed of his various romances despite the fact that he was now forced into being chaste. She had learned early that Moses had been her mother's lover long before she was born. That relationship was suspended when the McCarthy family traveled to Ireland, where she was born the daughter of a Peter Brown. Her years in Ireland were very few and certainly not memorable. Mother Mary, having been widowed soon after the birth of her daughter, chose to return to Trois-Rivières in 1811 along with her half-brother Alexander. Soon after he was transferred to his father's care on Rue Alexandre and she remained with her mother. It was fated that she would eventually become the mistress of the house on Rue Alexandre and the mother of other children sired by Moses Hart.

* * *

The ice in the river had broken by the time Mary entertained another guest arriving at the house. In this case it with an unambiguous welcome. Adolphus, somewhat younger than she, had long been an object of her secret admiration. He, however, had eyes for Hannah Constance only and ten years before had decided to leave Trois-Rivières for Montreal. This day he was dressed in the height of fashion. The high collar, the neatly arranged cravat. However, he had yet to cultivate a beard of moustache. Mary led him to the most comfortable seat in the parlor. She was eager to know what was transpiring upriver. "We are told that your municipal elections were not without incident."

"The Annexation issue consumes us all in Montreal. The municipal elections in Montreal are over at last. My friend Benjamin Holmes was contesting the seat representing the West Ward but ran as an Annexationist and that caused him much trouble. The Doric Club people have declared themselves in favor of the British American League and worked against him. There was indeed some violence. Needless to say, he didn't succeed in replacing Fabre as mayor."

Mary sighed. "It has been very quiet here. Your uncle asks about what is happening in Montreal but we don't have a lot to tell him."

"He may be losing his brother to the United States. You may not have heard that Benjamin is moving to New York. Soon after *pesach*."

"That will be bad news for Moses. The last of his brothers gone. How happy is Mr. Benjamin to leave Montreal?"

Adolphus dropped his voice to a half whisper. "He is very much beaten down. Stripped of his magisterial and militia commissions, he feels disgraced. And of course his health is not good. He is fortunate that Harriot owned property in Manhattan. The rental income plus his proximity to Wellington and family should make his life there at least bearable."

"Let us hope!"

"I myself may soon be practicing law in New York rather than in Canada. Constance is once more pregnant. She expects to give birth in late summer. We plan not to depart Montreal until then."

"Why New York?" Mary wondered if the Hart family still regarded that metropolis as a haven of sorts.

"There is probably more opportunity for me in the west. St. Louis perhaps. But Constance and I may have to wait until her papa is properly settled in the big city."

Mary chuckled. "You are not going to wait for Annexation, are you? Will American politics not bother you?"

"Slavery has become a major bone of contention now that the southern states are threatening secession. I may use my writing skills to author pamphlets in favor of the abolitionists."

"And you have given up on Canada."

Adolphus frowned. "I am not hopeful. Not only does *Monsieur* La Fontaine have a jaundiced view of Annexation. He and his fellow *Bleus* have adopted Bourget's opposition to any reform that might weaken the position of the Catholic bishopric. We have the ultramontane influence firmly established in the governing party."

"Areli tells me that La Fontaine favors abolishing the seigneuries."

"That is what he said ten years back. But the Church fears any such trends to secularization. It already opposes the breaking up of the clergy reserves in Upper Canada. I understand La Fontaine will not support doing away with the seigneuries unless there is adequate compensation for the landowners. Moses and Areli would be reasonably satisfied with such a compromise."

"I can attest to that." Mary nodded vigorously.

Adolphus was caught up in the moment. "It isn't all going the way Moffatt and MacNab would like it. MacNab was told in no uncertain terms when in London that the Russell administration would not disallow the Rebellion Losses Bill. That would be a contravention of responsible government. I was told this by Hincks, who was also in direct contact with the Colonial Office."

"Isn't that what you have always wanted?"

"Quite right! But I worry about the direction La Fontaine and his people are heading. You are probably aware of the fact that the Parliament is now meeting in Toronto this very week. On Front Street. I wouldn't have minded being there to hear the debate on the fate of the seigneurial system. Or on the clergy reserves, if it comes to that. These are strange times, Mary. I look forward to see how my uncle interprets them. He has been a witness to everything that has happened here on the St Lawrence since the British conquest."

PART SIX

Dénoument
1850–1852

*Traveling from Quebec to Montreal for Passover was a most hazardous
and often dangerous undertaking. The ice would begin to break up,
creating a very precarious situation. Reached Berthier 3 pm ..my business
occupied me till 10 o'clock. Left Berthier next morning for Sorel.
Was to have gone up the Richelieu to Chambly but could
not on account of the badness of ice.*
ABRAHAM JOSEPH
(diary, April 2, 1850)

*Much water on the ice prevented the driver from seeing the air holes;
into one of them we were very near being sent having come within
2 ft of the edge. Notwithstanding 2 or 3 accidents – narrow escape
from a watery grave, etc – I reached Montreal at 5 pm...
Friday 29th.. evening at Mother's a holiday. Sat 30th, Synagogue 9 ..
minister expected from Home [England].. I visited David's today..
Second night.. Sunday 2nd Day.. Synagogue at 9 out 10 1/2*
ABRAHAM JOSEPH
(diary, April 2, 1850)

Fifty one

The decision to cross the river this Thursday morning was not taken
without some trepidation. Abraham Joseph was, of course, cognizant
of the danger inherent in traveling by sledge during a spring thaw. The ice
surface, already covered with water, seemed solid enough but it was near
the end of March. The milder weather of recent days could spell trouble.
However, there was no other easy way to get to Sorel from Berthier or to
proceed up the Richelieu to Chambly, where he had business to transact.

The trip from Quebec to Berthier had been without incident. Abraham
found himself quite comfortable, Berthier being where he was born and
where old business acquaintances still existed. He spent the night there and
was able to get away from his obligations by ten in the morning. The journey
across the St Lawrence to Sorel was a little scarier. The pools of water looked
ominous.

His itineraries had altered considerably since the previous summer
following an adjustment in the relationship with his brother Jacob Henry.

He was now doing business in Quebec City as a wholesale distributor of provisions under the name of Abraham Joseph and Company.

Sorel wasn't quite the same town he had known as a youth. No longer was it called William-Henry, the military establishment having abandoned it in recent years. In 1845 the original French character of the community had so returned that the government agreed to refer to it by its old name. For Abraham it was a bit of a wrench; his father, arriving in Lower Canada in the previous century, had worked for a period of time in Moses Hart's store there. William Henry with its British garrison and a summer residency for the Governor was then one of the few outposts of an Anglo culture.

The remnants of the fortifications were still evident as Abraham left the stable to enter the inn he usually frequented. The atmosphere inside, however, was very different. He had arranged to have his business associate meet him at the noon hour and he wasn't disappointed. The fellow, lightly dressed because of the milder weather, was pleasant enough. He did, however, sound concerned about Abraham having travelled across the river with ice conditions worsening. "The ice on the Richelieu has been cracking in the last couple of days. I wouldn't chance going upriver if I were you."

The advice was not to be ignored. Traveling the Richelieu south, given the condition of the ice, would be folly. The land route wasn't a reasonable option; roads would be a morass at this time of year. *I must write my client once I'm in Montreal. I'll try coming back home via the south bank if he can find his way to Sorel.*

Despite his assurances that all was safe, the driver was very deliberate in his pace as he proceeded upriver on the St Lawrence. However, the layer of water on the ice obscured any air holes that might have developed. When a sudden halt by the horses, an action that lurched Abraham's torso forward until he almost fell out of the seat, left the sledge within two feet of an ice surface break, he wished he had never left Sorel. Abraham's heart was pounding. There were bound to more accidents of this sort. *Am I destined for a watery grave?*

But what choice did he have but to continue his course? Being stranded on the south shore in the middle of nowhere was a most unattractive outcome. Indeed, he was counting on being at his mother's home in time to sit at the *seder* table this very evening. *God willing, I shall do that!*

It was an early Passover this year; the first day was on March 29 whereas more often than not it occurred in April. He had given thought to having Sophia accompany him in order for her to be with the family during the holiday. But little Henry, their third child and the first boy, was still an infant and not likely to fare well on an extended trip. And it had to be an extended trip if Abraham was to combine business with the celebration.

The danger I have just managed to avoid reminds me that I made the right decision before leaving Quebec.

* * *

It was late afternoon before Abraham reached the hostelry in Montreal – just enough time to have his valises carried to Rue Lagauchetière and the *cul-de-sac* in which the Joseph family had established itself over the last couple of decades. He succeeded in relieving Rachel Joseph's anxiety; she couldn't be certain that her son would be arriving in time whereas much of the meal had to be cooked during the afternoon.

She was joined in the vestibule by just about everybody that had assembled for the traditional Passover meal. Four of his siblings actually lived at #8 Près-de-Ville. Three were sisters who had never married. Abraham had dwindling hopes for either Rebecca or Sarah finding the same "marital bliss" as did Catharine, who had given Dr. Aaron David nine children over a fourteen-year period and had yet to reach menopause. In contrast, Rebecca and Sarah were already in their thirties. Esther, the youngest of his sisters, was still in her late twenties and also had not yet found a mate. Nevertheless, Abraham had been informed that the *chazzan* – Abraham De Sola was ensconced at #1 Près-de-Ville – was paying her much attention. He was two years younger than she, but to Abraham's mind that should not be a serious obstacle to a match.

There was a male presence as well at #8. His brother Jesse shared the house despite having the resources to support a residence of his own. He was showing no inclination for finding a wife though he was already thirty three (two years younger than Abraham himself). The most enthusiastic of the greeters at the door proved to be Jesse; they not only collaborated in business but also were in frequent correspondence. Curiously, the same affection did not come from the older brother, Jacob Henry. The latter, now living next door at #7, would be at the head of the *seder* table. At that moment he was carrying his infant daughter Rebecca and didn't hand her off to Sara, the mother, until Abraham removed his outerwear. There had been no opportunity to embrace.

Mother Rachel hurried everybody into the dining room. Servants were waiting to dispense the pre-cooked lamb that had been carefully reheated for the eating. First the traditional Hebrew blessings; the wine in the *kiddush* cup, the references to the *matzoh*, bitter herbs and other symbols of biblical deliverance. Abraham monitored Jacob Henry carefully to check whether he was up to the task.

The chance to talk to his brothers didn't come till later in the evening. They chatted while settled in Jesse's study and sipping more wine. Initially the talk was about politics. How were the parliamentary sessions in Toronto working out? They missed not having proximity to the government functions that once accompanied the meeting of legislators at Place d'Youville in previous years. Eventually the talk shifted to family matters.

"Has Gershom written?" Abraham himself had not heard from his younger brother since he went to San Francisco the previous autumn. Was the Gold Rush proving to be to his benefit or would the adventure be no more than a bitter experience as had been the case for so many?

Neither of his brothers was better informed. They were more interested in how Abraham and Sophia were making a life for themselves in Quebec City. Abraham assured them that all was going well. "I've been involved in the management of the District Bank of Quebec since it was formed three years ago."

Jacob Henry looked puzzled. "Isn't that the Provident and Savings Bank that we have heard about?"

"It is! Are you interested in more financing?" Jacob Henry had certainly made a success of distributing manufactures to the region's retailers. Tobacco products were his main stock in trade. Nevertheless, Abraham was aware that his older brother had begun to invest in real estate.

"I can't hold a candle to Jesse here. He's very busy building warehouses on Lemoyne. He has studied some law so that he is well versed in real estate documents." Jacob Henry's comment drew a round of laughter. Jesse was well known for his activities on Rue Lemoyne, the street between Rue Saint-Pierre and Rue McGill just north of Rue Saint-Paul. But Jesse had something else to talk about.

"You will be surprised to learn, Abe, that a note has arrived from Brussels. *Monsieur* Rogier has arranged for me to be the first Belgian Consul in Canada. What an honor!" Jesse was not joking and Abraham was indeed impressed. True, both of the brothers had been developing close commercial ties with the young kingdom. Not too long before Jesse was chartering cargo ships to sail between Montreal and Antwerp. King Leopold and his prime minister were obviously grateful. Rogier, who had assumed the nation's top post in 1847, was originally the governor of Antwerp.

Abraham lifted his glass. "An honor without doubt, brother dear."

* * *

The Saturday morning was taken up in the main with prayer. Abraham was to learn that De Sola had not yet returned from London. He wasn't surprised. Vessels directly from Portsmouth wouldn't be arriving for at least another month. And any trip from New York via the Hudson, the lakes and the Richelieu, was hazardous and open to delay. *I know full well what can happen when there is mud and ice.*

Abraham did see Dr. David at the services. In fact, his brother-in-law made a point of engaging him once the congregation began to disperse. "I have something to discuss with you, Abe. Can you drop by at our house on Craig Street in the afternoon?"

Abraham wasn't the only guest when he complied with the invitation. His sister Catharine met him at the door and the reunion went well. She was pregnant again; a tenth child was in the offing. She led him to the parlor where another David, Moses Samuel, had seated himself. There was some suspense; why was an attorney present?

Aaron David explained. He had encountered his older brother, Eleazar, at a downtown inn. Moses Samuel was the one other male David who had a stake in what was about to develop. Abraham was presumably there as the husband of Sophia. Phoebe, however, was in Trois-Rivières and therefore absent from this family gathering.

"You probably have read that Major Harris perished in the Battle of Chillianwala over a year ago. That has consequences we didn't anticipate." Dr. David was referring to Henry William Harris of the British 24th Regiment, the soldier husband of Eliza LockeWalker who had been cuckolded by Eleazar David, Aaron David's older brother.

This particular infantry regiment was stationed in Toronto for some years but had been sent to Lower Canada in October 1837 to suppress the uprising there. Eleazar David, a Captain in the cavalry at the time, became acquainted with Harris and his wife Eliza.

Abraham was about twelve when the exploits of Eleazar David were being feted in Montreal. He imagined himself in command of the cavalry and being able to escape injury should his horse be shot from under him.

The battle of Saint-Charles on the Richelieu was now history and Eleazar's heroism were soon forgotten in the wake of his disgrace but a couple of years later. In May, 1840 Eleazar eloped with Eliza; the couple moved to New York and had several children. The late Aaron Philip Hart had even represented Harris when he sued in court to facilitate a divorce. The action was left in abeyance. In 1846 the 24th regiment was transferred to India and thrown into the Punjab campaign. Harris was killed in action at the age of 34.

In his methodical way Dr. David elaborated on the dilemma facing the family. Eleazar was counting on its support as he worked towards reestablishing himself as a professional in Montreal. And there were five children to consider with more offspring reasonably expected. Do the David brothers subsidize the prodigal son? Do they forgive him?

Moses David stated where he stood. "Eleazar is almost forty years old. It may be too late for him to rehabilitate himself. I would advise him to look elsewhere instead of Montreal if he wants to spare his family much grief. I can offer some succor, but there is a limit to how much of a burden I am willing to assume."

Dr. David, whose career at the Montreal General was in the ascendancy, was not about to offer much more than his younger brother. Abraham didn't declare himself. *Let Sophia dictate how far I should go on behalf of her family.*

God knows that I detest slavery, but it is an existing evil, for which we
are not responsible, and we must endure it, till we can get rid of it without
destroying the last hope of free government in the world.
US PRESIDENT MILLARD FILLMORE
(signing of the Fugitive Slave Act, September 18, 1850)

Said party of the first part, will lithograph in the best style of the art
with suitable columns, and devices, tho property of the said party
of the second part, dated from the years 1746, up to the year
1776 inclusive, which the said party of the second part hath
this day delivered into the possession of said party of the
first part, the receipt of which they hereby acknowledge.
AGREEMENT BETWEEN MESSRS E & C ROBYN AND A.M. HART
(signed in St Louis, August 11, 1851))

Fifty two

Constance insisted. She and Adolphus had received an invitation from her older brother to celebrate the first night of Chanukah at his home. Arthur Wellington Hart had settled in New York the year before and had just taken on the responsibility of caring for his aging father. Now that his younger sister had also arrived in New York, he wanted to include her and her husband in the festivities. Wellington's wife Selena and daughter, Harriet Blanche, had had no contact with other members of the Benjamin Hart family. This would their first opportunity to do so. Constance empathized. "Besides, Papa will be there, my dear, and he would be hurt if we didn't show up."

It had been a difficult autumn for both Constance and Adolphus. She was burdened with a new infant (Asher had been born in early September and named a month later), not to mention three other male children four years old or less. Adolphus was scrambling to make a name for himself in the United States.

Adolphus' ambivalence when the invitation came had stemmed less from having to endure another encounter with his fractious father-in-law than with the fact that he had just returned to New York after an extended trip to St. Louis. He could use some rest and there was also the need to review the manuscript he was working on. In any case, Chanukah wasn't that meaningful to him. It certainly didn't rank with the High Holidays of last September.

What could he expect when he got there? It was Friday night and he knew that his cousin as a stickler for maintaining rituals. Wellington was his contemporary but had sailed to England a dozen years ago and the two of them had little or nothing to do with each other since. By the time Adolphus moved to Montreal in 1840 the only information on his cousin that he was able to glean from Benjamin related to the stories of how Wellington was acting on his father's behalf. From Liverpool the son had been pressing the Colonial Secretary to give his father proper respect as a devoted agent of the Crown during the uprising of 1837.

The sun was already dipping below the Jersey horizon before the couple came down the stairs. The early December weather was turning nasty; heavy clouds gathering in the East suggested rain. Adolphus noted that a horse-drawn vehicle was at rest in the front of the building. He recognized it as one of the new Hansoms that had been introduced to the city earlier in the year. It was two-wheeled and could accommodate two passengers under a protective roof. Assisting his wife through the side door, he gave the necessary instructions to the driver who was mounted on an elevated seat behind. Constance was of course grateful that her finery would escape possible disarray.

Wellington met them at the door. They were quickly informed that the family patriarch was still upstairs engaged in his prayers. Meanwhile the host had drinks available in the parlor. Adolphus relaxed. *So far so good!*

Selena brought the daughter into the room and introductions were made. "We had hoped, of course, that Raphael could join us for the celebration. But the Schoyers, father and children, are still in mourning."

"We had looked so forward to being with Fanny when we decided to move to New York. What a tragedy!" Constance's mention of her older sister was not without an emotional display. Frances Hart Schoyer had seemingly made a remarkable success of running a household in New York. She was a frequent hostess for friends in her circle. Her music and language talents redounded to her advantage and she had a large family to boot. Five sons in succession over a twelve-year period. Alas, the last of the five, Ernest, did not long survive the birth process. Nor did she! A stroke of fate: she died two months ahead of her mother in Montreal.

Wellington handed Constance a glass of sherry in an attempt to divert her from breaking down. She apologized. "I feel depressed. I have been without Dolph for weeks. He has just returned from St Louis."

Adolphus was the recipient of the next question. "You were in Missouri? Not to live there, I trust. I had understood that you were admitted a counselor-at-law here in New York."

"I have taken the same examinations in St. Louis. I am accredited to practice there as well."

"Does that mean you will be writing no more polemics for the New York papers?" Wellington's tone reflected some disapproval of Adolphus' recent activities.

"I've always taken an interest in politics and particularly now that there is a new president in Washington. True, I have written some pamphlets in favor of the Democrats. A Whig government doesn't please me. When I read that President Taylor died in July, my immediate reaction was that the so-called Compromise of 1850 would soon be signed into law. It is ironic that the General, a Southerner once owning 100 or more slaves, should oppose the legislation and threaten federal intervention if rebellious states seceded whereas the Vice President, coming from the state of New York and protesting that he is anti-slavery, signs the five bills that make up the Compromise. The possibility of civil war obviously scares Fillmore despite his sentiments."

"A civil war that could draw in the British colonies! You ought to read my treatise on the subject of Empire. It was my last contribution to English polity. In the future I may have to adopt an American view in my writing." Wellington was signaling that he regarded himself as more learned that his cousin in this area.

The conversation came to a sudden end. Benjamin Hart was coming down the stairs, the thumping cane heralding his arrival.

*   *   *

The lighting of the candles, the Hebrew prayers and the other devotional steps associated with the Sabbath occupied those gathered at the table for the next while. Adolphus had not grown up with this level of orthodoxy in his home in Trois-Rivières. But Benjamin Hart would have it no other way and son Arthur Wellington was just as devout.

The eating commenced with Selena supervising the servant actually apportioning the food. Constance considered it appropriate to commend her sister-in-law for the selection of dishes. Benjamin said nothing until they were at the desserts. Then he addressed Adolphus. "I have yet to see you at the Shearith Israel. I am there every day."

"It's a long walk from where the family is staying." The Shearith Israel was no longer on Mill Street. It had been replaced several years before by a synagogue built on cobbled Crosby, which was south of Houston Street and east of Broadway. It was still called the Spanish and Portuguese by most people outside the congregation.

Benjamin seemed not to hear. "You have not met with Rabbi Lyons? He would have told me if you had."

There was a momentary silence. Constance looked ready to intervene but Adolphus was ready to take the bull by the horns. "Actually, sir, I've been talking to certain members of the congregation who think that the Rabbi, young as he is, is too inflexible in his philosophy. They say that in Germany some rabbis are preaching reform of our religion."

Wellington interrupted. "Men like Geiger and Holdheim seek to open the Jewish pulpit for the occupancy of Christian clergymen ostensibly to explain 'the doubtful truths' which seize the mind. Alas, to what are we drifting? Is a religion unshaken in trust or creed for 6000 years to be set aside for the free religious sentiments which pervade certain critics of the present day?"

"You have a point, Wellington. I will say no more." Adolphus realized that he had no allies at the table. But the conversation did eventually stray to other, albeit profane, issues. Who could avoid talking about slavery when the country was in a crisis? Adolphus once more made remarks about the spinelessness of the Fillmore administration. "I don't know what drives him. Britain abolished slavery almost twenty years ago."

Benjamin admitted to be of two minds on the subject. "My daughter writes from California that the people there insist on being a free state. The pro-slavery South will agree to that only if the remainder of the territory acquired from Mexico comes into the union without a ban on the slave trade. Will the compromise work?"

Nobody else at the table was prepared to speculate. They were all transplanted British subjects who conceded that they probably didn't fully comprehend the American ethos. Meanwhile Benjamin was showing his age. His eyes were half closed and his head drooped. Everybody took pity on him. He was once a force to be reckoned with in the political arena but now he came across as a dispirited old man.

Constance chose at that moment to indicate that they ought to be returning to their abode. There were four rambunctious little boys who would be waking up early in the morning. Besides, it could be raining outside. "Dolph, can you find another of those Hansom cabs to take us home?"

* * *

Adolphus was at his makeshift writing table when Constance interrupted. "You have been at this for hours. I and your children need your attention. Besides, I still question why you are so engaged in this opus."

The same question had occurred to Adolphus in recent days. He ought to be advertising his services. He found a ready excuse in the fact that business activity in New York slowed during the Christmas break. Perhaps by the time Americans were well into 1851 it would be timely for him to assert himself. Raphael Schoyer had assured Adolphus that certain counselors in the city could use a junior colleague. In the meanwhile he could use the time to complete his manuscript. Once more he had to explain to Constance that the project made sense. "I believe I'm well suited for being the one describing how the valley of the Mississippi was discovered in the last century. Very few Americans have a working knowledge of French and thus able to recognize all the subtleties of the historical documents available to us. My visit to St Louis reinforced my interest in how the banks of the big river were settled over time."

Constance was not mollified and Adolphus appreciated why. Their living quarters were rather shabby and dealing with four children, one very much at the infant stage, was quite a chore though they did have one maid in their employ. But that was the lot of a married woman. Did she not know that when she consented to come under the *chupah*? "I have hopes that my literary efforts will bring us the extra income that will make your life easier. Eventually you will be proud that I am author as well as lawyer."

"Don't you think I too wanted to be an author? I was educated to be more than a matron. But what chance is there for me when I'm told the family comes first?" The pained expression on her face bothered Adolphus but he could think of no way to giving her anything but false hope. "We must play the hand we are dealt. I too have fantasies. If I had the means I would travel to California. Gershom Joseph is there. As are the Horts. The Gold Rush fascinates me."

Constance's face softened. Her husband was admitting that he too was prone to unrequited dreams. "You have a point, my dear. Emily writes me that there are now 25,000 full-time residents in San Francisco. Two years ago there were perhaps a thousand. I once worried about my two sisters. Had the Hort brothers led them into more misery?"

Adolphus took Constance's hand. "People's luck changes. The Horts may be better off than we are." Emily Abigail Hart had married Samuel Hort in 1841. She was less than twenty at the time and undoubtedly not too excited about trading her comfortable home on Rue des Récollets for frontier life on the Pacific Coast. But what could she do? Her Samuel was too handy with his pen; forgery led to bankruptcy. With his indebtedness in the thousands of pounds he opted to take his wife and their twin girls as far away from Montreal as they could reasonably go.

The younger Hort, Alfred, had a different history. An Englishman who departed New Zealand in 1844 for North America, he won the hand of Adolphus' sister-in-law despite the reputation of his brother Samuel. Dora Hart was forceful, outspoken and blessed with a sublime sense of self-importance even at her tender age. When Alfred migrated to California, she had no objections to making the move. The last that Constance had heard, the two brothers were investing in mining properties in the Sierra Nevada.

"You aren't going to gamble everything on finding a fortune in California, are you?"

"No, I am not, darling. But I do intend to take my manuscript to Cincinnati. I showed a few pages to a publisher operating there. He happened to be visiting St Louis last month and he thinks such a treatise should be made available to the public.

Sara is very pleasantly situated in a retired part of the city,
has good neighbors on the street, and a large garden opposite belonging
to the Friars, where fruit & vegetables are abundant
and the black robed inhabitants, are daily seen from my chamber window
– book in hand strolling for hours together – as no woman kind
is admitted into their dwelling I cannot vouch for the good order
of their household but the garden appears well cared for.
REBECCA GRATZ
(letter to sister Ann, September 3, 1851)

During the last Session of the Lafontaine Administration
a select committee was appointed to consider the complaints
that had been made in regard to the seigniorial tenure in
Lower Canada…. It was contended at the period to which I have
adverted, 1851, and for several years previously,
by those who held that the censitaires had substantial
grievances to complain of, that excessive rents had been
charged by many seigniors, and the legislation was
read in the interests of the people.
FRANCIS HINCKS
(Reminiscences of his Public Life, 1884)

Fifty three

On his way to the new offices of the City and District Savings Bank, Jesse Joseph happened to pass the fledgling bank's old quarters on Great St. James Street with its exaggerated number 46 on the front door. His destination this spring morning, however, was 29 Rue Saint-François-Xavier, which was farther down the street. Jesse fully appreciated the reason the investors in City and District had selected this latter address. The building was still close to the other financial houses: the Bank of Montreal and the City Bank, both off Place d'Armes, and the Banque du Peuple, which had moved into the old Bank of Montreal edifice, also on Rue Saint-Jacques. Griffintown was nearby albeit not as close as it had been before. It had been the vacancy created by the Banque du Peuple move that prompted the president of City and District, William Workman, to transfer operations to the corner of Saint-Jacques and Saint-François-Xavier.

Would this augur well when Jesse came face to face with the savings bank's general manager? He had spoken with Henry Judah, his second cousin who happened to be a director of the City and District Savings Bank. Judah chose to point out that the institution had not fared nearly as well since its maiden year, which ended in March 1847. The economic slump, combined with the influx of Irish immigrants, pandemics (typhus and cholera) and political unrest, encouraged customer withdrawals at the same time as new deposits declined. In fact the directors had been called upon to put up funds to offset the deficits in each of the following two years. Given that the savings institution accepted deposits as small as a shilling, it could not be termed a bank of deposit for only the wealthy.

Once through the entrance and accosted by a bank employee, Jesse announced that he had an appointment with Mr. Collins. He was accordingly ushered into an office at the rear of the main hall. Jesse had met John Collins at various times but he couldn't say he really knew the "cashier", who had overall management responsibility for the bank ever since it opened its doors five years before. Actually few in commerce appeared to be close to Collins, who apparently had been engaged elsewhere on his own account before entering service with the bank. That he was Anglo Irish one could be certain. He was treasurer of the St. Patrick's Society and resided in Griffintown on the western side of Rue McGill.

Coincidentally the St. Patrick's Society was presided over by William Workman, the hardware merchant who was also the bank's president. Theodore Hart had once introduced Workman to him as a fellow Unitarian. Apparently, not all members of the Society were Catholic.

Collins lit a cigar and offered one to Jesse. They puffed for a few minutes before they got down to business.

Jesse had told himself he had a strong case for bank credit. His stature as a participant in the burgeoning economy of Belgium, which had culminated in his being designated as the Belgian consul in Canada, was certainly an asset. He could cite his chartering of a ship because he regularly arranged the movement of goods to Antwerp and back. But his main preoccupation was with the *Magasins* Jesse Joseph, the seven buildings he was having constructed on Rue Le Moyne. These stores and warehouses were designed as a rental property capable of earning a regular income for its landlord. The architect had assured him that the grey limestone frame concept was the prototype for many more commercial buildings in the future. With the economy recovering, there would be little difficulty in finding tenants. Jesse said as much. Unfortunately, neither the Bank of Montreal nor the City Bank was convinced that trade would come back that much in the immediate future.

"You didn't go to De Witt, did you?" Collins inquisition annoyed Jesse. It was true that he had approached the Banque du Peuple for a loan albeit politically he had found that somewhat awkward. Jacob De Witt was in

Parliament as the member representing Beauharnois. In fact, his association with the *Patriotes* coupled with his partnership with Louis-Michel Viger as the two principals in the bank made him much disliked by Anglo merchants in the city. Viger, a cousin of Papineau, had actually been jailed twice after the uprisings of 1837-38.

Collins didn't seem that interested in pursuing the matter. He had already come to a conclusion. "Like you, Mr. Joseph, I am operating on the principle that the crisis has passed. Deposits are once more regular and steady. If we can get free trade with the United States, prosperity will return to the colony. The bank is, of course, very careful about loans after what happened to the Provident. We don't get into railway financing, for example. But we should be able to work something out."

Jesse rose from his seat and extended his hand. His decision to seek help from the City & Savings was paying off. "By the way, sir, I would have thought that with railroads being now regarded as the most attractive investment, you would be looking in that direction."

Collins sighed. "As we all know, a stagecoach journey to Bytown is most uncomfortable. And yet for over ten years we have seen plans for a portage railway on the north shore of the Ottawa being proposed but never acted upon. Two charters to build such a line have lapsed in succession. Now Joseph Masson and associates are trying their hand at putting together a project. Tell me, do you believe this Montreal and Ottawa Valley trunk line will get off the ground?"

"Your president seems to think so. Mr. Judah says that Mr. Workman is one of Masson's associates." Jesse knew that Henry Judah too was involved in the project.

"That may be. But we are a savings bank. The risk would be too great for us."

Leaving the banking establishment, Jesse ruminated on the conversation just completed. He himself had invested heavily in Montreal real estate as had others in the Joseph-Hart-David clan. They were no different in that respect than many of the leading merchants in the city. Workman, for example, had bought a large number of lots in the west-end residential suburb and had teamed up with another entrepreneur, Alexandre-Maurice Delisle, to buy properties elsewhere. Nevertheless, Jesse had to wonder if he weren't being aggressive enough in the transportation sector. His elder brother, Jacob Henry, had been involved in the Champlain-St Lawrence line fifteen years before. Theodore Hart had intimated that he would be one of the incorporators of the Grand Trunk Railway now being organized to establish a necessary link between Montreal and Toronto. Jesse wouldn't be astonished if his cousin also got into the Ottawa valley enterprise.

* * *

The summer months of 1851 were pleasant enough weather-wise but there were thunder claps emanating from a distance. Jesse heard them first from his mother. "Mr. Baldwin has resigned. Legislators are coming back from Toronto in an unhappy state."

Jesse was increasingly disturbed the more he mulled over some of the consequences of any disarray in the Reform administration. A national election was scheduled for October and for the first time in a decade Baldwin and La Fontaine would no longer be working in tandem. Jesse had previously been told that La Fontaine himself was not well. The Clear Grits in Upper Canada and the *Rouge* east of the Ottawa might take advantage. *Is the union of the Canadas in jeopardy? If it is not preserved, would the province's credit be undermined? I owe it to Monsieur Rogier to inform him of that possibility.*

In early July he accidentally encountered Theodore at a downtown function. Jesse reckoned that his cousin, long involved in Reform politics, could give him more insight. They repaired to a nearby coffeehouse when Jesse begged for a private talk.

Theodore was quite forthcoming. The immediate cause of the resignation was a cabinet decision to abandon Baldwin's reform of the Court of Chancery. "It goes further than that. Baldwin was not keen on railway financing by local governments but Hincks had already put through measures that allowed municipalities to have taxing and borrowing powers. And then there was the opposition of both the Church and La Fontaine to disposition of the clergy reserves. Lafontaine is backtracking on the issue of seigneurial tenure. No matter what he has said in the past, he isn't happy about giving Papineau an excuse to champion *Canadien* traditions. La Fontaine probably won't accept anything less than full compensation for the *seigneurs.* The Bishop will undoubtedly support him if he takes that stance. Finally, Baldwin has been in a funk since his mother died last January. All in all, not a happy situation!"

"So Hincks is now the minister speaking for Upper Canada? You should be happy with that, Theo. He has been your favorite for years. You helped bring him to Montreal to publish his journal."

Theodore produced a contorted smile. "That was before I signed the Annexation Manifesto. Hincks has been doing everything possible to maintain the connection with the Old Country. Much to my dismay! I fear I no longer have any influence over him."

"But life goes on!" Jesse drained the last of the beer in the mug.

"Yes, I now have a second son, born last Thursday, the 26th. Mary and I have decided to call him Frederick l'Étrange."

"Because he is strange?" Jesse found this bizarre.

"You probably don't know your medieval history. Frederick was a Holy Roman emperor in the 12th century. But he was also a religious skeptic. Hence the strangeness. He is said to have denounced Moses, Jesus and Muhammed as frauds. Mary was in her whimsical mood. Here was a man who mocked Christian sacraments and beliefs while being a German holding one of the highest titles in the Christian world. She couldn't resist adopting the name for our family. The christening is later this month. It's on a Monday. You are welcome to attend although I suspect you would find that awkward."

Jesse had never visited #4 Metcalfe Terrace. The townhouses, built on Côte-Sainte-Antoine a dozen years before, had become a haven for the well-to-do wishing to escape the squalor of *Vieux-Montréal. Theo is quite right. It would be awkward.*

Theodore inquired about how Abraham was doing in Quebec City. "He would have been my brother-in-law if Fanny had lived."

"My brother and Sophia are doing very well. She is pregnant with her fourth child, which is due in September."

"Meanwhile, you are without a spouse. Your mother already has three daughters who are still single. It makes for a big household. But I do understand that the Reverend next door is courting Esther."

Theodore was teasing, which Jesse didn't mind. He was a confirmed bachelor. *Who would want to wed a man whose pleasures did not include the marital bliss others took for granted?* He could also confirm that Abraham de Sola was seriously wooing his youngest sister. His best guess was that they would marry in the coming year.

* * *

The same question that Theodore was asking of Jesse came up weeks later from an unusual source. Next door at #7 Près-de-Ville the aunt of Sara Joseph was staying for a fortnight at the end of August. Rebecca Gratz had accompanied Sara and her two daughters when they returned from Philadelphia. This matron had no qualms about demanding answers from Jesse on subjects he thought to be quite personal. Jacob Henry seemed prepared to accept this role for his wife's blood relation.

The visitor was returning a favor. Lizette had been born in mid-February. Now being called Lizzie Lee, the infant girl was transported to Philadelphia to be inspected by her grand aunts. The Gratz family had wealth and stature in that city and Jacob Henry would have been the last person to oppose his wife undertaking this summer sojourn.

Rebecca Gratz had been in Montreal the previous year when her grandniece, also called Rebecca, was born. She evidently relished in examining landscapes and cities outside of Philadelphia. Jesse was amused at how easily she was enraptured by the sights of Montreal. For instance, she couldn't help but notice that the narrow streets and imperfect pavements, the one-story houses in parts of the city, contrasted so markedly with magnificent churches, the occasional monasteries and fine gardens that also could be found within walking distance. She enjoyed hearing as much French as English as she made these outings.

One evening Jesse's mother invited her relative by marriage to spend the evening with Jesse and his sisters. They were impressed with Rebecca's worldliness. She might be a spinster by choice but like Jesse she had broadened her interests to include men of letters. Moreover, Montreal seemed not to arouse any apprehension in her. She actually demonstrated that later in the evening. "Let me read from a letter I just wrote to my sister Ann! 'The approach to Montreal is beautiful – the City lies on the bosom of the noble River St Lawrence and stretches more than a mile along the shore, where a fine quay fronted by large buildings present themselves, the domed market place and numerous steeples of churches have a very imposing appearance and the beautiful mountains in their verdant covering bound the whole view, the day we arrived the heavens were dressed in fantastic white clouds which reflected in the water and crowning the mountain tops added greatly to the prospect, and gave a fine first impression.'"

She stayed on well after the other women in the room chose to retire. It was then that she delved into seeking a reason for Jesse's bachelorhood. Why was he so different than his older brothers? Both Jacob Henry and Abraham had married and both had selected Jewish women as mates. "That is God's wish – to multiply the Jewish race."

Jesse had had some empathy for the woman in that she too had never married. Apparently four more of her siblings were without a spouse. Also interesting to him was the fact that the sisters who did marry, chose Jewish husbands whereas the brothers opted for Christian women. Rebecca herself was a devout Jew. Over thirty years before she had organized the Female Hebrew Benevolent Society to involve poor Jewish girls in the activities of the Sephardic Mikveh Israel congregation in Philadelphia. *But multiplying the Jewish race is for me no reason to circumscribe my life style.*

*I am very sorry indeed you have lost Lafontaine from your Cabinet,
he seems to me to have had more of the Gentleman about him
than any other of public men of Canada*
COLONIAL SECRETARY EARL GREY III
(letter to Governor Lord Elgin, October 2, 1851)

*...the Earl of Elgin sent for me and entrusted me with the task
of forming a new one [Cabinet]. I at once put myself in communication
with Mr. Morin... and we had no difficulty in agreeing on a programme
embracing the secularization of the Clergy Reserves, the increase
of the Representation, the extension of the franchise, the abolition
of the seigniorial tenure, the extension of the principle of election
to the Legislative Council, and the encouragement of railway enterprises.*
FRANCIS HINCKS
(Reminiscences of his Public Life, 1884)

Fifty four

It being a temperate Sunday morning, Theodore Hart convinced Mary Kent to walk together with him from Metcalfe Terrace to the Unitarian church on Beaver Hall Hill. The foliage, though showing the colors of autumn, had yet to descend in mass onto the streets leading to *Vieux-Montréal.*

The Reverend John Cordner stood at the door greeting all as they entered the church. His sideburns melded into a thin beard, which made up for some of the hair loss on his crown. He was in his mid-thirties, Theodore's age, but his lean features and heavy-browed eyes gave him a more mature look. He was Irish by birth and had a Calvinist background. Yet his theology was liberal and progressive. The Montreal congregation, which included businessmen such as Holton, Holmes, Young and Workman, constituted a sympathetic milieu. Even Francis Hincks had attended on Sundays when he lived in Montreal as publisher of the *Pilot.*

Theodore had come to enjoy Cordner's sermons. The subjects could vary from the Fugitive Slave Act in the United States to British

Imperialism worldwide. Mary Kent compared him to Theodore Parker, the Transcendentalist in Boston who preached to parishioners such as Louisa May Alcott, William Lloyd Garrison and Julia Ward Howe.

Theodore Hart recognized that in this allegiance he was in the minority. His father, like so many others committed to religious faiths not Unitarian, had denounced Cordner in predictable terms. Benjamin Hart was not prepared to accept that reason rather than religious belief is the final arbiter. Most Christians were offended that Jesus was described repeatedly as a human being rather than someone divine. Benjamin, of course, agreed with Cordner on the latter point.

In the early '40s the congregation had first met in a house on Fortification Lane that was converted into a chapel seating 150 people. Once the Unitarians had a permanent minister, they committed themselves to building a more substantial church on Beaver Hall Hill. It could accommodate over 400 Montrealers if and when the membership grew to that size.

Luther Hamilton Holton was present in the hall this morning. Once the sermon had been delivered and the rites of the church adhered to, Holton sought out Theodore before he and Mary Kent could don their cloaks. "You may not have heard, Theo. La Fontaine has just handed in his resignation to Lord Elgin and will not contest the upcoming election. It will be Hincks and Morin from now on if the Reformers triumph again."

"If they do, I suppose there will be immediate action on railway building."

"You are so right, Theo. Construction is well along on the Great Western. Hincks will see to it that others benefit from his Guarantee Act, especially now that his greatest rival, MacNab, has a head start with the Great Western." The Great Western was scheduled to be completed from Niagara Falls to London by 1853.

Mary Kent joined them at that moment. Holton repeated the news. Her immediate question: "Why is La Fontaine retiring from the government? Is it his health?"

"Not directly. I've been told that his wife is suffering from rheumatism and he needs time to care for her." Holton's information was given *sotto voce*.

Mary Kent had another question. "Do you think the Reformers will prevail? Baldwin has been getting it from both ends. MacNab speaks for the Tories and the Clear Grits are growing in strength."

Neither Holton nor Theodore Hart had a certain answer. Without doubt Hincks was betting that his success in getting legislative support for the St. Lawrence & Atlantic scheme before Parliament was prorogued in the summer would impress the electorate. Nevertheless, with William Lyon Mackenzie recently back in the Parliament following his amnesty, he and other "Grits" were denouncing Hincks as more of a railway man than a true liberal. Would the voters in Upper Canada respond to this double-pronged attack on Baldwin's successor?

*   *   *

All was quiet in the railway station at this time of night. Theodore resented having to sally out to this downtown location on such a cold and drizzly evening. The Indian summer was no longer. Sodden leaves covered the section of sidewalk between where the cab driver had dropped him off and the entrance many yards away. His trousers would be soiled before he got indoors.

But he had little choice. It was an extraordinary meeting of the Lake St Louis and Province Railway being held upstairs in the Bonaventure Station, which had been recently built just off Rue Saint-Jacques. Theodore had extensive real estate in the Place d'Armes area and almost naturally became involved in setting up the Bonaventure and the operation of what was then called the Montreal and Lachine Railroad. That was four years before when it was deemed worthwhile to build a rail link bypassing the Lachine Rapids. The track was less than eight miles long. Bigger stakes, however, were in the offing and they could not be ignored.

Anticipating that this piece of transportation would eventually be expanded to give Montreal better access to the upper St Lawrence, the Ottawa valley and Plattsburgh on Lake Champlain, the board of directors agreed to merge with another firm and become the Lake St Louis and Province and so expand its vision. Lac Saint-Louis, after all, was the confluence of two mighty waterways. From Sault Saint-Louis a link was to be established to Prescott in Upper Canada, where steamers could carry traffic from there up and down the St Lawrence without the hindrance of rapids. Another line would begin at Huntington and connect with the Champlain transportation route through New York.

Speaking with a pronounced Scottish burr, the chairman brought the meeting to order. He was direct in his exposition. "We have always considered our enterprise as a launching pad for further expansion. Our Montreal and New York Railroad is encountering opposition from rivals and we must decide whether or not we participate in the St Lawrence and Ottawa Grand Junction."

As president of the company James Ferrier left no doubt where he stood on the subject. Repeating the common complaint that bottling up the "aorta of the North", the St Lawrence River, during the frigid winters at the same time as steam whistles sounded south of the border was an intolerable condition. "The lifeblood of commerce is being curdled in winter when we rely on stagecoaches for travel on snow-covered roads and contend with river locks sealed in ice."

The St Lawrence and Ottawa Grand Junction would allow freight to go northwest from Lachine into the hinterland of the St Lawrence and Ottawa rivers. But the charter of this new company called for track being laid within three years. Ferrier was insisting that the board of directors act decisively in joining with the "Grand Junction" in raising capital.

Like Theodore, Ferrier was heavily engaged in real estate. Already in his fifties, he had accumulated much wealth not only from his land holdings but also from a large shop on Rue Notre-Dame and from income earned by leasing the Saint-Maurice ironworks five years before. He was generally regarded as one of the three richest men in Montreal. He had served a term as mayor of the city and was now a member of the Legislative Council.

Theodore had already discussed the matter with men such as Holton and Workman. "I beg to differ, Mr. Ferrier. There isn't the financial wherewithal to support competing lines. I've spoken to Mr. Hincks. He is working towards government support of a railroad connecting Montreal, Toronto and beyond. He foresees the emergence of what he calls the Grand Trunk railway. Links to Halifax and Portland. A link to Bytown. A system more rational than what the Americans have."

Ferrier grunted. "He first has to be elected. Next week we shall know whether our ineffable Mr. Hincks has the backing of all our citizens for spending so much on transportation."

The debate was more spirited than usual. Theodore, who knew he was respected as a director of many corporations, had willing ears from several at the table. In the end there was no consensus that the "Grand Junction" would ever get off the ground. Theodore considered that result a victory.

It was already dark when Theodore left the meeting. The streetlights would normally give sufficient illumination for him to proceed to the carriage waiting for him down the street. But Rue Saint-Jacques was strangely dark. He cursed to himself. *That is the trouble with coal gas. The lamp can be extinguished with the slightest breath of wind.* He guessed that a lamp lighter would come around soon to reestablish the flame. Yet it bothered him that the Montreal Gas Co. was constantly being criticized for such safety problems. Customers also complained that the lanterns were dirty and emitted foul odors. Although he didn't own stock in the company, he understood its concerns. Moreover, he was a director of the Consumers'

Gas Company in Toronto and had to deal with the same problems there. *Manufacturing coal gas has its downside.*

*   *   *

It was well into the evening of October 27 when Mary Kent returned to Metcalfe Terrace. She had spent much of the day at the election headquarters of John Young, the bearded Scot who was running under the *Rouge* banner in Montreal. It had been a long day but before she settled for some tea in the study, Mary Kent felt it necessary to look in on her sleeping children. Both Charles and Frederick seemed quite content in their cribs.

Theodore, who had opted to remain home reading despite the election excitement, waited impatiently for his wife's report. She didn't have him wait long. "We shall have a Tory and a Radical representing Montreal. Young is winning and Badgley was also well ahead in votes when I departed. Papineau failed to get enough French support to win." Mary Kent was only confirming what Theodore expected. John Young, liberal-minded and a personal friend of Theodore, was well-enough respected in the Anglophone community to offset the charge that he was an annexationist. As for William Badgley, he was a successful lawyer who had served as Solicitor General under Draper and Sherwood and represented Missisquoi in Parliament until the current election was called.

Theodore's immediate comment: "The Tories have little hope of ending domination of the *Patriotes* in Lower Canada even if the *Rouges* gain a foothold in the province. The *Bleus* are now calling themselves Ministeralists instead of *Patriotes*. That makes sense. They no longer regard themselves as radicals even if they also claim to be reformers.

"Still, it is important that the *Rouges* have at least one voice when Parliament meets in Quebec City next year." Mary Kent was not put off.

"Don't you believe Valois will win the Montreal county seat? And I wouldn't be surprised if Papineau runs elsewhere at his first opportunity to get elected again. Nevertheless, it is true, my dear, that our friend John will take a progressive stand when he speaks in the House. Hincks and Morin may even listen to him because he has the experience that comes with being on the Montreal Harbour Commission. He is dedicated to improving our transportation system." Theodore had already discussed with Young the prospects for a Grand Trunk project.

Mary Kent continued sipping her tea. "It has indeed been a long day, Theo. I shall retire earlier than usual."

"It must have been tiring waiting around for messengers to bring you the counts from the polling stations. John was probably wishing that Allan would get his telegraph system up and running. But all is well that ends well. At least you didn't have you walk up the mountain to John's Rosemount estate." Theodore didn't want to admit that he was a bit jealous that Young could afford to build a magnificent home on the southern slope of the Westmount hill. That was only last year. If his investments went well in the near future, Theodore Hart could conceivably move his family up the mountain.

*I am directed by the Governor General to inform you, that His Excellency
has received a Communication from Sir John Pakington..that looking
to the amount of support which the Bishop of Toronto has met, in his
endeavour to establish a College in connection with the Church of
England (in Upper Canada) and to other circumstances, the Canadian
Government do not feel it advisable to offer further opposition to
the grant of the Royal Charter in favour of Trinity University.*
ROBERT BRUCE
(letter from Lord Elgin's military secretary to Bishop Strachan, April 23, 1852)

*And so it began. A fire broke out, apparently by accident, at Brown's
Tavern on St Lawrence. Fanned by the wind, it soon was roaring out
of control, leaping inexorably northeast from street to crowded street
… By late afternoon, just when the fire looked to be in retreat, church
bells pealed out in alarm. Once more sparks had ignited a new fire closer
to the waterfront at the eastern edge of the business district. The Hays
House, Montreal's finest hotel, as well as several military buildings
on Dalhousie Square were damaged. So were some mansions and other
buildings farther east. Only by about 4 am Friday were flames defeated.*
MONTREAL GAZETTE, JUNE 7
(reporting the great fire of June 4-5, 1852)

Fifty five

Catharine Joseph David listened sympathetically as her youngest sister blurted out the trepidations perhaps typical of a prospective bride. Esther Joseph had come over to the David house on Rue Craig in the early afternoon. For her part Catharine had completed supervision of the daily chores required to run her extensive household. It being almost summer, the two sisters sat next to an open window to bathe in the sunlight and feel the gentle breeze.

The wedding was scheduled to be held at the end of the June. Catharine had not paid as much attention to the upcoming event as she ought to have. Husband Aaron was in the midst of making a major career move. He needed all the support she could give him.

Esther had appeared at the door in the most up-to-date Victorian style. Her blouse and flowing skirt were obviously recent purchases. Catharine's first response was an invitation to have tea together. She rang for a servant.

Once seated, it was Esther's disconcerted expression that first alerted Catharine to having a distressed sister on her hands. An attempt was made to delve into extraneous subjects as they sipped their tea but suddenly Esther's eyes showed tears. "Am I doing the right thing, Katie?"

"Marrying? Why would you say that?"

"You think so highly of Abraham but I see him almost every day living as he does almost next door to us. At times imperious, more often too absorbed in his own thoughts to remember that I am a different person. I am easily hurt when he is so condescending. He is younger than me but that should not make that much of a difference."

Catharine had noticed a certain lack of warmth and their relationship. From her perspective Alexander Abraham de Sola ought to be quite a catch for Esther. He was born into an accomplished Sephardic family originating in Amsterdam. Abraham had grown up in London under the influence of his maternal grandfather, who was the chief rabbi of the Spanish and Portuguese congregation in the city. His education, directed by the father as well as by an Oriental scholar, had prepared him well for the task of being the *chazzan* to Montreal's Shearith Israel. Only a half dozen years in that position he had made himself a name in the general community. "Perhaps the affection will grow once the two of you are intimate. If you think not, now is your last opportunity to step back."

"But what else can I do? I'll be thirty next year. Both Becky and Sarah have missed their chance."

"I appreciate that, Esther." Catharine had also been forced to wait longer than normal for marriage. Back in the early thirties her intended, Aaron, was off in Scotland getting his medical degree. She was already 27 when she bore Samuel, her first child. There was nothing tardy about her next fifteen years -- ten more babies, seven of them male. Catharine had been heartbroken when her second boy, Henry, died in infancy. Otherwise the children, protected by a physician as a father, had been remarkably healthy. Harline, still less than a year old, was especially full of life and vigor - even precocious. But would she be the last of the brood; Catharine expected no more pregnancies.

"And mama would never forgive me, Katie. I dread even raising the matter with her."

Catharine was well aware that their mother had striven to have the marriage happen. *How many unwed daughters can mama abide?* Rachel Joseph had already talked to her sons, particularly Jacob Henry, about contributing to a suitable dowry should a marriage contract be negotiated. In the end the two parties agreed to a *kiddushin*; the sanctification and dedication of Abraham and Esther to each other. The obligations of each pertaining to the *ketuvah*, the pre-nuptial agreement, and to the date for the wedding were delineated forthwith. For Catharine it was reminiscent of what she and Aaron went through so many years before. "All I can say, Esther, is that you probably need to make the best of it. It should all work out."

The two women rose from the table and embraced. Esther then resumed her seat. "There is another problem. Jacob Henry has asked me to invite Eleazar to the wedding but to make no mention of his wife and children in the note. That I've done yet I fear that Eleazar will certainly decline under those conditions."

Catharine was startled. Eleazar David had come back into their lives at a most awkward time. "I'll talk to Aaron. He has met recently with his brother. He'll have a better sense of how Eleazar would behave."

∗ ∗ ∗

Aaron was home earlier than usual that afternoon and lo and behold he was accompanied by his older brother. *What a coincidence!* Aaron looked a bit sheepish. "Katie, I bumped into Eleazar on Sherbrooke. Invited him here for dinner. I trust you don't mind."

Catharine under normal circumstances would have minded. The evening meal was already being cooked. Hopefully there would be enough for one extra. Still, it was fortuitous that Eleazar was on hand so that she could resolve Esther's little dilemma. She surreptitiously studied her brother-in-law's visage while the two of them engaged in some private banter. *He has certainly aged over the last ten years. Do I really know him?*

While the two brothers took over the parlor, Catharine hurried to the kitchen. They would eat after the children were fed but the menu had to be altered. By the time she returned to the parlor, Aaron had dispensed some sherry in glasses and offered her to imbibe with them. This was not the usual routine for the last while. More often than not, he would be seeing patients after hours because he had to teach during the day. Aaron had resigned as a member of the staff of Montreal General Hospital in December. As one of the founders of the St Lawrence School of Medicine and as its secretary, he had been preoccupied with the winter course of lectures. It wouldn't have been too difficult physically to remain at Montreal General since the building being used for the school was close enough to the hospital. Nevertheless, the administration there had ties with the medical faculty at McGill College. The latter institution had established the Edinburgh curriculum and conducted six-month courses of basic science lectures to complement those taken by the students walking the wards at Montreal General. Aaron recognized that he and the other physicians associated with the new school would have trouble maintaining a separate curriculum. Yet he had cast his lot with the young clinicians such as Gibb, MacDonnell, Jones and the Howards who wanted to do more research. Only days before Aaron had reported having met with the new superior of the religious Hospitaller of Saint Joseph of Montreal. *Soeur* Mance, as she was called, was intent on launching a new hospital and was receptive to the idea of medical doctors using its patients for research purposes.

Catharine made a point of mentioning Esther's visit. "The wedding is but weeks away and she is counting on me to help with the arrangements. She tells me that an invitation has gone out to you, Eleazar. I have not seen you at *shul* since your return from abroad but your attendance, I trust, will not be a problem."

"Not a problem at all. You haven't forgotten, have you, that I was legal adviser to the trustees of the synagogue soon after I was admitted to the bar? That was twenty years ago but I fervently hope that I shall soon be reinstated as a member of the *shul*."

"Will Eliza convert?" Catharine asked the question before she had time to consider whether it was appropriate at this point in the conversation. Aaron gave a sharp look. They had never had any social contact with the former Eliza Lock Walker. While she was the wife of Major Harris, Catharine and David had studiously avoided the military set. And, of course, the elopement had put an end to Eleazar's stay in Montreal.

"You must understand, Katie, that Eliza takes her Christian faith quite seriously. The children have been baptized and they have attended church even when we lived in France, Italy and the West Indies. I still regard myself as a Jew but I have not sought to impose my faith on the little ones. You may not know that Eliza is pregnant again. It will be our eighth child."

Catharine said no more. Eleazar evidently wasn't interpreting the lack of an invitation to his wife and family as an insult. They sat at the supper table without another mention of the wedding. Instead he enquired about the whereabouts of her family. She brought him up to date on the activities of Jacob Henry, Abraham, Jesse and Gershom. He seemed especially interested in what Jacob Henry was doing beyond running his tobacco business. "Is your brother involving himself in railway policy? I remember him being connected with the building of the Champlain-St Lawrence line back in the '30s. He is probably wondering how our first minister is doing in London."

Eleazar like so many others were following reports that Hincks, now confirmed along with Morin as the first ministers in the province, was out of the country. Catharine also understood that Hincks had been dealing with the premiers of New Brunswick and Nova Scotia on the joint financing of a railway from Halifax to Windsor or Sarnia. The arrangement had suddenly come apart because the British government was refusing to guarantee the interest on any loan if the line did not follow the more defensible route along the Gaspé Peninsula. Hincks and the Maritime politicians revised the plan and Hincks sailed to England at the end of February to consult with the Russell administration. Unfortunately Russell had just resigned his post, the unauthorized British acceptance of Napoleon III's coup of the previous December having left the prime minister in an untenable position. A new colonial secretary, John Pakington, had replaced Lord Grey and signaled that the Tories were even more cautious on financing than were the Whigs. Eleazar had seen the latest report in a New York daily. He was convinced that Britain would never accept a route that was too close to the US border.

Aaron appeared uninterested in the subject of railways. His silence warned Catharine that she should encourage conversation in a different direction.

* * *

On the Friday morning Catharine woke to the acrid smell of burning wood. Little did she know that at six in the morning at the corner of Rue Saint-Pierre and Rue Lemoyne a fire had consumed the carpenter shop of a J. Martin. His destroyed residence had led to fatal consequences. One child was already dead and the other died later in the day from his burns. Had she known the origin of the conflagration, she would have immediately thought of her brother Jesse. He had invested heavily on real estate along Rue Lemoyne.

This was no isolated occurrence. A stiff wind from the southwest was driving the flames toward the heart of Montreal's business section. Roofs on buildings along busy Rue Saint-Paul were not easily protected. Firemen did save the store of Frothingham & Workman but some of its outbuildings perished. Commercial buildings occupied by the Imperial Customs Department were among the many in the downtown area that were not spared. Several houses facing the steamboat landings went down. On Commissioner St the Vermont Central Railroad office burned to the ground. The same fate befell the Champlain and St Lawrence Railroad office, the Harbor Commissioners office and Trinity House. Public houses did not fare well. Gone were the Liverpool Tavern, the Boston Inn and the Old Countrymen's Inn.

Catharine only learned of the extent of the destruction later in the day when Aaron returned from the river front. No more fatalities were being reported but he had felt it necessary to show his presence in any case.

This was an epidemic of a different kind. She for her part had kept the children indoors despite the hot weather. *Who knows what will be in this path of destruction?*

The fire was indeed moving in a northeast direction and seemed certain to touch Dalhousie Square, which was to the east of where the Joseph family lived. Aaron sought to comfort her. He had been told that the fire was being contained on the east side of Rue Saint-Laurent.

He was wrong. The fire was not extinguished and Dalhousie Square, a prestigious residential area featuring the hotel and other structures owned by Moses Judah Hays, became the target of a new outbreak. It was late afternoon by this time and the firemen were being overwhelmed by the heat and the exertion required in pumping an inadequate supply of water. Aaron once more ventured out and witnessed the flames leaping out of the windows of the Hays hotel and the theatre attached. It was a sight to behold: Montreal's most celebrated entertainment center, the stage for international performers, going up in smoke. The blowing sparks were already igniting homes and shops that had only recently been built in the shadow of the hotel complex. The firemen and soldiers were fighting a losing battle and the end did not come till the early morning, by which time hundreds of properties were lost in the eastern suburb. Montreal had suffered its worst conflagration ever and the cost would be in the millions of pounds. Aaron could not resist commenting to Catharine that thank goodness they had decided not to buy the house they had looked at when Dorchester Square was in its heyday.

It appears that the number of intern patients amounted to 211, and that of the externs to 306, making a total of 517...and is sure of being watched and tended through his illness with more than a mother's care; he can command a visit from his medical man as often as he pleases, and when necessary to take exercise, he can do so on the grounds connected with the establishment.
AARON HART DAVID, R.L.MACDONNELL, H.HOWARD
(quarterly report, St. Patrick Hospital, April 30, 1852)

One of the first questions which the new Government was obliged to consider was the expediency of aiding in the establishment of a line of ocean steamers.. The lowest offer was from the Liverpool firm of McKean, McLarty & Co., and it was deemed expedient to enter into a contract with that firm... It is well known that the service was not satisfactorily performed, owing, probably to the war with Russia. ..In later years other lines have been established without having been subsidized, but no capitalist could have been induced in 1851 to embark in such an enterprise without a considerable subsidy.
FRANCIS HINCKS
(Reminiscences of his Public Life, 1884)

Fifty six

Aaron Hart David surveyed his new office. It was new in a couple of senses: the room was part of a relatively modern edifice on Rue Saint-Paul and Aaron had not set foot in it before. It had escaped the fire that had raged earlier in the month. Built as a college for Anglophone Baptists, it was meant to fulfill the dream of ambitious British missionaries resident in London. As the fledgling St Patrick's Hospital, it was now slated to be opened for patients next week on the Monday, June 21, the day of the summer solstice. For Aaron this space was quite different from what he had at the Montreal General.

The patients in the hospital would in all likelihood be the Irish immigrants living in Griffintown, Pointe-Saint-Charles or Goose Village. The staff had been recruited from the Hôtel-Dieu – nuns who had had excellent experience in handling the sick and infirm. Aaron would be collaborating with Marie-Julie-Marguerite Céré de la Colombière, better know as Sister Mance, who became superior of the religious Hospitallers of Saint-Joseph as of the previous year.

When in late 1851 Aaron was approached by Sister Mance with the offer, the idea bothered him at first of converting the old Baptist College to a facility able to handle the indigent in downtown Montreal. Couldn't the Hôtel Dieu and/or the Montreal General be modified to accomplish the same purpose? A teaching hospital, however, did fit in so well with the recently established St Lawrence School of Medicine. Thus he had accepted being appointed physician and clinical lecturer in medicine in this new establishment.

It had been Aaron's intention to wait a week before beginning his duties in the hospital wards on the 21st. He had agreed, however, to meet with John Mockett Cramp, his predecessor in this office. As president of the Baptist College of Montreal the middle-aged clergyman was now reduced to writing for the *Pilot*, the journal once owned by Francis Hincks. The man had, however, an intimate knowledge of how the maintenance of the building had been carried out over the time it was operational. Aaron would have some responsibility in running the hospital.

Cramp appeared at the door on time. The man appeared no worse for wear despite being deprived of his presidency. He explained that in recent months he had gained a new perspective on the ills of the world. "I commend you for what you are undertaking, Dr. Hart. I see what has been happening to our Irish refugees. They arrived at the worst possible time. Diseased, jobless, without hope. Orphans from Grosse-Île have had to be sent to families in the countryside. Thank God they are Catholic, for what else could have been done for them? I say this despite being a committed Protestant."

Aaron was heartened by this outburst. "We agree, sir. I think thousands perished when the typhus struck at Windmill Point. That was almost five years ago. I felt almost helpless at the time. Perhaps I can do more good in this new hospital. But tell me! Why did your college fail?"

"A bitter tale. We had such high hopes for an institution that would combine classical and biblical studies with language training. John Gilmour in London had in mind duplicating what we Baptists have in Stepney. Unfortunately the student enrolment was low and the library not quite up to snuff. There has been no support from the New England Baptists, who are so devoted to communalism that they reject all innovation. Then came the economic depression. Our English brethren withdrew their support and we were short $10,000. What else could we do but sell the building?"

"What puzzles me is why the Baptists in Montreal are so isolated. Surely you would have been better off as a bilingual institution."

Cramp looked down at his hands before replying. "Language is indeed a barrier to cooperation. There is the Baptist school at Grande Ligne led by

Henrietta Odin. It is but ten miles south of Saint-Jean so that one would think that she would join the French Canadian Missionary Society that we have established here in Montreal. But that hasn't happened."

"Henrietta Odin has been mentioned to me. Isn't she the one who converted Côté to the Baptist cause?" During the 1837 insurrection Aaron had been posted in Napierville and had often been informed of the exploits of the local doctor, Cyrille Côté, who had become quite the revolutionary.

Cramp nodded. "She has attracted many to the cause but Swiss Protestantism has yet to make much of an impact in our metropolis. As for Côté, he would not have fared well in Montreal. The Catholic priests feared him because he is an apostate with great appeal to the average *habitant*. And the English community hadn't forgotten his deeds during the insurrections. They have nothing to fear any more. He died of a heart attack in October '50. He was barely forty years old."

The conversation finally reverted to practical matters. Cramp seemed open to discussing the troubles he had running things until the school closed. Aaron took notes.

Being the longest day of the year, it was still sunlight when Aaron emerged from his new office. He had much to think about as he passed some of the gutted buildings that had been caught up in the fire. What a world we live in? He didn't get back to Rue Craig until well past the supper hour.

Catherine had finished feeding the children, all ten of them, but she had news for him. Harline, their third daughter, had succeeded in walking about the downstairs floor on her own two feet. That was at the earliest age that accomplishment was recorded in the David family. He was jubilant. "We shall have the chance to let her perform at the wedding."

* * *

The Wednesday at the end of the month proved to be another hot, sticky day but those attending the wedding at the synagogue were generally in a good mood. Their *chazzan* was marrying the girl next door.

There was less dancing than Aaron would have guessed. Undoubtedly the heat had something to do with so much restraint. Otherwise he had the pleasure of observing the rituals common to Jewish weddings. Once the supper had been served, he slipped out of the main room in hope that there was a breeze outdoors. Coincidentally his brother Eleazar was also seeking some fresh air. He extracted a cigar from his jacket and lit it.

Aaron sighed. "Half the year has gone. Perhaps now that Hincks is back in Canada, this year '52 will be more meaningful. I've been told that

371

he signed an agreement with a private British company that will give us a railway from Montreal to Toronto."

"I've heard the same story. Apparently this firm – Peto, Brassey, Jackson and Betts – has promised to lay 330 miles of track at an acceptable price. Presumably the Grand Trunk will therefore not proceed as a public venture." Eleazar's information was new to Aaron.

Aaron grunted. He was convinced that Hincks in his obsession with railways was biting off more than he could chew. But there was nothing more said on the subject.

Eleazar had a different question. "I understand there are none of your medical lectures being advertised. Your school is no more?"

"My colleagues and I agreed. We can't compete on equal terms with the McGill faculty. Besides, the work at St Patrick's keeps us busy. I have already done some surgical operations at the hospital. Even those as complicated as removal of a parotid tumor and the amputation of patient's breast."

"You personally did that?"

"We have a rule at the hospital. The patient is permitted to select any of the physicians on the medical staff. I insist on the nurses being vigilant in their tending of the patients throughout their illness. They provide more than even a mother's care."

"You are doing good work, brother. I wonder if I have the diligence to be so self-sacrificing. Now that I'm back in Montreal, I do have to reestablish my law practice. And I have made other commitments. Resuming my post as a Major in the Montreal cavalry and I plan to offer my services to De Sola as a legal adviser to the congregation. I shall need more income to do all that."

"I have wondered, Eleazar. How were you able to afford living in New York and traveling abroad as well?"

"Both papa and Uncle David did provide some funds for me in their respective wills. You too got something when they died, what is it?, almost thirty years ago. I, however, didn't apply my inheritance to a medical education."

Aaron gazed at his older brother. *You are indeed the prodigal son.*

*   *   *

Aaron's assistant caught his attention while he was perusing a medical report. "We are about to be visited by a member of the press." The statement was accurate if somewhat disconcerting. In the waiting room sat the publisher of *La Minerve*, the renowned Ludger Duvernay who had specifically asked to see him. Aaron, who didn't usually see patients in the mornings, concluded that he would make an exception in this case. The visitor was seated in his office almost immediately. Aaron lifted the blind covering the window despite it being a sunny July day.

Aaron had had little personal contact with Duvernay despite the man's prominence. Aaron knew of him as the political radical exiled for his participation in the rebellion and one rehabilitated as the current president of the Association Saint-Jean-Baptiste de Montréal. An occasional reading of *La Minerve* editorials was the closest Aaron had gotten to knowing what Duvernay thought or did as an individual.

A quick survey of the man's physique told Aaron that this was not someone in the best of health. The back was slightly stooped, the facial skin blotched, the eyes bloodshot. Duvernay quickly explained his presence. "I have been having sharp pains in the chest complicated by coughing spells. The pain occurs when I walk and disappears as soon as I rest. There is no shortness of breath and my heart beat seems unaffected. The doctors I have seen agree that it is a case of *angina pectoris* but they differ on how it should be treated."

He had spoken in French but that posed no problem for Aaron. The latter thought to himself that this is somebody quite aware of his condition but desperate for guidance. Almost as if to prove the point, Duvernay began coughing for a minute or two.

"How old are you, *monsieur*? I ask that because *angina pectoris* most often affects men in their fifties, especially those who are overweight."

"I was fifty-three in January."

"You condition is not uncommon. The original diagnosis of *angina pectoris* came eighty years ago when William Heberden in England published a paper based on his experience at the Royal College. He was convinced then that a disease of the nervous system is involved, especially if it coincides with ossification of the coronary arteries, of the valve or the aorta. There is still some mystery about how these problems are related." Aaron suggested that Duvernay visit an examining room next door and submit to a test. A new binaural stethoscope had become commercially available that very year and this was a good occasion on which to listen to the heart rhythms.

The examination took but a few minutes. Aaron returned Duvernay to his office and gave him the unpleasant news. "Your doctors are probably correct in their diagnoses. There is a blockage of one or more of the arteries. If only we could clear it out but we don't have the tools. The best that one can do for you is to prescribe as much rest as possible and to simplify your diet. No alcohol! Ferocious therapies such as bleeding don't apply in this case despite your coughing. That may not be what you want to hear, being a man of your temperament and your engagement with the public. You must accept, however, that you are not a well man."

Duvernay took the news without any show of dismay. Aaron guessed that he probably expected no less a verdict. But he had a question unrelated to the case. "You are obviously related to Aaron Hart of Trois-Rivières."

"He was my grandfather."

Aaron's patient suddenly became quite detached. "I began my journalism career in Trois-Rivières. I knew Aaron Hart's sons. Louis-Joseph Papineau was then striving to change Lower Canada into a new kind of country. Today Papineau is an outsider and we have come to live with double majorities in Parliament. I meet with *Monsieur* Morin quite often. He is the insider even if he is not certain how Canada will evolve. He and Francis Hincks will have the task next month in Quebec of showing us the way."

Aaron didn't like engaging in political debate with a patient but again he decided to make an exception in this case. "It seems to me that our new government has the responsibility of returning our colony to prosperity. Unless one is an annexationist, the way forward has yet to be defined. If Britain is able to negotiate a reciprocity treaty with the United States, the outlook would be much better."

Duvernay smiled wryly. "We shall not get trade reciprocity any time soon. Hincks tried to convince Pakington that a deal with the Americans would at the minimum let us pick up revenue from canal tolls. But our Colonial Secretary wants to hold out for an even better deal. Will the governments succeed in striking a bargain? I have my doubts."

*I stated, a little while ago, that you had courted a bad principle.
If it were simply bad, I should not complain of it, but it is dangerous
and pernicious in its consequences. It is the same principle which
I have combated and am combating with all my force in Lower Canada,
and against which moderate and conscientious men of all parties
in Europe have united. Clear Gritism is, in my opinion, neither more
or less than Socialism and Socialism of the worse kind, ardently
desiring the destruction of our institutions, and expressing this desire,
without blushing, every hour of the day, through the medium of its press.*
JOSEPH CAUCHON
(letter to Francis Hincks, October 31, 1851)

*His Excellency Lord Elgin, the Governor General, opened the
proceedings of the session of Legislature of Canada, on the 19th day of
August 1852, with the usual Speech from the Throne, but in which he
made no reference to the subject of Education.*
**EDUCATIONAL PROCEEDINGS OF THE LEGISLATURE OF CANADA
1852, 1853**

Fifty seven

Aaron Ezekiel Hart dreaded making the journey despite the summer
weather being quite conducive to travel. Professional duty had to
prevail over distaste for becoming involved in family disputes. The ferry had
taken him across the river to Nicolet earlier in the morning and now came
the need to direct his *calèche* along a dusty and somewhat winding trail to
the Courval seigneury.

The village of Saint-Zépherin-de-Courval was but a pimple on the
rump of this south-side territory. Why his cousin Alexander had chosen to
settle here confounded him. Yes, "Aleck" had become the *seigneur* of this
particular district courtesy of his father Moses and he did have a thriving
timber business utilizing the remaining tree growth on the seigneury and
beyond. But the village had little else to boast about other than the parish
church, and that was built only in the past few years. No matter; Alexander
had been carried as a dying man to Trois-Rivières to be buried in the family

cemetery on Rue Alexandre. *What mark has he left in Saint-Zépherin other than a struggling family who was demanding help?*

This demand actually surfaced months after the funeral in April. Mary McCarthy Brown had come to see not only Aaron Ezekiel but the whole Hart family on Rue des Forges bearing a letter she received from the widow. Miriam Judah Hart was insisting that she had proof that in 1840 her prospective father-in-law Moses had written to her in New York that she would be paid fifteen hundred pounds if she married Alexander Thomas Hart. No such payment had seemingly occurred. Mary was adamant; Moses, though virtually bed-ridden these days, was denying any commitment of cash. On the other hand, Miriam had been mentioned in the will written by Moses in 1847. At the time Moses had made a formal donation *inter vivos* of the seigneury of Courval, a property of six square leagues, to Alexander for life, "with remainder to his children in fee and, in default of children, to one half, to his wife for her life."

It was not easy to reach consensus among Aaron Ezekiel and his siblings. Samuel Bécancour and Ira Craig had no patience with Miriam's implicit threat to challenge the Hart estate even while Moses was still alive. Esther Elizabeth saw it from Miriam's perspective; her cousin had three children to raise and diminishing sources of income with which to do so.

The church steeple finally appeared on the horizon. As expected the Hart house turned out to be the most substantial in this community of hundreds. Turning over the *calèche* and horse to a stable boy, Aaron Ezekiel entered through the front door. He and Miriam embraced; they had known each other for a dozen years and they happened to be cousins who grew up in two different lands. There was scarcely much difference in age.

Miriam's three offspring hovered about them. Moses was the oldest at age eleven and Lewis the youngest at five. They seemed excited seeing one of their relatives from Trois-Rivières come into their isolated lives. Aaron Ezekiel handed out small presents to them and they soon disappeared outdoors. They weren't too interested in staying for tea. The atmosphere in the house was much too humid to their liking.

Aaron Ezekiel made some small talk. "I found Saint Zépherin a rather quaint name. Did some reading to learn that Zephyrinus was a bishop of Rome in the third century AD. Apparently he called for full forgiveness in the church whereas some believed that some sins could never be forgiven."

"Most of the parishioners here wouldn't know that. Yet they are glad to have their new sanctuary and a priest to listen to them."

"I noticed the church. It looks adequate."

"You may not realize that though the villagers used wood for the church, it relied on the architect Thomas Baillairgé for its design."

Aaron Ezekiel finally got down to business. "Is it your intention, Miriam, to remain here indefinitely? The boys will need schooling very shortly if that is not the situation already."

"That is precisely why I am looking for financial help. Help that is coming to me by right."

"That has yet to be established. Your father-in-law believes he has done well by both you and Aleck. He was, after all, a *seigneur*. Rents from the seigneury have undoubtedly brought you a good living."

"What does a title matter if seigneuries are to be done away with?" Miriam too had undoubtedly been following the newspaper reports on the government move to end seigneurial tenure. Legislation had already been passed allowing *censitaires* to switch to freehold status but compensating the *seigneurs* for loss of dues and services was a stumbling block to widespread shift away from the seigneurial system. Lewis Drummond, the Attorney General in Lower Canada, was expected to push for limiting seigneurial privileges and in effect eliminate the system altogether. The issue would be joined when Parliament met in Quebec City during the following month.

"There will be compensation if that should happen. I don't think you are as badly off as you suggest." Aaron Ezekiel realized he was being argumentative.

Miriam responded by going to a strongbox sitting on a sideboard. "In my letter to Mary I cited proof. Here is the letter written in Uncle Moses' own hand promising me money if I married Aleck. I've shown it to cousins Tom and Henry in Montreal. They confirm it is in his handwriting."

"That may not be enough to establish your document as proof. I would hate to see this matter having to go to the courts." Nevertheless, after perusing the contents of the letter, Aaron Ezekiel recognized that his cousin had reason to believe that she had the advantage. Yet the other party (his client) was not be ready to concede. *Family disputes are the hardest to arbitrate.*

* * *

A letter arriving in Trois-Rivières the next day lightened Aaron Ezekiel's mood considerably. The Chief Justice John Beverley Robinson notified him that he was being appointed commissioner for receiving affidavits in Lower Canada. Aaron Ezekiel hadn't fully appreciated that somebody in Toronto could honor him without the two having ever met. He would be fifty years old next year and this was the first time he had been singled out for government recognition.

After dinner Aaron Ezekiel and Phoebe retired to their room in the house on Rue des Forges. He then chose to propose something he had been thinking about all day. "This is July, Phoebe. I have no urgent cases on my schedule. You have been asking me so often for the two of us to visit your sister in Quebec. Little Fanny will have her chance to interact with at least four of her cousins, including her namesake."

Aaron Ezekiel was referring to the eldest of Sophia's children, Fanny David Joseph, who had already reached the age of five. Their own daughter, Frances Lazarus Hart, born the previous August, had yet to be viewed by any of the Josephs. He noted, however, that his wife was suspicious. Usually it was she who suggested travel, albeit with a small child to care for, the conditions seldom seemed right.

She finally voiced her skepticism. "This is not like you, Eze."

"I admit, dear, that there is method to my madness. One of my clients has property that would increase in value if a railroad were built along the north shore to Quebec City. I have been asked to call on Joseph Cauchon, who has spoken vigorously on such a project and will presumably do it again when Parliament meets next month."

So it was agreed. A letter was dispatched to Abraham Joseph declaring their intentions. And two days later the threesome, man, woman and child, boarded the steamer bound for Quebec City. Hours later they were at their destination. Abraham Joseph had come down to the Lower Town from his residence on Clapham Terrace to greet Aaron Ezekiel, sister-in-law Phoebe and child at the dock. Soon the carriage was on its way up the hill.

There was much tumult when the sisters finally came face to face. Aaron Ezekiel carried little Fanny Lazarus while Phoebe introduced herself to the Joseph children. Besides Fanny David, there were Rachel Sarah, Henry and Montefiore. Sophia was well into her next pregnancy, which was obviously more advanced than that of Phoebe's. The latter, almost in her mid-thirties, could never match her younger sister in fecundity.

Aaron Ezekiel waited until the evening meal before drawing his brother-in-law aside. "By the way, Abe, could you arrange for me to call on Joseph Cauchon? I know that you have loaned money to the Le Journal de Québec over the years. You would be doing me a favor if you could convince its proprietor and editor to see me." Aaron Ezekiel had watched with great interest the ability of Joseph Cauchon to avoid the financial difficulties that had plagued Neilson's Quebec Gazette during its last years. Neilson had died in 1848 but Le Journal de Québec, launched in 1842 had made Cauchon an important figure in Canadian politics. He had in fact been invited by Hincks to join his administration. Cauchon, an ardent nationalist, had refused because Hincks was also negotiating with the "Clear Grits", the liberals linked with William Lyon Mackenzie.

Abraham was puzzled. What business could a Hart have with the editor of a francophone journal? The explanation satisfied him. It was widely known that Hincks entertained the idea of the Grand Trunk being built east as well as west of Montreal. But the plan was to lay track along the south shore of the St Lawrence as far as Lévis, across the river from Quebec. That would fit in with the ultimate goal of linking Montreal with the Maritime Provinces. Cauchon, on the other hand, was supporting the promoters of a north-shore railway, which too would be subsidized by government if they had their way.

Aaron Ezekiel didn't get an answer to his request until two days later. No, Cauchon would not find the time to see a lawyer representing an indirect interest in the project. Abraham apologized for his lack of success but Aaron Ezekiel had met rebuffs before and learned to live with them.

∗   ∗   ∗

Mary McCarthy was once more at the entrance to the house on Rue des Forges. She reported that Moses Hart was dying. The doctor gave him a few weeks to live at best. Aaron Ezekiel was the most affected by the news. He recalled himself leaving the chamber of the Chief Justice in Quebec in the autumn of 1824. The first Jew to qualify as an advocate, barrister, attorney, solicitor, proctor and counsel in all His Majesty's Courts of Justice in Lower Canada, he had to make a career choice. It was to go to work for his uncle Moses Hart, who was in frequent litigation with tenants, business rivals and the government bureaucracy.

Moses would eventually have other nephews to represent him. Aaron Philip Hart, Benjamin's son, actually did act for Moses in certain instances and there were always the Judah brothers, nephews of his wife Sarah, and later on two sons of his sister Sarah Hart David and finally Adolphus, Aaron Ezekiel's younger brother. Moses could always count on legal advice within the clan. But Aaron Ezekiel was the first and the longest to serve, especially after he returned from Quebec to live in Trois-Rivières. Now was the time to show his respect.

The home on Rue Alexandre seemed ghostly to Aaron Ezekiel. It was also not properly tended. The October shedding of the trees was well advanced and no attempt had been made to gather the leaves that had accumulated. Not too many candles had been lit in the rooms leading to the master bedroom. He wondered why; Mary was too good a housekeeper to let things slide. It did occur to him that with the two minors in the household – Samuel and Reuben – off to prep school and with Moses so ill, there was very little incentive to show the place at its best.

At almost eighty-four years of age (his birthday was in November) Moses was but a shell of a man. Propped up with pillows piled high on his bed, he could see only shadows. But his mind seemed clear and his memory particularly acute when it came to his early life. Aaron Ezekiel listened patiently as Moses offered a narrative that included his travel to New York after the American Revolution, his sojourn in London soon after the French Revolution and his venture into brewing in the final decade of that century and into the next. He didn't, however, talk of his many women friends. Aaron Ezekiel never did know how many of them gave Moses children. Ezekiel Hart, his own father, would have kept track but he was dead.

Aaron Ezekiel interjected at this point. "Uncle Moses, you are the scion of a great family. I regard myself as part of it. Aaron Hart had children and grandchildren that have made the name honored throughout the land."

"I hear you, son. My siblings, though younger than me, are almost all gone and buried. There is, of course, Kitty in New York." He hesitated as if he weren't quite sure whether Catharine Hart Judah was still alive. (His sister was born in 1776.)

He forced himself to continue. "And then there is Benjamin. He still goes on. We have not written since he moved to New York. What could we write about? We disagree on religion. We disagree on politics. We disagree on money. And yet for years we worked together. Benjy, I miss you."

Aaron Ezekiel swore to himself at that moment that he would contact Benjamin Hart in New York. Maybe there was still time for reconciliation.

*That the said A.M.Hart of the first part being author, translator
and proprietor of a certain manuscript by him written and compiled,
entitled by him "French Writers and Warriors in America during
the Revolutionary War" has for good and sufficient consideration, to wit,
two hundred dollars by him in hand received, assigned, sold and
conveyed unto the said Ward & Taylor the sole and
exclusive right to copyright, print publish and sell the said
manuscript or any part thereof in such manner and under
such title as may to them seem proper and expedient...*
A. M. HART, WARD & TAYLOR
(Cincinnati contract, May 28, 1852)

*We have strolled off to moralize, but our history of this worthy family
must close. Benjamin Hart was committed to the silent dust
in February, 1855, and his remains lie interred in the family plot
at Long Island of Col. A. Wellington Hart, his eldest surviving
son residing in New York, and a member of the third
generation of worshippers with this Synagogue.*
ARTHUR WELLINGTON HART
(letter to the American Jewish Historical Society, 1873)

Fifty eight

The St George's Hotel on Broadway wasn't that far from the home of
Arthur Wellington Hart. It had become probably the last haven for
Benjamin Hart, who was three years into his eightieth decade. The son,
Wellington, the eldest surviving male in Benjamin's immediate family, was
thus able to monitor the father without having to deal with his perversity
on a daily basis.

Entering the hotel lobby, Adolphus was quickly able to ascertain
which floor his father-in-law had found his refuge. It had been months
since Adolphus interacted with Benjamin, in part because the former had
become involved in the political campaigning preceding the November
presidential election. Prior to that, he and Constance had been residents of
Missouri and his prime concern then was getting his book published. The
Passover holiday had passed before they returned to New York. There had
been no social occasion to bring him together with Benjamin Hart though
Constance had made a point of visiting her father.

Benjamin greeted Adolphus at the door. The handshake was firm enough although the old man's visage did not belie his years. Adolphus felt obliged to give him some explanation of why he had become an author as well as a practicing lawyer while living in St Louis. This city on the Mississippi was booming and there was hunger for knowledge of the valley's origins. Having a good acquaintance with both history and the French language had stood him in good stead. "Constance probably told you that I sold my manuscript on French writers and warriors in America during the Revolutionary War to a Cincinnati publisher."

"She also mentioned that you fraternized with Henry while living there. My son stopped writing me years ago. Married a Christian." Benjamin showed a pained expression.

Adolphus sighed. "He deplores the rift in the family. This is partly why I am here. I have just received a communication from my brother Ezekiel. He writes that my uncle Moses is near the end of his tether. You know that both I and Ezekiel worked closely with him for many years. Apparently he has expressed regret that you and your brother have drifted apart in recent years. Ezekiel feels strongly that if there is enough time the two of you might reconcile. I'm prepared to travel to Three Rivers with you if you are similarly inclined."

"You seem to suggest that he is on his deathbed. Surely there is not enough time for us to reach Three Rivers to see him alive. It would be a case of standing at his graveside, would it not?"

"There is now rail service from here all the way to Montreal. We could catch a steamer from there to Three Rivers." Adolphus had anticipated such an objection to his scheme.

Benjamin appeared intrigued by the proposal albeit Adolphus had not foreseen a serious interest in his traveling to Lower Canada at this stage in his life. "It is true that we are the last of a generation. Incidentally, your Aunt Kitty would be less inclined than me to visit him. She is in touch with her daughter in Saint-Zépherin. Miriam is not painting a flattering picture of Moses Hart."

Walking back to his own dwelling in lower Manhattan, Adolphus had to reconsider his personal commitment to return if only temporarily to his place of birth. It would be awkward to explain to the election team associated with Horatio Seymour that he was withdrawing his active participation in the campaign for family reasons. And yet the prospect of not only reacting to Aaron Ezekiel's request but also of once more being under the roof of the house on Rue des Forges excited him.

Constance was busy nursing their latest addition to the family. Harriot Judith, named after Constance's deceased mother, was the first girl in a family of five. Adolphus related the gist of the plan he and her father had agreed to. He then expressed a sense of disappointment at abandoning his comrades battling for electoral success.

Constance had her own take on New York politics. She had previously contended that there was an air of unreality about the whole process. "Do you believe that the Compromise of 1850 has indeed settled the issue of slavery? In my view there are too many anti-slavery people in both parties to let the question remain dormant."

"You may not be wrong, my dear. Nevertheless, I still have been supporting Franklin Pierce for the presidency. He backs the Compromise and stands a very good chance to win. The Democrats are once more united."

"And your friend Horatio Seymour is also running for the governorship of New York. Can he win this time?"

He's a Hunker, though in the end he is supporting Pierce in the upcoming election." Adolphus was chuckling, amused that the New York Democratic Party had adopted such labels to identify its split over policy. The Hunker faction was the more conservative and committed to the former state governor, William Marcy. The Barnburners leaned to a previous President, Martin Van Buren. In their determination to give Pierce a victory over the Whigs, Seymour and his friends were downplaying their policy differences.

"Frankly, Dolph, I couldn't care less who wins in November so I am not displeased that you have reason to turn away from political activity. Whether papa is ready for engaging with Uncle Moses is another question. My preference, of course, is that both you and he stay put in New York. It certainly would make life easier for me."

*   *   *

The October landscape kept shifting as the train moved north. The New York and Harlem line took Adolphus and Benjamin up the east side of the Hudson River, enabling them to gaze at the slopes of the Highlands. Earlier in the year the tracks has been extended north to Chatham Four Corners for a connection to the Albany and West Stockbridge Railroad and then to the Hartford & New Haven. Their destination was Windsor, the town on the Connecticut River giving them access to the Vermont Central. The latter railway offered a direct link at the Canadian border with the St Lawrence and Atlantic. The journey was proving shorter than if they traveled by stagecoach but Benjamin was soon grumbling about the frequent changes of trains to get to Montreal.

Any steamboat plying the St Lawrence didn't depart Montreal until the morning so that Adolphus had arranged for his cousin Theodore to meet them at the station with a carriage that would take them to Metcalfe Terrace. Benjamin was near exhaustion so that there was little conversation between father and son. Theodore made certain that Benjamin was bedded down for the night.

Adolphus enquired whether there was any word from Trois-Rivières on the condition of their Uncle Moses. Theodore disclaimed any knowledge of a change in circumstance. Rather he appeared interested in the details of the train trip from New York through the New England states. There was almost jubilation with the prospect that Canada would be catching up with the United States on railway construction. "The time is right, cousin, to make one's fortune. The depression is behind us and leading the country is a man dedicated to revolutionizing transportation."

Theodore elaborated. Francis Hincks had come back from London possessing a private deal with Peto, Brassey, Jackson and Betts. By the autumn Hincks had told the Parliament in Quebec City that he was expanding the project to include a western terminal in Sarnia and an eastern one in Portland. "Now that the government is on record supporting a railway beyond Montreal and Toronto, the Grand Trunk Railway will soon come into being. The St Lawrence and Atlantic will undoubtedly be part of that entity."

"You and Hincks are old collaborators and it is paying off."

"Think of it, Dolph! He has already taken steps to have 1,100 miles of track financed. Stocks and debentures will be floated next spring. I am one of those involved in incorporating the new firm. My friend Luther will in all likelihood also be a director for the Grand Trunk and will therefore be well placed to bid for the right to lay track for any extensions of the main line beyond Toronto or Montreal. He is negotiating with Galt to create a company for that express purpose. If you were a gambling man, you too would be investing in the Grand Trunk."

"In other words, Theo, I would be getting in on the ground floor just as you are doing." Adolphus was impressed with the audacity of these *entrepreneurs*. Holton teaming up with Galt? He remembered when the Englishman Alexander Tilloch Galt was but a local bigwig. But married to a Torrance, related by blood to Hugh Allan, the shipping magnate, and ensconced as the commissioner of the British American Land Company, Galt was seemingly too ambitious to limit himself to being top dog in Sherbrooke, where he maintained his major enterprises and lived luxuriously. He had first involved himself in the St Lawrence & Atlantic and now was allied with the Hincks-Morin administration in planning more railroads.

His legal mind always looking for contradictions, Adolphus wondered if Hincks and his friends were not opening themselves up for adverse reactions to their ambitions. "He will not escape criticism in the press. My guess is that George Brown in the *Globe* and Daoust in *L'Avenir* will find scandal in the way Hincks is running the country. Even Duvernay in *La Minerve* will not be quiet."

"Strange that you should mention Duvernay! There is some talk of him not lasting even another month or two. It's his heart. He intends to leave *La Minerve* to his son Louis Napoléon but the paper will never be the same without Ludger Duvernay."

* * *

The gathering in and about the house on Rue Alexandre was large enough to warn Adolphus that the desired meeting of the two old men would not happen. Everybody was warmly dressed – it was after all the middle of October – but the clothing's dominant color was black. A death scene without doubt! Family constituted much of the crowd but Adolphus also spotted several leading citizens of Trois-Rivières who were obviously there to pay their respects to the richest man in the district.

The family cemetery was on the grounds so that the coffin holding the body of Moses Hart hadn't been moved too far. What surprised Adolphus was the presence of the *chazzan* who oversaw the local synagogue. *A Jewish burial! So unexpected a choice for the Deist uncle I knew.* Nevertheless, Adolphus did remember that in recent years Moses Hart made occasional donations to the Shearith Israel congregations in both Montreal and New York. He had been playing it safe with his soul.

As the funeral came to its conclusion, Benjamin Hart never looked graver. Adolphus accompanied him inside the house and had him seated in the parlor. Mary McCarthy appeared at the door asking if she could offer him something to drink. Benjamin deigned to notice her; in other circumstances he would have cut her dead.

Within minutes family members, especially the nieces and nephews, filled the room. Adolphus greeted his siblings warmly. Esther Elizabeth, Harriet and Caroline were tear-stricken but their brothers, Samuel and Ira Craig in particular, showed complete composure. Aaron Ezekiel and Adolphus embraced. "Thank you for coming, Dolph."

What occurred to Adolphus was the absence of so many of the offspring sired by his uncle. Areli Blake and family were in the parlor but there was no sign of Louise. As for Moses' "natural" children, only those borne by

Mary McCarthy were there. By Adolphus' count, altogether eighteen had been born out of wedlock. Several had died over the years and a few were scattered across the continent. Moses Hart could never have claimed having a close-knit family.

Adolphus found Mary busying herself in the kitchen. She obviously felt out of place despite her semi-status as the widow. He sought to console her. "You have been catering to his needs over so many years. You deserve everything that is coming to you."

She put up a wan smile. "Moses has willed the house to his son Areli Blake. It is not certain whether I shall continue living here. There are enough rooms and Areli is a generous man. Like his father, he is a Deist at heart and quite tolerant of all faiths. Some of his children will probably embrace Catholicism. But who knows if my step-son and I are compatible in the long run?"

Dusk had soon settled on Trois-Rivières and Adolphus had yet to determine where he would sleep for the night. It had been a frustrating day. Benjamin and Adolphus had disembarked from the steamer at about noon. The vessel had made good time so there had been no other option but being patient. But it hadn't been patience rewarded; they hadn't been in time to say their goodbyes to Moses Hart.

Adolphus knew where he wanted to sleep. Hopefully his siblings on Rue des Forges had left his old bedroom undisturbed. Some of the disappointments of the day would not appear quite as disturbing if he had the chance to dream of other times. Even now he recalled how Samuel would tease him because as the youngest of the boys he was no match physically for his brothers. *What would Sammy say now?*

Aaron Ezekiel did have something to say about his uncle. "Things will be quite different for his progeny than it was for him. Drummond, our Attorney General, has already proposed legislation that will limit seigneurial privileges and put a ceiling on the steady rise in *cens et rentes*. Take it from me: in the next few years most *censitaires* will commute to freehold tenure."

"That is possible, even likely. But at least the *seigneurs* will be indemnified from public funds for some of their losses. Life will go on for them." Adolphus was thinking not only of those inheriting the properties of Moses Hart. Ezekiel Hart too had had extensive land holdings bequeathed to his sons. Samuel Bécancour Hart, however, would eventually have no rents to collect in Bécancour on the south shore.

"We miss having you here in Three Rivers. Do you intend to live out your years in New York?" Aaron Ezekiel's question was rendered with much emotion.

"I do have a new life, Eze. Constance and I have children to raise and my income from writing must be expanded to give them a future. But don't bet against me ever returning to my homeland. The Hart family has made a mark in this country and I wish to contribute to making it permanent."